by Paul Bowles

Novels

The Sheltering Sky (1949)
Let It Come Down (1952, 1980)
The Spider's House (1955)
Up Above the World (1966)

Collections of Stories

The Delicate Prey (1950)
A Hundred Camels in the Courtyard (1962)
The Time of Friendship (1967)
Things Gone & Things Still Here (1977)
Collected Stories 1939-1976 (1979)
Midnight Mass (1981)

Travel Essays

Yallah (Photographs by Peter W. Haeberlin) (1957)
Their Heads Are Green and Their Hands Are Blue (1963)

Poetry

Two Poems (1933)
Scenes (1968)
The Thicket of Spring (1972)
Next to Nothing (1977)
Next to Nothing, Collected Poems 1926-1977 (1981)

Texts Edited and Translated from the Moghrebi

A Life Full of Holes (Driss ben Hamed Charhadi) (1964)
Love with a Few Hairs (Mohammed Mrabet) (1968)
The Lemon (Mohammed Mrabet) (1968)
M'Hashish (Mohammed Mrabet) (1970)
The Boy Who Set the Fire (Mohammed Mrabet) (1974)
Look & Move On (Mohammed Mrabet) (1976)
Harmless Poisons, Blameless Sins (Mohammed Mrabet) (1976)
Five Eyes (Abdeslam Boulaich, Mohamed Choukri, Larbi
   Layachi, Mohammed Mrabet and Ahmed Yacoubi) (1979)
The Beach Café & The Voice (Mohammed Mrabet) (1980)

Autobiography

Without Stopping (1972)

PAUL BOWLES

LET IT COME DOWN

With a Preface
by the Author

BLACK SPARROW PRESS
Santa Rosa ~ 1992

LIBRARY OF CONGRESS CATALOGING IN PUBLICATION DATA

Bowles, Paul Frederic, 1911-
   Let it come down.

   I. Title.
PS3552.Q874L47   1980   813'.54   80-24825
ISBN 0-87685-479-X (pbk.)

Fifth Printing

Thirty Years Later

FROM THE TIME when I was a boy of eight or nine, I had been fascinated by that brief passage in *Macbeth* where Banquo comes out of the castle with his son and makes a passing remark to the men outside about the approaching rain, to be answered by the flash of a blade and the admirable four-word sentence, succinct and brutal: "Let it come down."

The novel to which I gave that title was first published early in 1952, at the very moment of the riots which presaged the end of the International Zone of Morocco. Thus, even at the time of publication the book already treated of a bygone era, for Tangier was never the same after the 30th of March 1952. The city celebrated in these pages has long ago ceased to exist, and the events recounted in them would now be inconceivable. Like a photograph, the tale is a document relating to a specific place at a given point in time, illumined by the light of that particular moment.

The book was begun in what was perhaps an unusual manner. In December 1949 I boarded a Polish freighter in Antwerp, bound for Colombo. We entered the Strait of Gibraltar at night, and I stood on deck watching the flashes of the lighthouse at Cape Spartel, the northwestern corner of Africa. As we sailed eastward I could distinguish the lights of certain houses on the Old Mountain. Then when we came nearer to Tangier, a thin fog settled over the water, and only the glow of the city's lights was visible, reflected in the sky. That was when I felt an unreasoning and powerful desire to be in Tangier. Up until that moment it had not even occurred to me to write a book about the international city. But I went below, got into my hard bunk, and started a scene which took place on the cliffs beneath which we had just passed. This was not the beginning of the book, but it served as a point of geographical contact, from which I was able to work backward and forward in time.

Notes are useless to me unless there is a portion of the finished text to which they can be applied; I knew I must write enough of that text to serve as an umbilical cord between me and the novel before I landed in an unfamiliar place, otherwise I should lose it all. As the ship drew nearer to Ceylon I found myself recalling Kafka's well-known aphorism: *From a certain point onward there is no longer any turning*

7

8 PAUL BOWLES

back. That is the point that must be reached. I doubt that he meant it to be applied to the writing of a book, nevertheless it seemed relevant to the situation. I strained to pass that crucial point; only then could I be sure of not having to turn back and abandon the book when I tried to continue work on it later.

Sri Lanka (of which Ceylon is a latter-day mispronunciation) was as counterproductive of further work on the novel as I had anticipated; there was too much to see and learn, and the landscape was too seductive to allow much time for contemplation. I led a nomadic life, seldom staying more than a few days in one place. It was not until I crossed over into India that I was able to get back to work.

In India the daytimes were devoted to exploration; I wrote at night, and my windowless workroom was far from satisfactory. The air was always several degrees above blood temperature, and the oil lamp felt like a furnace on my face. (The indicated place to work, of course, would have been the bed in the next room, save that no light could be lit there for the thousands of winged insects that would immediately enter. I went to bed in the dark.) But as writers know, intense discomfort often helps to induce intensive work.

At the end of 1950 I was back in Tangier; it was a memorably stormy winter and I was living in a newly opened *pension*. It was also newly (read *badly*) built, so that the rain ran down the walls of my room, across to the door into the corridor, and thence down the stairs into the reception hall below. Since moving around the room meant splashing through cold water, I stayed in bed most of the time while I completed *Fresh Meat and Roses*. Then I traveled for eight months in Morocco, Algeria and Spain, working sporadically on the third section, *The Age of Monsters*.

In the autumn of 1951 when I returned to Tangier, I went up to Xauen to write the final section. Here in the absolute silence of the mountain nights, I accomplished what I had hoped to be able to do when I reached this place in the book. I shut off the controls and let *Another Kind of Silence* guide itself, without supplying any conscious direction. It went as far as it could go, then stopped, and that was the end of the book.

The hero is a nonentity, a "victim," as he describes himself, whose personality, defined solely in terms of situation, elicits sympathy only to the extent to which he is victimized. He is the only totally invented character; for all the others I used as models actual residents of Tangier. Some of these people have moved away and the rest have died. The sole character whose model remains here is Richard Holland, and this is because I am still here and he is a caricature of myself.

The theft of the money as it actually occurred was so improbable that I had to modify it to give it credibility. About three years after the end of World War II the son of a famous English writer came to Tangier with his wife and decided to buy a piece of land and build a house. There was a ban on removing sterling from the United Kingdom, so, like many others, he went to see an Indian merchant in Gibraltar, to whom he gave a check on his London bank. The Indian was to instruct his son in Tangier to deliver the money in pesetas to Mr. X. But Mr. X was a grand gentleman who employed an English secretary to attend to such matters. When the secretary went to fetch the money from the younger Indian, he found the cash waiting for him, but it was in sterling rather than in pesetas, and sterling could not be spent in the International Zone because of the financial restrictions. The Indian put him in touch with a money-changer around the corner, who agreed to buy the sterling. The money-changer filled a box with pesetas and took it to the Indian, saying that he was on his way to lunch and did not want to carry it with him, and that he would call by in the afternoon on his way back to his office and pick up the pounds.

In the afternoon the secretary called at the Indian's shop to say that he had just left the money-changer in the Zoco Chico and that he had asked him to do him the favor of taking the pounds around to his office immediately. He went out with the box, and was back five minutes later. There, that's done, he said. Then he picked up the pesetas, thanked the Indian, and stepped out into the throng passing through the Siaghines. An hour later he was on a plane bound for Madrid, with both pesetas and pounds. The last report on him, which I heard a year or so later, was from Buenos Aires, where he was playing the races.

P.B.

BANQUO: It will be Rayne to Night.

1ST MURDERER: Let it come downe.
                  (*They set upon Banquo.*)
                  MACBETH *Act III, Scene 3*

Let It Come Down

1

International Zone

1

IT WAS NIGHT by the time the little ferry drew up alongside the dock. As Dyar went down the gangplank a sudden gust of wind threw warm raindrops in his face. The other passengers were few and poorly dressed; they carried their things in cheap cardboard valises and paper bags. He watched them standing resignedly in front of the customs house waiting for the door to be opened. A half-dozen disreputable Moroccans had already caught sight of him from the other side of the fence and were shouting at him. "Hotel Metropole, mister!" "Hey, Johnny! Come on!" "You want hotel?" "Grand Hotel, hey!" It was as if he had held up his American passport for them to see. He paid no attention. The rain came down in earnest for a minute or so. By the time the official had opened the door he was uncomfortably wet.

The room inside was lighted by three oil lamps placed along the counter, one to an inspector. They saved Dyar until last, and all three of them went through his effects very carefully, without a gleam of friendliness or humor. When he had repacked his grips so they would close, they marked them with lavender chalk and reluctantly let him pass. He had to wait in line at the window over which was printed *Policia*. While he was standing there a tall man in a visored cap caught his attention, calling: "Taxi!" The man was decently dressed, and so he signaled yes with his head. Straightway the man in the cap was embroiled in a struggle with the others as he stepped to take the luggage. Dyar was the only prey that evening. He turned his head away disgustedly as the shouting figures followed the taxi-driver out the door. He felt a little sick anyway.

17

And in the taxi, as the rain pelted the windshield and the squeaking wipers rubbed painfully back and forth on the glass, he went on feeling sick. He was really here now; there was no turning back. Of course there never had been any question of turning back. When he had written he would take the job and had bought his passage from New York, he had known his decision was irrevocable. A man does not change his mind about such things when he has less than five hundred dollars left. But now that he was here, straining to see the darkness beyond the wet panes, he felt for the first time the despair and loneliness he thought he had left behind. He lit a cigarette and passed the pack to the driver.

He decided to let the driver determine for him where he would stay. The man was a Moroccan and understood very little English, but he did know the words cheap and clean. They passed from the breakwater onto the mainland, stopped at a gate where two police inspectors stuck their heads in through the front windows, and then they drove slowly for a while along a street where there were a few dim lights. When they arrived at the hotel the driver did not offer to help him with his luggage, nor was there any porter in sight. Dyar looked again at the entrance: the façade was that of a large modern hotel, but within the main door he saw a single candle burning. He got down and began pulling out his bags. Then he glanced questioningly at the driver who was watching him empty the cab of the valises; the man was impatient to be off.

When he had set all his belongings on the sidewalk and paid the driver, he pushed the hotel door open and saw a young man with smooth black hair and a dapper moustache sitting at the small reception desk. The candle provided the only light. He asked if this were the Hotel de la Playa, and did not know whether he was glad or sorry to hear that it was. Getting his bags into the lobby by himself took a little while. Then, led by a small boy who carried a candle, he climbed the stairs to his room; the elevator was not working because there was no power.

They climbed three flights. The hotel was like an enormous concrete resonating chamber; the sound of each footstep, magnified, echoed in all directions. The building had the kind of intense and pure shabbiness attained only by cheap new constructions.

Great cracks had already appeared in the walls, bits of the decorative plaster mouldings around the doorways had been chipped off, and here and there a floor tile was missing.

When they reached the room the boy went in first and touched a match to a new candle that had been stuck in the top of an empty Cointreau bottle. The shadows shot up along the walls. Dyar sniffed the close air with displeasure. The odor in the room suggested a mixture of wet plaster and unwashed feet.

"Phew! It stinks in here," he said. He looked suspiciously at the bed, turned the stained blue spread back to see the sheets.

Opposite the door there was one large window which the boy hastened to fling open. A blast of wind rushed in out of the darkness. There was the faint sound of surf. The boy said something in Spanish, and Dyar supposed he was telling him it was a good room because it gave on the beach. He did not much care which way the room faced: he had not come here on a vacation. What he wanted at the moment was a bath. The boy shut the window and hurried downstairs to get the luggage. In one corner, separated from the rest of the room by a grimy partition, was a shower with gray concrete walls and floor. He tried the tap marked *caliente* and was surprised to find the water fairly hot.

When the boy had brought the valises, piled them in the wrong places, received his tip, had difficulty in closing the door, and finally gone away leaving it ajar, Dyar moved from the window where he had been standing fingering the curtains, looking out into the blackness. He slammed the door shut, heard the key fall tinkling to the floor in the corridor. Then he threw himself on the bed and lay a while staring at the ceiling. He must call Wilcox immediately, let him know he had arrived. He turned his head and tried to see if there was a telephone on the low night table by the bed, but the table lay in the shadow of the bed's footboard, and it was too dark there to tell.

This was the danger point, he felt. At this moment it was almost as though he did not exist. He had renounced all security in favor of what everyone had assured him, and what he himself suspected, was a wild goose chase. The old thing was gone beyond recall, the new thing had not yet begun. To make it begin he had to telephone Wilcox, yet he lay still. His friends had told him he was crazy, his family had remonstrated with him both indignantly and sadly, but for some reason about which he himself knew very little, he had shut his ears to them all. "I'm fed up!" he would cry, a little hysterically. "I've stood at that damned window in the bank for ten years now. Before the war, during the war, and after the war. I can't take it any longer, that's all!" And when the suggestion was made that a visit to a doctor might be indicated, he laughed scornfully, replied: "There's nothing wrong with me that a change won't cure. Nobody's meant to be confined in a cage like that year after year. I'm just fed up, that's all." "Fine, fine," said his father. "Only what do you think you can do about it?" He had no answer to that. During the depression, when he was twenty, he had been delighted to get a job in the Transit Department at the bank. All his friends had considered him extremely fortunate; it was only his father's friendship with one of the vice-presidents which had made it possible for him to be taken on at such a time. Just before the war he had been made a teller. In those days when change was in the air nothing seemed permanent, and although Dyar knew he had a heart murmur, he vaguely imagined that in one way or another it would be got around so that he would be given some useful wartime work. Anything would be a change and therefore welcome. But he had been flatly rejected; he had gone on standing in his cage. Then he had fallen prey to a demoralizing sensation of motionlessness. His own life was a dead wight, so heavy that he would never be able to move it from where it lay. He had grown accustomed to the feeling of intense hopelessness and depression which had settled upon him, all the while resenting it bitterly. It was not in his nature to be morose, and his family noticed it. "Just do things as they come along," his father would say. "Take it easy. You'll find there'll be plenty to fill each day. Where does it get you to worry about the future? Let it take care of itself." Continuing, he would issue the familiar warning about heart trouble. Dyar would smile wryly. He was quite willing to let each day take care of itself—the future was the farthest from his thoughts. The present stood in its way; it was the minutes that were inimical. Each empty, overwhelming minute as it arrived pushed him a little further back from

life. "You don't get out enough," his father objected. "Give yourself a chance. Why, when I was your age I couldn't wait for the day
to be finished so I could get out on the tennis court, or down to the
old river fishing, or home to press my pants for a dance. You're
unhealthy. Oh, I don't mean physically. That little heart business
is nothing. If you live the way you should it ought never to give
you any trouble. I mean your attitude. That's unhealthy. I think
the whole generation's unhealthy. It's either one thing or the
other. Overdrinking and passing out on the sidewalk, or else
mooning around about life not being worth living. What the hell's
the matter with all of you?" Dyar would smile and say times had
changed. Times always change, his father would retort, but not
human nature.

Dyar was not a reader; he did not even enjoy the movies.
Entertainment somehow made the stationariness of existence more
acute, not only when the amusement was over, but even during the
course of it. After the war he made a certain effort to reconcile
himself to his life. Occasionally he would go out with two or three
of his friends, each one taking a girl. They would have cocktails at
the apartment of one of the girls, go on to a Broadway movie, and
eat afterward at some Chinese place in the neighborhood where
there was dancing. Then there was the long process of taking the
girls home one by one, after which they usually went into a bar and
drank fairly heavily. Sometimes, not very often, they would pick
up something cheap in the bar or in the street, take her to Bill
Healy's room, and lay her in turn. It was an accepted pattern; there
seemed to be no other to suggest in its place. Dyar kept thinking:
"Any life would be better than this," but he could find no different
possibility to consider. "Once you accept the fact that life isn't *fun*,
you'll be much happier," his mother said to him. Although he lived
with his parents, he never discussed with them the way he felt; it
was they who, sensing his unhappiness, came to him and, in
vaguely reproachful tones, tried to help him. He was polite with
them but inwardly contemptuous. It was so clear that they could
never understand the emptiness he felt, nor realize the degree to
which he felt it. It was a progressive paralysis, it gained on him
constantly, and it carried with it the fear that when it arrived at a

certain point something terrible would happen.

He could hear the distant sound of waves breaking on the beach outside: the dull roll, a long silence, another roll. Someone came into the room over his, slammed the door, and began to move about busily from one side of the room to the other. It sounded like a woman, but a heavy one. The water was turned on and the wash basin in his room bubbled as if in sympathy. He lit a cigarette, from time to time flicking the ashes onto the floor beside the bed. After a few minutes the woman—he was sure it was a woman—went out the door, slammed it, and he heard her walk down the hall into another room and close that door. A toilet flushed. Then the footsteps returned to the room above.

"I must call Wilcox," he thought. But he finished his cigarette slowly, making it last. He wondered why he felt so lazy about making the call. He had taken the great step, and be believed he had done right. All the way across on the ship to Gibraltar, he had told himself that it was the healthy thing to have done, that when he arrived he would be like another person, full of life, delivered from the sense of despair that had weighed on him for so long. And now he realized that he felt exactly the same. He tried to imagine how he would feel if, for instance, he had his whole life before him to spend as he pleased, without the necessity to earn his living. In that case he would not have to telephone Wilcox, would not be compelled to exchange one cage for another. Having made the first break, he would then make the second, and be completely free. He raised his head and looked slowly around the dim room. The rain was spattering the window. Soon he would have to go out. There was no restaurant in the hotel, and it was surely a long way to town. He felt the top of the night table; there was no telephone. Then he got up, took the candle, and made a search of the room. He stepped out into the corridor, picked his key off the floor, locked his door and went downstairs thinking: "I'd have him on the wire by now if there'd only been a phone by the bed."

The man was not at the desk. "I've got to make a call," he said to the boy who stood beside a potted palm smirking. "It's very important.—Telephone! Telephone!" he shouted, gesturing, as the other made no sign of understanding. The boy went to the desk, brought an old-fashioned telephone out from behind and set it on top. Dyar took the letter out of his pocket to look for the number of Wilcox's hotel. The boy tried to take the letter, but he copied the number on the back of the envelope and gave it to him. A fat man wearing a black raincoat came in and asked for his key. Then he stood glancing over a newspaper that lay spread out on the desk. As the boy made the call Dyar thought: "If he's gone out to dinner I'll have to go through this all over again." The boy said something into the mouthpiece and handed Dyar the receiver.

"Hello?"

"Hotel Atlantide."

"Mr. Wilcox, please." He pronounced the name very carefully. There was a silence. "Oh, God," he thought, annoyed with himself that he should care one way or the other whether Wilcox was in. There was a click.

"Yes?"

It was Wilcox. For a second he did not know what to say. "Hello?" he said.

"Hello. Yes?"

"Jack?"

"Yes. Who's this?"

"This is Nelson. Nelson Dyar."

"Dyar! Well, for God's sake! So you got here after all. Where are you? Come on over. You know how to get here? Better take a cab. You'll get lost. Where are you staying?"

Dyar told him.

"Jesus! That—" Dyar had the impression he had been about to say: that dump. But he said: "That's practically over the border. Well, come on up as soon as you can get here. You take soda or water?"

Dyar laughed. He had not known he would be so pleased to hear Wilcox's voice. "Soda," he said.

"Wait a second. Listen. I've got an idea. I'll call you back in five minutes. Don't go out. Wait for my call. Just stay put. I just want to call somebody for a second. It's great to have you here. Call you right back. O.K.?"

"Right."

He hung up and went to stand at the window. The rain that was beating against the glass had leaked through and was running down the wall. Someone had put a rag along the floor to absorb it, but now the cloth floated in a shallow pool. Two or three hundred feet up the road from the hotel there was a streetlight. Beneath it in the wind the glistening spears of a palm branch charged back and forth. He began to pace from one end of the little foyer to the other; the boy, standing by the desk with his hands behind him, watched him intently. He was a little annoyed at Wilcox for making him wait. Of course he thought he had been phoning from his room. He wondered if Wilcox were making good money with his travel agency. In his letters he had said he was, but Dyar remembered a good deal of bluff in his character. His enthusiasm need have meant nothing more than that he needed an assistant and preferred it to be someone he knew (the wages were low enough, and Dyar had paid his own passage from New York), or that he was pleased with a chance to show his importance and magnanimity; it would appeal to Wilcox to be able to make what he considered a generous gesture. Dyar thought it was more likely to be the latter case. Their friendship never had been an intimate one. Even though they had known each other since boyhood, since Wilcox's father had been the Dyars' family doctor, each had never shown more than a polite interest in the other's life. There was little in common between them—not even age, really, since Wilcox was nearly ten years older than he. During the war Wilcox had been sent to Algiers, and afterward it never had occurred to Dyar to wonder what had become of him. One day his father had come home saying: "Seems Jack Wilcox has stayed on over in North Africa. Gone into business for himself and seems to be making a go of it." Dyar had asked what kind of business it was, and had been only vaguely interested to hear that it was a tourist bureau.

He had been walking down Fifth Avenue one brilliant autumn twilight and had stopped in front of a large travel agency. The wind that moved down from Central Park had the crispness of an October evening, carrying with it the promise of winter, the season that paralyzes; to Dyar it gave a foretaste of increased unhappiness. In one side of the window was a large model ship, black and white, with shiny brass accessories. The other side represented a tropical beach in miniature, with a sea of turquoise gelatin and tiny palm trees bending up out of a beach of real sand. BOOK NOW FOR WINTER CRUISES, said the sign. The thought occurred to him that it would be a torturing business to work in such a place, to plan itineraries, make hotel reservations and book passages for all the places one would never see. He wondered how many of the men who stood inside there consulting their folders, schedules, lists and maps felt as trapped as he would have felt in their place; it would be even worse than the bank. Then he thought of Wilcox. At that moment he began to walk again, very fast. When he got home he wrote the letter and took it out to post immediately. It was a crazy idea. Nothing could come of it, except perhaps that Wilcox would think him a god-damned fool, a prospect which did not alarm him.

The reply had given him the shock of his life. Wilcox had spoken of coincidence. "There must be something in telepathy," he had written. Only then did Dyar mention the plan to his family, and the reproaches had begun.

Moving regretfully away from the desk, the fat man walked back to the lift. As he shut the door the telephone rang. The boy started for it, but Dyar got there ahead of him. The boy glared at him angrily. It was Wilcox, who said he would be at the Hotel de la Playa in twenty minutes. "I want you to méet a friend of mine," he said. "The Marquesa de Valverde. She's great. She wants you to come to dinner too." And as Dyar protested, he interrupted. "We're not dressing. God, no! None of that here. I'll pick you up."

"But Jack, listen—"

"So long."

Dyar went up to his room, nettled at not having been given the opportunity of deciding to accept or refuse the invitation. He asked himself if it would raise him in Wilcox's estimation if he showed independence and begged off. But obviously he had no intention of doing such a thing, since when he got to his room he tore off his clothes, took a quick shower, whistling all the while, opened his bags, shaved as well as he could by the light of the lone candle, and put on his best suit. When he had finished he blew out the candle and hurried downstairs to wait at the front entrance.

2

DAISY DE VALVERDE sat at her dressing table, her face brilliant as six little spotlights threw their rays upon it from six different angles. If she made up to her satisfaction in the pitiless light of these sharp lamps, she could be at ease in any light later. But it took time and technique. The Villa Hesperides was never without electricity, even now when the town had it for only two hours every other evening. Luis had seen to that when they built the house; he had foreseen the shortage of power. It was one of the charms of the International Zone that you could get anything you wanted if you paid for it. Do anything, too, for that matter;—there were no incorruptibles. It was only a question of price.

Outside, the wind was roaring, and in the cypresses it sounded like a cataract. The boom of waves against the cliffs came up from far below. Mingled with the reflections of the lights in the room, other lights, small, distant points, showed in the black sheets of glass at the windows: Spain across the strait, Tarifa and Cape Camariñal.

She was always pleased to have Americans come to the house because she felt under no constraint with them. She could drink all she pleased and they drank along with her, whereas her English guests made a whiskey last an hour—not to mention the French, who asked for a Martini of vermouth with a dash of gin, or the Spanish with their glass of sherry. "The Americans are the nation of the future," she would announce in her hearty voice. "Here's to 'em. God bless their gadgets, great and small. God bless Frigidaire, Tampax and Coca-Cola. Yes, even Coca-Cola, darling." (It was generally conceded that Coca-Cola's advertising was ruining the picturesqueness of Morocco.) The Marqués did not share her enthusiasm for Americans, but that did not prevent her from asking them whenever she pleased; she ran the house to suit herself.

She had a Swiss butler and an Italian footman, but when Americans were invited to dinner she let old Ali serve at table because he owned a magnificent Moorish costume; although he was not very competent she thought his appearance impressed them more than the superior service the two Europeans could provide.

The difficulty was that both the butler and footman disapproved so heartily of this arrangement that unless she went into the kitchen at the last moment and repeated her orders, they always found some pretext for not allowing poor old Ali to serve, so that when she looked up from her plate expecting to see the brilliant brocades and gold sash from the palace of Sultan Moulay Hafid, she would find herself staring instead at the drab black uniform of Hugo or Mario. Their faces would be impassive; she never knew what had been going on. There was a chance that this would happen tonight, unless she went down now and made it clear that Ali must serve. She rose, slipped a heavy bracelet over her left hand, and went out through the tiny corridor which connected her room with the rest of the house. Someone had left a window open at the end of the upper hall, and several of the candles in front of the large tapestry had been blown out. She could not bear the anachronism of having electricity in the rooms where tapestries were hung. Ringing a bell, she waited until a breathless chambermaid had appeared, then she indicated the window and the candles with a stiff finger. "*Mire*," she said disapprovingly, and moved down the stairway. At that moment there was the sound of a motor outside. She hurried down the rest of the way, practically running the length of the hall to disappear into the kitchen, and when she came back out Hugo was taking her guests' raincoats. She walked toward the two men regally.

"Darling Jack. How sweet of you to come. And in this foul weather."

"How kind of you to have us. Daisy, this is Mr. Dyar. The Marquesa de Valverde."

Dyar looked at her and saw a well-preserved woman of forty with a mop of black curls, china blue eyes, and a low-cut black satin dress, to squeeze herself into which must have been somewhat painful.

"*How* nice to see you, Mr. Dyar. I think we've got a fire in the drawing room. God knows. Let's go in and see. Are you wet?" She felt Dyar's sleeve. "No? Good. Come along. Jack, you're barman. I want the stiffest drink you can concoct."

They sat before a scorching log fire. Daisy wanted Wilcox to mix sidecars. At the first sip Dyar realized how really hungry he was; he glanced clandestinely at his watch. It was nine-forty. Observing Daisy, he thought she was the most fatuous woman he had ever met. But he was impressed by the house. Hugo entered. "Now for dinner," thought Dyar. It was a telephone call for Madame la Marquise. "Pour me another, sweet, and let me take it with me as consolation," she said to Wilcox.

When she had gone Wilcox turned to Dyar.

"She's one grand girl," he said, shaking his head.

"Yes," Dyar replied, without conviction, adding: "Isn't she a little on the beat-up side for you?"

Wilcox looked indignant, lowered his voice. "What are you talking about, boy? She's got a husband in the house. I said she's grand fun to be with. What the hell did you think I meant, anyway?" Mario's arrival to add a log to the fire stopped whatever might have followed. "Listen to that wind," said Wilcox, sitting back with his drink.

Dyar knew he was annoyed with him; he wondered why. "He's getting mighty touchy in his old age," he said to himself, looking around the vast room. Mario went out. Wilcox leaned forward again, and still in a low voice, said: "Daisy and Luis are practically my best friends here." There were voices in the hall. Daisy entered with a neat dark man who looked as though he had stomach ulcers. "Luis!" cried Wilcox, jumping up. Dyar was presented, and the four sat down, Daisy next to Dyar. "This can't last long," he thought. "It's nearly ten." His stomach felt completely concave.

They had another round of drinks. Wilcox and the Marqués began to discuss the transactions of a local banker who had got himself into difficulties and had left suddenly for Lisbon, not to return. Dyar listened for a moment.

"I'm sorry, I didn't hear," he said to Daisy; she was speaking to him.

"I said: how do you like our little International Zone?"

"Well, I haven't seen anything of it yet. However—" he looked around the room with appreciation—"from here it looks fine." He smiled self-consciously.

Her voice assumed a faintly maternal note. "Of course. You just came today, didn't you? My dear, you've got so much ahead of you! So much ahead of you! You can't know. But you'll love it, that I promise you. It's a madhouse, of course. A complete, utter madhouse. I only hope to God it remains one."

"You like it a lot?" He was beginning to feel the drinks.

"Adore it," she said, leaning toward him. "Absolutely worship the place."

He set his empty glass carefully on the table beside the shaker. From the doorway Hugo announced dinner.

"Jack, one more drop all around." She held forth her glass and received what was left. "You've given it all to me, you monster. I didn't want it all." She stood up, and carrying her glass with her, led the men into the dining room, where Mario stood uncorking a bottle of champagne.

"I'm going to be drunk," thought Dyar, suddenly terrified that through some lapse in his table etiquette he would draw attention to himself.

Slowly they advanced into a meal which promised to be endless.

Built into the wall opposite him, a green rectangle in the dark paneling, was an aquarium; its hidden lights illumined rocks, shells and complex marine plants. Dyar found himself watching it as he ate. Daisy talked without cease. At one point, when she had stopped, he said: "I don't see any fish in there."

"Cuttle-fish," explained the Marqués. "We keep only cuttle-fish." And as Dyar seemed not to understand, "You know—small octopi. You see? There is one there on the left, hanging to the rock." He pointed; now Dyar saw the pale fleshy streamers which were its tentacles.

"They're rather sweeter than goldfish," said Daisy, but in such a way that Dyar suspected she loathed them. He had never met anyone like her; she gave the impression of remaining uninvolved in whatever she said or did. It was as if she were playing an intricate game whose rules she had devised herself.

During salad there was a commotion somewhere back in the house: muffled female voices and hurrying footsteps. Daisy set down her fork and looked around the table at the three men.

"God! I know what that is. I'm sure of it. This storm has brought in the ants." She turned to Dyar. "Every year they come in by the millions, the tiniest ones. When you first see them on the wall you'd swear it was an enormous crack. When you go nearer it looks more like a rope. Positively seething. They all stick together. Millions. It's terrifying." She rose. "Do forgive me; I must go and see what's happening."

Dyar said: "Is there anything I can do?" and got a fleeting glance of disapproval from Wilcox.

She smiled. "No, darling. Eat your salad."

Daisy was gone nearly ten minutes. When she returned she was laughing. "Ah, the joys of living in Morocco!" she said blithely. "The ants again?" asked the Marqués. "Oh, yes! This time it's the maids' sewing room. Last year it was the pantry. That was *much* worse. And they had to shovel the corpses out." She resumed eating her salad and her face grew serious. "Luis, I'm afraid poor old Tambang isn't long for this world. I looked in on him. It seemed to me he was worse."

The Marqués nodded his head. "Give him more penicillin."

Daisy turned to Dyar. "It's an old Siamese I'm trying to save. He's awfully ill. We'll go and see him after dinner. Luis refuses to go near him. He hates cats. I'm sure you don't hate cats, do you, Mr. Dyar?"

"Oh, I like all kinds of animals." He turned his head and saw the octopus. It had not moved, but a second one had appeared and was swaying loosely along the floor of the tank. It looked like something floating in a jar of formaldehyde—a stomach, perhaps, or a pancreas. The sight of it made him feel vaguely ill, or else it was the mixture of sidecars and champagne.

"Then you won't mind helping me with him, will you?" pursued Daisy.

"Be delighted."

"You don't know what you're letting yourself in for," said Wilcox, laughing unpleasantly.

"Nonsense!" Daisy exclaimed. "He'll wear enormous thick gloves. Even Tambang can't claw through those."

"The hell he *can't!* And he's got teeth too, hasn't he?"

"Just for this," said the Marqués, "we must make *Jack* go and be the attendant."

"No," Daisy said firmly. "Mr. Dyar is coming with me. Does anyone want fruit? I suggest we go in and have coffee immediately. We'll have our brandy afterward when we come down." She rose from the table.

"You'll need it," said Wilcox.

From the drawing room now they could hear the storm blowing louder than before. Daisy gulped her coffee standing up, lit a cigarette, and went toward the door.

"Tell Mario to keep the fire blazing, Luis, or it'll begin to smoke. It's already begun, in fact. Shall we go up, Mr. Dyar?"

She went ahead of him up the stairs. As she passed each candelabrum the highlights of her satin flashed.

From a small cloakroom at the head of the stairs she took two pairs of thick gardening gloves and gave one to Dyar.

"We don't really need these," she said, "but it's better to be protected."

The walls of the little room were lined with old French prints of tropical birds. On an antique bed with a torn canopy over it lay a large Siamese cat. An enamal pan containing lumps of raw liver had been pushed against its head, but it looked wearily in the other direction. The room smelled like a zoo. "God, what a fug!" Daisy exclaimed. "But we can't open the window." The storm raged outside. From time to time the house trembled. A branch beat repeatedly against the window like a person asking to be let in. The cat paid no attention while Daisy filed off the ends of ampoules, filled the syringe, and felt along its haunches for the right spot.

"He's got to have four different injections," she said, "but I can give the first two together. Now, stand above, and be ready to push down on his neck, but don't push unless you have to. Scratch him under the chin."

The old cat's fur was matted, its eyes were huge and empty. Once as the needle flashed above his head Dyar thought he saw an expression of alertness, even of fear, cross its face, but he scratched harder, with both hands, under the ears and along the jowls. Even when the needle went in tentatively, and then further in, it did not move.

"Now we have only two more," said Daisy. Dyar watched the sureness of her gestures. No veterinarian could have been more deft.

He said as much. She snorted. "The only good vets are amateurs. I wouldn't let a professional touch an animal of mine." The odor of ether was very strong. "Is that ether?" Dyar asked; he was feeling alarmingly ill. "Yes, for sterilizing." She had filled the syringe again. "Now, hold him." The wind roared; it seemed as though the branch would crack the windowpane. "This may burn. He may feel it." Dyar looked up at the window; he could see his own head reflected vaguely against the night beyond. He thought he might throw up if he had to watch the needle go into the fur again. Only when Daisy stepped away from the bed did he dare lower his gaze. The cat's eyes were half shut. He bent down: it was purring.

"Poor old beast," said Daisy. "Now for the last. This will be easy. Tambang, sweet boy, what is it?"

"He's purring," said Dyar, hoping she would not look at his face. His lips felt icy, and he knew he must be very pale.

"You see how right I was to bring you? He likes you. Jack would have antagonized him in some way."

She did look at him, and he thought her eyes stayed an instant too long. But she said nothing.

"Don't tell me he's going to faint," she thought. "The wretched man is completely out of contact with life." But he was making a great effort.

"The cat doesn't seem to feel anything," he said.

"No, I'm afraid he won't live."

"But he's purring."

"Will you hold him, please? This is the last."

He wanted to talk, to take his mind off his dizziness, away from what was going on just below his face on the bed. He could think of nothing to say, so he kept silent. The cat stirred slightly. Daisy straightened up, and at the same moment there was a splitting sound and a heavy crash somewhere outside in the darkness. They looked at each other. Daisy set the syringe on the table.

"I know what that was. One of our eucalyptus. God, what a night!" she said admiringly.

They shut the door and went downstairs. In the drawing room there was no one. "I daresay they've gone out to look. Let's go into the library. The fireplace draws better in there. This one's smoking."

The library was small and pleasant; the fire crackled. She pushed a wall button and they sat down on the divan. She looked at him, musing.

"Jack told me you were coming, but somehow I never thought you'd actually arrive."

"Why not?" He felt a little better now.

"Oh, you know. Such things have a way of not coming off. Frightfully good idea that misses fire. And then, of course, I can't see really why Jack needs anyone there in that little office."

"You mean it's not doing well?" He tried to keep his voice even.

She laid a hand on his arm and laughed. As though she were imparting a rather shameful secret, she said in a low voice: "My dear, if you think he makes even his luncheon money there, you're gravely mistaken."

She was studying him too carefully, trying to see the effect of her words. He would refuse to react. He felt hot all over, but did not speak. Hugo entered carrying a tray of bottles and glasses. They both took brandy, and he set the tray down on a table at Dyar's elbow and went out.

She was still looking at him.

"Oh, it's not going well," he said. He would not say what he was sure she was waiting for him to say: How does he keep going?

"Not at all. It never has."

"I'm sorry to hear that," said Dyar.

"There's no need to be. If it had gone well I daresay he wouldn't have sent for you. He'd have had just about all he could manage by himself. As it is, I expect he needs you far more."

Dyar made a puzzled face. "I don't follow *that*."

Daisy looked pleased. "Tangier, Tangier," she said. "You'll follow soon enough, my pet."

They heard voices in the hall.

"You'll be wanting a good many books to read, I should think," she said. "Do feel free to borrow anything here that interests you. Of course there's a circulating library run by the American Legation that's far better than the English library. But they take ages to get the new books."

"I don't read much," said Dyar.

"But my dear lamb, whatever are you going to *do* all day? You'll be bored to distraction."

"Oh, well. Jack—"

"I doubt it," she said. "I think you'll be alone from morning to night, every day."

The voices were no longer audible. "They've gone into the kitchen," she said. He pulled out a pack of cigarettes, held it up to her.

"No, thank you. I have some. But seriously, I can't think what you'll do all day, you know." She felt in her bag and withdrew a small gold case.

"I'll probably have work to do," he replied, getting a match to the end of her cigarette before she could lift her lighter.

She laughed shortly, blew out the flame, and seized his hand, the match still between his fingers. "Let me see that hand," she said, puffing on her cigarette. Dyar smiled and held his palm out stiffly for her to examine. "Relax it," she said, drawing the hand nearer to her face.

"Work!" she scoffed. "I see no sign of it here, my dear Mr. Dyar."

He was incensed. "Well, it's a liar, then. Work is all I've ever done."

"Oh, standing in a bank, perhaps, but that's so light it wouldn't show." She looked carefully, pushing the flesh of the hand with her fingers. "No. I see no sign of work. No sign of anything, to be quite honest. I've never seen such an empty hand. It's terrifying." She looked up at him.

Again he laughed. "You're stumped, are you?"

"Not at all. I've lived in America long enough to have seen a good many American hands. All I can say is that this is the worst."

He pretended great indignation, withdrawing his hand forcibly. "What do you mean, worst?" he cried.

She looked at him with infinite concern in her eyes. "I mean," she said, "that you have an empty life. No pattern. And nothing in you to give you any purpose. Most people can't help following some kind of design. They do it automatically because it's in their nature. It's that that saves them, pulls them up short. They can't help themselves. But you're safe from being saved."

"A unique specimen. Is that it?"

"In a way." She searched his face questioningly for a moment. "How odd," she murmured presently. This empty quality in him pleased her. It was rather as if he were naked,—not defenseless, exactly—merely unclothed, ready to react, and she found it attractive; men should be like that. But it struck her as strange that she should think so.

"How odd what?" he inquired. "That I should be unique?" He could see that she believed all she was saying, and since it was flattering to have the attention being paid him, he was ready to argue with her, if necessary, just to prolong it.

"Yes."

"I've never been able to believe all this astrology and palmistry business," he said. "It doesn't hold water."

She did not answer, and so he continued. "Let's leave hands for a minute and get down to personalities." The brandy was warming him; he felt far from ill now. "You mean you think each individual man's life is different and has its own pattern, as you call it?"

"Yes, of course."

"But that's impossible!" he cried. "It stands to reason. Just look around you. There never was any mass production to compare with the one that turns out human beings—all the same model, year after year, century after century, all alike, always the same person." He felt a little exalted at the sound of his own voice. "You might say there's only one person in the world, and we're all it."

She was silent for a moment; then she said: "Rubbish." What he was saying made her vaguely angry. She wondered if it were because she resented his daring to express his ideas at all, but she did not think it was that.

"Look, my pet," she said in a conciliatory tone, "Just what do you want in life?"

"That's a hard question," he said slowly. She had taken the wind out of his sails. "I suppose I want to feel I'm getting something out of it."

She was impatient. "That doesn't mean anything."

"I want to feel I'm alive, I guess. That's about all."

"Great God in heaven. Give me some more brandy."

They let the subject drop, turning to the storm and the climate in general. He was thinking that he should have answered anything that came to mind: money, happiness, health, rather than trying to say what he really meant. As an accompaniment to these thoughts there recurred the image of his room back at the Hotel de la Playa, with its spotted bedspread, its washstand that gurgled.

"He has nothing, he wants nothing, he is nothing," thought Daisy. She felt she ought to be sorry for him, but somehow he did not evoke pity in her—rather, a slight rancor which neutralized her other emotions. Finally she stood up. "We must see what has happened to Luis and Jack."

They found them in the drawing room talking.

"Which eucalyptus was it?" said Daisy. "I know it was one of them."

The Marqués frowned. "The great one by the gate. It's not the whole tree. Only one branch, but a big one, the one overhanging the road. The road is blocked."

"Why do they always manage to fall into the road?" demanded Daisy.

"I don't know," said Wilcox. "But it screws me up fine. How am I going to get out of here?"

She laughed merrily. "You and Mr. Dyar," she said, with very clear enunciation, "will spend the night, and in the morning you'll call for a taxi. It's that simple."

"Out of the question," said Wilcox irritably.

"I assure you no taxi will come now, in this weather. That goes without saying. And it's eight kilometers to walk."

He had no answer to this.

"There are plenty of rooms for just such emergencies. Now, stop fretting and make me a whiskey and soda." She turned to Dyar and beamed.

When she had been served, Wilcox said shortly: "What about it, Dyar? Same for you?" Dyar looked quickly at him, saw that he seemed annoyed. "Please." Wilcox handed him his drink without turning to face him. "That's easy," Dyar thought. "He's afraid I'm getting on too well with her."

They talked about the house. "You must come back sometime

during the daylight and see the rose garden," said Daisy. "We have the most divine rose garden."

"But what you've really got to see is that glass bedroom," said Wilcox, leaning back in his chair and yawning toward the ceiling. "Have you seen that?"

The Marqués laughed uncomfortably.

"No, he hasn't," Daisy said. She rose, took Dyar's arm. "Come along and see it. It's a perfect opportunity. Jack and Luis will discuss the week's bankruptcies."

The bedroom reminded Dyar of a vast round greenhouse. He scuffed at the zebra skins scattered about on the shining black marble floor. The bed was very wide and low, its heavy white satin spread had been partially pulled back and the sheets were turned down. The place was a gesture of defiance against the elements that clamored outside the glass walls; he felt distinctly uncomfortable. "Anybody could see in, I should think," he ventured.

"If they can see all the way from Spain." She stood staring down toward the invisible waves that broke on the rocks below. "This is my favorite room in the world," she declared. "I've never been able to abide being away from the sea. I'm like a sailor, really. I take it for granted that salt water is the earth's natural covering. I must be able to see it. Always." She breathed deeply.

"What's *this* act all about?" he thought.

"It's a wonderful room," he said.

"There are orange trees down in the garden. I call the place Hesperides because it's here to this mountain that Hercules is supposed to have come to steal the golden apples."

"Is that right?" He tried to sound interested and impressed. Since he had started on the whiskey he had been sleepy. He had the impression that Wilcox and the Marqués would be coming upstairs any minute; when they came he felt that Daisy and he ought not to be found standing here in her bedroom in this tentative, absurd attitude. He saw her stifle a yawn; she had no desire to be showing him the room anyway. It was merely to irk Wilcox, a game they were in together. It occurred to him then that it might be fun to play around a little with her, to see which way the wind was blowing. But he was not sure how to begin; she was a little overwhelming. Something like:

That's a big bed for one small person. She would probably reply: But Luis and I sleep here, my dear. Whatever he said or did she would probably laugh.

"I know what you're thinking," she said. He started a bit. "You're sleepy, poor man. You'd like to go to bed."

"Oh," he said. "Well—"

A youngish woman hurried into the room, calling: "*On peut entrer?*" Her clothes were very wet, her face glistened with rain. She and Daisy began a lively conversation in French, scraps of which were thrown to Dyar now and then. She was Daisy's secretary, she was just returning from a dance, the taxi had been obliged to stop below the fallen tree, but the driver had been kind enough to walk with her to the house and was downstairs now having a cognac, she was soaked through, and did anyone want the cab?

"Do we!" cried Dyar, with rather more animation than was altogether civil. Immediately he felt apologetic and began to stammer his thanks and excuses.

"Rush downstairs, darling. Don't stop to say good night. Hurry! I'll call you tomorrow at the office. I have something to talk to you about."

He said good night, ran down the stairs, meeting the Marqués on the way.

"Jack is waiting for you outside. Good night, old boy," said the Marqués, continuing to climb. When he reached the top of the stairs, Daisy was blowing out the candles along the wall. "*Estamos salvados,*" she said, without looking up. "*Qué gentuza más aburrida,*" sighed the Marqués.

She continued methodically, holding her hand carefully behind each flame as she blew on it. She had the feeling her evening had somehow gone all wrong, but at what point it had begun to do that she could not tell.

The malevolent wind struck out at them as they fought their way to the taxi. They crawled under one end of the great branch that lay diagonally across the road. The driver had some difficulty turning the car; at one point he backed into a wall and cursed. When they were on their way, going slowly down the dark mountain road, Wilcox said: "Well, did you see the bedroom?"

"Yes."

"You've seen everything. You can go back to New York. Tangier holds no secrets for you now."

Dyar laughed uneasily. After a pause he said: "What's up tomorrow? Do I come around to the agency?"

Wilcox was lighting a cigarette. "You might drop in sometime during the late afternoon, yes."

His heart sank. Then he was angry. "He knows damned well I want to start work. Playing cat and mouse." He said nothing.

When they arrived in the town, Wilcox called: "Atlantide." The cab turned right, climbed a crooked street, and stopped before a large doorway. "Here's fifty pesetas," said Wilcox, pressing some notes into his hand. "My share."

"Fine," said Dyar. "Thanks."

"Good night"

"Good night."

The driver looked expectantly back. "Just wait a minute," said Dyar, gesturing. He could still see Wilcox in the lobby. When he had gone out of sight, Dyar paid the man, got out, and started to walk downhill, the rain at his back. The street was deserted. He felt pleasantly drunk, and not at all sleepy. As he walked along he muttered: "Late afternoon. Drop in, do. Charmed, I'm sure. Lovely weather." He came to a square where a line of cabs waited. Even in the storm, at this hour, the men spied him. "Hey, come! Taxi, Johnny?" He disregarded them and cut into a narrow passageway. It was like walking down the bed of a swiftly running brook; the water came almost to the tops of his shoes, sometimes above. He bent down and rolled up his trousers, continued to walk. His thoughts took another course. Soon he was chuckling to himself, and once he said aloud: "Golden apples, my ass!"

3

THAMI WAS FURIOUS with his wife: she had a nosebleed and was letting it drip all over the patio. He had told her to get a wet rag and try to stanch it with that, but she was frightened and seemed not to hear him; she merely kept walking back and forth in the patio with her head bent over. There was an oil lamp flickering just inside the door, and from where he lay on his mattress he could see her hennaed feet with their heavy anklets shuffle by every so often in front of him. Rain fell intermittently, but she did not seem to notice it.

That was the worst part of being married, unless one had money—a man could never be alone in his own house; there was always female flesh in front of him, and when he had had enough of it he did not want to be continually reminded of it. "Yah latif!" he yelled. "At least shut the door!" In the next room the baby started to cry. Thami waited a moment to see what Kinza was going to do. She neither closed the door nor went to comfort her son. "Go and see what he wants!" he roared. Then he groaned: "Al-lah!" and put a cushion over his abdomen, locking his hands on top of it, in the hope of having an after-dinner nap. If it were not for his son, he reflected, he would send her back where she belonged to her family in the Rif. That might pave the way, at least, to his being taken back by his brothers and permitted to live with them again.

He had never considered it just of Abdelmalek and Hassan to have taken it upon themselves to put him out of the house. Being younger than they, he had of course to accept their dictum. But certainly he had not accepted it with good grace. It was typical of him to consider that they had acted out of sheer spite, and he behaved accordingly. He committed the unpardonable offense of speaking against them to others, dwelling upon their miserliness and their lecherousness; this trait had gradually estranged him from practically all his childhood friends. Everyone knew he drank and had done so since the age of fifteen, and although that was generally considered in the upper-class Moslem world of Tangier sufficient grounds for his having been asked to leave the Beidaoui residence, still, in itself it would not have turned his friends against him. The trouble was that Thami had a genius for doing the wrong thing; it was as if he took a perverse and bitter delight in cutting himself off from all he had ever known, in making himself utterly miserable. His senseless marriage with an illiterate mountain girl—surely he had done that only in a spirit of revenge against his brothers. He must certainly have been mocking them when he rented the squalid little house in Emsallah, where only laborers and servants lived. Not only did he take alcohol, but he had recently begun to do it publicly, on the terraces of the cafés in the Zoco Chico. His brothers had even heard, although how much truth lay in the report they did not know, that he had been seen going on numerous trips by train to Casablanca, an activity which usually meant only one thing: smuggling of one sort or another.

Thami's friends now were of recent cultivation, and the relationships between him and them not particularly profound ones. Two were professors at the Lycée Français, ardent nationalists who never missed an opportunity during a conversation to excoriate the French, and threw about terms like "imperialist domination," "Pan-Islamic culture" and "autonomy." Their violence and resentment against the abuses of an unjust authority struck a sympathetic chord in him; he felt like one of them without really understanding what they were talking about. It was they who had given him the idea of making the frequent trips to the French Zone and (—for it was perfectly true: he had been engaging in petty smuggling—) carrying through with him fountain pens and wrist watches to sell there at a good profit. Every franc out of which the French customs could be cheated, they argued, was another nail in the French economic coffin; in the end the followers of Lyautey would be forced to abandon Morocco. There were also the extra thousands of francs which it was agreeable to have in his wallet at the end of such a journey.

Another friend was a functionary in the Municipalité. He too approved of smuggling, but on moral grounds, because it was important to insist on the oneness of Morocco, to refuse to accept the three zones into which the Europeans had arbitrarily divided it. The important point with regard to Europeans, he claimed, was to sow chaos within their institutions and confuse them with seemingly irrational behavior. As to the Moslems, they must be made conscious of their shame and suffering. He frequently visited his family in Rabat, always carrying with him a large bunch of bananas, which were a good deal cheaper in Tangier. When the train arrived at Souk el Arba the customs officers would pounce on the fruit, whereupon he would begin to shout in as loud a voice as possible that he was taking the bananas to his sick child. The officers, taking note of the growing interest in the scene on the part of the other native passengers, would lower their voices and try to keep the altercation as private and friendly as they could. He, speaking excellent French, would be polite in his language but noisy in his protest, and if it looked at any point as though the inspectors might be going to placate him and let the bananas by, he would slip into his speech some tiny expression of defiant insult, imperceptible to the other passengers but certain to thrown the Frenchmen into a fury. They would demand that he give up the bananas then and there. At this point he would appear to be making a sudden decision; he would pick up the bunch by the stem and break the fruit off one by one, calling to the fourth-class passengers, mostly simple Berbers, to come and eat, saying sadly that since his sick son was not to have the bananas he wanted to give them to his countrymen. Thus forty or fifty white-robed men would be crouching along the platform munching on bananas, shaking their heads with pity for the father of the sick boy, and turning their wide accusing eyes toward the Frenchmen. The only trouble was that the number of customs inspectors was rather limited. They all had fallen into the trap again and again, but now they remembered the functionary only too well, and the last time he had gone through they had steadfastly refused to notice the bananas at all. When Thami heard this he said: "So you went through to Rabat with them?" "Yes," said the other a little dejectedly. "That's wonderful," said Thami with enthusiasm. The functionary looked at him. "Of course!" Thami cried. "You broke the law. They knew it. They didn't dare do anything. You've won." "I suppose that's true," said the other after a moment, but he was not sure Thami understood what it was all about.

*

Thami opened his eyes. It was five minutes later, although he thought it was an hour or more. She had taken the lamp; the room was in darkness. The patio door was open, and through it he could hear the splatter of rain on the tiles. Then he realized that the baby was still crying, wearily, pitifully. *"Inaal din—"* he said savagely under his breath. He jumped up in the dark, slid his feet into his slippers, and stumbled out into the wet.

The lamp was in the next room. Kinza had picked the baby up and was holding him clumsily while she prepared to nurse him. The blood still ran down her face and was dripping slowly, regularly, from the end of her chin. It had fallen in several places on the baby's clothing. Thami stepped nearer. As he did so, he saw a drop of blood fall square in the infant's face, just above his lips. A cautious tongue crept out and licked it in. Thami was beside himself. *"Hachouma!"* he cried, seizing the baby and holding it out of her reach so that it began to scream in earnest. He laid it carefully on the floor, got an old handkerchief, stood in the doorway for a moment with his hand out in the rain, and when the cloth was soaked, he threw it to her. She had let blood drip over everything: the matting, the cushions, the floor, the brass tray on the tea table, and even, he noted with a shiver of disgust, into one of the tea glasses. He picked up the tiny glass and threw it outside, heard it smash and tinkle. Now he wanted to get out of the house. At each moment it seemed to be raining harder. So much the worse, he thought. He would go anyway. He pulled his raincoat down from the nail where it hung, put on his shoes, and without saying a word, went out the door into the street. Only when he had shut it behind him did he notice that there was a violent wind to accompany the downpour.

It was late. From time to time he met a man hurrying along, face hidden under the hood of his djellaba, head bent over, eyes on the ground. The streets of Emsallah were unpaved; the muddy water ran against him all the way to the boulevard. Here a solitary cautious car moved by under the rain's onslaught, sounding its horn repeatedly.

He passed along the Place de France under the low overhanging branches of the liveoaks in front of the French Consulate. Neither the Café de Paris nor the Brasserie de France was open. The city was deserted, the Boulevard Pasteur reduced to two converging rows of dim lights leading off into the night. It was typical of Europeans, he

thought, to lose courage and give up all their plans the minute there
was a chance of getting themselves wet. They were more prudent than
passionate; their fears were stronger than their desires. Most of them
had no real desire, apart from that to make money, which after all is
merely a habit. But once they had the money they seemed never to
use it for a specific object or purpose. That was what he found difficult
to understand. He knew exactly what he wanted, always, and so did
his countrymen. Most of them only wanted three rams to slaughter at
Aïd el Kebir and new clothing for the family at Mouloud and Aïd es
Seghir. It was not much, but it was definite, and they bent all their
efforts to getting it. Still, he could not think of the mass of Moroccans
without contempt. He had no patience with their ignorance and
backwardness; if he damned the Europeans with one breath, he was
bound to damn the Moroccans with the next. No one escaped save him,
and that was because he hated himself most of all. But fortunately he
was unaware of that. His own dream was to have a small speedboat; it
was an absolute necessity for the man who hoped to be really successful
in smuggling.

Right now he wanted to get to the Café Tingis in the Zoco Chico
and have a coffee with cognac in it. He turned into the Siaghines and
strode rapidly downhill between the money changers' stalls, past the
Spanish church and the Galeries Lafayette. Ahead was the little
square, the bright lights of the gasoline lamps in the cafés pouring into
it from all four sides. It could be any hour of the day or night—the
cafés would be open and crowded with men, the dull murmuring
monotone of whose talking filled the entire zoco. But tonight the
square was swept by the roaring wind. He climbed the steps to the
deserted terrace and pushed inside, taking a seat by the window. The
Tingis dominated the square; from it one could look down upon all the
other cafés. Someone had left an almost full pack of Chesterfields on
the table. He clapped his hands for the waiter, took off his raincoat. He
was not very dry underneath it: a good deal of water had run down his
neck, and below his knees he was soaked through.

The waiter arrived. Thami gave his order. Pointing at the cigarettes he said: "Yours?" The waiter looked vaguely around the café, his
forehead wrinkled with confusion, and replied that he thought the
table was occupied. At that moment a man came out of the washroom

and walked toward Thami, who automatically started to rise in order to sit somewhere else. As the man reached the table he made several gestures indicating that Thami remain there. "That's okay, that's okay," he was saying. "Stay where you are."

Thami had learned English as a boy when his father, who often had English people of rank staying at the house, had insisted he study it. Now he spoke it fairly well, if with a rather strong accent. He thanked the man, and accepted a cigarette. Then he said: "Are you English?" It was curious that the man should be in this part of the town at this hour, particularly with the weather the way it was.

"No. I'm American."

Appraisingly Thami looked at him and asked if he were from a boat: he was a little afraid the American was going to ask to be directed to a bordel, and he glanced about nervously to see if anyone he knew was in the café. One rumor he could not have circulating was that he had become a guide; in Tangier there was nothing lower.

The man laughed apologetically, saying: "Yeah, I guess you could say I'm from a boat. I just got off one, but if you mean do I work on one, no."

Thami was relieved. "You stay in a hotel?" he asked. The other said he did, looking a little bit on his guard, so that Thami did not ask him which hotel it was, as he had intended to do.

"How big is Tangier?" the man asked Thami. He did not know. "Are there many tourists now?" That he knew. "It's very bad. No one comes any more since the war."

"Let's have a drink," the American said suddenly. "Hey, there!" He leaned backward, looking over his shoulder for the waiter. "You'll have one, won't you?" Thami assented.

He looked at Thami for the first time with a certain warmth. "No use sitting here like two bumps on a log. What'll it be?" The waiter approached. Thami still had not decided what kind of man this was, what he could afford. "And you?" he asked.

"White Horse."

"Good," said Thami, having no idea what this might be. "For me, too."

The two men looked at each other. It was the moment when they were ready to feel sympathy for one another, but the traditional formula of distrust made it necessary that a reason be found first.

"When have you come to Tangier?" asked Thami.

"Tonight."

"Tonight, for the first time?"

"That's right."

Thami shook his head. "What a wonderful thing to be an American!" he said impetuously.

"Yes," said Dyar automatically, never having given much thought to what it would be like not to be an American. It seemed somehow the natural thing to be.

The whiskey came; they drank it, Thami making a face. Dyar ordered another set-up, for which Thami half-heartedly offered to pay, quickly slipping his money back into his pocket at Dyar's first "no."

"What a place, what a place," said Dyar, shaking his head. Two men with black beards had just come in, their heads wrapped in large Turkish towels; like all the others they were completely engrossed in unceasing and noisy conversation. "They sit here talking all night like this? What are they talking about? What is there to talk about so long?"

"What are people talking about in America?" said Thami, smiling at him.

"In a bar, usually politics. If they talk. Mostly they just drink."

"Here, everything: business, girls, politics, neighbors. Or what we are talking about now."

Dyer drained his glass. "And what are we talking about?" he demanded. "I'm damned if I know."

"About them." Thami laughed and made a wide gesture.

"You mean they're talking about us?"

"Some, perhaps."

"Have fun, chums," Dyar called loudly, turning his head toward the others. He looked down at his glass, had difficulty in getting it into clear focus. For a second he forgot where he was, saw only the empty glass, the same little glass that was always waiting to be refilled. His toe muscles were flexing, and that meant he was drunk. "Which is the nearest subway?" he thought. Then he stretched his legs out in front of him voluptuously and laughed. "Jesus!" he cried. "I'm glad to be here!" he looked around the dingy bar, heard the meaningless chatter, and felt a wave of doubt break over him, but he held firm. "God knows where this is, but I'd rather be here than there!" he insisted. The sound of the words being spoken aloud made him feel more sure; leaning back, he looked up at the shadows moving on the high yellow ceiling. He did not see the badly dressed youth with the sly expression who came in the door and began to walk directly toward the table. "And I mean it, too," he said, suddenly sitting upright and glaring at Thami, who looked startled.

The first Dyar knew of his presence was when Thami grudgingly responded to his greeting in Arabic. He glanced up, saw the young man looking down at him in a vaguely predatory fashion, and immediately took a dislike to him.

"Hello, mister." The youth grinned, widely enough to show which of his teeth were of gold and which were not.

"Hello," replied Dyar apathetically.

Thami said something in Arabic; he sounded truculent. The youth paid no attention, but seized a chair and drew it up to the table, keeping his eyes fixed on Dyar.

"Spickin anglish you like wan bleddy good soulima yah mister?" he said.

Thami looked around the bar uncomfortably, relaxing somewhat when he saw no one watching the table at the moment.

"Now," said Dyar, "just start all over again and take your time. What was that?"

The youth glared at him, spat. "You no spickin anglish?"

"Not that kind, buddy."

"He wants you to go and see a film," explained Thami. "But don't go."

"What? At this hour?" cried Dyar. "He's nuts."

"They show them late because they are forbidden by the police," said Thami, looking as though the whole idea were highly distasteful to him.

"Why? What kind of movies are they?" Dyar was beginning to be interested.

"Very bad. You know." Since Thami had the Moroccan's utter incomprehension of the meaning of pornography, he imagined that the police had placed the ban on obscene films because these infringed upon Christian doctrine at certain specific points, in which case any Christian might be expected to show interest, if only to disapprove. He found it not at all surprising that Dyar should want to know about them, although he himself was as totally indifferent as he would have expected Dyar to be had they treated of the question as to whether the pilgrim at Mecca should run around the Qaâba clockwise or counter-clockwise. At the same time, their being prohibited made them disreputable, and he was against having anything to do with them.

"They are very expensive and you see nothing," he said.

The young man did not understand Thami's words, but he knew the drift of his argument, and he was displeased. He spat more vehemently and carefully avoided turning his head in his direction.

"Well, you must see something, at least," objected Dyar with logic. "Let's get this straight," he said to the youth. "How much?" He got no reply. The youth looked confused; he was trying to decide how far above the usual tariff he could safely go. "Ch'hal?" pursued Thami. "How much? The man says how much. Tell him."

"Miehtsain."

"Achrine duro," said Thami sternly, as if he were correcting him. They argued a while. Presently Thami announced triumphantly: "You can go for one hundred pesetas." Then he glanced about the bar and his face darkened. "But it's no good. I advise you, don't go. It's very late. Why don't you go to bed? I will walk with you to your hotel."

Dyar looked at him and laughed lightly. "Listen, my friend. You don't have to come anywhere. Nobody said you had to come. Don't worry about me." Thami studied his face a second to see if he were angry, decided he was not, and said: "Oh, no!" There was no question of leaving the American to wander off into Benider with the pimp. Even though he would have liked more than anything at the moment to go home and sleep, and despite the fact that the last thing he wanted was to be seen in the street at this hour with a foreigner and this particular young man, he felt responsible for Dyar and determined not to let him out of his sight until he had got him to his hotel door. "Oh, no!" he said. "I'll go with you."

"Suit yourself."

They rose, and the youth followed them out onto the terrace. Dyar's clothes were still wet and he winced when the wind's blast struck him. He asked if it were far; Thami conferred with the other and said that it was a two-minute walk. The rain had lessened. They crossed the zoco, took a few turnings through streets that were like corridors in an old hotel, and stopped in the dimness before a high grilled door. Thami peered uneasily up and down the deserted alley as the youth hammered with the knocker, but there was no one to see them.

"I'm going to quit singin', I'm worried in my shoes —" sang Dyar, not very loud. But Thami gripped his arm, terrified. "No, no!" he whispered. "The police!" the song had echoed in the quiet interior of the street.

"Jesus Christ! So we're going to see a dirty movie. So what?" But he did not sing again.

They waited. Eventually there were faint sounds within. A muffled voice spoke on the other side of the door, and the youth answered. When the grille opened there was nothing at all to see but the blackness inside. Then a figure stepped from behind the door, and at the same time there came an odor which was a combination of eau de cologne, toothpaste and perspiration. The figure turned a flashlight in their faces, ordered the young man with them, in broken Spanish, to fetch a lamp, and shut the grille behind them. For a moment they all stood without moving in complete darkness. Thami coughed nervously; the sharp sound reverberated from wall to wall. When the young man appeared carrying the lamp the figure in white retired silently into a side room, and the three started up a flight of stairs. At the top, in a doorway, stood a fat man with a grayish complexion; he wore pyjamas and held a hand that was heavy with rings in front of his mouth to cover his yawns. The air up here was stiff with the smell of stale incense; the dead smoke clogged the hall.

The fat man addressed them in Spanish. Between words he wheezed. When he discovered that Dyar spoke only English he stopped, bowed, and said: "Good night, sir. Come these way, please." In a small room there were a few straight-backed chairs facing a blank wall where a canvas screen hung crookedly. On each side of the screen was a high potted palm. "Sit, please," he said, and stood above them breathing heavily. To Dyar he said: "We have one off the men with ladies, one from prists-nuns, and one boys altogether, sir. Very beautiful. All not wearing the clothing. You love, sir. You can looking all three these with one combination price, yes. Sir wishing three, sir?"

"No. Let's see the nuns."

"Yes, sir. Spanish gentleman liking nuns. Taking always the nuns. Very beautiful. Excuse."

He went out, and presently was heard talking in an adjoining room. Dyar lit a cigarette; Thami yawned widely. "You ought to have gone to bed," said Dyar.

"Oh, no! I will go with you to your hotel."

Dyar exploded. "God damn it, I'm not going to my hotel! Can't you get that through your head? It's not so hard to understand. When I get through here I'll go somewhere else, have another drink, maybe a little fun, I don't know. I don't know what I'll be doing. But I won't be going to the hotel. See?"

"It doesn't matter," said Thami calmly.

They were quiet for a moment, before Dyar pursued in a conciliatory tone: "You see, I've been on a ship for a week. I'm not sleepy. But you're sleepy. Why don't you go on home and call it a night?"

Thami was resolute. "Oh, no! I can't do that. It would be very bad. I will take you to your hotel. Whenever you go." He sat as low as the chair permitted and closed his eyes, letting his head fall slowly forward. The projector and film were brought and installed by another man in pyjamas, equally fat but with a full, old-fashioned moustache. By the time the whirring of the machine had started and the screen was lighted up, Thami's immobility and silence had passed over into the impetuously regular breathing of the sleeper.

4

THERE HAD BEEN a minor volcanic eruption in the Canaries. For several days the Spanish had been talking about it; the event had been given great prominence in the newspaper *España*, and many of them, having relatives there, had been receiving reassuring telegrams. On the disturbance everyone blamed the sultry weather, the breathless air and the grayish yellow light which had hung above the city for the past two days.

Eunice Goode had her own maid whom she paid by the day—a slovenly Spanish girl who came in at noon and did extra work the hotel servants could not be expected to do, such as keeping her clothes pressed and in order, running errands, and cleaning the bathroom daily. The girl had been full of news of the volcano that morning and had chattered on about it, much to her annoyance, for she had decided she was in a working mood. *"Silencio!"* she had finally cried; she had a thin, high voice which was quite incongruous with her robust appearance. The girl stared at her and then giggled. "I'm working," Eunice explained, looking as preoccupied as she could. The girl giggled again.

"Anyway," she went on, "this bad weather is simply the little winter arriving." "They say it's the volcano," the girl insisted. There was the little winter first, thus termed only because it was shorter, and then the big winter, the long rainy season which came two months or so afterward. They both made for dim days, wet feet and boredom; those who could escaped southward, but Eunice disliked movement of any kind. Now that she was in contact with what she called the inner reality, she scarcely minded whether the sun shone or not.

The girl was in the bathroom scrubbing the floor; she sang shrilly as she pushed the wet rag back and forth on the tiles. "Jesus!" moaned Eunice after a moment. "Conchita," she called. *"Mande,"* said the girl. "I want you to go and buy a lot of flowers in the market. Immediately." She gave her a hundred pesetas and sent her out in order to have solitude for a half-hour. She did not go out much herself these days; she spent most of her time lying in her bed. It was wide and the room was spacious. From her fortress of pillows she could see the activity of the small boats in the inner port, and she found it just enough of a diversion to follow with her eyes when she looked up from her writing. She began her day with gin, continuing with it until she went to sleep at night. When she had first come to Tangier she had drunk less and gone out more. Daytimes she had sunbathed on her balcony; evenings she had gone from bar to bar, mixing her drinks and having eventually to be accompanied to the entrance of her hotel by some disreputable individual who usually tried to take whatever small amount of money was left in the handbag she wore slung over her shoulder. But she never went out carrying more than she minded losing. The sunbathing had been stopped by the hotel management, because one day a Spanish lady had looked (with some difficulty) over the concrete partition that separated her balcony from the adjoining one, and had seen her massive pink body stretched out in a deckchair with nothing to cover it. There had been an unpleasant scene with the manager, who would have put her out if she had not been the most important single source of revenue for the hotel: she had all her meals served in bed and her door was always unlocked so the waiters could get in with drinks and bowls of ice. "It's just as well," she said to herself. "Sun is anti-thought. Lawrence was right." And now she found that lying in bed she drank more evenly; when night came she no longer had the urge to rush through the streets, to try to be everywhere at once for fear she would miss what was going to happen. The reason for this of course was that by evening she was too drunk to move very much, but it was a pleasant drunkenness, and it did not stop her from filling the pages of her notebooks with words— sometimes even with ideas.

Volcanoes angered her. The talk about this one put her in mind of a scene from her own childhood. She had been on a boat with her parents, going from Alexandria to Genoa. Early one morning her father had knocked on the door of the cabin where she and her mother slept, calling excitedly for them to go immediately on deck. More asleep than awake they arrived there to find him pointing wildly at Stromboli. The mountain was vomiting flames, and lava poured down its flanks, already crimson with the rising sun. Her mother had stared an instant, and then in a voice made hoarse by fury she had cried out one word: "Dis—gusting!" turned on her heel and taken Eunice below. In retrospect now, although she still could see her father's crestfallen face, she shared her mother's indignation.

She lay back, closed her eyes, and thought a bit. Presently she opened them and wrote: "There is something in the silly human mind that responds beautifully to the idea of rarity—especially rarity of conditions capable of producing a given phenomenon. The less likely a thing is to happen, the more wonderful it seems when it does, no matter how useless or even harmful it may be. The fact of its having happened despite the odds makes it a precious event. It had no right to occur, yet it did, and one can only blindly admire the chain of circumstances that caused the impossible to come to pass."

On reading over the paragraph she noted with a certain satisfaction that although it had been meant with reference to the volcano, it also had a distinct bearing upon her personal life at that moment. She was still a little awed by what seemed to her the incredible sequence of coincidences which had made it suddenly possible for her to be happy. A strange thing had happened to her about a fortnight back. She had awakened one bright morning and made a decision to take daily exercise of some kind. (She was constantly making decisions of one sort or another, each of which she was confident was going to re-volutionize her life.) The exercise would be mentally stimulating and would help her to reduce. Accordingly she had donned an old pair of slacks which were too small around the waist to be fastened, and set out for the top of the Casbah. She went through the big gate and, using her cane, climbed down the steep path to the long dirty beach below where only Moroccans bathed.

From there she had followed the coastline to the west, along the foot of the Casbah's lower buildings, past the stretch where all the sewers emptied and the stink was like a solid object in the air, to a further rocky beach which was more or less deserted. And here an old Moroccan fisherman had stopped her, holding forth a small piece of paper, and asked her with great seriousness in his halting Spanish to read him what was written on it.

It said: "Will the finder kindly communicate with C. J. Burnett, Esq., 52, Ashurst Road, North Finchley, London, England. April 12, 1949." She translated the request, indicating the address, and could not restrain herself from asking him where he had got the paper.

"Bottle in water," he replied, pointing to the small waves that broke near their feet. Then he asked her what he should do. "Write the man, if you like," she said, about to go on.

Yes, mused the old man, stroking his beard, he must write him, of course. But how, since he couldn't write? "A friend," she said. He looked at her searchingly and in a hesitant voice asked her if she would do it. She laughed. "I'm going for a walk," she said, pointing up the beach away from the town. "Perhaps when I come back." And she started walking again, leaving the old man standing there, holding his bit of paper, staring after her.

She had forgotten the incident by the time she arrived back at the same spot, but there was the fisherman sitting on a rock in his rags, looking anxiously toward her as she approached. "Now you write it?" he said. "But I have no paper," she objected. This was the beginning of a long episode in which he followed her at a distance of a few paces, all the way back along the shore, up the side hill and through the Casbah from one bacal to another in quest of an envelope and a sheet of paper.

When they had finally found a shopkeeper able to provide them with the two objects, she tried to pay for them, but the old man proudly laid his own coins on the counter and handed hers back to her. By then she thought the whole incident rather fun; it would make an amusing story to tell her friends. But she also felt in need of an immediate drink, and so she refused his invitation to go into a neighboring Moroccan café for tea, explaining that she must sit in a European café in order to write the letter for him properly. "Do you know one near here?" she asked him; she hoped they would not need to resort to one of the cafés in the Zoco Chico, to reach which they would have to go down steep streets and innumerable steps. He led her along several extremely narrow alleys where the shade was a blessing after the midday sun, to a small dingy place called *Bar Lucifer*. An extremely fat woman sat behind the counter reading a French movie magazine. Eunice ordered a gin and the old man had a gaseosa. She wrote the letter quickly, in the first person, saying she had found the bottle off Ras el Ihud, near Tangier, and was writing as requested, signing herself Abdelkader ben Saïd ben Mokhtar and giving his address. The fisherman thanked her profusely and went off to post the letter, first having insisted on paying for his gaseosa; she however stayed on and had several more gins.

The fat woman began to take an interest in her. Apparently she was not used to having women come into the bar, and this large foreigner who wore trousers and drank like a man aroused her curiosity. In French she asked Eunice a few questions about herself. Not being of a confiding nature, Eunice answered by improvising falsehoods, as she always did in similar circumstances. Then she countered with her own queries. The woman was only too eager to reply: she was Greek, her name was Madame Papaconstante, she had been eleven years in Tangier, the bar was a recent acquisition and had a few rooms in the back which were at the disposal of clients who required them. Presently Eunice thanked her and paid, promising to return that evening. She considered the place a discovery, because she was sure none of her friends knew about it.

At night the Bar Lucifer was quite a different matter. There were two bright gasoline lamps burning, so that the posters announcing bulls in San Roque and Melilla were visible, the little radio was going, and three Spaniards in overalls sat at the bar drinking beer. Madame Papaconstante, heavily made up and wearing an orange chiffon dress, walked to welcome her, her gold teeth glowing as she smiled. Behind the bar stood two Spanish girls with cheap permanent waves. Pretending to be following the men's conversation, they simpered when the men laughed.

"Are they your daughters?" asked Eunice. Madame Papaconstante said with some force that they were not. Then she explained that they served at the bar and acted as hostesses in the private rooms. A third girl stuck her head through the beaded curtain in the doorway that led into the back; she was very young and extraordinarily pretty. She stared at Eunice for a moment in some surprise before she came out and walked across to the entrance door.

"Who's that?" said Eunice.

A *fille indigène*, said Madame Papaconstante—a Moroccan girl who worked for her. "Very intelligent. She speaks English," she added. The girl turned and smiled at them, an unexpected smile, warming as a sudden ray of strong sunlight on a cloudy day.

"She's a delightful creature," said Eunice. She stepped to the bar and ordered a gin. Madame Papaconstante followed with difficulty and stood at the end beaming, her fleshy hands spread out flat on the bar so that her numerous rings flashed.

"Won't you have something?" suggested Eunice.

Madame Papaconstante looked astonished. It was an unusual evening in the Bar Lucifer when someone offered her a drink. *"Je prendrais bien un machaquito,"* she said, closing her eyes slowly and opening them again. They took their drinks to a small rickety table against the wall and sat down. The Moroccan girl stood in the doorway looking out into the dark, occasionally exchanging a word with a passerby.

"*Hadija, ven acá,*" called Madame Papaconstante. The girl turned and walked lightly to their table, smiling. Madame Papaconstante took her hand and told her to speak some English to the lady.

"You spickin English?" said the girl.

"Yes, of course. Would you like a drink?"

"I spickin. What you drink?"

"Gin." Eunice held up her glass, already nearly empty. The girl made a grimace of disgust.

"Ah no good. I like wan Coca-Cola."

"Of course." She caught the eye of one of the girls at the bar, and shouted to her: "*Una Coca-Cola, un machaquito y un gin!*" Hadija went to the bar to fetch the drinks.

"She's exquisite," said Eunice quickly to Madame Papaconstante. "Where did you find her?"

"Oh, for many years she has been playing in the street here with the other children. It's a poor family."

When she returned to the table with the glasses Eunice suggested she sit with them, but she pretended not to hear, and backed against the wall to remain there looking calmly down at them. There was a desultory conversation for twenty minutes or a half hour, during which Eunice ordered several more gins. She was beginning to feel very well; she turned to Madame Papaconstante. "Would you think me rude if I sat with her alone for a bit? I should like to talk with her."

"*Ça va,*" said Madame Papaconstante. It was unusual, but she saw no reason to object.

"She is absolutely ravishing," added Eunice, flinging her cigarette across the room so that it landed in the alley. She rose, put her arm around the girl, and said to her in English: "Have another Coca-Cola and bring it inside, into one of the rooms." She gestured. "Let's sit in there where it's private."

This suggestion, however, outraged Madame Papaconstante. "*Ah, non!*" she cried vehemently. "Those rooms are for gentlemen."

Eunice was unruffled. Since to her mind her aims were always irreproachable, she rarely hesitated before trying to attain them. "Come along, then," she said to the girl. "We'll go to my hotel." She let go of Hadija and stepped to the bar, fumbling in her handbag for money. While she was paying, Madame Papaconstante got slowly to her feet, wheezing painfully.

"She works here, *vous savez!*" she shouted. "She is not free to come and go." As an afterthought she added: "She owes me money."

Eunice turned and placed several banknotes in her hand, closing the fingers over them gently. The girls behind the bar watched, their eyes shining.

"*Au revoir, madame,*" she said with warmth. An expression of great earnestness spread over her face as she went on: "I can never thank you enough. It has been a charming evening. I shall stop by tomorrow and see you. I have a little gift I should like to bring you."

Madame Papaconstante's large mouth was open, the words which had intended to come out remained inside. She let her gaze drop for a second to her hand, saw the corners of two of the bills, and slowly closed her mouth. "Ah," she said.

"You must forgive me for having taken up so much of your time," Eunice continued. "I know you are busy. But you have been very kind. Thank you."

By now Madame Papaconstante had regained control of herself. "Not at all," she said. "It was a real pleasure for me."

During this dialogue Hadija had remained unmoving by the door, her eyes darting back and forth from Eunice's face to that of her *patronne*, in an attempt to follow the meaning of their words. Now, having decided that Eunice had won in the encounter, she smiled tentatively at her.

"Good night," said Eunice again to Madame Papaconstante. She waved brightly at the girls behind the bar. The men looked around for the first time, then resumed their talk. Eunice took Hadija's arm and they went out into the dark street. Madame Papaconstante came to the door, leaned out, saying softly: "If she does not behave herself you will tell me tomorrow."

"Oh, she will, I'm certain," said Eunice, squeezing the girl's arm. "*Merci mille fois, madame. Bonne nuit.*"

"What he sigh you?" demanded Hadija.

"She said you were a very nice girl."

"Sure. Very fine." She slipped ahead, since there was not room for them to walk abreast.

"Don't go too fast," said Eunice, panting from her attempt to keep up with her. When they came out on to the crest of the hill at Amrah, she said: "Wait, Hadija," and leaned against the wall. It was a moment she wanted to savor. She was suddenly conscious of the world outside herself—not as merely a thing that was there and belonged to other people, but as something in which she almost felt she could share. For the first time she smelled the warm odor of fulfillment on the evening air, heard the nervous beating of drums on the terraces with something besides indifference. She let her eyes range down over the city and saw clearly in the moonlight the minaret on the summit of the Charf with its little black cypress trees around it. She pounded her cane on the pavement with pleasure, several times. "I insist too hard on living my own life," she thought. The rest of the world was there for her to take at any moment she wished it, but she always rejected it in favor of her own familiar little cosmos. Only sometimes as she came out of sleep did she feel she was really *in* life, but that was merely because she had not had time to collect her thoughts, to become herself once more.

"What a beautiful night," she said dreamily. "Come and stand here a minute." Hadija obeyed reluctantly. Eunice grasped her arm again. "Listen to the drums."

"*Drbouka.* Women make."

"Aha." She smiled mysteriously, following with her eye the faint line of the mountains, range beyond range, blue in the night's clarity. She did not hope Hadija would be able to share her sensations; she asked only that the girl act as a catalyst for her, making it possible for her to experience them in their pure state. As a mainspring for her behavior there was always the aching regret for a vanished innocence, a nostalgia for the early years of life. Whenever a possibility of happiness presented itself, through it she sought to reach again that infinitely distant and tender place, her lost childhood. And in Hadija's simple laughter she divined a prospect of return.

The feeling had persisted through the night. She exulted to find she had been correct. At daybreak, while Hadija was still asleep beside her, she sat up and wrote in her notebook: "A quiet moment in the early morning. The pigeons have just begun to murmur outside the window. There is no wind. Sexuality is primarily a matter of imagination, I am sure. People who live in the warmer climates have very little of it, and so society there can allow a wide moral latitude in the customs. Here are the healthiest personalities. In temperate regions it is quite a different matter. The imagination's fertile activity must be curtailed by a strict code of sexual behavior which results in crime and depravity. Look at the great cities of the world. Almost all of them are in the temperate zone." She let her eyes rest a moment on the harbor below. The still water was like blue glass. Moving cautiously so as not to wake Hadija, she poured herself a small amount of gin from the nearly empty bottle on the night table, and lit a cigarette. "But of course all cities are points of infection, like decayed teeth. The hypersensitivity of urban culture (its only virtue) is largely a reaction to pain. Tangier has no urban culture, no pain. I believe it never will have. The nerve will never be exposed."

She still felt an itch of regret at not having been allowed to go into a back room of the Bar Lucifer with Hadija. That would have given her a certain satisfaction; in her eyes it would have been a pure act. Perhaps another time, when she and Madame Papaconstante had come to know each other better, it would be possible.

Not until Hadija awoke did she telephone down for breakfast. It gave her great pleasure to see the girl, wearing a pair of her pyjamas, sitting up crosslegged in the bed daintily eating buttered toast with a knife and fork, to show that she knew how to manage those Western accessories. She sent her home a little before noon, so she would not be there when the Spanish maid arrived. In the afternoon she called by the Bar Lucifer with a small bottle of perfume for Madame Papaconstante. Since then almost every other night she had brought Hadija back with her to the hotel. She had never seen the old fisherman again—she could hardly expect to see him unless she returned to the beach, and she was not likely to do that. She had forgotten about getting exercise; her life was too much occupied at the moment with Hadija for her to be making resolutions and decisions for improving it. She taxed her imaginative powers devising ways of amusing her, finding places to take her, choosing gifts that would please her. Faintly

she was conscious through all this that it was she herself who was
enjoying these things, that Hadija merely accompanied her and accepted the presents with something akin to apathy. But that made no
difference to her.

When she was happy she invariably invented a reason for not
being able to remain so. And now, to follow out her pattern, she
allowed an idea to occur to her which counteracted all her happiness.
She had made an arrangement with Madame Papaconstante whereby
it was agreed that on the nights when Hadija did not go with her to the
Metropole she was to remain at home with her parents. Madame
Papaconstante had assured her that the girl did not even put in
appearance at the bar those evenings, and up until now Eunice had not
thought to question the truth of her statements. But today, when
Conchita returned from the market with her arms full of flowers,
notwithstanding the fact that Hadija had left the room only three
hours before and did not expect to return until tomorrow night,
Eunice suddenly decided she wanted her back again that same evening. She would get her some very special gift in the Rue du Statut, and
they would have a little extra celebration, surrounded by the lilies and
poinsettias. She would go to the Bar Lucifer and have Madame
Papaconstante send someone to fetch her.

It was at this moment that the terrible possibility struck her:
what if she found Hadija in the bar? If she did, it could only mean that
she had been there all along, that the parent story was a lie, that she
lived in one of the rooms behind the bar, perhaps. (She was working
up to the climax.) Then the place was a true bordel, in which case—it
had to be faced—there was a likelihood that Hadija was entertaining
the male customers in bed on those other nights.

The idea stirred her to action: she threw her notebook on the
floor and jumped out of bed with a violence that shook the room and
startled Conchita. When she had dressed she wanted to start out
immediately for the Bar Lucifer, but she reflected on the uselessness of
such a procedure. She must wait until night and catch Hadija *in
flagrante delicto*. By now there was no room in her mind for doubt.
She was convinced that Madame Papaconstante had been deceiving
her. Assailed by memories of former occasions when she had been
trusting and complacent only to discover that her happiness had rested
wholly on falsehoods, she was all too ready this time to seek out the

deception and confront it.

As the afternoon advanced toward evening she grew more rest-less, pacing back and forth from one side of the room to the other, again and again going out onto the balcony and looking toward the harbor without seeing it. She even forgot to walk up to the Rue du Statut for Hadija's present. A black cloud gathered above the harbor and twilight passed swiftly into night. Gusts of rain-laden wind blew across the balcony into the room. She shut the door and decided, since she was dressed, to go downstairs for dinner rather than have it in bed. The orchestra and the other diners would help to keep her mind occupied. She could not hope to find Hadija at the bar before half-past nine.

When she got downstairs it was too early for dinner. There was no electricity tonight; candles burned in the corridors and oil lamps in the public rooms. She went into the bar and was engaged in conversa-tion by an elderly retired captain from the British Army, who insisted on buying her drinks. This annoyed her considerably because she did not feel free to order as many as she wanted. The old gentleman drank slowly and reminisced at length about the Far East. "Oh God oh *God* oh God," she said to herself, "Will he ever shut up and will it ever be eight-thirty?"

As usual the meal was execrable. However, eating in the dining-room she at least found the food hot, whereas by the time it reached her bed it generally had ceased being even warm. Between orchestral numbers she could hear the wind roaring outside, and the rain streamed down the long French windows of the dining room. "I shall get soaked," she thought, but the prospect was in no way a deterrent. On the contrary, the storm rather added to the drama in which she was convinced she was about to participate. She would plod through the wet streets, find Hadija, there would be an awful scene, perhaps a chase through the gale up into a forsaken corner of the Casbah or to some solitary rock far out above the strait. And then would come the reconciliation in the windy darkness, the admissions and the prom-ises, and eventually the smiles. But this time she would bring her back to the Metropole for good.

After she had finished eating she went up to her room, changed into slacks, and slipped into a raincoat. Her hands were trembling with excitement. The air in her room was weighted down with the thick sweetness of the lilies. The candle flames waved back and forth as she moved about in haste, and the shadows of the flowers crouched, leapt to the ceiling, returned. From a drawer in one of her trunks she took a large flashlight. She stepped out, closing the door behind her. The candles went on burning.

5

IT LOOKED LIKE a bright spring day. The sun shone on the laurel that lined the garden path where Sister Inez strolled, clutching her prayer book. Until she arrived at the fountain her long black skirts hid the fact that she was barefoot. It was the sort of garden whose air one would expect to be heavy with the sweet smell of jasmine, and although they did not appear, one could imagine birds twittering and rustling their wings with nervous delight in the shadow of the bushes. Sister Inez stretched forth one shining foot and touched the water in the basin; the sky glimmered whitely. From the bushes Father José watched, his eyes bright as he followed the two little feet moving one behind the other through the clear water. Suddenly Sister Inez undid her cowl, which was fastened with a snap-hook under her chin: her black tresses fell over her shoulders. With a second brusque gesture she unhooked her garments all the way down (it was remarkably easy), opened them wide, and turned to reveal a plump young white body. A moment later she had tossed her apparel upon a marble bench and was standing there quite naked, still holding her little black book and her rosary. Father José's eyes opened wider and his gaze turned heavenwards: he was praying for the strength to resist temptation. In fact, the words PIDIENDO EL AMPARO DIVINO appeared in print across the sky, and remained there, shaking slightly, for several seconds. What followed was not a surprise to Dyar, since he had not expected the divine aid to be forthcoming, nor was he startled when a moment later three other healthy young nuns made their entrances from as many different directions to join the busy couple in the fountain, thus making the pas de deux into an ensemble number.

Subsequently the scene of activities was shifted to an altar in a nearby church. Dyar, sensing that the frenzy of this episode announced the imminent end of the film, nudged Thami and offered him a cigarette which, after awakening with a jolt, he accepted automatically and allowed to be lighted. By the time he was really conscious, the images had come to an abrupt finish and the screen was a blinding square of light. Dyar paid the first fat man, who stood in the hallway still yawning, and they went downstairs. "If two gentlemen wishing room one hour—" the fat man began, calling after them. Thami shouted something up at him in Spanish; the young man let them out into the empty street where the wind blew.

*

When Eunice Goode stepped into the little bar she was disappointed to see that Hadija was not in sight. She walked up to the counter, looking fixedly at the girl who stood behind, and noted with pleasure the uneasiness her sudden appearance was causing in the latter's behavior. The girl made an absurd attempt to smile, and slowly backed against the wall, not averting her gaze from Eunice Goode's face. And, indeed, the rich foreign lady's mien was rather formidable: her plump cheeks were suffused with red, she was panting, and under her heavy brows her cold eyes moved with a fierce gleam.

"Where is everyone?" she demanded abruptly.

The girl began to stammer in Spanish that she did not know, that she thought they were out that way. Then she made for the end of the bar and tried to slip around it to get to the door that led back to the other rooms. Eunice Goode pushed her with her cane. "Give me a gin," she said. Reluctantly the girl returned to where the bottles were and poured out a drink. There were no customers.

She emptied the glass at one gulp, and leaving the girl staring after her in dismay, walked through the beaded curtain, feeling ahead of her with the tip of her cane, for the hallway was dark.

"Madame!" cried the girl loudly from behind her. "Madame!"

On the right a door opened. Madame Papaconstante, in an embroidered Chinese kimono, stepped into the hall. When she saw Eunice Goode she gave an involuntary start. Recovering, she smiled feebly and walked toward her uttering a series of voluble salutations which, as she was delivering them, did not prevent the visitor from noticing that her hostess was not only blocking the way to further progress down the hall, but was actually pushing her firmly back toward the bar. And standing in the bar she talked on.

"What weather! What rain! I was caught in it at dinner time. All my clothes soaking! You see." She glanced downward at her attire. "I had to change. My dress is drying before the heater. Maria will iron it for me. Come and have a drink with me. I did not expect you tonight. *C'est un plaisir inattendu.* Ah, yes, madame." She frowned furiously at the girl. "Sit down here," said Madame Papaconstante, "and I shall serve you myself. Now, what are we having tonight?"

When she saw Eunice finally seated at the little table she heaved a sigh of relief and rubbed her enormous flabby arms nervously, so that her bracelets clinked together. Eunice watched her discomfiture with grim enjoyment.

"Listen to the rain," said Madame Papaconstante, tilting her head toward the street. Still Eunice did not answer. "The fool," she was thinking. "The poor old god-damned fool."

"What are *you* having?" she said suddenly, with such violence that Madame Papaconstante looked into her eyes terrified, not quite sure she had not said something else. "Oh, me!" she laughed. "I shall take a *machaquito* as always."

"Sit down," said Eunice. The girl brought the drinks, and Madame Papaconstante, after casting a brief worried glance toward the street, sank onto a chair opposite Eunice Goode.

They had two drinks apiece while they talked vaguely about the weather. A beggar crawled through the door, moving forward by lifting himself on his hands, leaned against the wall, and with expressive gestures indicated his footless lower limbs, twisted like the stumps of a mangrove root. He was drenched with rain.

"Make him go away!" cried Eunice. "I can't bear to see deformed people. Give him something and get rid of him. I hate the sight of suffering." Since Madame Papaconstante did not move, she felt in her handbag and tossed a note to the man, who thrust his body forward with a reptilian movement and seized it. She knew perfectly well that one did not give such large sums to beggars, but the Bar Lucifer was a place where the feeling of power that money gave her was augmented to an extent which made the getting rid of it an act of irresistible voluptuousness. Madame Papaconstante shuddered inwardly as she watched the price of ten drinks being snatched up by the clawlike hand. Vaguely she recognized Eunice's gesture as one of hostility toward her; she cast a resentful glance at the strange woman sprawled out opposite her, thinking that God had made an error in allowing a person like that to have so much money.

Up to her arrival Eunice had fully intended to ask in a straightforward fashion whether or not Hadija was there, but now such a course seemed inadvisable. If she were in the establishment, eventually she would have to come out through the front room, since the back of the building lay against the lower part of the Casbah ramparts and thus had no other exit.

Without turning her head, Madame Papaconstante called casually in Spanish to the girl behind the bar. "Lolita! Do you mind bringing me my jersey? It's in the pink room on the big chair." And to Eunice in French: "With this rain and wind I feel cold."

"It's a signal," thought Eunice as the girl went beneath the looped-up beaded curtain. "She wants to warn Hadija so she won't come out or talk loud." "Do you have many rooms?" she said.

"Four." Madame Papaconstante shivered slightly. "Pink, blue, green and yellow."

"I adore yellow," said Eunice unexpectedly. "They say it's the color of madness, but that doesn't prevent me. It's so brilliant and full of sunshine as a color. *Vous ne trouvez pas?*"

"I like all colors," Madame Papaconstante said vaguely, looking toward the street with apprehension.

The girl returned without the sweater. "It's not there," she announced. Madame Papaconstante looked at her meaningfully, but the girl's face was blank. She returned to her position behind the bar. Two Spaniards in overalls ducked in from the street and ordered beer; evidently they had come from somewhere nearby, as their clothes were only slightly sprinkled with raindrops. Madame Papaconstante rose. "I'm going to look for it myself," she announced. "One moment. *Je reviens à l'instant.*" As she waddled down the hallway, running her hand along the wall, she murmured aloud: "*Qué mujer!*

Qué mujer!"

More customers entered. When she came out, wearing over the kimono a huge purple sweater which had been stretched into utter formlessness, she looked a little happier. Without speaking to Eunice she went to the bar and joked with the men. It was going to be a fairly good night for business, after all. Perhaps if she ignored the foreign lady she would go away. The men, none of whom happened to have seen Eunice before, asked her in undertones who the strange woman was, what she was doing, sitting there alone in the bar. The question embarrassed Madame Papaconstante. "A tourist," she said nonchalantly. "Here?" they exclaimed, astonished. "She's a little crazy," she said, by way of explanation. But she was unhappy about Eunice's presence; she wished she would go away. Naively she decided to try and get her drunk, and not wishing to be re-engaged in conversation with her, sent the drink, a double straight gin, over to her table by Lolita.

"*Ahí tiene,*" said Lolita, setting the glass down. Eunice leered at her, and lifting it, drained it in two swallows. Madame Papaconstante's ingenuousness amused her greatly.

A few minutes later Lolita appeared at the table with another drink. "I didn't order this," said Eunice, just to see what would happen.

"A gift from Madame."

"*Ah, de veras!*" said Eunice. "Wait!" she cried sharply as the girl started away. "Tell Madame Papaconstante I want to speak to her."

Presently Madame Papaconstante was leaning over her table. "You wanted to see me, madame?"

"Yes," said Eunice, making an ostensible effort to focus her eyes on the fleshy countenance. "I'm not feeling well. I think I've had too much to drink." Madame Papaconstante showed solicitude, but not very convincingly. "I think," Eunice went on, "that you'll have to take me to a room and let me lie down."

Madame Papaconstante started. "Oh, impossible, Madame! It's not allowed for ladies to be in the rooms."

"And what about the girls?"

"*Ah, oui, mais ça c'est naturel!* They are my employees, madame."

"As you like," said Eunice carelessly, and she began to sing, softly at first, but with rapidly increasing stridency. Madame Papaconstante returned to the bar with misgivings.

Eunice Goode sang on, always louder. She sang: "I Have to Pass Your House to Get to My House" and "Get Out of Town". By the time she got to "I Have Always Been a Kind of Woman Hater" and "The Last Round-Up" the sound that came from her ample lungs was nothing short of a prolonged shriek.

Noticing Madame Papaconstante's expression of increasing apprehension, she said to herself with satisfaction: "I'll fix the old bitch, once and for all." She struggled to her feet, managing as she did so to upset not only her chair, but the table as well. Pieces of glass flew toward the feet of the men who stood at one end of the bar.

"*Aaah, madame, quand-même!*" cried Madame Papaconstante in consternation. "Please! You are making a scandal. One does not make scandals in my bar. This is a respectable establishment. I can't have the police coming to complain."

Eunice moved crookedly toward the bar, and smiling apologetically, leaned her arm on Madame Papaconstante's cushion-like shoulder. "*Je suis navrée,*" she began hesitantly. "*Je ne me sens pas bien. Ça ne va pas du tout.* You must forgive me. I don't know. Perhaps a good large glass of gin——"

Madame Papaconstante looked around helplessly. The others had not understood. Then she thought: perhaps now she will leave, and went behind the bar to pour it out herself. Eunice turned to the man beside her and with great dignity explained that she was not at all drunk, that she merely felt a little sick. The man did not reply.

At the first sip of her drink she raised her head, looked at Madame Papaconstante with startled eyes, and put her hand to her forehead.

"Quick! I'm ill! Where's the toilet?"

The men moved a little away from her. Madame Papaconstante seized her arm and pulled her through the doorway down the hall. At the far end she opened a door and pushed her into a foul-smelling closet, totally dark. Eunice groaned. "I shall bring a light," said Madame Papaconstante, hurrying away. Eunice lit a match, flushed the toilet, made some more groaning sounds, and peered out into the corridor. It was empty. She stepped out swiftly and went into the next room, which was also dark. She lit another match, saw a couch against the wall. She lay down and waited. A minute or two later there were voices in the hallway. Presently someone opened the door. She lay still, breathing slowly, deeply. A flashlight was turned into her face. Hands touched her, tugged at her. She did not move.

"*No hay remedio,*" said one of the girls.

A few more halfhearted attempts were made to rouse her, and then the group withdrew and closed the door.

*

As he climbed behind Thami through the streets that were half stairways, Dyar felt his enthusiasm for their project rapidly diminishing. The wet wind circled down upon them from above, smelling of the sea. Occasionally it splashed them with rain, but mostly it merely blew. By the time they had turned into the little street that ran level, he was thinking of his room back at the Hotel de la Playa almost with longing. "Here," said Thami.

They walked into the bar. The first thing Dyar saw was Hadija standing in the back doorway. She was wearing a simple flannel dress that Eunice had bought her on the Boulevard Pasteur, and it fitted her. She had also learned not to make up so heavily, and even to do her hair up into a knot at the back of her neck, rather than let it stand out wildly in hopeless imitation of the American film stars. She looked intently at Dyar, who felt a slight shiver run down his spine.

"By God, look at that!" he murmured to Thami.

"You like her?"

"I could use a little of it, all right."

A Spaniard had placed a portable radio on the bar; two of the girls bent over listening to faint guitar music behind a heavy curtain of static. Three men were having a serious drunken discussion at a table in the corner. Madame Papaconstante sat at the end of the bar, smoking listlessly. "*Muy buenas,*" she said to them, beaming widely, mistaking them in her sleepiness for Spaniards.

Thami replied quietly without looking at her. Dyar went to the bar and ordered drinks, keeping his eye on Hadija, who when she saw his attention, looked beyond him to the street. Hearing English being spoken, Madame Papaconstante rose and approached the two, swaying a little more than usual.

"Hello, boys," she said, patting her hair with one hand while she pulled her sweater down over her abdomen with the other. Apart from figures and a few insulting epithets, these words were her entire English vocabulary.

"Hello," Dyar answered without enthusiasm. Then he went over to the door and holding up his glass, said to Hadija: "Care for a drink?" But Hadija had learned several things during her short acquaintance with Eunice Goode, perhaps the most important of which was that the more difficult everything was made, the more money would be forthcoming when payment came due. If she had been the daughter of the English Consul and had been accosted by a Spanish fisherman in the middle of the Place de France she could not have stared more coldly. She moved across the room and stood near the door facing the street.

Dyar made a wry grimace. "My mistake," he called after her ruefully; his chagrin, however, was nothing compared to Madame Papaconstante's indignation with Hadija. Her hands on her hips, she walked over to her and began to deliver a low-pitched but furious scolding.

"She works here, doesn't she?" he said to Thami. Thami nodded.

"Watch," Dyar went on, "the old madam's giving her hell for being so snotty with the customers." Thami did not understand entirely, but he smiled. They saw Hadija's expression grow more sullen. Presently she ambled over to the bar and stood sulking near Dyar. He decided to try again.

"No hard feelings?"

She looked up at him insolently. "Hello, Jack" she said, and turned her face away.

"What's the matter? Don't you like strange men?"

"Wan Coca-Cola" She did not look at him again.

"You don't have to drink with me if you don't want to, you know," he said, trying to make his voice sound sympathetic. "If you're tired, or something——"

"How you feel?" she said. Madame Papaconstante was watching

her from the end of the bar.

She lifted her glass of Coca-Cola. "Down the hotch," she said, and took a sip. She smiled faintly at him. He stood closer to her, so he could just feel her body alongside his. Then he turned slightly toward her, and moved in a bit more. She did not stir.

"You always as crazy as this?" he asked her.

"I not crazy," she said evenly.

They talked a while. Slowly he backed her against the bar; when he put his arm around her he thought she might push him away, but she did nothing. From her vantage-point Madame Papaconstante judged that the right moment for intervention had arrived; she lumbered down from her stool and went over to them. Thami was chatting with the Spaniard who owned the radio; when he saw Madame Papaconstante trying to talk to Dyar he turned toward them and became interpreter.

"You want to go back with her?" he asked him.

Dyar said he did.

"Tell him fifty pesetas for the room," said Madame Papaconstante hurriedly. The Spaniards were listening. They usually paid twenty-five. "And he gives the girl what he likes, afterward."

Hadija was looking at the floor.

*

The room smelled of mildew. Eunice had been asleep, but now she was awake, and she noticed the smell. Certain rooms in the cellar of her grandmother's house had smelled like that. She remembered the coolness and mystery of the enormous cellar on a quiet summer afternoon, the trunks, the shelves of empty mason jars and the stacks of old magazines. Her grandmother had been an orderly person. Each publication had been piled separately: *Judge, The Smart Set, The Red Book, Everybody's, Hearst's International* —— She sat up in the dark, tense, without knowing why. Then she did know why. She had heard Hadija's voice outside the door. Now it said: "This room O.K."; she heard a man grunt a reply. The door into the adjacent room was opened, and then closed.

She stood up and began to walk back and forth in front of the couch, three steps one way and three steps the other. "I can't bear it," she thought. "I'll kill her. I'll kill her." But it was just the sound of the words in her head; no violent images came to accompany the refrain. Crouching on the floor with her neck twisted at a painful angle, she managed to place her ear flush against the wall. And she listened. At first she heard nothing, and she thought the wall must be too thick to let the sound through. But then she heard a loud sigh. They were not saying anything, and she realized that when something was said, she would hear every word.

A long time went by before this happened. Then Hadija said: "No." Immediately the man complained: "What's the matter with you?" In his voice Eunice recognized a fellow American; it was even worse than she had expected. There were sounds of movement on the couch, and again Hadija said very firmly: "No."

"But, Baby—" the man pleaded.

After more shifting about, "No," said the man halfheartedly, as if in faint protest. Eunice's neck ached; she strained harder, pushing against the wall with all her strength. For a while she heard nothing. Then there was a long, shuddering groan of pleasure from the man. "As if he were dying," thought Eunice, gritting her teeth. Now she told herself: "I'll kill *him*," and this time she had a satisfactorily bloody vision, although her imaginary attack upon the man fell somewhat short of murder.

Suddenly she had drawn her head back and was pounding on the wall with her fist. And she was calling out to Hadija in Spanish: "Go on! *Haz lo que quieres! Sigue!* Have a good time!" Her own knocking had startled her, and the sound of her voice astonished her even more; she would never have known it was hers. But now she had spoken; she caught her breath and listened. There was silence in the next room for a moment. The man said lazily: "What's all that?" Hadija answered by whispering. "Quick! Give money!" She sounded agitated. "One other time I fix you up good. No like tonight. No here. Here no good. Listen, boy—" And here apparently she whispered directly into his ear, as if she knew from experience just how thin the walls were and how easily the sound carried. The man, who seemed to be in a state of profound lassitude, began nevertheless to grunt: "Huh? When? Where's that?" between the lengthy inaudible explanations.

"Okay?" said Hadija finally. "You come?"

"But Sunday, right? Not Friday—" The last word was partially muffled, she supposed by Hadija's hand.

Painfully Eunice got to her feet. She sighed deeply and sat down on the edge of the couch in the dark. Everything she had suspected was perfectly true: Hadija had been working regularly at the Bar Lucifer; probably she had often come to her fresh from the embrace of a Spanish laborer or shopkeeper. The arrangement with Madame Papaconstante was clearly a farce. Everyone had been lying to her. Yet instead of resentment she felt only a dimly satisfying pain—perhaps because she had found it all out at first-hand and through her own efforts. It was an old story to her and she did not mind. All she wanted now was to be alone with Hadija. She would not even discuss the evening with her. "The poor girl," she thought. "I don't give her enough to live on. She's forced to come here." She began to consider places where she might take her to get her away from the harmful environment, places where they could be alone, unmolested by prying servants and disapproving or amused acquaintances. Sospel, perhaps, or Caparica; somewhere away from Moroccans and Spaniards, where she would have the pleasure of feeling that Hadija was wholly dependent upon her.

"But, Baby, that's all I've got," the man was protesting. They talked normally now; she could hear them from where she sat.

"No, no," said Hadija firmly. "More. Give."

"You don't care *how* much you take from a guy, do you? I'm telling you, I haven't *got* any more. Look."

"We go spick you friend in bar. He got."

"No. You got enough now. That's damn good money for what you did."

"Next time I fix—"

"I know! I know!"

They argued. It astonished Eunice to hear an American refusing to part with an extra fifty pesetas under such circumstances. Typically, she decided he must be an extremely vicious man, one who got his true pleasure from just such scenes, to whom it gave a thrill of evil delight to withhold her due from a helpless girl. But it amused her to observe the vigor with which Hadija pursued the discussion. She bet herself drinks for the house that the girl would get the extra money. And after a good deal of pointless talk he agreed to borrow the sum from the friend in the bar. As they opened the door and went out Hadija said: "You good man. I like." Eunice bit her lip and stood up. More than anything else, that remark made her feel that she was right in suspecting this man of being a particular danger. And now she realized that it was not the possibility of professional relationships on Hadija's part that distressed her most. It was precisely the fear that things might not remain on that footing. "But I'm an idiot," she told herself. "Why this man? the very first one I happen to have caught her with?" The important thing was that it be the last; she must take her away. And Madame Papaconstante must not know of it until they were out of the International Zone.

A quarter of an hour later she went out into the hallway; it was gray with the feeble light of dawn which came through the curtain of beads from the bar. There she heard Madame Papaconstante and Hadija arguing bitterly. "You let me go into the very next room!" Hadija was shouting. "You knew she was in there! You wanted her to hear!"

"It's not my fault she woke up!" cried Madame Papaconstante furiously. "Who do you think you are, yelling at me in my own bar!"

Eunice waited, hoping Madame Papaconstante would go further, say something more drastic, but she remained cautious, obviously not wishing to provoke the girl too deeply: — she brought money into the establishment.

Eunice walked quietly down the passageway and stepped into the bar, blinking a little. Her cane was lying across one of the tables. The two ceased speaking and looked at her. She picked up the cane, turned to face them. "Drinks for the house," she remembered. "Three double gins," she said to Madame Papaconstante, who went without a word behind the bar and poured them out.

"Take it," she said to Hadija, holding one of the glasses toward her. With her eyes on Eunice, she obeyed.

"Drink it."

Hadija did, choking afterward.

Madame Papaconstante hesitated and drank hers, still without speaking.

Eunice placed five hundred pesetas on the bar, and said: "*Bonne nuit, madame.*" To Hadija she said: "*Ven.*"

Madame Papaconstante stood looking after them as they walked slowly up the street. A large brown rat crept from a doorway opposite and began to make its way along the gutter in the other direction, stopping to sample bits of refuse as it went. The rain fell evenly and quietly.

6

WILCOX SAT on the edge of his bed in his bathrobe. Mr. Ashcombe-Danvers was concentrating his attention upon opening a new tin of Gold Flakes; a faint hiss came out as he punctured the top. Rapidly he cut around the edge and removed the light tin disc, which he dropped on the floor beside his table.

"Have one?" he said to Wilcox, holding up the tin to him. The odor of the fresh tobacco was irresistible. Wilcox took a cigarette. Mr. Ashcombe-Danvers did likewise. When both had lights, Mr. Ashcombe-Danvers went on with what he had been saying.

"My dear boy, I don't want to seem to be asking the impossible, and I think if you try to look at it from my point of view you'll see soon enough that actually I'm only asking the inevitable. I expect you knew that sooner or later I should require to move sterling here."

Wilcox looked uncomfortable. He ran his finger along the edge of the ash tray. "Well, yes. I'm not surprised," he said. Before the other could speak again he went on. "But if you'll excuse my saying so, I can't help feeling you've chosen a rather crude method of getting it here."

Mr. Ashcombe-Danvers smiled. "Yes. If you like, it's crude. I don't think that militates against its success in any way."

"I wonder," said Wilcox.

"Why should it?"

"Well, it's too large a sum to bring in that way."

"Nonsense!" Mr. Ashcombe-Danvers cried. "Don't be bound by tradition, my boy. That's simply superstitious of you. If one can do it that way with a small amount, one can do it in exactly the same way with a larger one. Can't you see how safe it is? There's nothing whatever in writing, is there? The number of agents is reduced to a minimum—all I need to be sure of is old Ramlal, his son and you."

"And all I need to be sure of is that nobody knows it when I go to Ramlal and take out nine thousand pounds in cash. That includes our British currency snoopers as well as the Larbi crowd. And I'd say it's impossible. They're bound to know. Somebody's bound to find out."

"Nonsense," said Mr. Ashcombe-Danvers again. "If you're afraid for your own skin," he smiled ingratiatingly, fearing that he might be treading on delicate ground, "and you've every right to be, of course, why—send someone else to fetch it. You must have someone around you can trust for a half hour."

"Not a soul," said Wilcox. He had just thought of Dyar. "Let's have some lunch. We can have it right here in the room. They have some good roast beef downstairs, or had yesterday." He reached for the telephone.

"Afraid I can't." Mr. Ashcombe-Danvers was half expecting Wilcox to raise his percentage, and he did not want to do anything which might help put him sufficiently at his ease to make him broach the subject.

"Sure?" said Wilcox.

"No, I can't," repeated Mr. Ashcombe-Danvers.

Wilcox took up the telephone. "A whiskey?" He lifted the receiver.

"Oh, I think not, thank you."

"Of course you will," said Wilcox. "Give me the bar."

Mr. Ashcombe-Danvers rose and stood looking out the window. The wet town below looked freshly built; the harbor and the sky beyond it were a uniform gray. It was raining indifferently. Wilcox was saying: "Manolo? Haig and Haig Pinch, two Perriers and ice for Two Forty Six." He hung up, and in the same breath went on: "I can do it, but I'll need another two percent."

"Oh, come," said Mr. Ashcombe-Danvers patiently. "I've been waiting for you to put it up. But I must say I didn't expect a two percent increase. That's a bit thick. Ramlal ten, and now you want seven."

"A bit thick? I don't think so," said Wilcox. "And I don't think you'll think so when you have your nine thousand safely in the Crédit Foncier. It's all very well for you to keep telling me how easy it is. You'll be safe in Paris—"

"My dear boy, you probably will think I'm exaggerating when I say I can think of six persons at this moment who I know would be delighted to do it for three percent."

Wilcox laughed. "Perfectly true. I can think of plenty who'd do it for one percent, too, if it comes to that. But you won't use them." To himself he was saying that Dyar was the ideal one to use in this connection: he was quite unknown in the town, his innocence of the nature of the transaction was a great advantage, and he could be given the errand as a casual part of his daily work and thus would not have to be paid any commission at all; the entire seven percent could be kept intact. "You'll have to meet the man I have in mind, of course, and take him around to young Ramlal yourself. He's an American."

"Aha!" said Mr. Ashcombe-Danvers, impressed.

Wilcox saw that he would have his way about the percentage. "Commission figures between ourselves, you understand," he went on.

"Obviously," said Mr. Ashcombe-Danvers in a flat voice, staring at him coldly. He supposed Wilcox intended to keep five and give the man two, which was just what Wilcox intended him to think.

"You can come around to my office this afternoon and size him up, if you like."

"My dear boy, don't be absurd. I'm perfectly confident in anyone you suggest. But I still think seven percent is a bit steep."

"Well, you come and talk with him," said Wilcox blandly, feeling certain his client had no desire to discuss the matter with anyone, "and if you don't like his looks we'll try and think up someone else. But I'm afraid the seven will have to stand."

There was a knock at the door, and a waiter came in with the drinks.

*

Dyar awoke feeling that he had not really slept at all. He had a confused memory of the morning's having been divided into many episodes of varying sorts of noise. There had been the gurgling of the plumbing as the early risers bathed and he tried to drop off to sleep, the train that shunted back and forth on the siding between his window and the beach, the chattering of the scrubwomen in the corridor, the Frenchman in the next room who had sung *"La Vie en Rose"* over and over while he shaved, showered and dressed. And through it all, like an arhythmical percussive accompaniment there had been the constant metallic slamming of doors throughout the hotel, each one of which shook the flimsy edifice and resounded through it like a small blast.

He looked at his watch: it was twenty-five past twelve. He groaned; his heart seemed to have moved into his neck and to be beating there. He felt breathless, tense and exhaused. In retrospect the night before seemed a week long. Going to bed by daylight always made him sleep badly. And he was bothered by two things, two ideas that he felt lodged in the pit of his stomach like unwanted food. He had spent twenty dollars during the evening, which meant that he now had $460 left, and he had borrowed a hundred pesetas from a Moroccan, which meant that he had to see the Moroccan again.

"God-damned idiot!" he said as he got out of bed to look in his bags for the aspirin. He took three, had a quick shower, and lay down again to relax. A chambermaid, having heard the shower running, knocked on the door to see when she could make up the room. "Who is it?" he yelled, and not understanding her reply, did not get up to let her in. Presently he opened his eyes again and discovered that it was twenty minutes past two. Still not feeling too well, he dressed and went down into the lobby. The boy at the desk handed him a slip that read: *Llamar a la Sra. Debalberde 28-01.* He looked at it apathetically, thinking it must be for someone else. Stepping outside, he began to walk along the street without paying attention to where he was going. It was good to be in the air. The rain dripped out of the low sky in a desultory fashion, as if it were falling from invisible eaves overhead.

Suddenly he realized he was extremely hungry. He raised his head and looked around, decided there would be no restaurant in the vicinity. A half-mile or so ahead of him, sprawling over a hill that jutted into the harbor, was the native town. At his right the small waves broke quietly along the deserted beach. He turned to his left up one of the many steep streets that led over the hill. Like the others it was lined with large new apartment houses, some of which were still under construction but inhabited, nonetheless. Near the top of the hill he came to a modest-looking hotel with the word *Restaurant* printed over the doorway. In the dining room, where a radio roared, several people were eating. The tables were small. He sat down and looked at the typewritten card at his place. It was headed *Menu à 30 p.* He counted his money and grinned a little to see that he still had thirty-five pesetas. As he ate his hors d'oeuvre he found his hunger growing rapidly; he began to feel much better. During the *merlans frits* he pulled out the piece of paper the boy at the desk had given him and studied it absently. The name conveyed nothing to him; suddenly he saw that it was a message from Daisy de Valverde. "Radio Internacional," boomed the imbecilic girl's voice. A harp glissando followed. He had no particular desire to see his hostess of last night, or to see anyone, for that matter. At the moment he felt like being alone, having an opportunity to accustom himself to the strangeness of the town. But for fear she might be waiting for his call he went out into the lobby and asked the desk clerk to make the call for him. "*Veinteyochocerouno,*" he heard him shout several times, and he wondered if he would ever be able even to make a telephone call by himself. After the man handed the instrument to him he had to wait a long time for her to come to the phone.

"Dear Mr. Dyar! How kind of you to ring me! Did you get back safely last night? What vile weather! You're seeing the place at its very worst. But keep a stiff upper lip. One of these days the sun will be out and dry up all this fearful damp. I can't wait. Jack is very naughty. He hasn't telephoned me. Are you there? If you see him, tell him I'm rather put out with him. Oh, I wanted to tell you, Tambang is better. He drank a little milk. Isn't that wonderful news? So you see, our little excursion to his room did some good." (He tried to dismiss the memory of the airless room, the needles and the smell of ether.) "Mr. Dyar, I want very much to see you." For the first time she paused to let him speak. He said: "Today?" and heard her laugh. "Yes, of course today. Naturally. I'm insatiable, yes?" As he stammered protests she continued. "But I don't want to go to Jack's office for a particular reason I shall have to tell you when I see you. I was thinking, we might meet at the Faro Bar on the Place de France. It's just around the corner from the tourist bureau. Darling old snobbish Jack wouldn't be caught dead in the place, so we shall be running no risk of seeing him. You can't miss it. Just ask anyone." She spelled out the name for him. "It's sweet of you to come. Shall we say about seven? Jack closes that establishment of his at half past six. I have so much to talk to you about. And one enormous favor to ask you, which you don't *have* to grant if you don't want." She laughed. "The Faro at seven." And as he was trying to decide quickly how to word his bread-and-butter phrase for last night's hospitality, he realized that she had hung up. He felt the blood rush to his face; he should have got the sentence in somehow at the beginning of the call. The man at the desk asked him for one peseta fifty. He went back to his table annoyed with himself, and wondering what she thought of him.

The check was for thirty-three pesetas, including the service. He had fifty céntimos left, which he certainly could not leave as a tip. He left nothing, and walked out whistling innocently in the face of the waiter's accusing stare. But after he had gone a short way he stopped under the awning of a tobacco shop and took out his two little folders of American Express checks. There was a book of fifties and one of twenties. On the ship he had counted the checks every few days; it made him feel a little less poor to see them and reckon their aggregate. He would have to stop into a bank now and get some money, but the examination of his fortune was to be done in the privacy of the street. Whatever one wants to do in a bank, there are always too many people there watching. There would be six left in the first book (he counted them and snapped the cover shut), which meant eight in the other. He shuffled them almost carelessly, and then immediately went through them again, to be certain. His expression became intense; he now counted them with caution, pushing his thumb against the edge of each sheet to separate a possible two. He still found only seven. Now he looked at the serial numbers: it was undeniable that he had only seven twenty-dollar checks—not eight. $440. His face assumed an expression of consternation as he continued to recount the checks uselessly, automatically, as though it were still an instant before he had made the discovery, as though it were still possible for something different to happen. In his mind he was trying to recall the time and place of the cashing of each check. And now he remembered: he had needed an extra twenty dollars on board the ship, for tips. The remembering, however, did not make the new figure emotionally acceptable; he put his checks away profoundly troubled, and began to walk along looking down at the pavement.

There were many banks, and each one he came to was closed. "Too late," he thought, grimly. "Of course."

He went on, found Wilcox's office easily. It was upstairs over a large tearoom, and the entire building smelled appetizingly of pastries and coffee. Wilcox was there, and made him feel a little better by saying with a wide gesture: "Well, here's your cage." He had half expected him to make some sort of drastic announcement like: "Listen, old man, I guess it's up to me to make a confession. I'm not going to be able to use you here. You can see for yourself why it's out of the question." And then he might have offered to pay his fare back to New York, or perhaps not even that. Certainly Dyar would not have been extremely astonished; such behavior would have been in keeping with his own feeling about the whole undertaking. He was prepared for just such a bitter blow. But Wilcox said: "Sit down. Take the load off your feet. Nobody's been in yet today, so there's no reason to think they'll come in now." Dyar sat down in the chair facing Wilcox at his desk, and looked around. The two rooms were uncomfortably small. In the antechamber, which had no window, there were a couch and a low table, piled with travel booklets. The office room had a window which gave on a narrow court; besides the desk and the two chairs there was a green filing cabinet. The room's inhospitable bareness was tempered by the colored maps covering the walls, drawing the eye inevitably to their irregular contours.

They talked for an hour or so. When Dyar remarked: "You don't seem to be doing a rushing business, do you?" Wilcox snorted disgustedly, but Dyar was unable to interpret his reaction as one of sincere discontent. The Marquesa was obviously correct: there was a slight mystery about his set-up. "I've got to change some money," he said presently. Wilcox might just possibly suggest an advance.

"What have you got?" asked Wilcox.

"Express checks."

"I'll cash whatever you want. I can give you a better rate than most of the banks, and a good deal better one than the money stalls."

Dyar gave him a fifty-dollar check. When he had his wallet stuffed with hundred-peseta notes and felt a little less depressed about his finances, he said: "When do I start work?"

"You've started," Wilcox replied. "You're working now.

There's a guy coming in here this afternoon, a customer of mine. He travels a lot, and always books through me. He'll take you down to meet young Ramlal. You'd have to meet him anyway, sooner or later. The Ramlals are great friends of mine. I do a hell of a lot of business with them." This monologue made no sense to Dyar; moreover he had the impression that Wilcox was on the defensive while delivering it, as if he expected to be challenged. Soon enough, he thought, he would know what it was all about. "I see," he said. Wilcox shot him a glance which he did not at all like: it was hard and unfriendly and suspicious. Then he went on. "I've got to be at somebody's house for drinks around five, so I hope to God he comes soon. You can go down with him and come right back. I'll wait till you get here. At six-thrity just go out and shut the door behind you. I'll have a set of keys for you tomorrow." The telephone rang. There ensued a long conversation in which Wilcox's part consisted mainly of the word "yes" uttered at irregular intervals. The door opened and a tall, slightly stooped gentleman wearing heavy tweeds and a raincoat stepped into the antechamber. Wilcox cut his telephone conversation short, stood up, and said: "This is Mr. Dyar. This is Mr. Ashcombe-Danvers. I sold him a ticket to Cairo the day after I opened this office, and he's been coming back ever since. A satisfied client. Or at least I like to think so."

Mr. Ashcombe-Danvers looked impatient. "Ah, yes. Quite." He put his hands behind his back and spun around to examine a large map of the world that hung above the filing cabinet. "I expect we'd better be going," he said.

Wilcox looked at Dyar significantly. He had meant to tell him a little more about Mr. Ashcombe-Danvers, above all to advise him not to ask any questions. But perhaps it was just as well that he had said nothing.

Dyar slipped into his raincoat as they descended the stairs. "We may as well walk," said Mr. Ashcombe-Danvers. "It's stopped raining for the present, and the shop's not very far." They went down the hill and came out into the wide square which had been empty last night save for the taxis; now it was a small city of natives engaged in noisy commerce. "Chaos," said Mr. Ashcombe-Danvers, a note of satisfaction in his voice. As they went under the bare trees in the center of the square the water dripped down upon their heads. The women huddled in rows along the pavement, wrapped in candy-striped woolen blankets, holding forth great bunches of drenched white lilies and calling out hoarsely for them to buy. The day was coming to a close; the sky was growing duller.

"Shrewd people, these mountain Berbers," remarked Mr. Ashcombe-Danvers. "But no match for the Indians."

"The Indians?" Dyar looked confused.

"Oh, not your redskins. Our Indians. Hindus, most of them, from India. Tangier's full of them. Hadn't you noticed? Young Ramlal, that we're on our way to see, he's one. Most shrewd. And his father, old Ramlal, in Gib. Amazing business acumen. Quite amazing. He's a bandit, of course, but an honest bandit. Never takes a shilling above what's been agreed upon. He doesn't need to, of course. His commission's enormous. He knows he has you and he piles it on because he knows he's worth it." Dyar listened politely; they were going between two rows of money changers. The men sat behind their small desks directly in the street. A few of them, spotting the two foreigners speaking English, began to call out to them. "Yes! Come on! Yes! Change money!"

"The devil of it is," Mr. Ashcombe-Danvers was saying, "the authorities are onto it. They know damned well Gib's one of the most important leakage points."

Dyar said tentatively: "Leakage?"

"Sterling leakage. They know there's probably twenty thousand pounds slipping out every day. And they're catching up with some of the chaps. It's only a question of time before they'll be able to put a stop to it altogether. Time is of the essence. Naturally it makes a man a bit nervous." He laughed apologetically. "It's a chance one must take. I like Morocco and my wife likes it. We're building a little villa here and we must have some capital, risk or no risk."

"Oh, sure," said Dyar. He was beginning to understand.

Ramlal's window was piled with cheap wrist watches, fountain pens and toys. The shop was tiny and dark; it smelled of patchouli. Once Dyar's eyes had got used to the lack of light inside, he realized that all the stock was in the window. The shop was completely empty. A swarthy young man sat at a bare desk smoking. As they entered he rose and bowed obsequiously.

"Good evening, Ramlal," said Mr. Ashcombe-Danvers in the tone of a doctor making his rounds through a ward of incurables.

"About to get under way?" Ramlal spoke surprisingly good English.

"Yes. Tomorrow. This is Mr. Dyar, my secretary." Dyar held out his hand to Ramlal, looking at Mr. Ashcombe-Danvers. "What the hell goes on?" he said to himself. He acknowledged the introduction.

"He'll arrange everything," went on Mr. Ashcombe-Danvers. "You'll give him the packet." Ramlal was looking carefully at Dyar all the while. Showing his very white teeth he smiled and said: "Yes, sir."

"Got him?" said Mr. Ashcombe-Danvers.

"Yes, indeed, sir."

"Well, we must be going. Your father's well, I hope?"

"Oh, yes, sir. Very well, thank you."

"Not too many worries, I hope?"

Ramlal smiled even more widely. "Oh, no, sir."

"That's good," grunted Mr. Ashcombe-Danvers. "Well, look after yourself, Ramlal. See you when I get back." Ramlal and Dyar shook hands again and they went out.

"Now if you'll come along with me to the Café España I'll present you to Benzekri."

Dyar looked at his watch. "I'm afraid I've got to get back to the office." It was twilight, and raining lightly. The narrow street was packed with people wearing djellabas, raincoats, Turkish towels, overalls, blankets and rags.

"Nonsense," said Mr. Ashcombe-Danvers sharply. "You've got to meet Benzekri. Come along. It's essential."

"Well, since I'm your secretary," Dyar smiled.

"In this matter you are." Mr. Ashcombe-Danvers walked as close to Dyar as he could, speaking directly into his ear. "Benzekri is with the Crédit Foncier here. I'll show you the entrance as we go by it in a moment." They had come out into the Zoco Chico, filled with the drone of a thousand male voices. This evening there was electricity and the cafés were resplendent.

Working their way among the clusters of men standing engaged in conversation, they crossed slowly to the lower end of the square. "There's the entrance," said Mr. Ashcome-Danvers, pointing at a high portal of iron grillework that stood at the top of a few steps in a niche. "That's the Crédit Foncier and that's where you'll take the packet. You'll just ask for Mr. Benzekri and go upstairs to his office. And here's the Café España."

Mr. Benzekri was there, sitting alone at one end of the terrace. He had a head like an egg—quite bald—and a face like a worried hawk. He did not smile when he shook hands with Dyar; the lines in his forehead merely deepened. "You will have a beer?" he inquired. His accent was thick.

"We'll sit for a moment. I'll not take anything," said Mr. Ashcombe-Danvers. They sat down. "None for me, either," Dyar said. He was not feeling too well, and he wanted a whiskey.

"Mr. Dyar will be bringing you a little present one of these days," said Mr. Ashcombe-Danvers. "He understands that he's to give it to no one but you."

Mr. Benzekri nodded gravely, staring down into his glass of beer. Then he lifted his head and looked sadly at Dyar for a moment. "Good," he said, as if there the matter ended.

"I know you are in a hurry," said Mr. Ashcombe-Danvers to Dyar. "So if you'd like to go on about your affairs go along. And many thanks. I shall be back in a few weeks."

Dyar said good evening. He had to fight his way across the Zoco Chico and up the narrow street; everyone was moving against him. "My new station in life: messenger-boy," he thought with a wry inner smile. He did not particularly like Mr. Ashcombe-Danvers: he had behaved exactly as though he had been paying him for his services. Not that he had expected payment, but still, the principal reason a man does not want to be paid for such things is to avoid being put into the position of an inferior. And he was in it anyway.

Wilcox was impatient when he got back to the office. "Took you long enough," he said.

"I know. He made me go on with him and meet some other guy from the bank."

"Benzekri."

"Yes."

"You didn't have to meet him. Ashcombe-Danvers is a fussy old buzzard. Be sure the window's shut, the door's locked and the lights are off. Stick around until six-thirty." Wilcox put on his coat. "Come by the Atlantide in the morning about nine and I'll give you the address where they're making the keys. If anyone calls tell 'em I had to go out and to call back tomorrow. See you."

7

THE DOOR CLOSED. Dyar sat looking around the room. He stood up and studied the maps a while, searched in the waiting room for magazines, and finding none, went and sat down again at the desk. A wild impatience kept him from feeling really alone in the room, an impatience merely to be out of it. "This isn't it," he told himself mechanically; he was not really sitting alone in the room because he did not believe he would ever work there. He was unable to visualize himself sitting day after day in this unventilated little box pretending to look after a non-existent business. In New York he had imagined something so different that now he had quite forgotten how he had thought it would be. He asked himself whether, knowing ahead of time what it would be like, he would have wanted to come, and he decided he would have, anyway, in spite of the profound apathy the idea of the job induced in him. Besides, the job was too chimerical and absurd to last. When it stopped, he would be free. He snorted, faintly. Free, with probably a hundred dollars between him and starvation. It was not a pleasant thought: it made him feel tense all over. He listened. Above the noise made by the automobile horns outside was the soft sound of rain falling.

He looked in the top drawer for a sheet of stationery, found it, and began to type a letter. The paper was headed EUROPE-AFRICA TOURIST SERVICE. "Dear Mother: Just a note. Arrived safely last night." He felt like adding: it seems like a month, but she would misunderstand, would think he was not happy. "The trip over was fine. We had fairly smooth weather all the way and I was not sick at all in spite of all you said. The Italians were not too bad." His parents had come to see him off, and had been upset to discover that he was to share a cabin with two Italians. "As you can see, I am writing this from the office. Jack Wilcox has gone for the day and I am in charge." He pondered a moment, wondering if the expression "in charge" looked silly, and decided to leave it. "I hope you're not going to worry about me, because there is no reason to. The climate is not tropical at all. In fact, it is quite chilly. The town seems to be clean, although not very modern." He ceased typing and gazed at a map of Africa in front of him, thinking of the crazy climb up through the dark alleys with the Moroccan, on the way to the bar. Then he saw Hadija's face, and frowned. He could not allow himself to think of her while he was writing his mother; there was a terrible disloyalty in that. But the memory, along with others more vivid, persisted. He leaned back in his chair and smoked a cigarette, wondering whether or not he would be able to find the bar by himself, in case he wanted to go back. Even if he were able, he felt it would be a bad idea. He had a date to meet Hadija in the Parque Espinel Sunday morning and it would be best to leave it at that; she might resent his trying to see her before then. He abandoned the attempt to write his letter, removed the paper from the machine, folded it and put it into his pocket to be continued the next day. The telephone rang. An Englishwoman was not interested in whether Mr. Wilcox was in or out, wanted a reservation made, single with bath, at the Hotel Balima in Rabat for the fourteenth through the seventeenth. She also wanted a round-trip plane passage, but she dared say that could be had later. The room however must be reserved immediately and she was counting on it. When she had hung up he wrote it all down and began studying a sheaf of papers marked *Hotels—French Zone*. At six-ten the telephone rang again. It was Wilcox. "Checking up on me," Dyar thought with resentment as he heard his voice. He wanted to know if anyone had stopped in. "No," said Dyar. "Well, that's all I wanted." He sounded relieved. Dyar told him about the Englishwoman. "I'll take care of that tomorrow. You might as well close up now. It's ten after six." He hesitated. "In fact, I wish you would. As soon as you can. Just be sure the catch is on the door."

"Right."

"Good night."

"What gives? What gives?" he murmured aloud as he slipped into his raincoat. He turned off the lights and stepped out into the corridor, shut the door and tried it vigorously.

At the pastry shop downstairs he stopped to inquire the way to the Faro Bar. When the proprietress saw him approaching the counter she greeted him pleasantly. *"Guten Abend,"* she said, and was a bit taken aback when he spoke to her in English. She understood, however, and directed him in detail, adding that it was only one minute's walk.

He found it easily. It was a very small bar, crowded with people most of whom seemed to know each other; there was a certain amount of calling from table to table. Since there was not room at the bar itself, even for those who were already there, and all the tables were occupied, he sat down on a bench in the window and waited for a table to be vacated. Two Spanish girls, self-conscious in their Paris models, and wearing long earrings which removed all trace of chic from their clothes, came in and sat next to him on the bench. At the table in front of him was a French couple drinking Bacardis. To his left sat two somewhat severe-looking middle-aged English ladies, and on his right, a little further away, was a table full of American men who kept rising and going back to the bar to talk with those installed there. In a far corner a small, bespectacled woman was seated at a tiny piano, singing in German. No one was listening to her. He rather liked the place; it seemed to him definitely high-class without being stuffy, and he wondered why the Marquesa had said that Wilcox would refuse to be caught dead in it.

"Y pensábamos irnos a Sevilla para la Semana Santa. . . ."
"Ay, qué hermoso!"

"Jesus, Harry, you sure put that one down quick!"

"Alors, tu ne te décides pas? Mais tu es marrante, toi!"

"I expect she's most frightfully unhappy to be returning to London at this time of year."

The woman at the piano sang: *"Wunderschön muss deine Liebe sein."*

"Y por fin nos quedamos aquí." "Ay, que lástima!"

"Ne t'en fais pas pour moi."

"Hey there, waiter! Make it the same, all the way around."

He waited, ordered a whiskey, drank it, and waited. The woman sang several old Dietrich songs. No one heard them. It was quarter past seven; he wished she would come. The Americans were getting drunk. Someone yelled: "Look out, you dumb bastard!" and a glass crashed on the tile floor. The English ladies got up, paid, and left. He decided they had timed their exit to show their disapproval. The two Spanish girls saw the empty table and gathering their things, made for it, but by the time they got there Dyar was already sitting in one of the chairs. "I'm waiting for a lady," he explained, without adding that he had arrived at the bar before they had, in any case. They did not bother to look at him, reserving all their energy for the registering of intense disgust. Presently another glass was broken. The woman in the corner played "God Bless America," doubtless with satirical intent. One of the Americans heard it and began to sing along with the music in a very loud voice. Dyar looked up: the Marquesa de Valverde was standing by the table in faded blue slacks and a chamois jacket.

"Don't get up," she commanded, as he hastily rose. "Ça va?" she called to someone at another table. He looked at her: she seemed less formidable than she had the preceding night. He thought it was because she was not made up, but he was mistaken. Her outdoor make-up was even more painstaking than the one she used for the evening. It merely did not show. Now she was all warmth and charm.

"I can't tell you how kind I think you are," she said when she had a whiskey-soda in her hand. "So few men have any true kindness left these days. I remember my father—what a magnificent man he was! I wish you could have known him—he used to say that the concept of nobility was fast disappearing from the face of the earth. I didn't know what he meant then, of course, but I do now, and, God, how heartily I agree with him! And nobility and kindness go together. You may not be noble—who knows?—but you certainly can't deny that it was damned kind of you to go out of your way to meet me when I had told you beforehand that I expected a favor of you."

He kept looking at her. She was too old, that was all. Every now and then, in the midst of the constantly changing series of expressions assumed by the volatile features, there was a dead instant when he saw the still, fixed disappointment of age beneath. It chilled him. He thought of the consistency of Hadija's flesh and skin, telling himself that to do so was scarcely just; the girl was not more than sixteen. Still, there were the facts. He considered the compensations of character and worldly refinement, but did they really count for much? He was inclined to think not, in such cases. "Nothing doing there," he thought. Or perhaps yes, if he had a lot of liquor in him. But why bother? He wondered why the idea had ever come to him, at all. There was no reason to think it had occurred to her, for that matter, save that he was sure it had.

The favor proved to be absurdly simple, he thought. He was merely to fill out a certain form in her name; he would find plenty of such forms in the office. This he was to send, along with a letter written on paper with the agency's letterhead, to the receptionist at the Mamounia Hotel in Marrakech, saying that a Mme. Werth's reservation for the twentieth of January had been canceled and that the room was to be reserved instead for the Marquise de Valverde. He was then to send her the duplicate of the filled-out form.

"Can you remember all that?" she said, leaning over the table toward him. "I think you're quite the most angelic man I know." He was making notes on a tiny pad. "During the season the Mamounia is just a little harder to get into than Heaven."

When he had it all written down he drained his glass and leaned over toward her, so that their foreheads were only a few inches apart. "I'll be delighted to do this for you—" he hesitated and felt himself growing red in the face. "I don't know what to call you. You know— the title. It's not *Mrs.* de Valverde. But I don't know—"

"If you're wise you'll call me Daisy."

He felt she was amusing herself at his expense. "Well, fine," he said. "What I was going to say is, I'm only too glad to do this for you. But wouldn't Jack be the man to do it? I'm just an ignoramus in the office so far."

She put her hand on his arm. "Oh, my God! Don't breathe a word of it to Jack, you silly boy! Why do you think I came to you in the first place? Oh, good God, no! He's not to know about it, naturally. I thought you understood that."

Dyar was disturbed. He said very slowly: "Oh, hell," emphasizing the second word. "I don't know about that."

"Jack's such an old maid about such things. It's fantastic, the way he runs that office. No, no. I'll give you the check for the deposit and you simply send it along with the letter and the form." She felt in her bag and brought forth a folded check. "It's all made out to the hotel. They'll understand that that's because the agency had already made its commission at the time the original reservation was made for Mme. Werth. Don't you see?"

What she was saying seemed logical, but none of it made any sense to him. If it had to be kept secret from Wilcox, then there was more to it than she admitted. She saw him running it over in his mind. "As I told you today," she said "you're not to feel under the least pressure about it. It's terribly unimportant, really, and I'm a beast even to have mentioned it to you. If someone else gets the reservation I can easily go to Agadir for my fortnight's rest. Please don't feel that I'm relying on your gallantry to do it for me."

Brusquely he cut her short. "I'll do it the first thing tomorrow morning and get it off my mind." He was suddenly extremely tired. He felt a million miles away. She went on talking; it was inevitable. But eventually he caught the waiter's eyes and paid the bill.

"I have a car down the street," she said. "Where would you like to go?" He thanked her and said he was going to stop into the nearest restaurant for dinner. When she had finally gone, he walked blindly along the street for a while, swearing under his breath now and then. After his dinner he managed to find his way to the Hotel de la Playa. Even with the electricity on, the place was dim and shadowy. He went to bed and fell asleep listening to the waves breaking on the beach.

In the morning there was a watery sky; a tin-colored gleam lay on the harbor. Dyar had awakened at eight-thirty and was rushing through his toilet, hoping not to arrive too late at the Atlantide. Daisy de Valverde's request still puzzled him; it was illogical. It occurred to him that perhaps it was merely part of some complicated scheme of hers:—a scheme for encouraging an imagined personal interest in her. Or maybe she thought she was flattering his vanity in appealing to him instead of to Wilcox. But even so, the mechanics of the procedure troubled him. He resolved not to think about it, merely to get it done as quickly as possible.

Wilcox looked perturbed, took no notice of his lateness. "Have

some coffee?" he asked, and indicated his breakfast tray. There was no
extra cup. "I'll have it in a few minutes, thanks, across the street."
Wilcox did not press him, but got back into bed and lit a cigarette.

"I have an idea the best thing right now would be for you to learn
a little something," he said meditatively. "You're not of much use to
me in the office as you are." Dyar stiffened, waited, not breathing.
"I've got a lot of reading matter here that it would help a lot for you to
know pretty much by heart. Take it on home and study it for a
while—a week or so, let's say—and then come back and I'll give you a
little test on it." He saw Dyar's face, read the question. "*With* salary.
Don't worry—you're working. I told you that yesterday. As of
yesterday." Dyar relaxed a little, but not enough. "The whole thing
smells," he thought, and he wanted to say: "Can't anyone in this
town tell the truth?" Instead, he decided to be a little bit devious
himself for a change, thinking that otherwise he would not be able to
get Daisy de Valverde's hotel reservation.

"I'd like to go over to the office for a few minutes and finish
typing a letter I was writing last night. Shall I go and get those keys
you're having made for me?"

He thought Wilcox looked uncomfortable. "To tell the truth, I
don't think there'll be time," he replied. "I'm going over there now,
and I'll be pretty busy there all day. For several days, in fact. A lot of
unexpected work that's come up. It's another good reason for you to
take this time off now and study up on the stuff. It fits in perfectly with
my schedule. Those keys like as not wouldn't be ready anyway. They
never have things when they promise them here."

Dyar took the pile of papers and booklets Wilcox handed him,
started to go out, and standing in the open doorway said: "What day
shall I get in touch with you?" (He hoped that somehow the words
would have ironic overtones; he also hoped Wilcox would say: "Ring
me up every day and I'll let you know how things are going.")

"You'll be staying on at the Playa?"

"As far as I know."

"I'll call you, then. That's the best way."

There was nothing to answer. "I see. So long," he said, and shut
the door.

Because he did not trust Wilcox, he felt he had been wronged by him. Feeling that, he had a natural and overwhelming desire to confide his trouble to someone. Accordingly, when he had eaten his breakfast and read a three-day-old copy of the Paris *Herald,* he decided to telephone Daisy de Valverde, believing that the true reason he was calling her was to tell her it would not be possible for him to do the little favor for her, after all. The annoyance he now felt with Wilcox made him genuinely sorry not to be able to help her in that particular fashion. He rang the Villa Hesperides: she was having breakfast. He told her the situation, and stressed Wilcox's peculiar behavior. She was silent a moment.

"My dear, the man's a raving maniac!" she finally cried. "I *must* talk to you about this. When are you free?"

"Anytime, it looks like."

"Sunday afternoon?"

"What time?" he said, thinking of the picnic with Hadija.

"Oh, sixish."

"Sure." The picnic would be over long before that.

"Perfect. I'll take you to a little party I know you'll enjoy. It's at the Beidaouis'. They're Moroccans, and I'm devoted to them."

"A party?" Dyar sounded unsure.

"Oh, not a party, really. A gathering of a few old friends at the Beidaoui Palace."

"Wouldn't I be a little in the way?"

"Nonsense. They love new faces. Stop being anti-social, Mr. Dyar. It just won't do in Tangier. My poor poached egg is getting cold."

It was agreed that she would call for him at his hotel at six on Sunday. Again he apologized for his powerlessness to help her.

"Couldn't care less," she said. "Good-bye, my dear. Until Sunday."

And as Sunday approached and the weather remained undecided, he was increasingly apprehensive. It would probably rain. If it did, they could not have a picnic and there would be no use in his going to the Parque Espinel to meet Hadija. Yet he knew he would go anyway, on the chance that she might be waiting for him. Even if the weather were clear, he must be prepared for her not being there. He began to train inwardly for that eventuality and to repeat to himself that it was of no importance to him whether she appeared or not. She was not a real person; it could not matter what a toy did. But there was no inner argument he could provide that would remove the tense expectancy he felt when he thought of Sunday morning. He spent the days learning the facts in the material Wilcox had given him, and when he got up on Sunday morning it was not raining.

8

WHERE THE LITTLE SIDE street ended they came out at the top of a high cliff. It was a windy day and the sky was full of fast-moving clouds. Occasionally the sun came through, a patch of its light spreading along the dark water of the strait below. Halfway down, where the gradient was less steep and brilliant green grass covered the slope, a flock of black goats wandered. The odor of iodine and seaweed in the air made Dyar hungry.

"This is the life," he said.

"What you sigh?" inquired Hadija.

"I like this."

"Oh, yes!" She smiled.

A long series of notches had been hewn in a diagonal line across the upper rock, forming a stairway. Slowly they descended the steps, he first, holding the picnic basket carefully, feeling a little dizzy, and wondering if she minded the steepness and height. "Probably not," he thought presently. "These people can take anything." The idea irritated him. As they got lower the sound of the waves grew louder.

On the way down, there was an unexpected grotto to their right, partially covered by a small growth of cane. A boy crouched there, the dark skin of his body showing through his rags. Hadija pointed.

"He got goats. The *guardia*."

"He's pretty young." The boy looked about six years old.

Hadija did not think so. "All like that," she said without interest.

Here and there in the strait, at varying distances from the shore, a seemingly static ship pointed eastward or westward. Dyar stopped a moment to count them: he could discern seven.

"All freighters," he said, gesturing, but it was half to himself that he spoke.

"What?" Hadija had stopped behind him; she was scanning the beach below, doubtless for natives who might recognize her. She did not want to be seen.

"Boats!" he cried; it seemed hopeless to elaborate. He moved his hand back and forth.

"America," said Hadija.

There were a few Moroccans fishing from the rocks. They paid no attention to the picnickers. It was high tide. Getting around certain of the points was not easy, since there was often very little space between the cliffs and the waves. At one spot they both got wet. Dyar was a little annoyed, because there was no sun to dry them, but Hadija thought it an amusing diversion.

Rounding a sharp corner of rock they came suddenly on a small stretch of sand where a dozen or more boys were running about stark naked. They were of an age when one would have expected them to want to cover their nudity at the arrival of a girl, but that seemed to be the last thing in their minds. As Dyar and Hadija approached, they set up a joyous cry, some assuming indecent postures as they called out, the others entering into group activities of an unmistakably erotic nature. Dyar was horrified and incensed. "Like monkeys," he thought, and automatically looked down for a stone to fling into their midst. He felt his face growing hot. Hadija took no notice of the antics. He wondered just what indignities they were shouting at her, but he did not dare ask. It was possible that she considered this frantic exhibitionism typical of male behavior, but it hurt him to see a delicate creature like her being obliged to witness such things, and he would not believe that she could accept them with equanimity. For a second he wondered if by chance she were so preoccupied with her thoughts that she had not noticed the boys. He stole a sidelong glance at her and was gratified at first to see that she was looking out across the strait, but then he caught the fixity of her stare.

"Son bitch," she muttered.

"The hell with them," he said, turning to smile at her. "Don't look at them."

They came to a long beach, completely deserted. Ahead of them rose a low mountain covered with cypress and eucalyptus; large villas sat comfortably among the trees toward the summit. The wind blew harder here. Dyar took her hand, from time to time lifted it to his lips and kissed the fingers lightly.

They rounded another rocky point. The wet wind blew with added force. A shore of boulders stretched before them into the distance. Dyar turned to her.

"Hey, where is this cave?"

"You tired now?"

"Do you know where it is or do you just think you know?"

She laughed gaily and pointed ahead to the farthest cliff jutting into the sea.

"Go past there." And she indicated a left turn with her hand.

"Oh, for God's sake! That'll take us an hour. You realize that?"

"One hour. Maybe. Too much?" She looked up at him mockingly.

"I don't care," he said with bad grace. But he was annoyed.

They walked for several minutes without speaking, devoting all their attention to choosing the easiest way of getting past each boulder. When they climbed down to a tiny cove where there was a spring among the rocks, he decided to kiss her. It took a long time; her response was warm but calm. Finally he drew away and looked at her. She was smiling. It was impossible to tell what she felt.

"By God, I'll get a rise out of you yet!" he said, and he pulled her to him violently. She tried to answer, but the sound of her voice came out into his mouth and died there. When he released her, the same smile was there. It was a bit disconcerting. He dug in his pockets and pulled out a pack of cigarettes which she took from him, tapping the bottom so that one cigarette appeared. She held up the pack to his mouth and let him take the end of the cigarette between his lips.

"Service," he said. "But now I've got to light it myself. Let's sit down a minute."

"O.K." She chose the nearest rock and he sat beside her, his left arm around her waist. They looked out across the strait.

He was glad she had chosen the shore of the strait here for their picnic, rather than the beach along the bay, although actually there would have been more assurance of privacy on the beach than here, where one never knew what would appear around the next point or who might be hiding among the rocks. But he liked the idea of being able to see Europe across the way while knowing he was in Africa.

He pointed to the big sand-colored crest directly opposite. "Spain."

She nodded, drew her finger across her throat significantly. "Bad. They kill you."

"What do you know about it?" he said banteringly.

"I know." She shook her head up and down several times. "I got friends come here never go back. No fackin good place."

"Hadija! I don't like to hear that kind of talk from girls."

"Huh?"

"Don't say that again when I'm around, you hear?"

She looked innocent and crestfallen. "What's the matter you?"

He tossed his cigarette away and got up. "Skip it. Come on, or we'll never get there." He picked up the basket. Conversation was by no means easy with Hadija. There were many things he would have liked to tell her: that a group of American boys would never have behaved like the young Moroccans they had passed a while ago. (But would she have believed him, her experience with Americans having been limited to the sailors who occasionally staggered into the Bar Lucifer, their faces smeared with lipstick and their hastily donned trousers held up by one button? He wondered.) He would have liked to tell her in his own way how lovely he thought she was, and why he thought so, and to make her understand how much more he wanted from her than she was used to having men want.

They came out onto a broad, flat shelf of land where on the side toward the cliffs there had at one time been a quarry. The surface was covered with dried thistle plants and a narrow path led straight across it. He still walked ahead of her, into the wind, feeling it push against him all the way from his face to his feet, like a great invisible, amorous body. The path, after it had traversed the field of thistles, rose and wound among the rocks. Suddenly they rounded a corner and looked out on the mountainous coastline to the west. Below them great blocks of stone rose sheer from the water.

"Be careful," said Dyar. "You go ahead here so I can keep an eye on you."

Ahead to the left he could see the cave, high in the vertical wall of rock. Birds flew in and out of smaller crevices above it; the roar of the waves covered all sound.

He was surprised to see that the cave was not dirty. Someone had made a fire in the center, and an empty tin can lay nearby. Toward the back of the cave in a corner there was a pallet of eucalyptus branches, probably arranged by some Berber fisherman months ago. Near the entrance there was one crumpled sheet of an old French newspaper. That was all. He set the basket down. Now, after all this, he felt shy.

"Well, here we are," he said with false heartiness, turning to Hadija.

She smiled as usual and carefully walked to the corner where the leaves covered the stone floor.

"Good here," she said, motioning to Dyar. She sat down, her legs akimbo, leaning against the wall of the cave. He had been about to light a cigarette to hide his confusion. Instead, he reached her in three strides, threw himself full length on the crackling leaves and twigs, and reached up to pull her face down to his. She cried out in surprise, lost her balance. Shrieking with laughter, she fell across him heavily. Even as she was still laughing she was deftly unbuttoning his shirt, unfastening the buckle of his belt. He rolled over and held her in a long embrace, expecting to feel her body hold itself rigid for a moment, and then slowly soften in the pleasure of surrender. But things did not happen like that. There was no surrender because there was no resistance. She accepted his embrace, returning his pressure with one arm while the other went on loosening his garments, attempting to slip them off. He pulled away, sat up.

"I'll fix that," he said, a little grimly, and straightway pulled off the remaining of his clothing.

"There. How's that?" His voice sounded unnatural; he was thinking: if she's going to act like a whore I'll damned well treat her like one.

"Now, you too," he said. And using both hands he began to pull her dress off over her head. She uttered a cry and struggled to a sitting position.

"No! No!"

He looked at her. It was disconcerting to be sitting there naked in front of this wild-eyed Moroccan girl pretending to defend her honor.

"What's the matter?" he demanded.

Her face softened; she leaned forward and kissed him on the lips. "You lie down," she said smiling. "Leave dress alone."

As he obeyed, perplexed, she added: "You one bad boy, but I fix you up good." And indeed, in another minute she made it clear that she was by no means attempting to protect her virtue; she merely had no intention of removing her dress. At the same time she appeared to find it perfectly natural that Dyar should be unclothed; furthermore she took obvious pleasure in running her hands over his body, patting and pinching his flesh. Yet he had the conviction that notwithstanding her occasional murmurs of endearment, for her it was all a game. She was unattainable even in the profoundest intimacy. "Still, here it is. I've got her," he thought. "What more did I expect?" Outside the cave beneath the cliffs, the sea pounded against the rocks; the air, even up here, was full of fine salt mist.

"The Garden of Hesperides. The golden apple," he thought, running his tongue over her smooth, fine teeth. Soon it was as if he were floating slightly above the water, out there in the strait, the wind caressing his face. The sound of the waves receded further and further. They slept.

Dyar's first thought on waking was that twilight had come. He raised himself a bit and surveyed Hadija: she was sleeping quietly, one hand under her cheek and the other resting on his arm. Like this she looked incredibly young—not more than twelve. Overcome with a great tenderness, he reached out, smoothed her forehead, and let his hand run softly over her hair. She opened her eyes. The bland, sweet smile appeared; was it an expression of friendship or a meaningless grimace? Reaching around among the branches and leaves, he assembled his clothing, leapt up and went outside the cave to dress. The sky was more heavily covered, the sun had completely disappeared, the light was muffled. A gull balanced itself in the wind before him, turning its head from time to time to look at the rocks below. Hadija called to him. When he went in she had moved to the center of the cave where she sat taking the parcels of food out of the basket.

"No radio?" she said. "Little radio?"

"No."

"One American lady I know she got one little radio. Little. Take it in beach. Take it in room. Take it on café in Zoco Chico. You hear music every time."

"I hate 'em. I wouldn't like it here. I like the waves better. Hear 'em?" He pointed outside and listened a moment. She listened, too, and appeared to be considering the sound she heard. Presently she nodded her head and said: "Good music."

"Couldn't be better," he answered, pleased that she understood so well.

"That's the beautiful. Come from God." She pointed casually upward. He was a little embarrassed, as he always was when a serious reference to God was made. Now he was not sure whether she had really understood him or not.

"Well, let's eat." He bit into a sandwich.

"*Bismil 'lah,*" said Hadija, doing likewise.

"What's that mean? Good appetite?"

"It mean we eat for God."

"Oh."

"*You* say."

She repeated it several times and made him say it until he had pronounced it to her satisfaction. Then they ate.

After lunch he went out and climbed among the rocks for a few minutes. It pleased him to see that there was not a soul in sight in either direction along the shore; he had half expected the gang of youths to follow them and perhaps continue their antics below on the rocks. But there was no one. When he returned to the cave he sat down outside it and called to Hadija.

"Come on out and sit here. It's too dark inside."

She obeyed. In a moment they were lying locked in each other's arms. When she complained of the cold rock beneath her, he got his jacket from inside the cave, put it under her, and lay down again.

"D'you know what I want?" he said, looking at the tiny black knob his head made against the sky in her eyes.

"You want?"

"Yes. D'you know what I want? I want to live with you. All the time. So we can be like this every night, every morning. You know? You understand?"

"Oh, yes."

"I'll get you a little room, a good room. You live in it and I'll come and see you every day. Would you like that?"

"I come every day?"

"No!" He moved one arm out from under her and gestured, pointing. "*I* pay for the room. *You* live in it. *I* come and see *you* every night. Yes?"

She smiled. "All right." It was as if he had said: "What do you say to starting back in about an hour?" As this occurred to him, he did say: "Want to start back pretty soon?"

"O.K."

His heart sank a little. He was right: it was the same voice, the same smile. He sighed. Still, she had agreed.

"But you promise?"

"What?"

"You'll live in the room?"

"Oh, yes." She took his head between her hands and kissed him on each cheek. "You come today?"

"Come where? The room?" He was about to begin again, to explain that he had not yet rented the room for her.

"No. No my room. Miss Goode. You come I take you. She very good friend. She got room Hotel Metropole."

"No. I don't want to go there. What would I want to do that for? You go if you want."

"She tell me you bring you drink whiskey."

Dyar laughed. "I don't think she said that, Hadija."

"Sure she say that."

"She's never heard of me and I've never heard of her. Who is she, anyway?"

"She got one little radio. I said you before. You know. Miss Goode. She got room Hotel Metropole. You come. I take you."

"You're crazy!"

Hadija tried to sit up. She looked very much upset. "I crazy? *You* crazy! You think I'm lie?" She pushed him in the chest with all her might, struggling to rise.

He was a little alarmed. To placate her he said: "I'll come! I'll come! Don't get so excited, for God's sake! What's the matter with you? If you want me to stop by and see her, I'll stop by and see her, I don't care."

"I no care. She tell me you bring you drink whiskey. You like whiskey?"

"Yes, yes. Sure. Now you lie back down there. I've got something to tell you."

"What?" she asked ingenuously, settling back, her great eyes wide.

"This." He kissed her. "I love you." His open lips touched hers all the way around as he said the words.

Hadija did not seem surprised to hear it. "Again?" she said, smiling.

"Huh?"

"You love me again now? This time quick one, yes? This time take few mintues. No take pants off. Then we go Hotel Metropole."

9

ON SATURDAY Hadija had told Eunice Goode that she would be out all the next day with a friend. After a certain amount of questioning Eunice had got an admission from her that it was the American gentleman and that they were going on a picnic. She did not think it wise to express any objections. For one thing Hadija had already made it clear that she did not by any means consider this sojourn at the Hotel Metropole a permanent arrangement, and that she would leave any time she felt like it. (What she hoped to be given eventually was an apartment of her own on the Boulevard.) And then, Eunice realized that in such a situation she was incapable herself of offering a quiet argument; she would straightway be precipitated into a violent scene. With her sometimes painfully acute objective sense she knew she would be the loser in any such quarrel: she was supremely conscious of being a comic figure. She knew which of her attributes operated against her, and they were several. Her voice, while pleasant and easily modulated when used with low dynamics, became a thin screech as soon as it was called upon to be more than mildly expressive. Her torso bulged in rather the same fashion as that of a portly old gentleman, her arms and legs were gigantic, and her hypersensitive

skin was always irritated and purplish, so that her face often looked as
though she had just finished climbing to the summit of a mountain.
She told herself she did not mind being a comic character; she accepted
the fact and used it to insulate herself from the too-near, ever-
threatening world. Dressed in a manner which accentuated the
deficiencies of her body, wherever she went she was a thing rather
than a person; she was determined to enjoy to the full the benefits of
that exemption.

From the first she had been an object of interest in the streets of
Tangier; now, appearing regularly in public with Hadija, whom a
great number of the lower-class native inhabitants knew and the rest
swiftly learned about, she became a full-fledged legendary figure in
the Zoco Chico. The Moroccans in the cafés there were delighted: it was
a new variation on human behavior.

In these four days Hadija had forced her to lead a much more
active life than was her wont, dragging her to all the bars and night
clubs the girl had always wanted to see. Eunice had met several people
she knew at these places. To them she had presented Hadija as Miss
Kumari from Nicosia. She thought it unlikely that they would come
across anyone who spoke modern Greek, and even if they did, she
planned to explain that the dialect of Cyprus was altogether a different
language.

Notwithstanding her outward coolness, Eunice was greatly disturbed when Hadija announced her projected outing. She lay back
against the pillows watching the harbor as usual, saying to herself
very firmly that action must be taken. It could not be against Hadija,
so it must be against the American. (Since she loathed travel, and
Mme. Papaconstante had so far given no sign that she was going to try
and get Hadija back, she had renounced the idea of spiriting the girl
away to Europe.) Going on from there, it was clear that one had to
know what one was fighting. She thought of dwelling on the idea that
the man had no money, but then she decided that there was no line of
reasoning which would carry any weight with Hadija, and she had
best keep still. And for all she knew, perhaps he did have money,
although she had reconsidered the overheard conversation at the Bar
Lucifer and decided that the man's reluctance to part with his money
had not been due to viciousness. And he had had to borrow the extra

sum from his friend. It seemed reasonable to think that he was not too well off. She hoped that was the case; it could be strongly in her favor. Poverty in other people generally was.

"I know your friend," she said casually.

"You know?" Hadija was surprised.

"Oh, yes. I've met him."

"Where?" asked Hadija skeptically.

"Oh, various places. At the Taylor's on the Marshan, at the Sphinx Club once, and I think at the Estradas' house on the mountain. He's very nice."

Hadija was noncommittal. "O.K."

"If you want, you can ask him back here when you've finished your picnic."

"He no like come here."

"Oh, I don't know," said Eunice meditatively. "He might easily. I imagine he'd like a drink. Americans do, you know. I thought you might like to invite him, that's all."

Hadija thought about it. The idea appealed to her because she considered the Hotel Metropole magnificent and luxurious, and she was tempted to let him see in what style she was living. She had set out for the Parque Espinel with that intention, but on the walk back with him it occurred to her (for the first time) that since the American seemed to be fully as possessive about her as Eunice Goode, he might not relish the discovery that he was sharing her with someone else. So she hastened to explain that Miss Goode was ill most of the time and that she often visited her. The possessiveness he manifested toward her had already prompted her to make the attempt to get him to buy her a certain wrist watch she greatly admired. Eunice had definitely refused to get it for her because it was a man's watch—an oversize gold chronograph with calendar and phases of the moon thrown in. Eunice was eminently careful to see that the girl looked respectable and properly feminine. Hadija mentioned the watch twice on the way to the Metropole; the American merely smiled and said: "We'll see. Keep your shirt on, will you?" She did not completely understand, but at least he had not said no.

When Dyar came into the room Eunice Goode looked at him and said to herself that even as a girl she would not have found him attractive. She had liked imposing men, such as her father had been. This one was not at all distinguished in appearance. He did not look like an actor or a statesman or an artist, nor yet like a workman, a businessman or an athlete. For some reason she thought he looked rather like a wire-haired terrier—alert, eager, suggestible. The sort of male, she reflected with a stab of anger, who can lead girls around by the nose, without even being domineering, the sort whose maleness is unnoticeable and yet so thick it becomes cloying as honey, the sort that makes no effort and is thereby doubly dangerous. Except that being accustomed to an ambiance of feminine adulation makes them as vulnerable, as easily crushed, as spoiled children are. You let them think that you too are taken in by their charm, you entice them further and further out on that rotten limb. Then you jerk out the support and let them fall.

Yet in her mad inner scramble to be exceptionally gracious, Eunice got off to rather a poor start. She had been away from most people for so long that she forgot there are many who actually listen to the words spoken, and for whom even mere polite conversation is a means of conveying specific ideas. She had planned the opening sentences with the purpose of keeping Hadija from discovering that this was her first meeting with the American gentleman. Wearing an old yellow satin négligé trimmed with mink (which Hadija had never seen before and which she immediately determined to have for herself), and being well covered by the bedclothes, she looked like any other stout lady sitting up in bed.

"This is a belated but welcome meeting!" she cried.

"How do you do, Miss Goode." Dyar stood in the doorway. Hadija pulled him gently forward and shut the door. He stepped to the bed and took the proffered hand.

"I knew your mother in Taormina," said Eunice. "She was a delightful woman. Hadija, would you call downstairs and ask for a large bowl of ice and half a dozen bottles of Perrier? The whiskey's in the bathroom on the shelf. There are cigarettes in that big box there. Draw that chair a little nearer."

Dyar looked puzzled. "Where?"

"What?" she said pleasantly.

"Where did you say you knew my mother?" It had not yet occurred to him that Eunice Goode did not know his name.

"In Taormina," she said, looking at him blandly. "Or was it Juan-les-Pins?"

"It couldn't have been," Dyar said, sitting down. "My mother's never been in Europe at all."

"Really?" She meant it to sound casual, but it sounded acid. To her, such stubborn insistence on exactitude was sheer boorishness. But there was no time for showing him she disapproved of his behavior, even if she had wanted to. Hadija was telephoning. Quickly she said: "Wasn't your mother Mrs. Hambleton Mills? I thought that was what Hadija said."

"What?" cried Dyar, making a face indicating that he was all at sea. "Somebody's *all* mixed up. My name is Dyar. D,Y,A,R. It doesn't sound much like Mills to me." Then he laughed good-naturedly, and she joined in, just enough, she thought, to show that she bore him no ill-will for his rudeness.

"Well, now we have that settled," she said. She had his name; Hadija believed they had known each other before. She pressed on, to get as many essentials as possible while Hadija was still chattering in Spanish to the barman.

"Passing through on a winter holiday, or are you staying a while?"

"Holiday? Nothing like it. I'm staying a while. I'm working here."

She had expected that. "Oh, really? Where?"

He told her. "I can't quite place it," she said, shutting her eyes as if she were trying.

Hadija put the receiver on the hook and brought a bottle of whiskey from the bathroom. Suddenly Dyar became conscious of the fact that preparations were being made for the serving of drinks. He half rose from his chair, and sat down again on its edge.

"Look, I can't stay. I didn't realize—I'm sorry—"

"Can't stay?" echoed Eunice, faintly dismayed.

"I have an appointment at my hotel. I've got to get back. Hadija told me you were sick so I just thought I'd stop by. She said you wanted me to come."

"So I did. But I don't call this a visit."

The waiter had come in, set the tray on the table, and gone out.

"I know." He was not sure which would be less impolite,—to

accept one drink and then go, or to leave without taking anything.
"One quick drink," Eunice urged him. He accepted it.

Hadija had ordered a Coca-Cola. She was rather pleased to see
her two protectors in the same room talking together. She wondered if
it were dangerous. After all, Eunice knew about the man and did not
seem to mind. It was possible that he would not care too much if he
knew about Eunice. But she would certainly prefer him not to know.
She became conscious of their words.

"Where you go?" she interrupted.

"Home," he said, without looking at her.

"Where you live?"

Eunice smiled to herself: Hadija was doing her work for her. But
then she clicked her tongue with annoyance. The girl had bungled it;
he had been put off.

"Too far," he had answered drily.

"Why you go there?" Hadija pursued.

Now he turned to face her. "Curiosity killed a cat," he said with
mock sternness. "I'm going to a party, Nosey." He laughed. To
Eunice he said: "What a girl, what a girl! But she's nice in spite of it."

"I don't know about that," Eunice replied, as if giving the matter
thought. "I don't think so, at all, as a matter of fact. I'll talk to you
about it some time. Did you say a party?" She remembered that the
Beidaouis were at home on Sunday evenings. "Not at the Beidaoui
Palace?" she hazarded.

He looked surprised. "That's right!" he exclaimed. "Do you
know them?"

She had never met any of the Beidaoui brothers; however, they
had been pointed out to her on various occasions. "I know them very
well," she said. "They're *the* people of Tangier." She had heard that
their father had held a high official positon of some sort. "The old
Beidaoui who died a few years ago was the Grand Vizier to Sultan
Moulay Hafid. It was he who entertained the Kaiser when he came
here in 1906."

"Is that right?" said Dyar, making his voice polite.

Presently he stood up and said good-bye. He hoped she would be
better.

"Oh, it's a chronic condition," she said cheerfully. "It comes and goes. I never think about it. But as my grandmother in Pittsburgh used to say: 'It'll be a lot worse before it's any better.'"

He was a little surprised to hear that she was American: he had not thought of her as having any nationality at all. And now he was worried about how to make another rendezvous with Hadija in the somewhat forbidding presence of Miss Goode. However, it had to be done if he was to see her again; he would never be able to get to the Bar Lucifer, where he supposed she was still to be found.

"How about another picnic next Sunday?" he said to her. He might be free all during the week, and then again Wilcox might telephone him tomorrow. Sunday was the only safe day.

"Sure," said Hadija.

"Same place? Same time?"

"O.K."

As soon as he had gone, Eunice sat up straight in the bed. "Hand me the telephone book," she said.

"What you sigh?"

"The telephone book!"

She skimmed through it, found the name. *Jouvenon, Pierre, ing.* Ingénieur, engineer. It sounded much more impressive in French, being connected with such words as genius, ingenuity. Engineer always made her think of a man in overalls standing in a locomotive. She gave the number and said peremptorily to Hadija: "Get dressed quickly. Put on the new black frock we bought yesterday. I'll fix your hair when I'm dressed." She turned to the telephone. "*Allô, allô? Qui est à l'appareil?*" It was a Spanish maid: Eunice shrugged with impatience. "*Quisiera hablar con la Señora Jouvenon. Sí! La Señora!*" While she waited she put her hand over the mouthpiece and turned again to Hadija. "Remember. Not a word of anything but English." Hadija had gone into the bathroom and was splashing water in the basin.

"I know," she called. "No spickin Arab. No spickin Espanish. I know." They both took it as a matter of course that if Eunice went out, she went with her. At the back of her mind Eunice vaguely imagined that she was training the girl for Paris, where eventually she would take her to live, so that their successful ménage would excite the envy of all her friends.

"Ah, chère Madame Jouvenon!" she cried, and went on to tell the person at the other end of the wire that she hoped she was unoccupied for the next few hours, as she had something she wanted to discuss with her. Madame Jouvenon did not seem at all surprised by the announcement or to hear that the proposed discussion would take several hours. *"Vous êtes tr-rès aimable,"* she said, purring the *"r"* as no Frenchwoman would have done. It was agreed that they should meet in a half hour at La Sevillana, the small tearoom at the top of the Siaghines.

Eunice hung up, got out of bed, and hurriedly put on an old, loosely-draped tea-gown. Then she turned her attention to clothing Hadija, applying her make-up for her, and arranging her hair. She was like a mother preparing her only daughter for her first dance. And indeed, as they walked carefully side by side through the narrow alleys which were a short cut to La Sevillana, sometimes briefly holding hands when the way was wide enough, they looked very much like doting mother and fond daughter, and were taken for such by the Jewish women watching the close of day from their doorways and balconies.

Madame Jouvenon was already seated in La Sevillana eating a meringue. She was a bright-eyed little woman whose hair, having gone prematurely white, she had unwisely allowed to be dyed a bright silvery blue. To complete the monochromatic color scheme she had let Mlle. Sylvie dye her brows and lashes a much darker and more intense shade of blue. The final effect was not without impact.

Evidently Madame Jouvenon had only just arrived in the tearoom, as heads were still discreetly turning to get a better view of her. Characteristically, Hadija immediately decided that this lady was suffering from some strange disease, and she shook her hand with some squeamishness.

"We have very little time," Eunice began in French, hoping that Madame Jouvenon would not order more pastry. "The little one here doesn't speak French. Only Greek and some English. No pastry. Two coffees. Do you know the Beidaouis?"

Madame Jouvenon did not. Eunice was only momentarily chagrined.

"It doesn't matter," she continued. "I know them intimately, and you're my guest. I want to take you there now because there's someone I think you should meet. It's possible that he could be very useful to you."

Madame Jouvenon put down her fork. As Eunice continued talking, now in lower tones, the little woman's shining eyes became fixed and intense. Her entire expression altered; her face grew clever and alert. Presently, without finishing her meringue, she reached for her handbag in a businesslike manner and laid some coins on the table. "*Tr-rès bien,*" she said tersely. "*On va par-rtir.*"

2

Fresh Meat and Roses

10

THE BEIDAOUIS' Sunday evenings were unique in that any member of one of the various European colonies could attend without thereby losing face, probably because the fact that the hosts were Moslems automatically created among the guests a feeling of solidarity which they welcomed without being conscious of its origin. The wife of the French minister could chat with the lowest American lady tourist and no one would see anything extraordinary about it. This certainly did not mean that if the tourist caught sight of Mme. D'Arcourt the next day and had the effrontery to recognize her, she in turn would be recognized. Still, it was pleasant and democratic while it lasted, which was generally until about nine. Very few Moslems were invited, but there were always three or four men of importance in the Moslem world: perhaps the leader of the Nationalist Party in the Spanish Zone, or the editor of the Arabic daily in Casablanca, or a wealthy manufacturer from Tunis, or the advisor to the Jalifa of Tetuan. In reality the gatherings were held in order to entertain these few Moslem guests, to whom the unaccountable behavior of Europeans never ceased to be a fascinating spectacle. Most of the Europeans, of course, thought the Moslem gentlemen were invited to add local color, and praised the Beidaoui brothers for their cleverness in knowing so well just what sort of Moroccan could mix properly with foreigners. These same people, who prided themselves upon the degree of intimacy to which they had managed to attain in their relationships with the Beidaoui, were nevertheless quite unaware that the two brothers were married, and led intense family lives with their women and children in a part of the house where no European had ever entered. The Beidaouis would

113

certainly not have hidden the fact had they been asked, but no one had ever thought to question them about such things. It was taken for granted that they were two debonair bachelors who loved to surround themselves with Europeans.

That morning, on one of his frequent walks along the waterfront, where he was wont to go when he had a hangover or his home life had grown too oppressive for his taste, Thami had met with an extraordinary piece of good luck. He had wandered out onto the breakwater of the inner port, where the fishermen came to unload, and was watching them shake out the black nets, stiff with salt. A small, old-fashioned motor-boat drew alongside the dock. The man in it, whom Thami recognized vaguely, threw a rope to a boy standing nearby. As the boatman, who wore a turban marking him as a member of the Jilala cult, climbed up the steps to the pier, he greeted Thami briefly. Thami replied, asking if he had been fishing. The man looked at him a little more closely, as if to see exactly who it was he had spoken to so carelessly. Then he smiled sadly, and said that he never had used his little boat for fishing, and that he hoped the poor old craft would be spared such a fate until the day it fell to pieces. Thami laughed; he understood perfectly that the man meant it was a fast enough boat to be used for smuggling. He moved along the dock and looked down into the motor-boat. It must have been forty years old; the seats ran lengthwise and were covered with decaying canvas cushions. There was an ancient two-cylinder Fay and Bowen engine in the center. The man noticed his scrutiny, and inquired if he were interested in buying the boat. "No," said Thami contemptuously, but he continued to look. The other remarked that he hated to sell it but had to, because his father in Azemmour was ill, and he was going back there to live. Thami listened with an outward show of patience, waiting for a figure to be mentioned. He had no intention of betraying his interest by suggesting one himself. Eventually, as he tossed his cigarette into the water and made as if to go, he heard the figure: ten thousand pesetas. "I don't think you'll get more than five," he replied, turning to move off. "Five!" cried the man indignantly. "Look at it," said Thami, pointing down at it. "Who's going to give more?" He started to walk slowly away, kicking pieces of broken concrete into the water as he went. The man called after him. "Eight thousand!" He turned around, smiling, and explained that he was not interested himself, but that if the Jilali really wanted to sell the boat, he should put a sensible price on it, one that Thami could quote to his friends in case one of them might know a possible buyer. They argued a while, and Thami finally went away with six thousand as an asking price. He felt rather pleased with himself, because although it was by no means the beautiful speed boat he coveted, it was at least a tangible and immediate possibility whose realization would not involve either an import license or any very serious tampering with his heritage. He had thought of asking the American, whom he liked, and who he felt had a certain sympathy for him, to purchase the boat in his name. It would have been a way around the license. But he thought he did not know him well enough, and beyond a doubt it would have been a foolish move: he would have had to rely solely on the American's honesty for proof of ownership. As to the price, it was negligible, even at six thousand, and he was positive he could get it down to five. There was even a faint possibility, although he doubted it, really, that he could get Abdelmalek to lend him the sum. In any case, among his bits of property there was a two-room house without lights or water at the bottom of a ravine behind the Marshan, which ought to bring just about five thousand pesetas in a quick sale.

The end of the afternoon was splendid: the clouds had been blown away by a sudden wind from the Atlantic. The air smelled clean, the sky had become intense and luminous. As Dyar waited in front of the door of his hotel, a long procession of Berbers on donkeys passed along the avenue on their way from the mountains to the market. The men's faces were brown and weather-burned, the women were surprisingly light of skin, with salient, round red cheeks. Dispassionately he watched them jog past, not realizing how slowly they moved until he became aware of the large American convertible at the end of the line, whose horn was being blown frantically by the impatient driver. "What's the hurry?" he thought. The little waves on the beach were coming in quietly, the hills were changing color slowly with the dying of the light behind the city, a few Moroccans strolled deliberately along the walk under the wind-stirred branches of the palms. It was a pleasant hour whose natural rhythm was that of leisure; the insistent blowing of the trumpet-like horn made no sense in that ensemble. Nor did the Berbers on their donkeys give any sign of hearing it. They passed peacefully along, the little beasts taking their measured steps and nodding their heads. When the last one had come opposite Dyar, the car swung toward the curb and stopped. It was the Marquesa de Valverde. "Mr. Dyar!" she called. As he shook her hand she said: "I'd have been here earlier, darling, but I've been bringing up the rear of this parade for the past ten minutes. Don't ever buy a car here. It's the most nerve-racking spot in this world to drive in. God!"

"I'll bet," he said; he went around to the other side and got in beside her.

They drove up through the modern town at a great rate, past new apartment houses of glaring white concrete, past empty lots crammed to bursting with huts built of decayed signboards, packing cases, reed latticework and old blankets, past new cinema palaces and night clubs whose sickly fluorescent signs already glowed with light that was at once too bright and too dim. They skirted the new market, which smelled tonight of fresh meat and roses. To the south stretched the sandy wasteland and the green scrub of the foothills. The cypresses along the road were bent by years of wind. "This Sunday traffic is dreadful. Ghastly," said Daisy, looking straight ahead. Dyar laughed shortly; he was thinking of the miles of strangled parkways outside New York. "You don't know what traffic is," he said. But his mind was not on what was being said, nor yet on the gardens and walls of the villas going past. Although he was not given to analyzing his states of mind, since he never had been conscious of possessing any sort of apparatus with which to do so, recently he had felt, like a faint tickling in an inaccessible region of his being, an undefined need to let his mind dwell on himself. There were no formulated thoughts, he did not even daydream, nor did he push matters so far as to ask himself questions like: "What am I doing here?" or "What do I want?" At the same time he was vaguely aware of having arrived at the edge of a new period in his existence, an unexplored territory of himself through which he was going to have to pass. But his perception of the thing was limited to knowing that lately he had been wont to sit quietly alone in his room saying to himself that he was here. The fact kept repeating itself to him: "Here I am." There was nothing to be deduced from it; the saying of it seemed to be connected with a feeling almost of anaes-

thesia somewhere within him. He was not moved by the phenomenon; even to himself he felt supremely anonymous, and it is difficult
to care very much what is happening inside a person one does not
know. At the same time, that which went on outside was remote and
had no relationship to him; it might almost as well not have been
going on at all. Yet he was not indifferent—indifference is a matter of
the emotions, whereas this numbness affected a deeper part of him.

They turned into a somewhat narrower, curving street. On the
left was a windowless white wall at least twenty feet high which went
on ahead, flush with the street, as far as the eye could follow. "That's
it," said Daisy, indicating the wall. "The palace?" said Dyar, a little
disappointed. "The Beidaoui Palace," she answered, aware of the
crestfallen note in his voice. "It's a strange old place," she added,
deciding to let him have the further surprise of discovering the
decayed sumptuousness of the interior for himself. "It sure looks it,"
he said with feeling. "How do you get in?"

"The gate's a bit farther up," replied Daisy, and without transition she looked directly at him as she said: "You've missed out on a
good many things, haven't you?" His first thought was that she was
pitying him for his lack of social advantages; his pride was hurt. "I
don't think so," he said quickly. Then with a certain heat he demanded: "What sort of things? What do you mean?"

She brought the car to a stop at the curb behind a string of others
already parked there. As she took out the keys and put them into her
purse she said: "Things like friendship and love. I've lived in America
a good deal. My mother was from Boston, you know, so I'm part
American. I know what it's like, Oh, God, only too well!"

They got out. "I guess there's as much friendship there as
anywhere else," he said. He was annoyed, and he hoped his voice did
not show it. "Or love."

"Love!" she cried derisively.

An elderly Sudanese swung the grilled gate. They went into a
dark room where several other bearded men were stretched out on
mats in a niche that ran the length of the wall. These greeted Daisy
solemnly, without moving. The old servant opened a door, and
they stepped out into a vast dim garden in which the only things Dyar
could identify with certainty were the very dark, tall cypresses, their

points sharp against the evening sky, and the very white marble
fountains in which water splashed with an uneven sound. They went
along the gravel walk in silence between the sweet and acid floral
smells. There were thin strains of music ahead. "I expect they're
dancing to the gramophone," said Daisy. "This way." She led him up
a walk toward the right, to a wide flight of marble stairs. "Evenings
they entertain in the European wing. And in European style. Except
that they themselves don't touch liquor, of course." Above the music
of the tango came the chatter of voices. As they arrived at the top of
the stairway a grave-faced man in a white silk gown stepped forward
to welcome them.

"Dear Abdelmalek!" Daisy cried delightedly, seizing his two
hands. "*What* a lovely party! This is Mr. Dyar of New York." He
shook Dyar's hand warmly. "It is very kind of Madame la Marquise to
bring you to my home," he said. Daisy was already greeting other
friends; M. Beidaoui, still grasping Dyar's hand, led him to a nearby
corner where he presented him to his brother Hassan, a tall
chocolate-colored gentleman also clothed in white robes. They spoke a
minute about America, and Dyar was handed a whiskey-soda by a
servant. As his hosts turned away to give their attention to a new
arrival, he began to look about him. The room was large, comfortable
and dark, being lighted only by candles that rested in massive candelabra placed here and there on the floor. It was irregularly shaped,
and the music and dancing were going on in a part hidden from his
vision. Along the walls nearby were wide, low divans occupied exclu-
sively by women, all of whom looked over forty, he noted, and certain
of whom were surely at least seventy. Apart from the Beidaoui
brothers there were only two other Moslems in view. One was
talking to Daisy by an open window and the other was joking with a
fat Frenchman in a corner. In spite of the Beidaouis, whom he rather
liked, he felt smothered and out of place, and he wished he had not
come.

As Dyar was about to move off and see who was taking part in the
dancing, Hassan tapped him on the arm. "This is Madame Werth,"
he said. "You speak French?" The dark-eyed woman in black to whom
he was being presented smiled. "No," said Dyar, confused. "It does
not matter," she said. "I speak a little English." "You speak very

well," said Dyar, offering her a cigarette. He had the feeling that someone had spoken to him about her, but he could not remember who, or what it was that had been said. They conversed a while, standing there with their drinks, in the same spot where they had been introduced, and the idea persisted that he knew something about her which he was unable to call to mind. He had no desire to be stuck with her all evening, but for the moment he saw no way out. And she had just told him that she was in mourning for her husband; she looked rather forlorn, and he felt sorry for her. Suddenly he saw Eunice Goode's flushed face appear in the doorway. "How do you do?" she said to Hassan Beidaoui. Behind her was Hadija, looking very smart indeed. "How do you do?" said Hadija, with the identical inflection of Eunice Goode. A third woman entered with them, small and grim-faced, who scarcely acknowledged the greeting extended to her, but immediately began to inspect the guests with care, one by one, as if taking a rapid inventory of the qualities and importance of each. There was not enough light for the color of her hair to be noticeable, so, since no one seemed to know her, no one paid her any attention for the moment. Dyar was too much astonished at seeing Hadija to continue his conversation; he stood staring at her. Eunice Goode held her by the hand and was talking very fast to Hassan.

"You'll be interested to know that one of my dearest friends was Crown Prince Rupprecht. We were often at Karlsbad together. I believe he knew your father." As the rush of words went on, Hassan's face showed increasing lack of comprehension; he moved backward a step after each few sentences, saying: "Yes, yes," but she followed along, pulling Hadija with her, until she had backed him against the wall and Dyar could no longer hear what she was saying. Somewhat embarrassed, he again became conscious of Madame Werth's presence beside him.

"—and I hope you will come to make a visit to me when I am returning from Marrakech," she was saying.

"Thank you, I'd like very much to." It was then that he recalled where he had heard her name. The canceled reservation at the hotel there which he had been going to give to Daisy had originally been Madame Werth's.

"Do you know Marrakech?" she asked him. He said he did not.

"Ah, you must go. In the winter it is beautiful. You must have a room at the Mamounia, but the room must have a view on the mountains, the snow, you know, and a terrace above the garden. I would love to go tomorrow, but the Mamounia is always full now and my reservation is not before the twenty of the month."

Dyar looked at her very hard. She noticed the difference in his expression, and was slightly startled.

"You're going to the Hotel Mamounia in Marrakech on the twentieth?" he said. Then, seeing the suggestion of bewilderment on her face he looked down at her drink. "Yours is nearly finished," he remarked. "Let me get you another." She was pleased; he excused himself and went across the room with a glass in each hand.

It all made perfectly good sense. Now at last he understood Daisy's request of him and the secrecy with which she had surrounded it. Madame Werth would simply have been told that there had been a most regrettable misunderstanding, and Wilcox's office would have been blamed, but the Marquise de Valverde would already have been installed in the room and there would have been no dislodging her. As he realized how close he had come to doing her the favor he felt a rush of fury against her. "The bitch!" he said between his teeth. The little revelation was unpleasant, and it somehow extended itself to the whole room and everyone in it.

He saw Daisy out of the corner of his eye as he passed the divan where she sat; she was talking to a pale young man with spectacles and a girl with a wild head of red hair. As he was on his way back she caught sight of him and called out: "Mr. Dyar! When you've made your delivery I want you to come over here." He held the glasses up higher and grinned. "Just a second," he said. He was wondering if Madame Werth would be capable of the same sort of throatslitting behavior as Daisy, and decided against the likelihood of it. She looked too helpless, which was doubtless precisely why Daisy had singled her out as a likely prospective victim.

Back, standing again beside Madame Werth, he said as she sipped her new drink: "Do you know the Marquesa de Valverde?"

Madame Werth seemed enthusiastic. "Ah, what a delightful woman! Such vivacity! And very kind. I have seen her pick out from the street young dogs, poor thin ones with bones, and take them to her home and care for them. The entire world is her charity."

Dyar laughed abruptly; it must have sounded derisive, for Madame Werth said accusingly: "You think kindness does not matter?"

"Sure it matters. It's very important." At the moment he felt expansive and a little reckless; it would be pleasurable to sit beside Daisy and worry her. She could not see whom he was talking to from where she sat, and he wanted to watch her reaction when he told her. Presently a Swiss gentleman joined them and began speaking with Madame Werth in French. Dyar slipped away, finishing his drink quickly and getting another before he went over to the divan where Daisy was.

"Two compatriots of yours," she said, moving over so he could squeeze in beside her. "Mr. Dyar. Mrs. Holland, Mr. Richard Holland." The two acknowledged the introduction briefly, with what seemed more diffidence than coldness.

"We were talking about New York," said Daisy. "Mr. and Mrs. Holland are from New York, and they say they feel quite as much at home here as they do there. I told them that was scarcely surprising, since Tangier is more New York than New York. Don't you agree?"

Dyar looked at her closely; then he looked at Mrs. Holland, who met his gaze for a startled instant and began to inspect her shoes. Mr. Holland was staring at him with great seriousness, like a doctor about to arrive at a diagnosis, he thought. "I don't think I see what you mean," said Dyar. "Tangier like New York? How come?"

"In spirit," said Mr. Holland with impatience. "Not in appearance, naturally. Are you from New York? I thought Madame de Valverde said you were." Dyar nodded. "Then you must see how alike the two places are. The life revolves wholly about the making of money. Practically everyone is dishonest. In New York you have Wall Street, here you have the Bourse. Not like the bourses in other places, but the soul of the city, its *raison d'être*. In New York you have the slick financiers, here the money-changers. In New York you have your racketeers. Here you have your smugglers. And you have every nationality and no civic pride. And each man's waiting to suck the blood of the next. It's not really such a far-fetched comparison, is it?"

"I don't know," said Dyar. At first he had thought he agreed, but then the substance of Holland's argument had seemed to slip away from him. He took a long swallow of whiskey. The phonograph was playing *"Mamá Inez."* "I guess there are plenty of untrustworthy people here, all right," he said.

"Untrustworthy!" cried Mr. Holland. "The place is a model of corruption!"

"But darling," Daisy interrupted. "Tangier's a one-horse town that happens to have its own government. And you know damned well that all government lives on corruption. I don't care what sort— socialist, totalitarian, democratic—it's all the same. Naturally in a little place like this you come in contact with the government constantly. God knows, it's inevitable. And so you're always conscious of the corruption. It's that simple."

Dyar turned to her. "I was just talking with Madame Werth over there." Daisy looked at him calmly for a moment. It was impossible to tell what she was thinking. Then she laughed. "I being the sort of person I am, and you being the sort of person you are, I think we can skip over *that*. Tell me, Mrs. Holland, have you read *The Thousand and One Nights?"*

"The Mardrus translation," said Mrs. Holland without looking up.

"All of it?"

"Well, not quite. But most."

"And do you adore it?"

"Well, I admire it terribly. But Dick's the one who loves it. It's a little direct for me, but then I suppose the culture had no nuances either."

Dyar had finished his drink and was again thinking of getting in to where the dancing was going on. He sat still, hoping the conversation might somehow present him with a possibility of withdrawing gracefully. Daisy was addressing Mr. Holland. "Have you ever noticed how completely illogical the end of each one of those thousand and one nights actually is? I'm curious to know."

"Illogical?" said Mr. Holland. "I don't think so."

"Oh, my dear! Really! Doesn't it say, at the end of each night: 'And Scheherazade, perceiving the dawn, discreetly became silent'?"

"Yes."

"And then doesn't it say: 'And the King and Scheherazade went to bed and remained locked in one another's arms until morning'?"

"Yes."

"Isn't that rather a short time? Especially for Arabs?"

Mrs. Holland directed an oblique upward glance at Daisy, and returned to the contemplation of her feet.

"I think you misunderstand the time-sequence," said Mr. Holland, sitting up straight with a sudden spasmodic movement, as if he were getting prepared for a discussion. Dyar got quickly to his feet. He had decided he did not like Mr. Holland, who he imagined found people agreeable to the extent that they were interested in hearing him expound his theories. Also he was a little disappointed to find that Daisy had met his challenge with such bland complacency. "She didn't bat an eyelash," he thought. It had been no fun at all to confront her with the accusation. Or perhaps she had not even recognized his remark as such. The idea occurred to him as he reached the part of the room where the phonograph was, but he rejected it. Her reply could have meant only that she admitted she had been found out, and did not care. She was even more brazen than he had imagined. For no particular reason, knowing this depressed him, put him back into the gray mood of despair he had felt the night of his arrival on the boat, enveloped him in the old uneasiness.

A few couples were moving discreetly about the small floor-space, doing more talking than dancing. As Dyar stood watching the fat Frenchman swaying back and forth on his feet, trying to lead an elderly English woman in a turban who had taken a little too much to drink, Abdelmalek Beidaoui came up to him bringing with him a tall Portuguese girl, cadaver-thin and with a cast in one eye. It was obvious that she wanted to dance, and she accepted with eagerness. Although she kept her hips against his as they danced, she leant sharply backward from the waist and peered at him fixedly while she told him bits of gossip about the people in the other part of the room. In speaking she kept her lips drawn back so that her gums were fully visible. "Jesus, I've got to get out of here," Dyar thought. But they went on, record after record. At the close of a samba, he said to her, panting somewhat exaggeratedly: "Tired?" "No, no!" she cried. "You are marvelous dancer."

Here and there candles had begun to go out; the room was chilly, and a damp wind came through the open door from the garden. It was that moment of the evening when everyone had arrived and no one had yet thought of going home; one could have said that the party was in full swing, save that there was a peculiar deadness about the gathering which made it difficult to believe that a party was actually in progress. Later, in retrospect, one might be able to say that it had taken place, but now, while it still had not finished, it was somehow not true.

The Portuguese girl was telling him about Estoril, and how Monte Carlo even at its zenith never had been so glamorous. If at that moment someone had not taken hold of his arm and yanked on it violently he would probably have said something rather rude. As it was, he let go of the girl abruptly and turned to face Eunice Goode, who was by then well primed with martinis. She was looking at the frowning Portuguese girl with a polite leer. "I'm afraid you've lost your dancing partner," she said, steadying herself by putting one hand against the wall. "He's coming with me into the other room."

Under ordinary circumstances Dyar would have told her she was mistaken, but right now the idea of sitting down with a drink, even with Eunice Goode along, seemed the preferable, the less strenuous of two equally uninteresting prospects. He excused himself lamely, letting her lead him away across the room into a small, dim library whose walls were lined to the ceiling with graying encyclopaedias, reference books and English novels. Drawn up around a fireplace with no fire in it were three straight-backed chairs, in one of which sat Mme. Jouvenon, staring ahead of her into the cold ashes. She did not turn around when she heard them come into the room.

"Here we are," said Eunice brightly, and she introduced the two, sitting down so that Dyar occupied the chair between them.

11

FOR A FEW MINUTES Eunice valiantly made conversation; she asked questions of them both and answered for both. The replies were doubtless not the ones that either Mme. Jouvenon or Dyar would have given, but in their respective states of confusion and apathy they said: "Ah, yes" and "That's right" when she took it upon herself to explain to each how the other felt. Dyar was bored, somewhat drunk, and faintly alarmed by Mme. Jouvenon's expression of fierce preoccupation, while she, desperately desirous of gaining his interest, was casting about frantically in her mind for a proper approach. With each minute that passed, the absurd situation in the cold little library became more untenable. Dyar shifted about on his chair and tried to see behind him through the doorway into the other room; he hoped to catch sight of Hadija. Someone put on a doleful Egyptian record. The groaning baritone voice filled the air.

"You have been to Cairo?" said Mme. Jouvenon suddenly.

"No." It did not seem enough to answer, but he had no further inspiration.

"You are inter-r-rested in the Middle East, also?"

"Madame Jouvenon has spent most of her life in Constantinople and Baghdad and Damascus, and other fascinating places," said Eunice.

"Not Baghdad," corrected Mme. Jouvenon sternly. "Bokhara."

"That must be interesting," said Dyar.

The Egyptian record was interrupted in mid-lament, and a French music-hall song replaced it. Then there was the sound of one of the heavy candelabra being overturned, accompanied by little cries of consternation. Taking advantage of the moment, which he felt might not present itself again even if he waited all night, Dyar sprang to his feet and rushed to the door. Directly behind him came Mme. Jouvenon, picking at his sleeve. She had decided to be bold. If, as Eunice Goode claimed, the young man was short of funds, it was likely he would accept an invitation to a meal, and so she promptly extended one for the following day, making it clear that he was to be her guest.

"That's a splendid idea," said Eunice hurriedly. "I'm sure you two will have a great deal to give each other. Mr. Dyar has been in the consular service for years, and you probably have dozens of mutual friends." He did not even bother to correct her: she was too far gone, he thought. He had just had a glimpse of Hadija dancing with one of the Beidaoui brothers, and he turned to Mme. Jouvenon to decline her kind invitation. But he was not quick enough.

"At two tomorrow. At the Empire. You know where this is. The food is r-rather good. I will have the table at end, by where the bar is. This will give me gr-reat pleasure. We cannot speak here." And so it was settled, and he escaped to the table of drinks and got another.

"You rather bungled that," Eunice Goode murmured.

Mme. Jouvenon looked at her. "You mean he will not come?"

"I shouldn't if I were he. Your behavior. . . ." She stopped on catching sight of Hadija engaged in a rumba with Hassan Beidaoui; they smiled fatuously as they wriggled about. "The little idiot," she thought. The sight was all too reminiscent of the Bar Lucifer. "She's surely speaking Arabic with him." Uneasily she walked toward the dance floor, and presently was gratified to hear Hadija cry: "Oh, yes!" to something Hassan had said.

Without being invited this time, Dyar went and sat down beside Daisy. The room seemed immense, and much darker. He was feeling quite drunk; he slid down into a recumbent position and stretched his legs out straight in front of him, his head thrown back so that he was staring up at the dim white ceiling far above. Richard Holland sat in a chair facing Daisy, holding forth, with his wife nestling on the floor at his feet, her head on his knee. The old English lady with the turban was at the other end of the divan, smoking a cigarette in a very long, thin holder. Eunice Goode wandered over to the group, followed by Mme. Jouvenon, and stood behind Holland's chair drinking a glass of straight gin. She looked down at the back of his head, and said in a soft but unmistakably belligerent voice: "I don't know who you are, but I think that's all sheer balls."

He squirmed around and looked up at her; deciding she was drunk he ignored her, and went on talking. Presently Mme. Jouvenon whispered to Eunice that she must go, and the two went toward the door where Abdelmalek stood, his robes blowing in the breeze.

"Who is that extraordinary woman with Miss Goode?" asked the English lady. "I don't recall ever having seen her before." No one answered. "Don't any of you know?" she pursued fretfully.

"Yes," said Daisy at length. She hesitated a moment, and then, her voice taking on a vaguely mysterious tone: "I know who she is."

But Mme. Jouvenon had left quickly, and Eunice was already back, dragging a chair with her, which she installed as close as possible to Richard Holland's, and in which she proceded to sit suddenly and heavily.

From time to time Dyar closed his eyes, only to open them again quickly when he felt the room sliding forward from under him. Looking at the multitude of shadows on the ceiling he did not think he felt the alcohol too much. But it became a chore to keep his eyes open for very long at a stretch. He heard the voices arguing around him; they seemed excited, and yet they were talking about nothing. They were loud, and yet they seemed far away. As he fixed one particular part of a monumental shadow stretching away into the darker regions of the ceiling, he had the feeling suddenly that he was seated there surrounded by dead people—or perhaps figures in a film that had been made a long time before. They were speaking, and he heard their voices, but the actual uttering of the words had been done many years ago. He must not let himself be fooled into believing that he could communicate with them. No one would hear him if he should try to speak. He felt the cold rim of his glass on his leg where he held it; it had wet through his trousers. With a spasmodic movement he sat up and took a long drink. If only there had been someone to whom he could have said: "Let's get out of here." But they all sat there in another world, talking feverishly about nothing, approving and protesting, each one delighted with the sound his own ideas made when they were turned into words. The alcohol was like an ever-thickening curtain being drawn down across his mind, isolating it from everything else in the room. It blocked out even his own body, which, like the faces around him, the candle flames and the dance music, became also increasingly remote and disconnected. "God damn it!" he cried suddenly. Daisy, intent on what Richard Holland was saying, distractedly reached out and took his hand, holding it tightly so he could not withdraw it without an effort. He let it lie in hers; the contact helped him a little to focus his attention upon the conversation.

"Oh no!" said Holland, "The species is not at all intent on destroying itself. That's nonsense. It's intent on being something which happens inevitably to entail its destruction, that's all."

A man came through the door from the garden and walked quickly across the room to where Abdelmalek stood talking with several of his guests. Dyar was not alert enough to see his face as he moved through the patches of light in the center of the room, but he thought the figure looked familiar.

"Give me a sip," said Holland, reaching down and taking his wife's glass out of her hand. "There's nothing wrong in the world except that man has persuaded himself he's a rational being, when really he's a moral one. And morality must have a religious basis, not a rational one. Otherwise it's just play-acting."

The old English lady lit another cigarette, throwing the match on the floor to join the wide pile of ashes she had scattered there. "That's all very well," she said with a touch of petulance in her cracked voice, "but nowadays religion and rationality are not mutually exclusive. We're not living in the Dark Ages."

Holland laughed insolently; his eyes were malignant. "Do you want to see it get dark?" he shouted. "Stick around a few years." And he laughed again. No one said anything. He handed the glass back to Mrs. Holland. "I don't think anyone will disagree if I say that religion all over the world is just about dead."

"*I* certainly shall," said the English lady with asperity. "But no matter."

"I'm sorry, but in most parts of the world today, professing a religion is purely a matter of politics, and has practically nothing to do with faith. The Hindus are busy letting themselves be seen riding in Cadillacs instead of smearing themselves with sandalwood paste and bowing in front of Ganpati. The Moslems would rather miss evening prayer than the new Disney movie. The Buddhists think it's more important to take over in the name of Marx and Progress than to meditate on the four basic sorrows. And we don't even have to mention Christianity or Judaism. At least, I hope not. But there's absolutely nothing that can be done about it. You can't *decide* to be irrational. Man is rational now, and rational man is lost."

"I suppose," said the English lady acidly, "that you're going to tell us we can no longer choose between good and evil? It seems to me that would come next on your agenda."

"God, the man's pretentious," Daisy was thinking. As she grew increasingly bored and restive, she toyed with Dyar's fingers. And to himself Dyar said: "I don't want to listen to all this crap." He never had been one to believe that discussion of abstractions could lead to anything but more discussion. Yet he did listen, perhaps because in his profound egotism he felt that in some fashion Holland was talking about him.

"Oh, that!" said Holland, pretending to sound infinitely patient. "Good and evil are like white and black on a piece of paper. To distinguish them you need at least a glimmer of light, otherwise you can't even see the paper. And that's the way it is now. It's gotten too dark to tell." He snickered. "Don't talk to *me* about the Dark Ages. Right now no one could presume to know where the white ends and the black begins. We know they're both there, that's all."

"Well, I must say I'm glad to hear we know that much, at least," said the English lady testily. "I was on the point of concluding that there was absolutely no hope." She laughed mockingly.

Holland yawned. "Oh, it'll work itself out, all right. Until then, it would be better not to be here. But if anyone's left afterward, they'll fix it all up irrationally and the world will be happy again."

Daisy was examining Dyar's palm, but the light was too dim. She dropped the hand and began to arrange her hair, preparatory to getting up. "*Enfin*, none of it sounds very hopeful," she remarked, smiling.

"It *isn't* very hopeful," Holland said pityingly; he enjoyed his role as diagnostician of civilization's maladies, and he always arrived at a negative prognosis. He would happily have continued all night with an appreciative audience.

"Excuse me. I've got to have another drink," said Dyar, lunging up onto his feet. He took a few steps forward, turned partially around and smiled at Daisy, so as not to seem rude, and saw Mrs. Holland rise from her uncomfortable position on the floor to occupy the place on the divan which he had just vacated. Then he went on, found himself through the door, standing on the balcony in the damp night wind.

There seemed to be no reason for not going down the wide stairs, and so he went softly down and walked along the path in the dark until he came to a wall. There was a bench; he sat down in the quiet and stared ahead of him at the nearby silhouettes of moving branches and vines. No music, no voices, not even the fountains could be heard here. But there were other closer sounds: the leaves of plants rubbed together, stalks and pods hardened by the winter rattled and shook, and high in a palmyra tree not far away the dry slapping of an enormous fan-shaped branch (it covered and uncovered a certain group of stars as it waved back and forth) was like the distant slamming of an old screen door. It was difficult to believe a tree in the wind could make that hard, vaguely mechanical noise.

For a while he sat quite still in the dark, with nothing in his mind save an awareness of the natural sounds around him; he did not even realize that he was welcoming these sounds as they washed through him, that he was allowing them to cleanse him of the sense of bitter futility which had filled him for the past two hours. The cold wind eddied around the shrubbery at the base of the wall; he hugged himself but did not move. Shortly he would have to rise and go back into the light, up the steps into the room whose chaos was only the more clearly perceived for the polite gestures of the people who filled it. For the moment he stayed sitting in the cold. "Here I am," he told himself once again, but this time the melody, so familiar that its meaning was gone, was faintly transformed by the ghost of a new harmony beneath it, scarcely perceptible and at the same time, merely because it was there at all, suggestive of a direction to be taken which made those three unspoken words more than a senseless reiteration. He might have been saying to himself: "Here I am and something is going to happen." The infinitesimal promise of a possible change stirred him to physical movement: he unwrapped his arms from around himself and lit a cigarette.

12

BACK IN THE ROOM Eunice Goode, on her way to being a little more drunk than usual (the presence of many people around her often led her to such excesses), was in a state of nerves. A recently arrived guest, a young man whom she did not know, and who in spite of his European attire was obviously a Moslem, had come up to Hadija as she and Eunice stood together by the phonograph, and greeted her familiarly in Arabic. Fortunately Hadija had had the presence of mind to answer: "What you sigh?" before turning her back on him, but that had not ended the incident. A moment later, while Eunice was across the room having her glass replenished, the two had somehow begun to dance. When she returned and saw them she had wanted terribly to step in and separate them, but of course there was no way she could do such a thing without having an excuse of some sort. "I shall make a fearful scene if I start," she said to herself, and so she hovered about the edge of the dance floor, now and then catching hold of a piece of furniture for support. At least, as long as she remained close to Hadija the girl would not be so likely to speak Arabic. That was the principal danger.

Hadija was in misery. She had not wanted to dance (indeed, she considered that her days of enforced civility to strange men, and above all Moslem men, had come to a triumphant close), but he had literally grabbed her. The young man, who was squeezing her against him with such force that she had difficulty in breathing, refused to speak anything but Arabic with her, even though she kept her face set in an intransigent mask of hauteur and incomprehension. "Everyone knows you're a Tanjaouia," he was saying. But she fought down the fear that his words engendered. Only her two protectors, Eunice and the American gentleman, knew. Several times she tried to push him away and stop dancing, but he only held her with increased firmness, and she realized unhappily that any more vehement efforts on her part would attract the attention of the other dancers, of whom there were now only two couples. Occasionally she said in a loud voice: "O.K."

or "Oh, yes!" so as to reassure Eunice, whom she saw watching her desperately.

"*Ch'âândek?* What's the matter with you? What are you trying to do?" the young man was saying indignantly. "Are you ashamed of being a Moslem? It's very bad, what you are doing. You think I don't remember you from the Bar Lucifer? Ha! *Hamqat, entina! Hamqat!*" His breath smelled strongly of the brandy he had been drinking all day.

Hadija was violently indignant. "*Ana hamqat?*" she began, and realized too late that she had given herself away. The young man laughed delightedly, and tried to get her to go on, but she froze into absolute silence. Finally she cried out in Arabic: "You're hurting me!" and breaking from his embrace hurried to Eunice's side, where she stood rubbing her shoulder. "Wan fackin bastard," she said under her breath to Eunice, who had witnessed her linguistic indiscretion and realized that as far as the young man was concerned the game was up.

"Shut up!" She seized Hadija's arm and pulled her off into an empty corner.

"I want wan Coca-Cola," objected Hadija. "Very hot. That lousy guy dance no good."

"Who is he, anyway?"

"Wan Moorish man live in Tangier."

"I know, but who? What's he doing in the Beidaoui Palace?"

"He plenty drunk."

Eunice mused a moment, letting go of Hadija's arm. With as much dignity as she could summon, she strode across the room toward Hassan Beidaoui, who, seeing her coming, turned around and managed to be talking animatedly with Mme. Werth by the time she reached him. The maneuver proved quite worthless, of course, since Eunice's piercing "I say" began while she was still ten feet away. She tapped Hassan's arm and he faced her patiently, prepared to listen to another series of incomprehensible reminiscences about Crown Prince Rupprecht.

"I say!" She indicated Hadija's recent dancing partner. "I say, isn't that the eldest son of the Pacha of Fez? I'm positive I remember him from Paris."

"No," said Hassan quietly. "That is my brother Thami. Would you like to meet him?" (This suggestion was prompted less by a feeling of amiability toward Eunice Goode than by one of spite toward Thami, whose unexpected appearance both Hassan and Abdelmalek considered an outrage. They had suggested he leave, but being a little drunk he had only laughed. If anyone present could precipitate his departure, thought Hassan, it was this outlandish American woman.) "Will you come?" He held out his arm. Eunice reflected quickly, and said she would be delighted.

She was not surprised to find Thami exactly the sort of Moroccan she most disliked and habitually inveighed against: outwardly Europeanized but inwardly conscious that the desired metamorphosis would remain forever unaccomplished, and therefore defiant, on the offensive to conceal his defeat, irresponsible and insolent. For his part, Thami behaved in a particularly obnoxious fashion. He was in a foul humor, having met with no success either in attempting to get the money for the boat from his brothers, or in persuading them to agree to the sale of his house in the Marshan. And again, this hideous woman was his idea of the typical tourist who admired his race only insofar as its members were picturesque.

"You want us all to be snake-charmers and scorpion-eaters," he raged, at one point in their conversation, which he had inevitably maneuvered in such a direction as to permit him to make his favorite accusations.

"Naturally," Eunice replied in her most provoking manner. "It would be far preferable to being a nation of tenth-rate pseudo-civilized rug-sellers." She smiled poisonously, and then belched in his face.

At that moment Dyar came in. The candlelight seemed bright to him and he blinked his eyes. Seeing Thami in the center of the room, he looked surprised for an instant, and then went up to him and greeted him warmly. Without seeming to see Eunice, he took him by the arm and led him aside. "I want to settle my little debt with you, from the other night."

"Oh, that's all right," said Thami, looking at him expectantly. And as the money changed hands, Thami said: "She's here. You have seen her?"

"Yeah, sure."

"You brought her?"

"No. Miss Goode over there." Dyar jerked his chin in her direction, and Thami fell to thinking.

From where she stood Eunice watched them, saw Dyar slip some notes into Thami's hand, and guessed correctly that Thami had been the friend who had lent him the money to pay Hadija at the Bar Lucifer. It was the realization of her worst fears, and in her present unbalanced state she built it up into a towering nightmare. The two men held her entire future happiness in their hands. If anyone had observed her face closely at that moment, he would unhesitatingly have declared her mad, and he would probably have moved quickly away from her. It had suddenly flashed upon her, the realization of how supremely happy she had been at the Beidaouis' this evening—at least, it seemed so to her now. Hadija belonged completely to her, she had been accepted, was even having a small success at the moment as Miss Kumari, chatting in monosyllables with Dr. Waterman in a corner. But Miss Kumari's feet were planted at the edge of a precipice, and it required the merest push from either of the two men there (she clenched her fists) to topple her over the brink. The American was the more dangerous, however, and she already had set in motion the apparatus that was destined to get rid of him. "It can't fail," she thought desperately. But of course it could fail. There was no particular reason to believe that he would keep the appointment so clumsily arranged by Mme. Jouvenon for tomorrow, nor were there any grounds for confidence in her ability to make matters go as they were supposed to go. She opened her mouth wide and after some difficulty belched again. The room was going away from her; she felt it draining off into darkness. Making a tremendous effort, she prevented herself from tipping sideways toward the floor, and took a few steps forward, perhaps with the intention of speaking to Dyar. But the effort was too much. Her final remaining energy was used in reaching a nearby empty chair; she slid into it and lost consciousness.

Daisy had joined Dyar, without, however, paying any notice to Thami, who unobtrusively walked away. "Good God!" she cried, seeing Eunice's collapse. "That's a lovely sight. I don't intend to be delegated to carry it home, though, which is exactly what will happen unless I leave." She paused, and seemed to be changing her mind.

"No! Her little Greek friend can just call a taxi and the servants can dump her in. I'm damned if I'll play chauffeur to Uncle Goode, and I'm damned if I'll go home to keep from doing it, either. Hassan— aren't they both sweet? don't you love them?—" Dyar assented. "—He's offered to show us the great room, and that doesn't happen every day. I've seen it only once, and I'm longing to see it again. So there's going to be no victim here, making a Red Cross ambulance out of the car, and going up that fiendish narrow street to the Metropole. God!" She paused, then went on. "They're not ready to take us yet. They want to wait till a few more people have left. But I must talk to you before you disappear again. I saw you run out, darling. You've got to stop acting like a pariah. Come over here and sit down. I've got two things to say to you, and both are important, and not very pleasant."

"What do you mean?"

"Just let me do the talking, and listen." They sat down on the same divan where they had been sitting a half hour ago. The fresh air had made him feel better, and he had decided not to take any more whiskey. She laid her hand on his arm; the diamonds of her bracelets shone in the candlelight. "I'm practically certain Jack Wilcox is about to get himself into trouble. It seems *most* suspicious, the fact that he's keeping you out of his office. The moment you told me that, I knew something peculiar was going on. He's always been an ass in his business dealings, and he's no less of one now. By ass I mean stupidly careless. God, the idiots and scoundrels he's taken into his confidence! You know, everyone here's got some little peccadillo he's hoping to hide. You know, *ça va sans dire.* Everyone has to make a living, and here no one asks questions. But Jack practically *advertises* his business indiscretions. He can't make a move now without the entire scum of the Zone knowing about it. Which would be all right if there were any protection, which obviously there can't be in such cases. You just have to take your chances."

Dyar was listening, but at the same time he was uneasily watching the other end of the room where he had observed Hadija and Thami engaged in what appeared to be an intense and very private conversation. "*What* are you talking about?" he demanded rudely, turning suddenly to stare at her.

Daisy misinterpreted his question. "My dear, certainly no one but an imbecile would think of trying to enlist the help of the Police in such matters. I love Jack; I think he's a dear. But I certainly think you should be warned. *Don't* get involved in any of his easy-money schemes. They crack up. There are plenty of ways of making a living here, and quite as easy, without risking getting stabbed or shot."

Now Dyar looked at her squarely and laughed.

"I know I'm drunk," she said. "But I also know what I'm saying. I can see you're going to laugh even more at the other thing I've got to tell you." Dyar cast a troubled glance behind him at Hadija and Thami.

Daisy's voice was suddenly slightly harsh. "Oh, stop breaking your neck. He's not going to run off with your girlfriend."

Dyar turned his head back swiftly and faced her, his mouth open a little with astonishment. "What?"

She laughed. "Why are you so surprised? I told you everyone knows everything here. What do you think I have a good pair of Zeiss field-glasses in my bedroom for, darling? You didn't know I had such a thing? Well, I have, and they were in use today. There's a short stretch of shore-line visible from one corner of the room. But that's not what I was going to tell you," she went on, as Dyar, trying to picture to himself just what incidents of his outing she might have seen, felt his face growing hot. "I'd like to sock her in that smug face," he thought, but she caught the unspoken phrase. "You're angry with me, darling, aren't you?" He said nothing. "I don't blame you. It was a low thing to do, but I'm making amends for it now by giving you some *very* valuable advice." She began to speak more slowly and impressively. "Madame Jouvenon, that frightful little woman you went off into the other room with, is a Russian agent. A spy, if you like the word better." She sat back and squinted at him, as if to measure the effect of that piece of news.

It seemed to have brought him around to a better humor, for he chuckled, took her hand and smoothed the fingers slowly; she made no effort to withdraw it. "At least," she continued, "I've heard it from two distinct sources, neither of which I have any reason to doubt. Of course, it's a perfectly honorable way of making a living, and we all have our agents around, and I daresay she's not even a particularly efficient one, but there you are. So those are my two little warnings for tonight, my dear young man, and you can take them or leave them, whichever you like." She pulled her hand away to smooth her hair. "I shouldn't have told you, really. God knows how much of a chatterbox you are. But if you quote me I shall deny ever having said a word."

"I'll *bet* you would. And the same goes for the room in Marrakech. Right?"

She took the tip of one of his fingers between her thumb and forefinger, squeezed it hard, and looked at him seriously a moment before she said: "I suppose you think that was immoral."

The company was thinning; people were leaving now in groups. Abdelmalek and Hassan Beidaoui stood one on each side of the door, bowing and smiling. There were not more than ten guests left, including the Hollands, who had found an old swing record in the pile, and were now doing some very serious jitterbugging, alone on the floor. One of the two Moroccan gentlemen stood watching them, an expression of satisfaction on his face, as though at last he were seeing what he had come here to see.

Thami and Hadija still conversed, but the important points in their talk had all been touched upon, with the result that Thami now suspected that the money for his boat might conceivably be donated by Eunice Goode. Many members of the lower stratum of society in Tangier naturally knew perfectly well who Hadija was, but there was next to no contact between that world of cast-off clothing, five-peseta cognac and cafés whose patrons sat on mats smoking kif and playing ronda, and this other more innocent world up here in which it was only one step from wanting a thing to having it. Nevertheless, he knew both worlds; he was the point of contact. It was a privileged position and he felt it could be put to serious use. Nothing of all this had been said to Hadija; encouraged by him she had told all the important facts. No Moroccan is foolish enough to let another Moroccan know that both are stalking the same prey—after all, there is only a limited amount of flesh on any given carcass. And while the tentative maximum set by Thami was only whatever the price of the boat should finally turn out to be, still, he knew that Hadija would consider as her rightful property every peseta that went to him. Like most girls with her training, basically Hadija thought only in terms of goods delivered and payment received; it did not occur to her that often the largest sums go to those who agree to do nothing more than stay out of the way. This is not to say that she was unaware of the position of power enjoyed by Thami in the present situation. "You won't say a word?" she whispered anxiously.

"We're friends. More than friends," he assured her, looking steadily into her eyes. "Like brother and sister. And Muslimin, both of us. How could I betray my sister?"

She was satisfied. But he continued. "And tonight, what are you doing?" She knew what that meant. If it had to be, there was nothing to do about it, and tonight was the most likely time, with Eunice in her present state. Hadija glanced across at the massive body sprawled on the chair.

"Call a taxi," went on Thami. "Get the servants to put her in. Take her home and see that she's in bed. Meet me outside the Wedad pastry shop in the dark part there at the foot of the steps to the garden. I'll be there before you, so you won't have to wait."

"Ouakha," she agreed. She was going to get nothing for it, yet it had to be done. To remain Miss Kumari she must go back and be the Hadija of the pink room behind the Bar Lucifer. She looked at him with undissimulated hatred. He saw it and laughed; it made her more desirable.

"Little sister," he murmured, his lips so close to the lobe of her hear that they brushed it softly in forming the word.

She got up. Save for Eunice they were alone in the room. The remaining guests had gone out, were being taken through the blue court, the jasmine court, the marble pavilion, to the vast, partially ruined ballroom where several sultans had dined. But Hadija was too much perturbed to notice that she had not been invited to make the tour along with the others.

"You call a taxi. The telephone is in there." He indicated the little library. "I'll take care of her." He went out to the entrance lodge and got two of the guards to come in and carry Eunice to the gate, where they laid her on a mat along one of the niches until the cab arrived. He sat in front with the driver and went along as far as

Bou Araqía, where he got out and after saying a word through the open window to Hadija, walked off into the dark in the direction of the Zoco de Fuera.

The European guests were not taken back into the European wing; Abdelmalek and Hassan led them directly to the gate on the street, bade them a gracious good-bye, and stepped behind the high portals which were closed and noisily bolted. It was a little like the expulsion from Eden, thought Daisy, and she turned and grinned at the Hollands.

"May I drive you to your hotel?" she offered.

They protested that it was nearby, but Daisy snorted with impatience. She knew she was going to take them home, and she wanted to start. "Get in," she said gruffly. "It's a mile at least to the Pension Acacias."

The final good nights were called as the other guests drove off.

"But it's out of your way," objected Richard Holland.

"Stuff and nonsense! Get in! How do you know where I'm going? I've got to meet Luis more or less in that neighborhood."

"Sh! What's that?" Mrs. Holland held up a silencing finger. From somewhere in the dark on the other side of the street came a faint chorus of high, piercing mews.

"Oh, God! It's a family of abandoned kittens," moaned Daisy. "The Moors are always doing it. When they're born they simply throw them out in a parcel into the street like garbage."

"The poor things!" cried Mrs. Holland, starting across the pavement toward the sound.

"Come back here!" shouted her husband. "Where do you think you're going?"

She hesitated. Daisy had got into the car, and sat at the wheel.

"I'm afraid it's hopeless, darling," she said to Mrs. Holland.

"Come *on!*" Holland called. Reluctantly she returned and got in. When she was beside him in the back seat he said: "What did you think you were going to do?"

She sounded vague. "I don't know. I thought we might take them somewhere and give them some milk." The car started up, skirting the wall for a moment and then turning through a park of high eucalyptus trees.

Dyar, sitting in front with Daisy, and infinitely thankful to be out of the Beidaoui residence, felt pleasantly relaxed. He had been listening to the little scene with detached interest, rather as if it were part of a radio program, and he expected now to hear an objection from Holland based on grounds of practicality. Instead he heard him say: "Why in hell try to keep them alive? They're going to die anyway, sooner or later."

Dyar turned his head sideways and shouted against the trees going by: "So are you, Holland. But in the meantime you eat, don't you?"

There was no reply. In the back, unprotected from the wet sea wind, the Hollands were shivering.

13

THE NEXT MORNING was cloudy and dark; the inescapable wind was blowing, a gale from the east. Out in the harbor the few freighters moored there rocked crazily above the whitecaps, and the violent waves rolled across the wide beach in a chaos of noise and foam. Dyar got up early and showered. As he dressed he stood in the window, looking out at the agitated bay and the gray hills beyond it, and he realized with a slight shock that not once since he had arrived had he gone to inquire for his mail. It was hard to believe, but the idea simply had not occurred to him. In his mind the break with the past had been that complete and definite.

At the desk downstairs he inquired the way to the American Legation, and set out along the waterfront on foot, stopping after ten minutes or so of battling against the wind, at a small café for breakfast. As he sat down at the teetering little table he noticed that his garments were sticky and wet with the salt spray in the air.

He found the Legation without difficulty; it was just inside the native town, through an archway cut in the old ramparts. In the waiting room he was asked by an earnest young man with glasses to sign the visitors' register, whereupon he was handed one letter. It was from his mother. He wandered a while in the twisting streets, pushing through crowds of small screaming children, and looking vaguely for a place where he could sit down and read his letter. From a maze of inner streets he came out upon the principal thoroughfare for pedestrians, and followed it downhill. Presently he arrived at a large flat terrace edged with concrete seats, overlooking the docks. He sat down, oblivious of the Moroccans who looked at him with their eternal insolent curiosity, and, already in that peculiarly unreal state of mind which can be induced in the traveler by the advent of a letter from home, tore open the envelope and pulled out the small, closely written sheets.

Dear Nelson:

I have neglected you shamefully. Since Tuesday for one reason or another I have put off writing, and here it is Saturday. Somehow after you left I didn't have much "gumption" for a few days! Just sat around and read and sewed, and did what light housework I could without tiring myself too much. Also had one of my rip-roaring sick-headaches which knocked me out for 24 hours. However, I am fine now, and have been for several days. Let me tell you it was a terrible moment when they pulled up that gangplank! Do hope you had no unpleasant experiences with your cabin mates on the way over. They didn't look too good to me. Your father and I both thought you were in for something, from the looks of them.

We are planning on driving down to Wilmington for Aunt Ida's birthday. Your father is quite busy these days and comes home tired, so I guess one trip will be enough for this winter. Don't want him to get sick again.

Tho't you might be interested in the enclosed clipping. That Williams girl certainly didn't lose any time finding a new fiancé, did she? Well, it seems as though practically all your old friends were married and settled down now.

We were over at the Mott's (Dr.) last evening after an early movie. He is in bed with a bad kidney and we have been several times to see them. Your father had a short visit upstairs with him, has two male nurses & is a very sick man. Louise, whom I don't think you have seen in twenty years, had come down unexpectedly to see how things were going. She is a very attractive young woman, two children now. She is most interested in your doings. Says she once stopped at Tangier for an afternoon on a Mediterranean Cruise when she was in college. Didn't think much of it. She was reminiscing about the good times you all used to have, and wondered if I still made the coconut macaroons I used to make. Says she never forgot them and the cookies. Naturally I had forgotten.

Well, I am getting this in the mail today.

Please take care of your health, just for my sake. Remember, if you lose that you lose everything. I have been reading up on Morocco in the Encyclopaedia and I must say it doesn't sound so good to me. They seem to have practically every sort of disease there. If you let yourself get run down in any way you're asking for trouble. I don't imagine the doctors over there are any too good, either, and the hospital conditions must be very primitive.

I shall be on tenterhooks until I hear from you. Please give Jack Wilcox my best. I hope he is able to make a go of his business. What with all the difficulties placed in the way of travel nowadays, both your father and I are very dubious about it. However, he must know whether he is making money or not. I don't see how he can.

May and Wesley Godfrey were in the other evening, told them all about your venture. They said to wish you good luck, as you probably need it. Your father and I join with them in the hope that everything goes off as you expect it to.

Well, here is the end of my paper so I will quit.

Love to you from
Mother

P.S. It seems it was Algiers that Louise Mott was in, not Tangier. Has never been in the latter. Your father told me just now when he came home for lunch. He is disgusted with me. Says I always get everything mixed up!

Love again.

When he had finished reading he folded the letter slowly and put it back into the envelope. He raised his head and looked around him. A little Moroccan boy, his face ravaged by a virulent skin disease, stood near him, studying him silently—his shoes, his raincoat, his face. A man wearing a tattered outmoded woman's coat, high-waisted, with peaked shoulders and puffed sleeves, walked up and stopped near the boy, also to stare. In one hand he carried a live hen by its wings; the hen was protesting noisily. Annoyed by its squawks, Dyar rose and went back into the street. Reading the letter had left him in an emotional no-man's land. The street looked insane with its cheap bazaar architecture, its Coca-Cola signs in Arabic script, its anarchic assortment of people in damp garments straggling up and down. It had begun to rain slightly. He put his hands into the pockets of his raincoat and walked ahead looking down at the pavement, slowly climbing the hill. An idea had been in his mind, he had intended to do something this morning, but now since reading his mother's letter he did not have the energy to stop and try to recall what it had been. Nor was he certain whether or not he would keep the luncheon appointment with the unpleasant woman he had met last night. He felt under no particular obligation to put in an appearance; she had given him no chance to accept or refuse, had merely ordered him to be at the Empire at two o'clock. He would either go or not go when the time came. He did not really believe Daisy's fantastic story about her being a Russian agent—as a matter of fact, he rather hoped she would turn out to be something of the sort, something a little more serious than the rest of the disparate characters he had met here so far, and a spy for the Soviet Government would certainly be that.

Under the trees of the Zoco de Fuera the chestnut vendors' fires made a fog of heavy, rich smoke. From time to time a rough gust of wind reached down and scooped the top layer out into the air above the trees, where it dissolved. He looked suspiciously at the objects offered for sale, spread out in patterns and mounds on the stone slabs of the market. There were little truncated bamboo tubes filled with kohl, an infinite variety of roots, resins and powders; rams' horns and porcupine skins, heavy with quills, and an impressive assortment of claws, bones, beaks and feathers. As the rain fell with more determination, those women whose wares were not protected by umbrellas began to gather them up preparatory to moving off toward more sheltered places. He still felt coreless—he was no one, and he was standing here in the middle of no country. The place was counterfeit, a waiting room between connections, a transition from one way of being to another, which for the moment was neither way, no way. The natives loped by in their rehabilitated European footgear which made it impossible for them to walk in a natural fashion, jostled him, stared at him, and tried to speak with him, but he paid them no attention. The new municipal buses moved into the square, unloaded, loaded, moved out, on their way to the edges of the city. A little way beyond the edges of the city was the border of the International Zone, and beyond that were the mountains. He said to himself that he was like a prisoner who had broken through the first bar of his cell, but was still inside. And freedom was not on sale for $390.

He decided it would do no harm to stop in and see Wilcox. A week or so, he had said, and this was the seventh day. He approached the entrance of the building with a rapidly increasing sensation of dread, although a moment ago he had not been conscious of any at all. Suddenly he found himself inside the pastry shop, sitting down at a table, ordering coffee. Then he asked himself what was worrying him. It was not so much that he realized Wilcox would be annoyed to see him come around without waiting to be telephoned, but that he knew the time had come to bring up the subject of money. And he knew that Wilcox knew it, would be expecting it, and so he was worried. He lit a cigarette to accompany his coffee; the hot liquid reinforced the savor of the smoke. When he had finished the coffee he slapped his knee and rose with determination. "We've got to have a showdown," he thought. But the Europe-Africa Tourist Service might as well have been a dentist's office for the reluctance with which he climbed the stairs and drew near its door.

He knocked. "*Sí*" cried Wilcox. He turned the knob; the door was locked. "*Quién?*" Wilcox called, with an edge of vexation or nervousness to his voice. Dyar hesitated, and was about to say: "Jack?" when the door was flung open.

As Dyar looked into Wilcox's face, he saw the expression in his eyes change swiftly to one of annoyance. But the first emotion he had caught there had been one of unalloyed fear. Involuntarily Wilcox made a loud clicking sound of exasperation. Then he stepped back a little.

"Come in."

They remained standing in the ante-room, one on each side of the low table.

"What can I do for you?"

"I've got all that stuff you gave me down pat, pretty much. I thought I'd drop around and say hello."

"Yeah." Wilcox paused. "I thought we said I'd call you. I thought you understood that."

"I did, but you didn't call."

"Any objection to waiting a few days? I've still got a lot of stuff here I've got to clear up. There's no room for you here now."

Dyar laughed; Wilcox broke in on his laughter, his voice a bit higher in pitch. "I don't *want* you here. Can't you get that through your head? I've got special reasons for that."

Dyar took a deep breath. "I've got special reasons for coming here. I need some cash."

Wilcox narrowed his eyes. "What happened to all those express checks you had last week? Damn it, I told you you were working for me. Do I have to sign a contract? I owe you a week's wages, right? Well, I'd planned to pay you by the month, but if you want, I can make it twice a month. I know you're short. It's a nuisance to me, but I can do it that way if you like."

"But Jesus Christ, I need it now."

"Yeah, but I can't give it to you now. I haven't got it."

"What do you mean, you haven't got it? It's not that much." Dyar leered a bit as he said this.

"Listen, Nelson," began Wilcox, his face taking on a long-suffering look—("Fake," thought Dyar)—"I'm telling you the truth. I haven't got it to give you. I've got a back bill at the Atlantide that would sink a ship. Whatever comes in goes to them now. If it didn't I'd be in the street. You can see for yourself how much business I'm doing in here."

There were footsteps in the corridor. Wilcox stepped to the door and tried it; it was locked, but a vestige of alarm flickered again across his face. Dyar said nothing.

"Look," he went on, "I don't want you to get the idea that I'm stalling or anything. You're working for me. It may just be a crazy idea of mine, but I think things are going to open up very soon, and I want you to be broken in and ready for the big day when it comes."

"I didn't say you were stalling. I just said I needed money. But if you haven't got one week's pay now, how the hell do you expect to have twice as much next week?"

"That's a chance we both have to take."

"Both!" He looked derisively at Wilcox.

"Unless you're a bigger God-damned fool than I think you are you've still got a few express checks left that'll last you at least till next week."

"That's got nothing to do with it. I'm trying to save those for an emergency."

"Well, this is your emergency."

"That's what you think." Dyar moved toward the door, opened it and stepped out into the corridor.

"Come here," said Wilcox, following him quickly. He stood in the doorway and held out a five-hundred peseta note. "You've got me all wrong. Jesus! They don't make 'em stubborner! You really think I'm trying to gyp you, don't you?" He glanced nervously up and down the corridor.

"I don't think anything," Dyar said. He was trying to decide whether or not to take the money; his first impulse had been to refuse it, but then that seemed like a gesture of childish petulance. He reached for it, and said: "Thanks." Immediately afterward he was furious with himself. This anger was not assuaged by Wilcox's next words.

"And now, for God's sake, keep out of here until I call you, will you? *Please!*" The last word was more of a shout of relief than of entreaty.

Again he cast a worried glance along the hall, and stepping inside the office, shut the door.

Slowly Dyar went down the stairs, still raging against himself for his blundering behavior. The money had been handed him as though he were a blackmailer come to exact more than the usual figure. Now it would be more difficult than ever to put the affair on a normal business basis.

As he stepped out in the street he realized that the rain was pouring down now. The sidewalks were empty; everyone had taken shelter under awnings, in doorways and arcades. Only an occasional Moroccan splashed along, seemingly oblivious of the storm. The pastry shop was crowded with people peering out into the street, most of them standing near the door so that if they were approached by a waitress they could move outside. He pushed through their ranks, sat down again and ordered another coffee. It was only then that he began to consider the aspect of Wilcox's behavior which was not concerned with him—the much more interesting fact that he seemed to be expecting an imminent unwelcome arrival. "Daisy's probably right," he thought. Jack had incurred the displeasure of some local hooligan and was awaiting reprisal. Either that or he was trying to avoid a creditor or two. Yet neither supposition quite explained his reluctance to have Dyar visit the office.

"No money!" he thought savagely. "Then why does he stay at the Atlantide?" But he knew the answer. Even if it were true that Wilcox was broke, which seemed unlikely, he would have felt obliged, and would have managed, to go on staying at the best hotel, because the town had agreed with his decision that he was one of the big shots, one of those who automatically get the best whether or not they can pay for it. But why? Every day in Tangier several new companies were formed, most of them with the intention of evading the laws of one country or another, and every day approximately the same number failed. And the reasons for their failure or success had very little to do with the business acumen of those connected with them. If you were really a winner you found ways of intercepting your competitors' correspondence, even his telegrams; you persuaded the employees at the French Post Office to let you have the first look at letters you were interested in seeing, which was how you got your mailing lists. You hired locals to break into other companies' offices and steal their stationery and examples of their directors' signatures for you; and when you sent your forged replies regretting your inability to supply the merchandise you prudently went all the way to Tetuan in the Spanish Zone to post them—only no customs official at the frontier got them away from you because somehow you were not stripped naked like the others, and the seams of your clothing were not ripped open. Not that you paid bribes in order to escape being molested—but everyone knew a winner on sight; he was the respected citizen of the International Zone. If one was not a winner one was a victim, and there seemed to be no way to change that. No pretense was of any avail. It was not a question of looking or acting like a winner—that could always be managed, although no one was taken in by it—it was a matter of conviction, of feeling like one, of knowing you belonged to the caste, of recognizing and being sure of your genius. For a long time he reflected confusedly upon these things; then he paid, got up, and went out into the rain, which now fell less heavily.

*

"I knew you would come," said Mme. Jouvenon. This was her way of saying that she had not been at all sure of it.

Dyar was more truthful. "*I* didn't," he said with a wry smile. And as he said it, he wondered why indeed he had come. Partly out of courtesy, perhaps, although he would not have wanted to admit that. He had found himself outside the restaurant three times during the late morning, but it had been too early for the rendez-vous. However, he had seen the bright displays of hors d'oeuvre through the window, and probably it was they more than anything else that had induced him finally to keep the appointment. It was the sort of place he never would have thought of eating in alone.

Mme. Jouvenon was much calmer today—even rather pleasant, he thought—and certainly she was nobody's fool. She held the reins of the conversation firmly, but directed it with gentleness so that there was no feeling of strain. When they had reached the salad course, with all the naturalness in the world she began to discuss the subject that interested her, and he found it difficult to see anything offensive in what she said or in the way she said it. He understood, she supposed, that most people in Tangier had to live as best they could, doing one thing and another, and precisely because there were so many governments represented in the Administration, there was a great need for a practical system of checking and counter-checking between each power and the others. This ought to have been worked out beforehand officially, but it had not been, and the old formula of private tallying had still to be adhered to. He nodded gravely, smiling to himself, wondering just how long it would take her to make her offer, and under what guise it would come.

He was aware, she said, that practically every Englishman in the Zone, even with a title, was constrained by his government to furnish whatever information he could gather, and that far from being a shameful pursuit, on the contrary this was considered to be a completely honorable activity.

"More than most others you could find here, I guess," Dyar laughed.

She did not know about the English, she said, but many people she knew managed to make the thing lucrative by supplying data to two or more offices simultaneously. At the moment her government (she did not specify which it was) had no representation on the Board of Administrators, which made adequate reports an even greater necessity. Inasmuch as it was common knowledge that the unseen power behind the Administration was the United States, it was particularly with regard to American activities that her government wished to be documented. The difficulty was that the American milieu in Tangier was peculiarly hermetic, not inclined to mix with the other diplomatic groups. And then of course Americans were especially unsusceptible to financial offers, simply because it was difficult to put the price high enough to make it worth the trouble to most of them.

"—But she makes the proposition to me," he thought grimly, "because I'm not a big shot."

And the proposition came out. She was empowered to offer him five hundred dollars a month, beginning with a month's advance immediately, in return for small bits of information which he might glean from conversations with his American friends, plus one or two specific facts about the Voice of America's set-up at Sidi Kacem,—things which Dyar need not even understand himself, she hastened to assure him, since her husband was a very good electrical engineer and would have no difficulty in interpreting them.

"But I don't know anything or anybody in Tangier!"

They would even provide introductions—indirectly, of course—to the necessary people, she explained. As an American he had entrée to certain places (such as the Voice of America, for instance) from which other nationals were excluded.

"R-r-really we ask very little," she smiled. "You must not have r-r-romantic idea this is spying. There is nothing to spy in Tangier. Tangier has no interest for anyone. Diplomatic, perhaps, yes. Military, no."

"How many months would you want me for?"

"Ah! How are we to know how good you are to us?" She looked archly across the table at him. "Maybe infor-r-rmation you give us is not accur-r-rate. We should not continue with you."

"Or if I couldn't get any dope for you at all?"

"Oh, I am not wor-r-ried about that."

From her handbag she pulled a folded check and handed it to him. It was a check on the Banco Salvador Hassan e Hijos, and was already made out to the order of Nelson Dyar, and signed in a neat handwriting by Nadia Jouvenon. It shocked him to see his name spelled correctly there on that slip of paper, the work of this intense little woman with blue hair; it was ridiculous that she should have known his name, but he was not really surprised, nor did he dare ask her how she had discovered it.

They ordered coffee. "Tomorrow evening you will take dinner at our home," she said. "My husband will be delighted to meet you."

A waiter came and asked for Mme. Jouvenon, saying she was wanted on the telephone. She excused herself and went through a small door behind the bar. Dyar sat alone, toying with his coffee spoon, smothered by an oppressive feeling of unreality. He had put the check into his pocket, nevertheless at the moment he had a strong impulse to pull it out and set a match to it in the ash tray in front of him, so that when she reappeared it would no longer exist. They would go out into the street and he would be free of her. Distractedly he took a sip of coffee and glanced around the room. At the next table sat four people chattering in Spanish: a young couple, an older woman who was obviously the mother of the girl, and a small boy who slouched low in his chair pouting, refusing to eat. The girl, heavily made-up and decked with what seemed like several pounds of costume jewelry, kept glancing surreptitiously in his direction, always looking rapidly at her mother and husband first to be sure they were occupied. This must have been going on since the family group had sat down, but now was the first he had noticed it. He watched her, not taking his gaze from her face; there was no doubt about it—she was giving him the eye. He tried to see what the husband looked like, but he was facing the other way. He was fat; that was all he could tell.

When Mme. Jouvenon returned to the table she seemed out of sorts about something. She called for the check, and occupied herself with pulling on her kid gloves, which were skin-tight.

The call had been from Eunice Goode, who, although she had not mentioned this fact to Mme. Jouvenon, had waked up early, and finding Hadija missing, had immediately suspected she was with Dyar. Thus she had first wanted to know if Dyar had kept the appointment, to which Mme. Jouvenon had replied shortly that he had, and made as if to draw the conversation to a close. But Eunice had not been satisfied; she wanted further to know if they had come to terms. Mme. Jouvenon had remarked that she appreciated her interest, but that she did not feel under any obligation to tender Mademoiselle Goode a report on the results of the luncheon interview. Eunice's voice had risen dangerously. "*Ecoutez, madame!* I advise you to tell me!" she had squealed. "*Je dois absolument savoir!*" Mme. Jouvenon had informed her that she did not intend to be intimidated by anyone, but then it had occurred to her that since after all it was Eunice who had supplied the introduction to Mr. Dyar, it might be just as well to retain her goodwill, at least for a little while. So she had laughed lamely and told her that yes, an understanding had been reached. "But has he accepted money?" insisted Eunice. "*Mais enfin!*" cried the exasperated Mme. Jouvenon. "You are incredible! Yes! He has taken money! Yes! Yes! I shall see you in a few days. *Oui! C'est ça! Au revoir!*" And she had added a few words in Russian under her breath as she had put the receiver back on the hook.

The Spanish family straggled to its feet, making a great scraping of chairs on the tile floor. As she fumbled for her coat and furpiece the young wife managed to throw a final desperate glance in Dyar's direction. "She's not only nympho but nuts," he said to himself, annoyed because he would not have minded being with her for an hour in a hotel room, and it was so manifestly impossible. He watched them as they went out the door, the girl pushing her small son impatiently ahead of her. "Typical Spanish nouveaux-riches," said Mme. Jouvenon disgustedly. "The sort Fr-r-ranco has put to r-r-run the nation."

They stood in the doorway being spattered by the blowing rain.

"Well, thank you for a very good lunch," Dyar said. He wished he were never going to have to see her again.

"You see that high building there?" She pointed to the end of the short street in front of them. He saw a large white modern apartment house. "Next door to that on the r-r-right, a small building, gr-r-ray, four floors high. This is my home. Top floor, number for-r-rty five. We wait for you tomorrow night, eight. Now I r-r-run, not to get wet too much. Goodbye."

They shook hands and she hurried across the street. He watched her for a moment as she walked quickly between the row of unfinished buildings and the line of small transplanted palm trees that never would grow larger. Then he sighed, and turned down the hill to the Boulevard; it led down to the Hotel de la Playa. There was practically no one in the rainy streets, and the shops were closed because it was not yet four. But on the way he passed the Banco Salvador Hassan e Hijos. It was open. He went in. In the vestibule a bearded Moroccan sitting on a leather pouf saluted him as he passed. The place was new, shining with marble and chromium. It was also very empty and looked quite unused. One young man stood behind a counter writing. Dyar walked over to him and handed him the check, saying: "I want to open an account." The young man glanced at the check and without looking at him handed him a fountain pen.

"Sign, please," he said. Dyar endorsed it and said he would like to withdraw a hundred dollars in cash.

"Sit down, please," said the young man. He pushed a button and a second later an enormous fluorescent lighting fixture in the center of the ceiling flickered on. It took about five minutes to make out the necessary papers. Then the young man called him over to the counter, handed him a checkbook and five thousand two hundred pesetas, and showed him a white card with his balance written on it. Dyar read it aloud, his voice echoing in the large, bare room. "Three hundred and ninety nine dollars and seventy five cents. What's the twenty five cents taken off for?"

"Checkbook," said the young man imperturbably, still not looking at him.

"Thanks." He went to the door and asked the Moroccan to get him a taxi. Sitting inside it, watching the empty wet streets go past, he thought he felt a little better, but he was not sure. At least he was out of the rain.

When he got to the hotel he asked at the desk to have a drink sent up to his room, but was told that the barman did not come in until six in the evening. He went up to the damp room and stood a while at the window, fingering the dirty curtain, staring out at the cold deserted beach so wet that it mirrored the sky. He took out the money and looked at it; it seemed like a lot, and five thousand two hundred pesetas could certainly buy a good deal more than a hundred dollars. Still, it did not give him the pleasure he wanted from it. The feeling of unreality was too strong in him, all around him. Sharp as a toothache, definite as the smell of ammonia, yet impalpable, unlocatable, a great smear across the lens of his consciousness. And the blurred perceptions that resulted from it produced a sensation of vertigo. He sat down in the armchair and lit a cigarette. The taste of it sickened him; he threw it into the corner and watched the smoke rise slowly along the wall until it came opposite the windowpane, when it rushed inward with the draught.

He was not thinking, but words came into his mind; they all formed questions: "What am I doing here? Where am I getting? What's it all about? Why am I doing this? What good is it? What's going to happen?" The last question stopped him, and he began unthinkingly to light another cigarette, laying it a moment later, however, unlighted on the arm of the chair. "What's going to happen?" Something was surely going to happen. It was impossible for everything just to continue as it was. All this was too unlikely, it was weighted down with the senseless, indefinable weight of things in a dream, the kind of dream where each simple object, each motion, even the light in the sky, is heavy with silent meaning. There had to be a break; some air had to come in. But things don't happen, he told himself. You have to make them happen. That was where he was stuck. It was not in him to make things happen; it never had been. Yet when he got to this point he realized that for the moment at any rate it was the bottom; from there the way went imperceptibly up. A tiny, distant pin-prick of hope was there. He had to probe to find where it came from. Triumphantly he dragged it out and examined it: it was simply that he had a blind, completely unreasonable conviction that when the

moment came if nothing happened, some part of him would take it
upon itself to make something happen. It seemed quite senseless
when he thought about it; it merely faded, grew weaker, and so to
save it he put it away again into the dark. He could not believe it,
but he liked to have it there. He rose and began to walk restlessly
about the room. Presently he threw himself on the bed, and lying
still, tried to sleep. A minute later he struggled out of his shoes and
trousers and pulled the bedspread up over him. But his thoughts
turned to Hadija with her perfect little face and her pliant body like
a young cat's.

"It was only yesterday," he thought incredulously. "God, not
till Sunday?" Six days to wait. There was only one way to find her,
and even that might not be possible. He would go to see the fat
woman, Miss Goode, at the Metropole, and see if she knew her
address. After a while he grew more calm. Waves, Hadija, seagulls.
When he awoke it was dark.

14

IT WAS AN OBSESSION of Eunice Goode's that there was very little time
left in the world, that whatever one wanted to do, one had better get it
done quickly or it would be too late. Her conception of that segment of
eternity which was hers to know was expressed somewhat bafflingly
in a phrase she had written in her notebook shortly after arriving in
Tangier: "Between the crackling that rends the air and the actual flash
of lightning that strikes you, there is a split second which seems
endless, and during which you are conscious that the end has come.
That split second is now." Yet the fact that her mind was constantly
recalled to this fixed idea (as a bit of wood floating in the basin of a
waterfall returns again and again to be plunged beneath the surface by
the falling water), rather than inciting her to any sort of action,
ordinarily served only to paralyze her faculties. Perhaps some of the
trouble was due merely to her size; like most bulky things she was set
in motion with difficulty. But when she began to move, she gathered
impetus. Her association with Hadija had started her off in a certain
direction, which was complete ownership of the girl, and until she had

the illusion of having achieved that, she would push ahead without looking right or left.

When she had finished telephoning Mme. Jouvenon, she scribbled a note to Hadija: *Espérame aquí. Vuelvo antes de las cinco,* and left it hanging crookedly from the edge of the center table, weighted down by a bowl of chrysanthemums. Hadija could get Lola the chambermaid to read it to her.

Eunice had not wept when she had awakened and found herself alone in the room. The thing was too serious, she felt, for that sort of self-indulgent behavior. It was horrible enough to find herself alone in the bed, with no sign that Hadija had been in the room at all during the night, but the real suffering had begun only when she went ahead to form her conjectures, one after the other, as to what might have happened. Even though Dyar had appeared at the Empire to lunch with Mme. Jouvenon, it was still perfectly possible that the girl had spent the night with him. She almost hoped that was the case; it would mean that the danger was all at one point—a point she felt she had at least partially under control. "The big idiot's in love with her," she said to herself, and it was some little solace to think that Hadija was unlikely to fall in love with him. But one could never count on how a girl was going to react to a man. Men had an extra and mysterious magnetism which all too often worked. She slammed her clothing around in a rage as she dressed. She had taken no breakfast—only a few small glasses of gin. Now she went to the high armoire and took down from the shelf half a dry spongecake that had been up there several days. She ate it all, fiercely crumpled the paper that had been around it, and threw the wad across the room, aiming at the wastebasket. It went in; her fleshy lips moved ever so slightly in the shadow of a grim little smile of passing satisfaction.

It was hard to know how to dress this afternoon. She felt well wearing only two kinds of uniform: slacks and shirt, or evening dress, both of which were out of the question. Finally she decided on a black suit with a cape that looked vaguely military under a good deal of gold frogging. Hoping to look as bourgeoise and proper as possible, she pulled out a choker of gold beads which she fastened around her neck. She even bothered to find a pair of stockings, and eventually squeezed into some shoes with almost two inches of heel. Looking in the mirror with extreme distaste, she powdered her face clumsily, not being able to avoid sprinkling the stuff liberally over the front of her suit, and applied a minimum of neutral-toned lipstick. The sight of her face thus disguised sickened her; she turned away from the mirror and began to brush the powder off the black flannel cape. The whole business was a ghastly bore, and she loathed going out alone into the wet streets and through the center of town. But there was no sense in doing a thing halfway. One had to see it through. She liked to remind herself that she came of pioneer stock; her grandmother had had an expression she had always loved to hear her use: "Marching orders have come," which to her meant that if a thing had to be done, it was better to do it without question, without thinking whether one liked the idea or not. Fortunately her life was such that it was very seldom anything really did have to be done, so that when such an occasion arose she played her part to the full and got the most out of it.

*

Eunice left the American Legation about four o'clock. They had been most civil, she reflected. (She was always expecting to intercept looks of derision.) They had listened to her, made a few notes, and thanked her gravely. She on her side thought she had done rather well: she had not told them too much,—just enough to whet their interest. "Of course, I'm passing on this information to you for what it may be worth," she had said modestly. "I have no idea how much truth there is in it. But I have a distinct feeling that you'll find it worth your while to follow it up." (When she had gone Mr. Doan, the Vice-Consul, had heaved an exaggerated sigh, remarked in a flat voice: "Oh, Death, where is thy sting?" and his secretary had smirked at him appreciatively.)

At the Metropole desk the manager handed Eunice an envelope which she opened on her way upstairs. It was a very short note written in French on the hotel stationery, suggesting that she meet the sender alone in the reading-room of the hotel at seven o'clock that evening. It added the hope that she would agree to receive the most distinguished sentiments of the signer, whose name when she saw it gave her an agreeable start. "Thami Beidaoui," she read aloud, with satisfaction. At the moment she recalled only the two brothers who lived in the palace; the entrance of the third brother had been effected too late in her evening to make any lasting impression on her. Indeed, at the moment she did not so much as suspect his existence. If she had not been so completely preoccupied with worry about Hadija she would have been delighted with the message.

When she opened the door of her room the first thing she noticed was that the note she had left was gone and the bowl of chrysanthemums had been moved back to the center of the table. Then she heard splashing in the bathtub, and the familiar wobbling vocal line of the chant that habitually accompanied Hadija's ablutions. "Thank God," she breathed. That stage of the ordeal was over, at least. There remained the extraction of the admission of guilt, and the scene. Because there was going to be a scene, of course—Eunice would see to that. Only it was rather difficult to make a scene *with* Hadija; she was inclined to sit back like a spectator and watch it, rather than participate in it.

Eunice sat down to wait, to calm herself, and to try to prepare a method of operations. But when Hadija emerged in a small cloud of steam, clad in the satin and mink négligé, it was she who led the attack. Shrilling in Spanish, she accused Eunice of thinking only of herself, of taking her to the Beidaoui Palace and embarrassing her in front of a score of people by passing out, leaving her not only to extricate herself from the unbelievably humiliating situation, but to see to the removal of Eunice's prostrate body as best she could. Eunice did not attempt to reply. It was all perfectly true, only she had not thought of it until now. However, to admit such a thing would be adding grist to Hadija's mill. She was curious to know how Hadija had managed to get her out of the palace and back to the hotel, but she did not ask her.

"What a disgrace for us!" cried Hadija. "What shame you have brought on us! How can we face the Beidaoui señores after this?"

In spite of the balm brought to her soul by this use of the plural pronoun, Eunice was suddenly visited by the terrible thought that perhaps the note she had just received had something to do with her behavior at the Beidaoui Palace; one of the brothers was coming to inform her discreetly that the hospitality of his home would henceforth not be extended to her and her friend Miss Kumari.

In a very thin voice she finally said: "Where did you spend the night?"

"I am lucky enough to have a few friends left," said Hadija. "I went and slept with a friend. I would not have anything to do with that mess." She called it *ese lio* with supreme disgust. So it had not been she who had seen to getting her back to the hotel. But Eunice was too upset to go into that; she was having a vision of herself in the act of misbehaving in some spectacular manner—breaking the furniture, throwing up in the middle of the dance floor, insulting the guests with obscenities. . . .

"But what did I *do?*" she cried piteously.

"*Bastante!*" said the other, glancing at her significantly.

The conversation dragged on through the waning light, until Hadija, feeling that she now definitely had the upper hand, lit the candles on the mantel and went to stand in front of the mirror where she remained a while, admiring herself in the négligé.

"I look beautiful in this?" she hazarded.

"Yes, yes," Eunice answered wearily, adding: "Hand me that bottle and the little glass beside it."

But before Hadija complied she was determined to pursue further the subject which preoccupied her. "Then I keep it?"

"Hadija! I couldn't care less what you do with it. Why do you bother asking me? You know what I told you about my things."

Hadija did, indeed, but she had wanted to hear it repeated with reference to this particular garment, just in case of a possible misunderstanding later.

"Aha!" She pulled it tighter around her, and still watching her reflection over her shoulder, took Eunice the bottle of Gordon's Dry and the tumbler.

"I very happy," Hadija confided, going into English because it was the language of their intimacy.

"Yes, I daresay," said Eunice drily. She decided to remain as she was, to receive M. Beidaoui. Seven o'clock was early; there was no need to dress more formally.

In order to obviate any possibility of Hadija's seeing him at the Metropole, Thami had made her promise to meet him at seven o'clock in the lobby of the Cine Mauretania, which was a good half-hour's walk from the hotel. She had demurred at first, but he still held the whip hand.

"She will want to come too," she complained. "She won't let me come alone."

"It's very important," he warned her. "If you try hard you'll find a way."

Now she had to break the news to Eunice, and she dreaded it. But strangely enough, when she announced that she was going out for a walk before dinner and would return about eight, Eunice merely looked surprised for an instant and said: "I'll expect you at eight, then. Don't be late." Eunice's acquiescence at this point had a twofold origin: she felt chastened by the idea of her behavior the preceding night, and she already had been vaguely wondering how she could keep Hadija away from the impending interview with M. Beidaoui. It seemed unwise to give him an opportunity to scrutinize her too closely.

Hidden among the kif-smokers, tea-drinkers and card-players in a small Moroccan café opposite the Metropole's entrance, Thami watched Hadija step out the door and pass along the street in the direction of the Zoco Chico. A quarter of an hour later Eunice's telephone rang. A M. Beidaoui wished to see Mlle. Goode; he would wait in the reading room.

"*Je déscends tout de suite*," said Eunice nervously. She gulped one more small glass of gin and with misgiving went down to meet M. Beidaoui.

When she went into the dim room with its bastard Moorish decorations she saw no one but a young Spaniard sitting in a far corner smoking a cigarette. She was about to turn and go out to the desk, when he rose and came toward her, saying in English: "Good evening."

Before anything else crossed her mind she had a fleeting but unsavory intuition that she knew the young man and that she did not want to speak with him. However, here he was, taking her hand, saying: "How are you?" And because she was looking increasingly confused, he said: "I am Thami Beidaoui. You know—"

Without actually remembering him, she knew in a flash, not only that this was the ne'er-do-well brother of the Beidaouis, but that she had had an unpleasant scene with him at the cocktail party. There were certain details in the face that seemed familiar: the strange eyebrows that slanted wildly upward, and the amused, mocking expression of the eyes beneath. Obviously, now that she saw him closely, she realized that no Spaniard could have a face like that. But it was not the grave figure clothed in white robes that she had expected to find. She was relieved, perplexed and apprehensive. "How do you do?" she said coldly. "Sit down."

Thami was not one to beat about the bush; besides, he took it for granted that it was only the dim light which had prevented her from recognizing him at once, that by now she remembered all the details of their exchange of insults, and had even more or less guessed the reason for his visit.

"You had a good time at my brothers' house yesterday?"

"Yes. It was very pleasant," she said haughtily, wondering what horrors of misbehavior he was remembering at the moment.

"My brothers like Miss Kumari, your friend. They think she's a very nice girl."

She looked at him. "Yes, she is."

"Yes. They think so." She heard the slight emphasis on the word *think*, but did not realize it was purposeful. He continued. "At the party Madame Vanderdonk ask me: Who is that girl?" (Mme. Vanderdonk was the wife of the Dutch Minister.) "She says she looks like a Moorish girl." (Eunice's heart turned over.) "I told her that's because she's Greek."

"Cypriot," corrected Eunice tonelessly. He stared an instant, not understanding. Then he lit a cigarette and went on. "I know who this girl is, and you know, too. But my brothers don't know. They think she's a nice girl. They want to invite both of you to dinner next week, a Moroccan style dinner with the British Minister, and Dr. Waterman and Madame de Saint Sauveur and a lot of many people, but I think that's a bad idea."

"Did you tell them so?" asked Eunice, holding her breath.

"Of course not!" he said indignantly. (Still safe! She thought; she was ready to go anywhere from here, at whatever cost, whatever hazard.) "That would not be nice to you. I wouldn't do that." Now his voice was full of soft reproof.

"I'm sure you wouldn't," she said. She felt so much better that she gave him a wry smile.

He had gone down to the port that afternoon and had managed to get the price of the boat down to five thousand seven hundred pesetas. When it came time to pay, he still hoped to be able to knock off the extra seven hundred, simply by refusing to give them.

There were roars of laughter from the next room which was the bar.

"Will you be at the dinner party?" said Eunice, not because she was particularly interested to know.

"I'm going away, I think," he said. "I want to go to Ceuta in my boat, do a little business."

"Business? You have a boat?"

"No. I want to buy one. Tomorrow. It costs too much money. I want to get out." He made the hideous grimace of disgust typical of the low-class Moroccan; he certainly had not learned that at the Beidaoui Palace. "Tangier's no good. But the boat costs a lot of money."

There was a silence.

"How much?" said Eunice.

He told her.

A little over a hundred dollars, she calculated. It was surely worth it, even if he did not leave Tangier, the likelihood of which she strongly doubted. "I should like to help you," she said.

"That's very kind. I didn't mean that." He was grinning.

"I know, but I'd like to help. I can give you a check." She wanted to finish the business and get rid of him.

In the bar someone began to play popular tunes on the piano, execrably. Several British sailors drinking in there looked into the reading room with undisguised curiosity, one after the other, like children.

"I'll write you a check. Excuse me. I'll be right back." She rose and went out the door into the foyer. With this native monster under control, and the American idiot out of the way, she told herself, life might begin to be bearable. She brought the checkbook downstairs with her, and made out the check in his presence, asking him how he spelled his name.

"Suppose we make it out for six thousand," she said. It was just as well to be generous.

"That's very kind. Thank you," said Thami.

"Not at all. I hope you have a good trip." She got up and walked toward the bar. Before she got to the door she paused and called to him: "Don't get drowned."

"Good night, Miss Goode," he said respectfully, her very personal irony having gone wide of the mark.

She went into the bar and ordered a gin fizz: the whole episode had been most distasteful. "What foul people they are!" she said to herself, finding it more satisfying to damn the tribe than the mere individual. The sailors moved a little away from her on each side when she ordered her drink.

Across the street Thami was back in the café, where he intended to stay in hiding until he saw Hadija return from her fruitless mission to the Cine Mauretania; he wanted to be sure and not meet her by accident in the street. With the eagerness of a small boy he looked forward to morning, when he could go to the bank, get the money, and rush to the waterfront to begin haggling once more for the boat. Watching the Metropole's entrance, he suddenly caught sight of the American, Dyar, about to go into the hotel. There was one Nesrani he liked. He had no reason for liking him, but he did. With a joviality born of the flush of victory, he rose and rushed out into the narrow street, calling: "Hey! Hey!"

Dyar turned and saw him without enthusiasm. "Hi," he said. They shook hands, but he did not let himself be enticed into the café by the other's blandishments. "I have to go," he explained.

"You want to see Miss Goode?" Thami guessed. Dyar was annoyed. "Yes," he said shortly. Thami was not the one to whom he would confide his business: the picture of him and Hadija talking so intensely and at such length at the party was too fresh in his memory. He had decided then that Thami was trying to make her.

"You'll be a long time in the hotel?"

"No, just a few minutes."

"I'll wait for you. When you come out you come in that café. You'll see me."

"Okay," said Dyar reluctantly. On the way he had bought a bracelet for Hadija; he swung the box on one finger by the little loop the saleswoman had tied in the string. "I'll look for you."

It was an absurd-looking old hotel, a gaudy vestige of the days when England had been the important power in Tangier. Still, he had to admit it was a lot more comfortable and pleasant than the new ones like his own Hotel de la Playa. At the desk they told him they thought he would find Miss Goode in the bar. That was good luck: he would not have to see her alone in her room. They could have one drink and he would be on his way. As he went into the crowded bar one of the sailors was pounding out "Oh Susannah." The room was full of sailors, but there was Eunice Goode in the midst of them, monumentally alone, sitting on a high stool staring straight in front of her.

"Good evening," he said.

It was as though he had slapped her in the face. She drew her head back and stared at him. First the Moor and now this one. She was horrified; in her imagination he was already out of the way, gone. And here he was, back from the dead, not even aware that he was a ghost.

"Oh," she said finally. "Hello."

"Drunk again," he thought.

"What are you doing here?" she asked him. She got down from the stool and stood leaning on the bar.

"I just thought I'd drop in and say hello."

"Oh? . . . Well, what are you drinking? Whiskey?"

"What are *you* drinking? Have one with me, please."

"Certainly not! Barman! One whiskey-soda!" She rapped imperiously on the top of the bar. "I'm just on my way upstairs," she explained. "I'm just having this one drink." She felt that she would jump out of her skin if she had to stay and talk with him another minute.

Dyar was a bit nettled. "Well, wait'll I've had my drink, can't you? I wanted to ask you something." The barman gave him his drink.

"What was that?" she said levelly. She was positive it had something to do with Hadija, and she looked at him waiting, mentally daring him to let it be that.

"Do you know where I can find Hadija, how I can get in touch with her? I know she comes by here every now and then to see you. Do you have her address, or anything?"

It was too much. Her face became redder than usual, and she stood perfectly still, scarcely moving her lips as she spoke.

"I do not! I don't know where she lives and I care less! Why don't you look for her in the whorehouse where you met her? Why do you come sneaking to me, trying to find her? Do you think I'm her madam? Well, I'm not! *I'm* not renting her out by the hour!"

Dyar could not believe his ears. "Now, wait a minute," he said, feeling himself growing hot all over. "You don't have to talk that way about her. All you have to say is no, you don't know her address. That's all I asked you. I didn't ask you anything else. I'm not interested in what you have to say about her. For my money she's a damned nice girl."

Eunice snorted. "For your money, indeed! Very apt! That little bitch would sleep with a stallion if you made it worth her while. And I daresay she has, for that matter. A special act for tourists. They love it." She was beginning to enjoy herself as she saw the fury spreading in his face. "I don't mind naïveté," she went on, "but when it's carried to the point—Aren't you finishing your drink?" He had turned away.

"Shove it up," he said, and walked out.

Considering the number of people in the street, he thought it might be possible for him to get by the café without being seen by Thami, but it was a vain hope. He heard him calling as he came opposite the entrance. Resignedly he stepped inside and sat down cross-legged on the mat beside Thami, who had had a few pipes of kif with friends, and felt very well. They talked a bit, Dyar refusing the pipe when it was passed him. Thami kept his eyes on the street, watching for Hadija. When presently he espied her walking quickly and angrily along in the drizzle, he called Dyar's attention to a large chromolithograph on the wall beside them.

"Do you know what that is?" he demanded. Dyar looked, saw a design representing a city of minarets, domes and balustrades. "No," he said.

"That's Mecca."

He saw the others watching him, awaiting his comment. "Very nice."

From the corner of his eye Thami saw Hadija disappear into the Metropole. "Let's go," he said. "Fine," agreed Dyar. They went out into the damp, and wandered up toward the Zoco Chico. In spite of the weather the streets were filled with Moroccans, standing in groups talking, or strolling aimlessly up and down.

"Do you want to go see some beautiful girls?" said Thami
suddenly.

"Will you quit trying to sell this town to me?" demanded Dyar.
"I don't want to go and see anything. I'm all fixed up with one
beautiful girl, and that's enough." He did not add that he would give a
good deal to be able to find her.

"What's in that?" Thami indicated the parcel containing the
bracelet.

"A new razor."

"What kind?"

"Hollywood," said Dyar, improvising.

Thami approved. "Very nice razor." But his mind was on other
things.

"You like that girl? Only that one? Hadija?"

"That's right."

"You want only that one? I know another very nice one."

"Well, you keep her, chum."

"But what's the difference, that one and another?"

"All right," said Dyar. "So you don't see. But I do. I tell you I'm
satisfied."

The trouble was that Thami, still tingling with memories of the
preceding night, did see. He became momentarily pensive. To him it
made perfect sense that he, a Moslem, should want Hadija to himself.
But it made no sense that a Nesrani, a Christian, should pick and
choose. A Christian was satisfied with anything—a Christian saw no
difference between one girl and another, as long as they were both
attractive—he took what was left over by the Moslems, without
knowing it, and without a thought for whether she was all his or not.
That was the way Christians were. But not this one, who obviously
not only wanted Hadija to himself, but was not even interested in
finding anyone else.

Dyar broke in on his reflections, saying: "D'you think she might
be at that place we saw her in that night?" He thought he might as well
admit that he would like to see her.

"Of course not—" began Thami, stopping when it occurred to
him that if Dyar did not know she was living with Eunice Goode, he
was not going to be the one to tell him. "It's too early," he said.

"So much the better," Dyar thought. "Well, let's go up there anyway and have a drink."

Thami was delighted. "Fine!"

This time Dyar was determined to keep track of the turns and steps, so that he could find his way up alone after dinner. Through a short crowded lane, to the left up a steep little street lined with grocery stalls, out into the triangular plaza with the big green and white arch opposite, continue up, turn right down the dark level street, first turn left again into the very narrow alley which becomes a tunnel and goes up steeply, out at top, turn right again, follow straight through paying no attention to juts and twists because there are no streets leading off, downhill to large plaza with fat hydrant in center and cafés all the way around (only they might be closed later, and with their fronts boarded up they look like any other shops), cross plaza, take alley with no streetlight overhead, at end turn left into pitch black street. . . . He began to be confused. There were too many details to remember, and now they were climbing an endless flight of stone steps in the dark.

At the Bar Lucifer Mme. Papaconstante leaned her weight on the bar, picking her teeth voluptuously. "Hello, boys," she said. She had had her hair hennaed. The place reeked of fresh paint. It was an off night. Of course it was very early. They had two drinks and Dyar paid, saying he wanted to go to his hotel. Thami had been talking about his brothers' stinginess, how they would not let him have any money—even his own. "But tomorrow I'll buy that boat!" he ended triumphantly. Dyar did not ask him where he had got the money. He was mildly surprised to hear that the other had been born and brought up in the Beidaoui Palace; he did not know whether he thought more or less of him now that he knew his origins. As they left, Thami reached across the bar and seizing Mme. Papaconstante's brilliant head, kissed her violently on each flaming cheek. "*Ay, hombre!*" she cried, laughing delightedly, pretending to rearrange her undisturbed coiffure.

In the street Dyar attempted to piece together the broken thread of the itinerary, but it seemed they were going back down by another route, as he recognized no landmark whatever until they were suddenly within sight of the smoke-filled Zoco de Fuera.

"You know, Dare—" (Dyar corrected him; "—some night I'll take you to my home and give you a real Moorish dinner. Couscous, bastila, everything. How's that?"

"That would be fine, Thami."

"Don't forget," Thami cautioned him, as if they had already arranged the occasion.

"I won't."

Just by the main gateway leading into the square, Thami stopped and indicated a native café, rather larger and more pretentious than most, inside which a very loud radio was roaring.

"I'm going here," he said. "Any time you want to see me you can always find me inside here. In a few days we'll go for a ride in my boat. So long."

Dyar stood alone in the bustling square. From the far end, through the trees, came the sound of drums, beating out a complicated, limping Berber rhythm from up in the mountains. He found a small Italian restaurant in a street off the Zoco, and had an indifferent meal. In spite of his impatience to get back into the streets and look for the Bar Lucifer, he relaxed over a café espresso and had two cigarettes before rising to leave. There was no point in getting there too early.

He wandered vaguely downhill until he came to a street he thought might lead in the right direction. Girls walked by slowly in clusters, hanging together as if for protection, staring at him but pretending not to. It was easy to tell the Jewish girls from the Spanish, although the two looked and dressed alike: the former loped, straggled, hobbled, practically fell along the street, as if they had no control and without a semblance of grace. And the Moslem women pushed by like great white bundles of laundry, an eye peering out near the top. Ahead of him, under a streetlight, a crowd of men and boys was gathering around two angry youths, each of whom held the other at arm's length by the lapels. The pose was as formal as a bit of frozen choreography. They glared, uttered insults, growled, and made menacing gestures with their free left hands. He watched a while; no blow was struck. Suddenly one jerked away. The other shot out of sight, and while the brief general conversation that followed was still in progress, returned from nowhere with a policeman—the classical procedure. The officer of the law separated the crowd and stepped in front of Dyar, tapping arms and shoulders very gently with his white billy. Dyar studied him:—he wore an American GI uniform and a metal helmet painted white. In a white leather holster he carried a revolver wrapped carefully in tissue paper, like a Christmas present.

As if he were a farmer urging his plow-horses, he murmured to the crowd softly: "Eh. Eh. Eh. Eh." And the crowd slowly dispersed, the two antagonists already having lost themselves in its midst.

Slowly he moved ahead in what seemed to him the right direction. All he needed was one landmark and he would be set. Sweet temple-incense poured out of the Hindu silk shops, a whole Berber family crouched in the shadow of a small mountain of oranges, mechanically calling out the price of a kilo. And then all at once the dark streets began, and the few stalls that remained open were tiny and lighted by carbide lamps or candles. At one point he stopped a man in European clothes and said: "Bar Lucifer?" It was a long chance, and he did not really expect a useful answer. The man grunted and pointed back the way Dyar had just come. He thanked him and continued. It was rather fun, being lost like this; it gave him a strange sensation of security, — the feeling that at this particular instant no one in the world could possibly find him. Not his family, not Wilcox, not Daisy de Valverde, not Thami, not Eunice Goode, not Mme. Jouvenon, and not, he reflected finally, the American Legation. The thought of these last two somewhat lowered his spirits. At the moment he was further from being free than he had been yesterday at this time. The idea horrified him; it was unacceptable. Yesterday at this time he had been leaving the Beidaoui Palace in a good humor. There had been the episode of the kittens, which now that he considered it, seemed to have had something to do with that good humor. It was crazy, but it was true. As he walked on, noticing less and less where he was, he pursued his memory of yesterday evening further, like a film being run backwards. When he got to the cold garden with the stone bench where he had sat in the wind, he knew he had found the setting. It had happened while he sat there. What Holland had said had started him off, feeling rather than thinking, but Holland had not said enough, had not followed through. "Here I am and something's going to happen." No connection. He said to Holland: "You're going to die too, but in the meantime you eat." No connection whatever, and yet it was all connected. It was all part of the same thing.

The fine rain came down, cold and smelling fresh. Then it became heavier and more determined. He had his raincoat. It if rained too hard he would get soaked anyway, but it made no difference. For quite a while now the streets had been almost empty. "The slums," he thought. "Poor people go to bed early." The places through which he was passing were like the tortuous corridors in dreams. It was impossible to think of them as streets, or even as alleys. There were spaces here and there among the buildings, that was all, and some of them opened into other spaces and some did not. If he found the right series of connections he could get from one place to the next, but only by going through the buildings themselves. And the buildings seemed to have come into existence like plants, chaotic, facing no way, topheavy, one growing out of the other. Sometimes he heard footsteps echoing when someone passed through one of the vault-like tunnels, and often the sound died away without the person's ever coming into view. There were the mounds of garbage and refuse everywhere, the cats whose raging cries racked the air, and that ever-present acid smell of urine: the walls and pavements were encrusted with a brine of urine. He stood still a moment. From the distance, through the falling rain, floated the sound of chimes. It was the clock in the belfry of the Catholic Church in the Siaghines striking the quarter of the hour. Ahead there was the faint roar of the sea breaking against the cliffs below the ramparts. And as he stood there, again he found himself asking the same questions he had asked earlier in the day: "What am I doing here? What's going to happen?" He was not even trying to find the Bar Lucifer; he had given that up. He was trying to lose himself. Which meant, he realized, that his great problem right now was to escape from his cage, to discover the way out of the fly-trap, to strike the chord inside himself which would liberate those qualities capable of transforming him from a victim into a winner.

"It's a bad business," he whispered to himself. If he was so far gone that when he came out to find Hadija, instead of making every effort to locate the place, he allowed himself to stumble along for an hour or so in the dark through stinking hallways like the one where he stood at the moment, then it was time he took himself in hand. And just how? It was a comforting idea, to say you were going to take yourself in hand. It assumed the possibility of forcing a change. But between the saying and the doing there was an abyss into which all the knowledge, strength and courage you had could not keep you from plunging. For instance, tomorrow night at this time he would be still more tightly fettered, sitting in the Jouvenons' flat after dinner, having some petty little plan of action prepared for him. At each moment his situation struck him as more absurd and untenable. He had no desire to do that kind of work, and he had no interest in helping Mme. Jouvenon or her cause.

However, it was nice to have the money; it was comfortable to be able to take a cab when it was raining and he was tired and wanted to get home; it was pleasant to go into a restaurant and look at the left hand side of the menu first; it was fun to enter a shop and buy a present for Hadija. (The box with the bracelet in it bulged in his raincoat pocket.) You had to make a choice. But the choice was already made, and he felt that it was not he who had made it. Because of that, it was hard for him to believe that he was morally involved. Of course, he could fail to put in an appearance tomorrow night, but that would do no good. They would find him, demand explanations, threaten him probably. He could even return the money by cashing express checks, depositing the hundred dollars back into the account and writing a check to Mme. Jouvenon for five hundred. It was still not too late for that. Or probably it was—all she had to do was to refuse. Her check had been cashed; that remained a fact, part of the bank's records.

It suddenly seemed to him that he could to some extent neutralize the harm he had done himself by reporting his action to the American Legation. He laughed softly. Then he would be in trouble, and also there would be no more money. He knew that was the action of a victim. It was typical: a victim always gave himself up if he had dared to dream of changing his status. Yet at the moment the prospect was attractive.

Right now he wanted to get out of this rubbish-heap and home to bed. By going toward the sound of the sea, he suspected, he could arrive at some sort of definite thoroughfare which would follow along inside the ramparts. That would lead him down to the port. The thing turned out to be more complicated than he had thought, but he did manage eventually to get down into the wider streets. Here there were men walking; they were always eager to point the way out of the Moroccan quarter, even in the pouring rain, and often even without being asked. Their fundamental hostility to non-Moslems showed itself clearly in this respect. "This way out," the children would call, in whatever language they knew. It was a refrain. Or if you were pushing your way in, "You can't get through that way," they would say.

He came out into the principal street opposite the great mosque. A little beyond, atop the ramparts, perched the Castle Club (Open All Night . . Best Wines and Liquors Served . . Famous Attractions . . Ernesto's Hawaiian Swing Band) through whose open windows spilled the sound of a high tenor wailing into a microphone.

From here on, the way was straight, and open to the sea wind. Twenty minutes later he was cursing in front of the entrance to the Hotel de la Playa, ringing the bell and pounding on the plate glass of the locked door in an attempt to waken the Moroccan who was asleep in a deck chair on the other side. When the man finally let him in he looked at him reproachfully, saying: "*Sí, sí, sí.*" In his mailbox with the key was a note. He went to his room, stripped off his wet clothes, and stepped into the corner to take a hot shower. There was no hot water. He rubbed himself down with the Turkish towel and got into his bathrobe. Sitting on the bed, he opened the note. *Where the hell are you?* it said. *Will be by at nine tomorrow morning. Jack.*

He laid the piece of paper on the night table and got into bed, leaving the window closed. He could tell by the sound that it was raining too hard to have it open.

3

The Age of Monsters

15

IN THE NIGHT the wind veered and the weather changed, bringing a luminous sky and a bright moon. In his bed at the Atlantide, Wilcox blamed his insomnia on indigestion. His dreams were turbulent and broken; he had to step out of a doorway into the street that was thronged with people who pretended to be paying him no attention, but he knew that among the passers-by were hidden the men who were waiting for him. They would seize him from behind and push him into a dark alley, and there would be no one to help him. Each time he awoke he found himself lying on his back, breathing with difficulty, his heart pounding irregularly. Finally he turned on the light and smoked. As he sat partially up in bed, looking around the room which seemed too fully lighted, he reassured himself, arguing that no one had seen Dyar in his office, and that thus no one would be able to know when he left Ramlal's shop that he was carrying the money. To look at the situation clearly, he forced himself to admit that the Larbi gang did have ways of finding things out. Ever since he had discovered that the dreaded El Kebir was back from his short term in jail at Port Lyautey (he had caught sight of him in the street the very afternoon he had left Dyar alone in the office), the fear that one of them might somehow learn of Dyar's connection with him had been uppermost in his mind. But this time he had been really circumspect; he did not think they knew anything. Only, it must be done immediately. With each hour that passed, they were more likely to get wind of the project. He wondered if it had been wise to go to the Hotel de la Playa and leave the note, if it might not have been better simply to keep telephoning all night until he had found Dyar in. He wondered if by any chance the British had had their suspicions aroused. He began to wonder all sorts of things, feeling at every moment less and less like sleeping. "That damned zabaglione," he thought. "Too rich." And he got up to take a soda-mint. While he was at the medicine cabinet he shook a gardenal tablet out of its tube as well, but then he reflected that it might make him oversleep, and he did not trust the desk downstairs to call him. They occasionally messed up, and it was imperative that he rise at eight. He got back into bed and began to read the editorial page of the Paris *Herald*.

It was about this time when Daisy de Valverde awoke feeling unaccountably nervous. Luis had gone to Casablanca for a few days on business, and although the house was full of servants she never slept well when she was alone. She listened, wondering if it had been a sudden noise which had brought her back from sleep: she heard only the endless sound of the sea against the rocks, so far below that it was like a shell being held to the ear. She opened her eyes. The room was bathed in brilliant moonlight. It came in from the west, but on all sides she could see the glow of the clear night sky out over the water. Slipping out of bed, she went and tried the door into the corridor, just to be positive it was locked. It was, and she got back into bed and pulled an extra blanket up over her, torturing herself with the fantasy that it might have been unlocked, so that it would have opened just a bit when she tried it, and she would have seen, standing just outside, a great ragged Moor with a beard, looking at her evilly through slits of eyes. She would have slammed the door, only to find that he had put one huge foot through the opening. She would have pushed against it with all her might, but. . . .

"Shall I never grow up?" she thought. Did one never reach a stage when one had complete control of oneself, so that one could think what one wanted to think, feel the way one wanted to feel?

Thami had gone home late. The considerable number of pipes of kif he had shared with his friends in the café throughout the evening had made him a little careless, so that he had made a good deal of noise in the process of getting his clothes off. The baby had awakened and begun to wail, and the kif, instead of projecting him through a brief region of visions into sleep, had made him wakeful and short of breath. During the small hours he heard each call to prayer from the minaret of the nearby Emsallah mosque, as well as the half-hourly chants of reassurance that all was well with the faithful; each time the arrowlike voice came out through the still air there was a sporadic outburst of cock-crows roundabout. Finally the fowls refused to go back to sleep, and their racket became continuous, up there on the roofs of the houses. Instinctively, when he had lain down, Thami had put Eunice's check under his pillow. At dawn he slept for an hour. When he opened his eyes, his wife was shuffling about barefoot and the baby was screaming again. He looked at his watch and called out: "Coffee!" He wanted to be at the bank before it opened.

Dyar slept fitfully for a while, his mind weighted down with half-thoughts. About four he sat up, feeling very wide-awake, and noticed the brightness outside. The air in the room was close. He went to the window, opened it, and leaned out, studying the moonlit details on the hills across the harbor: a row of black cypresses, a house which was a tiny cube of luminous white halfway between the narrow beach and the sky, in the middle of the soft brown waste of the hillside. It was all painted with meticulous care. He went back to his bed and got between the warm covers. "This is no good," he said to himself, thinking that if he were going to feel like this he would rather remain a victim always. At least he would feel like himself, whereas at the moment he was all too conscious of the pressure of that alien presence, clamoring to be released. "It's no good. It's no good." Miserable, he turned over. Soon the fresh air coming in the window put him to sleep. When he opened his eyes again the room was pulsing with sunlight. The sun was out there, huge and clear in the morning sky, and its light was augmented by the water, thrown against the ceiling, where it moved like fire. He jumped up, stood in the window, stretched, scratched, yawned and smiled. If you got up early enough, he reflected, you could get on board the day and ride it easily, otherwise it got ahead of you and you had to push it along in front of you as you went. But however you did it, you and the day came out together into the dark, over and over again. He began to do a few setting-up exercises there in front of the open window. For years he had gone along not being noticed, not noticing himself, accompanying the days mechanically, exaggerating the exertion and boredom of the day to give him sleep for the night, and using the sleep to provide the energy to go through the following day. He did not usually bother to say to himself: "There's nothing more to it than this; what makes it all worth going through?" because he felt there was no way of answering the question. But at the moment it seemed to him he had found a simple reply: the satisfaction of being able to get through it. If you looked at it one way, that satisfaction was nothing, but if you looked at it another way, it was everything. At least, that was the way he felt this morning; it was unusual enough so that he marveled at the solution.

The air's clarity and the sun's strength made him whistle in the shower, made him note, while he was shaving, that he was very hungry. Wilcox came at five minutes of nine, pounded heavily on the door and sat down panting in the chair by the window.

"Well, today's the big day," he said, trying to look both casual and jovial. "Hated to get you up so early. But it's better to get these things done as fast as possible."

"What things?" said Dyar into his towel as he dried his face.

"Ashcombe-Danvers's money is here. You're taking it from Ramlal's to the Crédit Foncier. Remember?"

"Oh." An extra and unwelcome complication for the day. He did not sound pleased, and Wilcox noticed it.

"What's the matter? Business breaking into your social life?"

"No, no. Nothing's the matter," Dyar said, combing his hair in front of the mirror. "I'm just wondering why you picked me to be messenger boy."

"What d'you mean?" Wilcox sat up straight. "It's been understood for ten days that you were going to take the job off my hands. You've been raising hell to start work. The first definite thing I give you to do, and you wonder why I give to you! I asked you to do it because it'll be a lot of help to me, that's why!"

"All right, all right, all right. I haven't raised any objection, have I?"

Wilcox looked calmer. "But Jesus, you've got a screwy attitude about the whole thing."

"You think so?" Dyar stood in the sunlight looking down at him, still combing his hair. "It could be the whole thing's a little screwy."

Wilcox was about to speak. Then, thinking better of it, he decided to let Dyar continue. But something in his face must have warned Dyar, for instead of going ahead and bringing in the British currency restrictions as he had intended, just to let Wilcox see that by "screwy" he meant "illegal" (since Wilcox seemed to think he was wholly ignorant of even that detail), said only: "Well, it ought not to take long, at any rate."

"Five minutes," said Wilcox, rising, "Have you had coffee?" Dyar shook his head. "Let's get going, then."

"God, what sun!" Dyar cried as they stepped out of the hotel. It was the first clear morning he had seen, it made a new world around him, it was like emerging into daylight after an endless night. "Smell that air," he said, stopping to stand with one hand on the trunk of a palm tree, facing the beach, sniffing audibly.

"For Christ's sake, let's get going!" Wilcox cried, making a point of continuing to walk ahead as fast as he could. He was letting his impatience run away with him. Dyar caught up with him, glanced at him curiously; he had not known Wilcox was so nervous. And in his insistence upon taking great strides, Wilcox stepped into some dog offal and slipped, coming down full length on the pavement. Picking himself up, even before he was on his feet, he snarled at Dyar. "Go on, laugh, God damn you! Laugh!" But Dyar merely looked concerned. There was no way of laughing in such a situation. (The sudden sight of a human being deprived of its dignity did not strike him as basically any more ludicrous and absurd than the constant effort required for the maintenance of that dignity, or than the state itself of being human in what seemed an undeniably non-human world.) But this morning, to be agreeable, he smiled as he helped dust off Wilcox's topcoat. "Did it get on me?" demanded Wilcox.

"Nope."

"Well, come on, God damn it."

They stopped for coffee at the place where Dyar had taken breakfast the previous day, but Wilcox would not sit down.

"We haven't got time."

"We? Where are you going?"

"Back to the Atlantide as soon as I know you're really on your way to Ramlal's, and not down onto the beach to sunbathe."

"I'm on my way. Don't worry about me."

They walked to the door. "I'll leave you, then," Wilcox said.

"You got everything straight?"

"Don't *worry* about me!"

"Come up to the hotel when you're finished. We can have some breakfast then."

"Fine."

Wilcox walked up the hill feeling exhausted. When he got to the Metropole he undressed and went back to bed. He would have time for a short nap before Dyar's arrival.

Following the Avenida de España along the beach toward the old part of town, Dyar toyed with the idea of going to the American Legation and laying the whole story of Madame Jouvenon before them. But who would "they" be? Some sleek-jowled individual out of the *Social Register* who would scarcely listen to him at first, and then would begin to stare at him with inimical eyes, put a series of questions to him in a cold voice, making notes of the replies. He imagined going into the spotless office, receiving the cordial handshake, being offered the chair in front of the desk.

"Good morning. What can I do for you?"

The long hesitation. "Well, it's sort of hard. I don't quite know how to tell you. I think I've gotten into some trouble."

The consul or vice-consul would look at him searchingly. "You *think?*" A pause. "Perhaps you'd better begin by telling me your name." Whereupon he would give him not only his name, but the whole stupid story of what had happened yesterday noon at the Empire. The man would look interested, clear his throat, put his hand out on the desk, say: "First of all, let's have the check."

"I haven't got it. I deposited it in the bank."

"That was bright!" (Angrily.) "Just about ten times as much work for us."

"Well, I needed money."

The man's voice would get unpleasant. "Oh, you needed money, did you? You opened an account and drew on it, is that it?"

"That's right."

Then what would he say? "So now you've got cold feet and want to be sure you won't get in trouble."

Dyar imagined his own face growing hot with embarrassment, saying: "Well, the fact that I came here to tell you about it ought to prove that I want to do the right thing."

The other would say: "Mr. Dyar, you make me laugh."

Where would it get him, an interview like that? Beyond making him an object of suspicion for the rest of the time he was in the International Zone, just what would going to the Legation accomplish?

As he started up the ramp that led to the taxi stand at the foot of the Castle Club he passed a doorway where a dog and a cat, both full-grown, lay in the sun, lazily playing together. He stopped and watched for a moment, along with several passers-by, all of whom wore the same half unbelieving, pleased smile. It was as if without their knowing it the spectacle served as proof that enmity was not inescapably the law which governed existence, that a cessation of hostilities was at least thinkable. He passed along up the street in the hot morning sun, through the Zoco Chico to Ramlal's shop. The door was locked. He went back to the Zoco, into the Café Central, and telephoned Wilcox, standing at the bar beside the coffee machine, being buffeted by all the waiters.

"Not open yet!" cried Wilcox, and he paused. "Well," he said finally, "hang around until he is. That's all you can do." He paused again. "But for God's sake don't hang around in front of the store! Just walk past every fifteen or twenty minutes and take a quick look."

"Right. Right." Dyar hung up, paid the fat barman for the call, and walked out into the square. It was twenty minutes of ten. If Ramlal was not open now, why would he be any more likely to be open at ten-thirty, or eleven? "The hell with that," he thought, starting to amble once more in the direction of the shop.

It was still closed. For him that settled it. He would go down to the beach for a while and lie in the sun. It was Wilcox who had put the idea into his head. All he had to do was to get back up here a little before half-past twelve, which was when the Crédit Foncier closed. First he stopped and had coffee and several slices of toast with butter and strawberry jam.

The beach was flat, wide and white, and it curved in a perfect semicircle to the cape ahead. He walked along the strip of hard sand that the receding tide had uncovered; it was a wet and flattering mirror for the sky, intensifying its brightness. When he had left behind the half-mile or so of boarded-up bathing cabins and bars, he took off his shoes and socks and rolled up his trousers. Until now the beach had been completely empty, but ahead two figures and a donkey were approaching. When they drew near he saw that it was two very old Berber women dressed as if it were zero weather, in red and white striped wool. They paid him no attention. Out here where no hill followed the shore line there was a small sharp wind to chill whatever surface was not in the sun. Before him now he saw several tiny fishing boats beached side by side. He came up to them. They had been abandoned long ago: the wood was rotten and the hulls were filled with sand. There was no sign of a human being in any direction. The two women and the donkey had left the beach, gone inland over the dunes, and disappeared. He undressed and got into a boat that was half buried. The sand filled the bow and sloped toward the center of the boat, making a perfect couch that faced the sun.

Outside the wind blew by; in here there was nothing but the beating of the hot sun on the skin. He lay a while, intensely conscious of the welcome heat, in a state of self-induced voluptuousness. When he looked at the sun, his eyes closed almost tight, he saw webs of crystalline fire crawling across the narrow space between the slitted lids, and his eyelashes made the furry beams of light stretch out, recede, stretch out. It was a long time since he had lain naked in the sun. He remembered that if you stayed long enough the rays drew every thought out of your head. That was what he wanted, to be baked dry and hard, to feel the vaporous worries evaporating one by one, to know finally that all the damp little doubts and hesitations that covered the floor of his being were curling up and expiring in the great furnace-blast of the sun. Presently he forgot about all that, his muscles relaxed, and he dozed lightly, waking now and then to lift his head above the worm-eaten gunwale and glance up and down the beach. There was no one. Eventually he ceased doing even that. At one point he turned over and lay face down on the hard-packed sand, feeling the sun's burning sheet settle over his back. The soft, regular cymbal-crash of the waves was like the distant breathing of the morning; the sound sifted down through the myriad compartments of the air and reached his ears long afterward. When he turned back and looked straight at the sky it seemed farther away than he had ever seen it. Yet he felt very close to himself, perhaps because in order to feel alive a man must first cease to think of himself as being *on his way*. There must be a full stop, all objectives forgotten. A voice says "Wait," but he usually will not listen, because if he waits he may be late. Then, too, if he really waits, he may find that when he starts to move again it will be in a different direction, and that also is a frightening thought. Because life is not a movement toward or away from anything; not even from the past to the future, or from youth to old age, or from birth to death. The whole of life does not equal the sum of its parts. It equals any one of the parts; there is no sum. The full-grown man is no more deeply involved in life than the new-born child; his only advantage is that it can occasionally be given him to become conscious of the substance of that life, and unless he is a fool he will not look for reasons or explanations. Life needs no clarifying, no justification. From whatever direction the approach is made, the result is the same: life for life's sake, the transcending fact of the living individual. In the meantime you eat. And so he, lying in the sun and feeling close to himself, knew that he was there and rejoiced in the knowledge. He could pretend, if he needed, to be an American named Nelson Dyar, with four thousand pesetas in the pocket of the jacket that lay across the seat in the stern of the boat, but he would know that it was a remote and unimportant part of the entire truth. First of all he was a man lying on the sand that covered the floor of a ruined boat, a man whose left hand reached to within an inch of its sun-heated hull, whose body displaced a given quantity of the warm morning air. Everything he had ever thought or done had been thought or done not by him, but by a *member* of a great mass of beings who acted as they did only because they were on their way from birth to death. He was no longer a member: having committed himself, he could expect no help from anyone. If a man was not on his way anywhere, if life was something else, entirely different, if life was a question of being, for a long continuous instant that was all one, then the best thing for him to do was sit back and be, and whatever happened, he still was. Whatever a man thought, said or did, the fact of his being there remained unchanged. And death? He felt that some day, if he thought far enough, he would discover that death changed nothing, either.

The pleasant bath of vague ideas in which his mind had been

soaking no longer sufficed to keep him completely dormant. Making an effort, he raised his head a little and turned his wrist to see the time. It was ten minutes past twelve. He sprang up, dressed quickly save for his socks and shoes, and started back along the still-deserted beach. Even though he walked so fast that he was painfully out of breath, by the time he reached the first buildings it was quarter of one. The Crédit Foncier would be closed; he would have to do the job after lunch. He came opposite the Hotel de la Playa, crossed the beach, climbed the steps to the street and went in barefooted. The boy at the desk handed him a message. "Jack has been phoning; he's going nuts," he thought, as he looked at the slip. But it said: "Sr. Doan, 25-16. Immediatamente." Still assuming that this was probably Wilcox trying frantically to reach him, perhaps from the office or home of someone else, he gave the boy the number and stood drumming with his fingers on the desk until the communication was made.

He took the telephone, heard a man's voice say: "American Legation." Quietly he hung up, and without explaining anything to the boy went and sat down in a corner where he put on his socks and shoes. After he had tied the second lace carefully he sat back and shut his eyes. Under the fingers of each hand he felt the smooth beveled wood of a chair-arm. A truck went by slowly, backfiring. The lobby smelled faintly of chloride of lime. For the first few minutes he felt neither calm or perturbation; he was paralyzed. Then when he opened his eyes he thought, almost triumphantly: "So this is what it's like." And immediately afterward he was conscious for the second time that day of being extremely hungry. He had no plan of action; he wanted to eat, he wanted to get the Ramlal business over with and let Wilcox know it was finished. After that, depending on how he felt, he might call Mr. Doan at the Legation and see what he wanted. (It consoled him to think there was no certainty that the call had to do with the Jouvenon nonsense; as a matter of fact, at moments he was almost certain it could not be that at all.) But as to the dinner at Mme. Jouvenon's apartment. . . .

He jumped up and shouted for the boy, who was hidden by the desk. "Taxi!" he cried, pointing at the telephone. He went to the door and stood looking up the avenue, trying to reassure himself by considering that if they had been going to handle the thing roughly they would not have begun by telephoning. But then he remembered something Daisy had said to him—that the Zone was so small it was generally possible for the police to put their finger on anyone in a few hours. The Legation could afford to sit back and be polite, at least until they saw how he intended to play it.

The taxi came coasting down the side street from the town above, drew up before the entrance. He hurried to get in, and leaning forward from the back seat directed it along the Avenida de España to the foot of the Medina.

*

The day moved by; the city lay basking in the hot bright air. About noon, up on the mountain in the rose garden of the Villa Hesperides Daisy de Valverde did a bit of weeding. Then when the exertion became too much for her she had a rubber mattress put by the pool and lay on it in her bathing suit. There were too few days like this in Tangier during the winter. When Luis came back from Casablanca she would talk with him again seriously about Egypt. Each year since the war they had spent part of the winter in Cairo, Luxor or Wadi Halfa, but this year for one reason and another they had not summoned the energy to set forth. Then she had tried at the last minute to get a room at the Mamounia in Marrakech, and finding it impossible, had hit on the idea of appropriating Mme. Werth's reservation, arguing that in any case that lady, always in poor health, was likely to be unable to avail herself of it when the time came. That little plan had of course been frustrated by Jack Wilcox's infuriating behavior.

"He's really rather sweet," she said to herself, thinking not of Wilcox, but of Dyar. Soon she rose, walked into the house and rang for Mario. "Get me the Hotel de la Playa on the telephone," she said.

Wilcox had gone to the Atlantide, undressed, and got into bed. There, in spite of his anxiety about the Ashcombe-Danvers sterling transfer, he had fallen into a deep slumber, exhausted finally by the wakeful night behind him. He awoke at twenty-five minutes past one (just as Dyar was entering Ramlal's shop), saw the time, and in a fury called downstairs to see what had happened. When anything went wrong, it was usually the fault of one of the employees at the desk.

"Have I had any calls?" he demanded. The young man did not know; he had just come on at one o'clock.

"Well, look in my box!" shouted Wilcox. The young man was rattled. He began to read him the messages for the person in the room on the floor beneath. "Oh, good Jesus Christ Almighty!" Wilcox yelled, and he dressed and went down to the desk to see for himself. His box was empty. There was nothing he could do, so he gave the youth at the desk a tongue-lashing and went into the bar to sit gloomily over a whiskey and grunt briefly now and then in answer to the barman's sporadic chatter, thinking how possible it was for Dyar to have come, announced himself at the desk, and been told that Mr. Wilcox was out.

16

PERSPIRING A LITTLE after his rapid climb up from the port, Dyar stepped from the street's yellow glare into the darkness of the shop. Young Ramlal was reading a newspaper; he sat dangling his legs from a high table which was the only piece of furniture in the tiny room. When he glanced up, no expression of recognition appeared on the features of his smooth face, but he jumped down and said: "Good morning. I expected you to come earlier."

"Well, I came by twice, but you were closed."

"Ah, *too* early. Will you have a cigarette?"

"Thanks."

Tossing his lighter onto the table, the Indian continued: "I have been waiting for you. You see, I could not leave the package here, and I did not want to carry it with me when I go to eat lunch. If you had not come I'd have waited. So you see I am glad to see you." He smiled.

"Oh," said Dyar. "I'm sorry to have kept you waiting."

"Not at all, not at all." Ramlal, happy to have extracted an apology, took a key from his trousers pocket and opened a drawer in the table. From this he lifted a large cardboard box marked *Consul. Twenty Tins of Fifty. A Blend of the Finest Matured Virginian Grown Tobaccos.* "I would not advise counting it here," he said. "But here it is." He opened the box and Dyar saw the stacks of thin white paper.

Then swiftly he closed it, as if more than this rapid exposure to air and light risked spoiling its delicate contents. Keeping one thin dark hand protectingly spread over the carton, Ramlal went on: "They were counted of course by my father in Gibraltar, and by me again last night. Therefore I assure you there are one thousand eight hundred five-pound notes in the box. If you wish to make a count now, it is quite all right. But—" He waved expressively at the throng passing in the street a few feet away, and smiled. "One never knows, you know."

"Oh, hell. That doesn't matter." Dyar tried to look friendly. "I'll take your word for it. If there's any mistake we know where to find you, I guess."

The other, looking faintly offended as he heard the last sentence, turned away and brought out a large sheet of shiny blue and white wrapping paper with the words "Galeries Lafayette" printed across it at regular intervals. With professional dexterity he made a smart package and tied it up with a length of immaculate white string.

"There we are," he said, stepping back and bowing slightly. "And when you write Mr. Ashcombe-Danvers please don't neglect to give him my father's greetings and my respects."

Dyar thanked him and went out into the street holding his parcel tightly. Half done, anyway, he thought. By the time he had eaten something the Crédit Foncier would be open. He strolled up through the Zoco de Fuera to the Italian restaurant where he had eaten the previous night. The bundles of big soiled white notes had not looked like money at all; the color of money was green, and real bills were small and convenient. It was no new sensation for him to have in his hands a large sum of banknotes which did not belong to him, so that the idea of his responsibility did not cause him undue nervousness. At the restaurant he laid the package on the floor near his feet and glanced down at it occasionally during the meal. Today of all days, he thought, he would have liked to be free, to rent a little convertible, perhaps, and drive out into the country with Hadija, or even better, to hop on a train and just keep going down into Africa, to the end of the line. (And from there? Africa was a big place and would offer its own suggestions.) He would even have settled for another pilgrimage to the beach, and this time he would have gone into the water and had a little exercise. Instead of which the best part of the afternoon would be occupied by the visits to the Crédit Foncier and the Hotel Atlantide, and Wilcox would find fault and yell at him, once he knew the money was safe in the bank. He decided to tell him he had gone by Ramlal's and found it closed three times, instead of twice.

A few minutes after two he got up, took his parcel, and paid the check to the stout *patronne* who stood behind the bar by the door. As he stepped into the brilliant sunlight he pitied himself a little for his obligations on such an afternoon. When he got to the Crédit Foncier the doors were open, and he went into the shabby gloom of its public room. Behind the iron grillework of the wickets the accountants were visible, seated on high stools at their chaotic desks. He started up the chipped marble staircase; a Moroccan in uniform called him back. "Mr. Benzekri," he said. The Moroccan let him continue, but looked after him suspiciously.

The buff walls of the little office were disfigured by rusty stains that spread monstrously from the ceiling to the floor. Mr. Benzekri sat in a huge black chair, looking even sadder than when they had met at the Café España. He nodded his head very slowly up and down as he unwrapped the box, as if he were saying: "Ah, yes. More of this dirty paper to count and take care of." But when he saw the carefully tied bundles inside, he looked up at Dyar sharply.

"Five-pound notes? We cannot accept these."

"What?" The loudness of his own voice surprised Dyar. "Can't accept them?" He saw himself embarking on an endless series of trips between an irascible Wilcox and a smiling Ramlal. However, Mr. Benzekri was very calm.

"Five-pound notes are illegal here, as you know." Dyar was about to interrupt, to protest his ignorance, but Mr. Benzekri, already wrapping the blue and white paper around the box, went on: "Choc-ron will change this for you. He will give you pesetas, and we will buy them for pounds. Mr. Ashcombe-Danvers of course wants pounds for his accounts. He will lose twice on the exchange, but I am sorry. These notes are illegal in Tangier."

Dyar was still confused. "But what makes you think this man—" he hesitated.

"Chocron?"

"—What makes you think *he's* going to buy illegal tender?"

A faint, brief smile touched Mr. Benzekri's melancholy lips. "He will take it," he said quietly. And he sat back, staring ahead of him as if Dyar had already gone out. But then, as Dyar gathered up the neatly tied parcel once again, he said: "Wait," bent forward and scribbled some words on a pad, tearing off the sheet and handing it to him. "Give this to Chocron. Come back before four. We close at four. The address is at the top of the paper." "A lot of good that's going to do me," Dyar thought. He thanked Mr. Benzekri and went downstairs, out into the Zoco Chico where the striped awning over the terrasse of the Café Central was being let down to shield the customers from the hot afternoon sun. There he approached a native policeman who stood grandly in the center of the plaza and inquired of him how to get to the Calle Sinagoga. It was nearby: up the main street and to the left, by what he could gather from the man's gestures. All hope of getting to the beach was gone. The next sunny day like this might come in another two weeks; there was no telling. Silently he cursed Ramlal, Wilcox, Ashcombe-Danvers.

Chocron's office was at the top of a flight of stairs, in a cluttered little room that jutted out over the narrow street below, and the gray-bearded Chocron, who looked distinguished in the long black tunic and skullcap worn by the older Jews of the community, beamed when he read Benzekri's note. His English, however, was virtually nonexistent. "Show," he said, pointing to the box, which Dyar opened. "Sit," suggested Chocron, and he removed the packets from the box and began to count the bills rapidly, moistening his finger on the tip of his tongue from time to time. "This one and Benzekri are probably crooks," Dyar thought uneasily. Still, the value of the pound in pesetas was posted on blackboards every few feet along the street; the rate could not go too far astray. Or perhaps it could, if the pounds were illegal. Even if the notes themselves had been valid, their very presence here was due to an infringement of the law; there was no possibility of recourse to any authority, whatever rates Chocron and Benzekri took it into their heads to charge. Below in the street the long cries of a candy-vendor passing slowly by sounded like religious chanting. Mr. Chocron's expert fingers continued to manipulate the corners of the notes. Occasionally he held one up to the light that came through the window and squinted at it. When he had finished with a bundle he tied it up again meticulously, never looking toward Dyar. Finally he placed all the bundles back in the box and taking the slip of paper Mr. Benzekri had sent him, turned it over and wrote on the other side: 138 pesetas. He pushed the paper toward Dyar and stared at him. This was a little higher than the street quotation, which varied between 133 and 136 to the pound. Still suspicious, making grimaces and gestures, Dyar said: "What do you do with money like this?" It seemed that Chocron understood more English than he spoke. "Palestina," he answered laconically, pointing out the window. Dyar began to multiply 138 by 9,000, just to amuse himself. Then he wrote the figures 1 4 2, and passed the paper back to the other, to see what the reaction would be. Chocron became voluble in Spanish, and it was easy to see that he had no intention of going that high. Somewhere along the flow of words Dyar heard the name of Benzekri; that, and the idea that one hundred forty two was too many pesetas to pay for a pound, was all he grasped of the monologue. However, he was warming to the game. If he sat quietly, he thought, Chocron would raise his offer. It took a while. Chocron pulled a notebook out of a drawer and began to do a series of involved arithmetical exercises. At one point he produced a small silver case and inhaled a bit of snuff through each nostril. Deliberately he put it away and continued his work. Dyar tapped his right toe against the red tile floor in a march rhythm, waiting. You could change the price of anything here, Wilcox had insisted, if you knew how, and the prime virtues in the affair were patience and an appearance of indifference. (He remembered Wilcox's anecdote of the country Moroccan in the post office who had tried for five minutes to get a seventy-five-céntimo stamp for sixty céntimos and finally had turned away insulted when the clerk refused to bargain with him.) In this case the indifference was more than feigned; he had no interest in saving Ashcombe-Danvers a few thousand pesetas. It was a game, nothing more. He tried to imagine how he would feel at the moment if the money were his own. Probably he would not have had the courage to attempt bargaining at all. There was a difference between playing with money that was not real and money that was. But at this point nothing was real. The little room crowded with old furniture, the bearded man in black opposite him, making figures mechanically in the notebook, the golden light of the waning afternoon, the intimate street sounds outside the window,—all these things were suffused with an inexplicable quality of tentativeness which robbed them of the familiar feeling of reassurance contained in the idea of reality. Above all he was aware of the absurdity of his own situation. There was no doubt now in his mind that the call from the American Legation had to do with a proposed questioning on the matter of Mme. Jouvenon. If he disregarded both the call and the dinner engagement, by tomorrow they would be pulling on him from both sides.

With each day as it passed Dyar had been feeling a little further from the world; it was inevitable that at some point he should make a voluntary effort to put himself back in the middle of it again. To be able to believe fully in the reality of the circumstances in which a man finds himself, he must feel that they bear some relation, however distant, to other situations he has known. If he cannot find this connection, he is cut off from the outside. But since his inner sense of orientation depends for its accuracy on the proper functioning, at least in his eyes, of the outside world, he will make any readjustment, consciously or otherwise, to restore the sense of balance. He is an instrument that strives to adapt itself to the new exterior; he must get those unfamiliar contours more or less into focus once again. And now the outside was very far away—so far that the leg of Chocron's desk could have been something seen through a telescope from an observatory. He had the feeling that if he made a terrible effort he could bring about a change: either the leg of the desk would disappear, or, if it stayed, he would be able to understand what its presence meant. He held his breath. Through the dizziness that resulted he heard Chocron's voice saying something that made no sense. *"Cientocuarenta. Mire."* He was holding up a piece of paper for him to look at. With the sense of lifting a tremendous weight, Dyar raised his eyes and saw figures written on it, conscious at the same time that inside himself a vast and irresistible upheaval was taking place. "Huh?" he said. Chocron had written "140."

"All right."

"One minute," said Chocron; he rose, took the box of money, and went into another room, closing the door behind him.

Dyar did not move. He stared out the window at the wall of the building opposite. The quake was quieting down; the principal strata had shifted positions, and their new places seemed more comfortable.

It was as if something which had been in his line of vision had now been removed, something that had been an obstacle to discovering how to change the external scene. But he distrusted this whole series of private experiences that had forced themselves upon him since he had come here. He was used to long stretches of intolerable boredom punctuated by small crises of disgust; these violent disturbances inside himself seemed no part of his life. They were much more a part of this senseless place he was in. Still, if that was the way the place was going to affect him, he had better get used to the effects and learn how to deal with them.

When Chocron returned he carried the box with him, but this time the bills in it were smaller, brownish-green, violet, and there were fewer of them. He set the box on the desk and still standing, wrote in his notebook for Dyar to see: 1260 @ 1000p. "Count," he said.

It took him a long time, even though most of the bills were new and crisp.

Well, this is fine, he thought, when he had finished. Twenty-five thousand two hundred bucks or thereabouts and no one to stop you. You just walk out. He looked up at Chocron's face, curiously, for a second. No one but Wilcox. It was true. And Wilcox alone—not Wilcox with the police. By God, what a situation, he thought. It's almost worth playing, just for the hell of it.

He did not pay much attention to Chocron's handshake and to the steep stairs that led down into the street. Walking along slowly, being jostled by water carriers and elderly Jewish women in fringed shawls, he kept his eyes on the pavement, not thinking. But he felt the glossy paper around the box, and knew that Chocron had wrapped it carefully, that it was once again a parcel from the Galeries Lafayette. He went beneath a high arch where Moroccans hawked bananas and thick glassware; to the left he recognized Thami's café.

When he looked inside the door the radio was not playing. It was dark in the café, and he had the impression that the place was practically empty.

"*Quiere algo?*" said the qahouaji.

"No, no." The air was aromatic with kif smoke. A hand grasped his arm, squeezed it gently. He turned.

"Hello," said Thami.

"Hi!" It was almost like seeing an old friend; he did not know why, except that he had been alone all during a day that had seemed endless. "I didn't think you'd be here."

"I told you I'm always here."

"What d'you have a home for?"

Thami made a face and spat. "To sleep when I have no other place."

"And a wife? What d'you have a wife for?"

"Same thing. Sit down. Take a glass of good tea."

"I can't. I have to go." He looked at his watch: it was quarter of four. "I have to go fast." The walk down to the Crédit Foncier was only a three-minute one, but he wanted to be sure and get there before they shut that iron grille.

"Are you going up or down?"

"To the Zoco Chico."

"I'll walk with you."

"Okay." He did not want Thami along, but there was no way out of it, and anyway, he thought they might have a drink afterward.

As they walked, Thami looked disparagingly down at his own trousers, which were very much out of press and smeared with grease.

"My old clothes," he remarked, pointing. "Very old. For working on my boat."

"Oh, you bought that boat?"

"Of course I bought it. I told you I was going to." He grinned. "Now I have it. Mister Thami Beidaoui, *propietario* of one old boat. One very old boat, but it goes fast."

"Goes fast?" Dyar repeated, not paying attention.

"I don't know how fast, but faster than the fishing boats down there. You know, it's an old boat. It can't go like a new one."

"No. Of course."

They passed Ramlal's shop. It was shut. Ramlal had added six batteries for portable radios to the array of fountain pens, celluloid toys and wrist watches. They passed El Gran Paris, its show windows a chaos of raincoats. It was always difficult to navigate the Zoco Chico with its groups of stationary talkers like rocks in the sea, around which the crowd surged in all directions. Arrived at what Dyar thought was

the entrance to the Crédit Foncier, at the top of some steps between
two cafés, he saw that even the way into the outer courtyard was
barred by high gates which were closed.

"This isn't it," he said, looking uneasily up and down the square.

"What do you want?" Thami asked, perhaps slightly annoyed
that Dyar had not already told him exactly where he was going and on
what errand. Dyar did not reply; his heart sank, because he knew now
that this was the Crédit Foncier and that it was closed. He ran up the
steps and shook the gate, pounded on it, wondering if the sound could
be heard through the vast babble of voices that floated in from the
zoco.

Thami slowly climbed the steps, frowning. "Why do you want
to get in? You want to go to the bank?"

"It's not even five to four yet. It shouldn't be closed."

Thami smiled pityingly. "Ha! You think this is America, people
looking at their watches all the time until they see if it is exactly four
o'clock, or exactly ten o'clock? Today they might stay open until
twenty minutes past four, tomorrow they might lock the door at ten
minutes before four. The way they feel. You know. Sometimes you
have a lot of work. Sometimes not much."

"God damn it, I've got to get in there!" Dyar pounded on the
gate some more, and called out: "Hey!"

Thami was used to this urgency on the part of foreigners. He
smiled. "You can get in tomorrow morning."

"Tomorrow morning hell. I *have* to get in now."

Thami yawned and stretched. "Well, I would like to help you,
but I can't do anything."

Pounding and calling out seemed fairly useless. Dyar continued
to do both, until a very thin Moroccan with a broom in his hand
appeared from a corner of the courtyard, and stood looking between
the bars.

"*Ili firmi!*" he said indignantly.

"Mr. Benzekri! I've got to see him!"

"*Ili firmi, m'sio.*" And to Thami: "*Qoullou rhadda f's sbah.*"
But Thami did not deign to notice the sweeper; he went back down the
steps into the zoco and shouted up to Dyar: "Come on!" Seeing that
the latter remained at the gate trying to argue with the man, he sat
down in a chair nearby on the sidewalk to wait until he had finished.

Presently Dyar came down to join him, muttering under his breath.
"The son of a bitch wouldn't even go and call Mr. Benzekri for
me."

Thami laughed. "Sit down. Have a drink. Be my guest." A
waiter had approached. Dyar threw himself into a chair. "Give me a
White Horse. No water," he said.

Thami ordered. Then he looked at Dyar and laughed again. He
reached over and slapped Dyar's knee. "Don't be so serious. No one is
going to die because you can't get in the bank today instead of
tomorrow. You can go tomorrow."

"Yes," said Dyar. Even as he said it he was thinking: Legally the
money belongs to whoever has it. And I've got it.

"You need money?" said Thami suddenly. "How much? I'll give
you some money. How much?"

"No thanks, Thami. I appreciate it. You're a good guy. Just let
me think. I just want to think a minute."

Thami was silent until the whiskey was brought. Then he began
to talk again, about an Englishman he had once known. The Englishman had invited him to go to Xauen with him, but for some
reason there had been difficulties at the frontier. Never very perceptive, he did not notice that Dyar was still sunk inside himself, for-
mulating, rejecting possibilities.

"*A votre santé, monsieur,*" said Thami, raising his glass expectantly.

"Yeah," said Dyar. "Yeah." And looking up suddenly: "Right.
Prosit." He drained his glass. He was thinking: if only Ramlal had
gotten the money yesterday morning instead of last night I'd be in the
clear. No Legation wondering when I'm going to phone. No Madame
Jouvenon. Damn Madame Jouvenon. He did not realize how illogical
his reasoning was at this point, how inextricably bound up with his
present decision was his involvement with that lady.

"Let's get out of here." He rose to his feet. The suddenness of the
remark and the tone in which it was said made Thami look up at him
wonderingly.

In the street, going down toward the port, he began to speak
confidentially, holding his mouth close to Thami's ear. "Can you run
that boat?"

"Well—"

"You can't run it. All right. Do you know anyone who can? How about the guy you bought it from? He can run it, can't he? Where is he now?"

"Where is he now?"

"Yes. Right now."

"He lives in Dradeb."

"Where's that?"

"You know," said Thami obligingly. "You go from the Zoco de Fuera into Bou Araqía. You go past the Moorish cemetery and you come to Cuatro Caminos—"

"Can we go there in a taxi?"

"Taxi? We don't need a taxi. We can walk. The taxi charges fifteen pesetas."

"We can get there in a taxi, though?"

Thami, looking increasingly surprised, said that they could.

"Come on!" Dyar rushed ahead, toward the cab-stand at the foot of the ramparts. Laughing and protesting, Thami followed. At last the American was behaving like an American. They got to the foot of the hill. Dyar looked at his watch. Ten after four. I'm glad I thought of *that*, he said to himself. "Hotel de la Playa," he told the driver. If Wilcox just happened to be at the hotel waiting for him, he could still have an alibi. Chocron had kept him so long that the Crédit Foncier was closed when he got there, so he had come back immediately to lock up the money until tomorrow. Wilcox could either take it with him, or leave it, as he liked. But if he returned to the hotel any later than this and happened to find Wilcox, there would be no way of explaining the time that had elapsed between four and whatever time he got there. "If you just do each thing as it comes along and keep calm you can get away with this. Get rattled and you're screwed for good," he told himself.

The sun had gone behind the high buildings on the hill, but it still shone on the freighters at anchor in the harbor; all their white paint was turning faintly orange in its light. Beyond them on its cliff stood the whitewashed tower of the lighthouse at Malabata.

At the hotel he had Thami wait in the cab. With his parcel he jumped out and went into the lobby. There was no sign of Wilcox. That was all right, but the more dangerous moment would be when he came back downstairs. Even then he could still say he had thought of locking it in one of his valises, then had decided to give it to the management to put into the hotel safe. The boy gave him his key and a telephone message, which he put into his pocket without reading. He ran upstairs. The air in his room was dead, colder by several degrees than the air outdoors. He laid his briefcase on the bed, quickly put into it his razor, shaving cream, blades, toothbrush, toothpase, comb and four handkerchiefs. Then he unwrapped the box and laid the bundles of bills in among the toilet articles. There was still room for a pair of shorts. The door was locked; if Wilcox rapped on it at this moment he would have time to take out the money and throw the briefcase into the closet. He felt in his pocket to see if his passport, wallet and express checks were all there. He stuffed a woolen scarf and a pair of gloves into the pocket of his overcoat and slung it over his arm, closed the briefcase, spun its Sesamee lock to triple zero, and looked once more around the room. Then, with a caution which he felt was absurd even as he used it, he unlocked the door and opened it. The corridor was empty. Through the window at the end he saw the distant dunes behind the beach; their shadows reached out along the flat sand toward the harbor. A radio upstairs was playing Flamenco music, but there was no sound in the halls or stairway.

"Let's go," he whispered, and he went quickly downstairs. Wilcox was not in the lobby. The taxi outside had not moved. He handed his key to the boy and walked out. "Good bye, Playa," he said under his breath.

"Now give that address to the driver."

"The Jilali?" Thami was mystified, but knowing something was in the air he had every intention of playing along until he satisfied his curiosity, both as to what Dyar was doing and as to whether there might be some money in it for him. He leaned forward and began to give the man complicated instructions.

"Come on! Let's get started!" Dyar cried, glancing anxiously down the Avenida de España. "You can do that on the way."

The cab backed and turned up the road that went over the hill. Now the setting sun shone directly into their faces; Dyar put on a pair of dark glasses, turned to Thami. "What did you pay for your boat?"

Thami gulped and floundered, saying: "Who, me?" which is

what any Moroccan would have said under similar circumstances; then, remembering that such an answer was calculated to infuriate any American, he quickly told him the only price he could think of, which was the true one.

"How's this?" said Dyar. "You rent the boat to me tonight for twenty-five hundred pesetas, and I'll give you another twenty-five hundred to come along and see that I get where I want to go. You'll have your boat and your five thousand."

The emotions engendered in Thami by the unfamiliar situation caused him further to abandon his European habits of thought. Good luck, like bad luck, comes directly from Allah to the recipient; the intermediary is of little importance save as a lever to help assure the extraction of the maximum blessing. "I have no money for *gasolina*," objected Thami.

By the time they got to the crowded main street of the suburb that was Dradeb, they had reached an agreement on all the main points of finance; the Jilali remained an uncertain factor, but Thami was optimistic. "I'll tell him seven hundred fifty and then we can go up to one thousand if we have to," he said, figuring on a fifty percent split (which might not be so easy to get, he reflected, considering that with his five thousand pesetas the Jilali was not immediately in need of money.)

The cab drew up to the curb and stopped in front of a grocery store. Thami leaped out, disappeared down one of the twilit alleys, was back to make inquiries at the shop, and hurried ahead up the main street. The driver got out and walked in the other direction.

Left alone in the taxi, oblivious of the inquisitive stares of passers-by, Dyar relaxed voluptuously, savoring the first small delights of triumph. It was already a very pleasant thing to have Thami rushing around out there, intent on helping him.

Then he remembered the message the boy at the hotel had given him. He took it out of his pocket and snapped on the overhead light. "*Llame Vd. al 28-01*", it said, and he knew that was Daisy de Valverde's number. The briefcase in his hand, he got out and stepped into the grocery store. By now it was fairly dark in the street, and there was only one candle in here to add to the failing blue daylight that still came through the door. A placid Soussi sat behind the counter, his eyes almost closed. Dyar saw the telephone on a crate behind the broken Coca-Cola cooler. It was a dial phone: he was thankful for that. He had to strike a match to see the numbers.

Surprisingly, Daisy herself answered. "You villain," she said. "You just got my message? I called hours ago. *Can* you come to dinner? All very informal, all very *private*, I might even add. Luis is in Casa. I'm in bed. Not really ill. Only sciatica. Just you and I, and I should love it if you could come. About seven? So we can talk? It'll be wonderful to see you, darling."

He laid the money for the call on the counter; the Soussi nodded his head once. When he got to the taxi, the driver was back at the wheel, opening a pack of cigarettes. He got in, slammed the door, and sat waiting. It seemed a perfect solution to the problem of dinner; it would keep him completely out of the streets, out of the town.

Presently he saw Thami coming along toward the cab. He had someone with him. He came up, opened the door and leaned in. "I found him," he announced, pleased with the financial arrangements he had just completed, on the way from Jilali's house.

"Fine. Now we go to your house," said Dyar. "Stick him in front and let's go."

The Jilali's name was Zaki; he was a man of thirty-five (which meant that he looked fifty), unkempt in his attire and very much in need of a shave, so that to Dyar his appearance suggested an extra in a pirate film.

"Does he understand any English?" he asked Thami.

"That man? Ha! He doesn't even understand Spanish!" Thami sounded triumphant. "*Verdad, amigo?*" he called to the one in front.

"*Chnou?*" said the Jilali, not turning around.

The street where Thami lived became increasingly bumpy and full of puddles whose depth it was impossible to judge; the driver suddenly stopped the car and announced that he would proceed no further. There ensued an argument which promised to be lengthy. Dyar got out and surveyed the street with distaste. The houses were ramshackle, some with second stories still in construction, and their front doors gave directly on to the muddy lane, no room having been left for a future laying of sidewalks. Impatiently he called to Thami. "Have him wait here, then. Hurry up!" The driver however, after locking the car, insisted on accompanying them. "He says we owe him sixty-five pesetas already," confided Thami. Dyar grunted.

Thami entered first, to get his wife out of the way, while the others waited outside in the dark.

"You stay here," Dyar said to the driver, who appeared satisfied once he had seen which house they were going to enter.

Soon Thami came to the door and motioned them in, leading the way through the unlit patio into a narrow room where a radio was playing. The mattress along the wall was covered with cheap green and yellow brocade; above it hung a group of large gilt-framed photographs of men wearing gandouras and fezzes. Three alarm clocks, all ticking, sat atop a hanging cupboard at the end of the room, but each one showed a different hour. Ranging along a lower shelf beneath them was a succession of dusty but unused paper cups which had been placed with care so as to alternate with as many small red figurines of plaster, representing Santa Claus; below and to both sides, the wall was papered with several dozen colored brochures, all identical, each bearing the photograph of an enormous toothbrush with a brilliant blue plastic handle. "DENTOLINE, LA BROSSE A DENTS PAR EXCELLENCE," they said, over and over. The radio on the floor in the corner was turned up to its full volume; Om Kalsoum sang a tortured lament, and behind her voice an orchestra sputtered and wailed.

"Sit down!" shouted Thami to Dyar. He knelt and reduced the force of the music a little. As Dyar stepped over to the mattress, the electric light bulb which swung at the end of a long cord from the center of the ceiling struck him on the forehead. "Sorry," he said, as the light waved crazily back and forth. The Jilali had removed his shoes at the door and was already seated at one end of the mattress, his legs tucked under him, swaying a bit from side to side with the music.

Dyar called across to Thami: "Hey! Cut off the funeral! Would you mind? We've got a lot to talk about, and not much time."

Out of the silence that followed came the sound of the baby screaming in the next room. Dyar began to talk.

17

WHAT DID IT MEAN, reflected Daisy, to be what your friends called a forceful woman? Although they intended to mean it as such, they did not manage to make it a flattering epithet; she knew that. It was adverse criticism. If you said a woman was forceful, you meant that she got what she wanted in too direct a manner, that she was not enough of a woman, that she was unsubtle, pushing. It was almost as much of an insult as to say that a man had a weak character. Yet her closest friends were in the habit of using the word openly to describe her; "even to my face," she thought, with mingled resentment and satisfaction. It was as if, in accepting the contemporary fallacy that women should have the same aims and capacities as men, they assumed that any quality which was a virtue in a man was equally desirable in a woman. But when she heard the word "forceful" being used in connection with herself, even though she knew it was perfectly true and not intended as derogation, she immediately felt like some rather ungraceful predatory animal, and the sensation did not please her. There were very concrete disadvantages attached to being classified that way: in any situation where it would be natural to expect an expression of concern for her well-being on the part of the males in the group, it was always the other women about whom they fretted. The general opinion, often uttered aloud, was that Daisy could take care of herself. And how many other husbands went off and left their wives for five or six days, alone in the house with the servants? It was not that she minded being alone—on the contrary, it was rather a rest for her, since she never entertained when Luis was away. But the fact that he took it so much as a matter of course that she would not mind—for some reason this nettled her, although she could not have found a logical explanation for her annoyance. "I suppose one can't have one's cake and eat it too," she would say to herself at least once during each of his absences. If you had spent your childhood astride a horse, riding with your four brothers around the fifty thousand acres of an estancia, it was natural that you should become the sort of woman she had become, and you could hardly expect men to feel protective toward you. As a matter of fact, it was often quite the reverse: she sometimes found her male friends looking to her for moral support, and she always gave it unhesitatingly even though she was aware as she did so that at each moment she was moving farther from the privileged position modern woman is expected to occupy vis-à-vis her male acquaintances.

The majority of Daisy's friends were men: men liked her and she prided herself on knowing how to handle them. Yet her first two husbands had died, the one leaving her with a child and the other with a considerable fortune. The little girl she had more or less abandoned to the care of her father's family in Buenos Aires; the fortune however she had kept. At loose ends in London, and for want of anything better to do, she had decided to set out in leisurely fashion around the world. The trip took three years; she ended up in the south of France 'during the autumn of 1938, where she took a small house at Saint Paul du Var, intensely conscious of her solitude and with the feeling that somehow her life had not yet begun.

It was at the Palm Beach in Cannes that she had first met Luis, a thin and dramatically dark Spaniard who wore an opera cape and handled it as arrogantly as a matador his muleta, who was rude to everyone without being actually offensive, who used incredibly obscene language and yet managed to remain very much a gentleman. He was the owner of several vast estates in Andalucía which he had very little hope of recovering, even assuming that Franco were able to put an end to the Republican resistance. "They are all eediot!" he would bellow to the entire casino. "All thee Spaniard can eat sheet!" Little by little Daisy found herself thinking with admiration of this strange man who bragged that he had never read a book and was unable to write more than his own signature. He managed horses as well as the most seasoned gaucho, was as good a marksman as she, and had not a trace of sentimentality or condescension in his character. He was as dry, hard and impersonal as a rock, and she once told him that he reminded her of certain Andalucían landscapes. She was scarcely prepared, however, for his reaction, which came immediately and with astonishing force. Turning to her with the violence of one who has just been insulted, he shouted: "That is a declaration of love!"

seized her in his arms, and began to make love to her with such brutality that she cried out and struck him in the face. The incident had taken place in the bar of the Carlton, in front of several people, and after a few moments of shame and fury in the ladies' room, to which she had retired when he had released her, she had come out and apologized to him for her behavior, expecting him, naturally enough, to do likewise. But he had laughed, paid the barman, and walked out.

Afterward, each time they met (since meetings were unavoidable in Cannes) he inquired if she still admired the Andalucían landscape as much as ever. It would have been a violation of her code to do anything but admit that she did. Her answers gave him immense satisfaction. "Aaah!" he would cry delightedly, *"Ya ves?"* for they had fallen into the habit of speaking Spanish together. He had a small villa at Le Cannet, packed with furniture and paintings he had succeeded in getting out of Spain, and she used to drive down sometimes in the late afternoon and visit him. Since it was well known that he sold a picture from time to time in order to go on living, she did not hesitate, when one day she saw a Goya she particularly admired, to ask him its price. The Marqués de Valverde went into a rare fury. "Andalucía is not for sale!" he yelled. "Don't be absurd," said Daisy. "I'll give you a good price for it. You need the money." But her host continued to rail, saying that he would rather put his foot through the Goya than let her have it, whatever sum she might be prepared to give him for it. Understanding that all this vehemence, although perfectly sincere, was merely a part of the abnormally developed pride which governs the behavior of the Spanish peasant or aristocrat, Daisy made an audacious suggestion. "I like that picture," she said, "and if you won't sell it to me you must give it to me." The Marqués had smiled with delight "Anything in my house is yours for the asking," he had replied. Their friendship had begun at that moment. The man was magnificent, she decided, and it was not surprising that from being inseparable friends they soon turned to being passionate lovers. Daisy was slightly over thirty, her face radiant with a healthy, strident kind of beauty that perfectly suited her statuesque figure. It was inevitable that a man like Luis should fall in love with her, that having done so he should perceive much more in her character than he had suspected, and thus determine to marry her, in order to own her completely. It was also inevitable that once having added her to his list of possessions he should cease to be in love with her, but Daisy knew this beforehand and did not care, because she also knew that she would never cease to admire him, whatever he might do, and she was sure she would be able to keep him, which for her, an eminently practical woman, was after all the main consideration.

And so to Daisy there was nothing surprising about Luis' first infidelities. After a very small wedding in the church at Saint Paul du Var they had closed their respective houses and shipped Luis' more valuable belongings to Rio, on the advice of Daisy's banker. "Jewish bankers always know when there's going to be a war," said Daisy. "You can trust them implicitly." They went off to Brazil, the war came, and they stayed there until it was over. Luis had begun with a nightclub dancer, had continued with chambermaids, and eventually had moved on to one of Daisy's own friends, a certain Senhora da Cunha, and Daisy never had said a word to show that she knew. Luis was perceptive enough to realize that she could not help being aware of his indiscretions, but whether she minded or not, he was bound to continue them, and they both knew this, so that the matter remained forever unmentioned, as if by mutual agreement. For a while, when they had first come to Tangier at the end of the war, there had been no one. Daisy knew this was merely a quiet interval; soon enough it would end. When his business trips to Casablanca had begun, she understood. Even now she had no idea who it was, nor, she kept telling herself, did she care too much. Still, somehow she always found herself making an effort to find out who the woman was, and if possible to meet her, because she felt each time that the knowledge gave her the key to yet another chamber of Luis' mysterious personality. The more she could learn about his mistress, the more she would know about him. Having been brought up in a world of Latins, Daisy believed that promiscuity was as proper for men as it was improper for women. She would have thought it shocking for her even to consider the idea of having a lover. For a decent woman there was no possibility of anyone but her husband, and since she was so firmly decided on this score, she allowed herself to follow a pattern of behavior which to women of less resolute character often seemed highly questionable. Her reputation among the feminine members of the English colony was not all that it might have been, precisely because she knew where she stood and could allow herself liberties that would have proven disastrous in the case of most of the others. Knowing herself, she had respect for herself; knowing the others, she had none for them, and thus it was of little importance to her what they whispered about her. What, she wondered, could they think but the very worst, if they heard that she had invited this young American to the Villa Hesperides during Luis' absence? And now as she lay in her bed and methodically searched to unearth her motives, she felt a tiny chill of apprehension. Was she completely safe from herself with regard to this young man? *He* was harmless enough; (she smiled as she remembered his ingenuousness, his apparent innocence of the world, and the impression she had of his utter helplessness in the face of it). But even the most innocuous element by itself could prove to be dangerous in its meeting with a different element. She thought about it, and felt small doubts rising. "Or am I really hoping that something will happen, and is this just my way of punishing myself?" It was hard to say. She reached for the bell button that lay on the table among a welter of perfume bottles and medicines, and pushed it. A maid knocked on the door. "Have Hugo come up," she told her.

"Ah, Hugo," she said when he appeared. "If the telephone rings this evening while Mr. Dyar is here, I've gone out to dinner and you don't know where, or what time I'll be back." After he had closed the door she got out of bed, wincing a little, more in anticipation of pain than because she felt it, and walked across the room to the window. It was a little before six and almost dark, the water down there was black and choppy, and the fading colorless sky made it look cold. Spain had disappeared, there were only the rocks and the sea, and soon there would be less than that: only the roar of the waves in the darkness. She pulled the curtains across all the windows carefully and turned on an electric heater by her dressing table. The little spotlights came on. She seated herself in front of the mirror and set to work on her face. It would be quicker than usual tonight because she knew exactly what light she would be in all during the evening. As she worked she found herself wondering exactly what this rather strange Mr. Dyar thought of her. "An aging nymphomaniac, most likely," she suggested, determining to be as realistic and ruthless with herself as she could.

But then she asked herself why she was being so violent; it could only be in order to kill whatever hope might be lurking within—hope that somehow he might find her attractive. "But that's nonsense," she objected. "What do I want of a callow, dull man like that? He's a definite bore." However, she could not convince herself. He did not bore her; he was like an unanswered riddle, a painting seen in semi-darkness, its subject only guessed at, which could prove to be of something quite different once one looked at it in the light. When she reminded herself that he could not possibly turn out to be anything worthwhile or interesting, even if she did manage to understand him, the fact that he was mysterious remained, and that, for her, was the important thing about him. But why should she find any mystery in a person like that? Again she experienced a feeling of misgiving, a pleasurable little shudder of fear. "I can manage him," she said to the half-finished face in the blinding mirror, "but can I manage *you?*"

The distant, multiple sounds of domestic activity came through the thick walls of the house, a series of muted, scarcely audible thuds rather than as noises actually distinguishable from one another; she, nevertheless, had learned through the years to interpret them. The pantry door swinging to, Mario's evening tour of the lower floor, closing the shutters and drawing the curtains, Inez climbing the staircase, Paco going out to the kennels with the dogs' dinner, she knew without question when each was happening, as the usher in a theatre knows from the dialogue exactly how the stage looks at any given moment, without needing to glance at it. Above these muffled sounds now emerged another, heard through the window: an automobile coming up the main road, turning into the driveway, stopping somewhere between the gate and the front door. Unconsciously she waited to hear it continue, to hear the car doors slam shut, the faint buzz of the bell in the kitchen, and the business of Hugo's getting to the front entrance. But nothing happened. The silence outside went on for so long that she began to doubt she had really heard any car come into the driveway; it must have continued up the mountain.

When she had finished she turned off the spots, slipped into a new black and white négligé that Balenciaga had made for her in Madrid, rearranged the pillows, and got back into bed, thinking that perhaps it had been a very bad idea, after all, to invite Mr. Dyar alone for dinner. He might easily be made shy by the absence of other guests, and particularly by the fact that Luis was not there. "If he's tongue-tied, what in God's name shall I talk to him about?" she thought. With drinks enough he might be more at ease, but there was the worse danger of his having too many. Spurred on by her nervousness to speculations of disaster, she began to wish she had not acted so quickly on her impulse to invite him. But he would arrive at any moment now. She shut her eyes and tried to relax in the way a Yogi at Benares had taught her to do. It was only partially successful; nevertheless, the effort made time pass.

Suddenly there was a knock at the door. Hugo entered, announcing Mr. Dyar.

18

DAISY STRUGGLED TO a sitting position, a little resentful at having been caught unawares. Dyar held a briefcase in his hand; he looked more wide-awake than she remembered him. She wondered in passing why Hugo had not taken the briefcase from him along with his coat, and even more fleetingly she wondered why she had not heard the taxi arrive, but he was advancing toward the bed, and Hugo was going out and closing the door.

"Hi!" he said, shaking her hand vigorously. "I hope you're sicker than you look, because you look fine." He bent over and pushed the briefcase under the table beside the bed.

"I'm not really sick at all. It's just a twinge of sciatica that comes now and then. Nothing at all, darling. But I'm such a God-damned crybaby and I loathe pain so, that I simply pamper myself. And here I am. Sit down." She indicated the foot of the bed.

He obeyed, and she looked at him attentively. It seemed to her that his eyes were unusually bright, that his whole face shone with an unaccustomed physical glow. At the same time he struck her as being nervous and preoccupied. None of these things tallied with what she remembered about him; he had been restless at the Beidaoui party, but it was a restlessness that came from boredom or apathy, whereas at the moment he looked uneasy, intense, almost apprehensive. They talked a bit; his remarks were not the sort she would have expected from him; neither more intelligent nor more stupid, they nevertheless seemed to come from a different person. "But then, how do I know what he's like? I scarcely know him at all," she reflected.

"It feels good to get inside where it's warm," he said. "It's chilly out."

"I take it your taxi wasn't heated. Unless the car was delivered last week the heater would be broken by now. The Moroccans have an absolute genius for smashing things. If you want to get rid of anything, just let a Moroccan touch it, and it'll fall to pieces as he hands it back to you. They're fantastic! *What* destructive people! God! Drinks will be along any minute. Tell me about yourself in the meantime." She pushed herself further back into the mound of pillows behind her and peered out at him with the expression of one about to be told a long story.

Dyar glanced at her sharply. "About myself," he said, looking away again. "Nothing much to tell. More of the same. I think you know most of it." Now that everything was arranged, with Thami waiting in the mimosa scrub below the garden, and the Jilali dispatched to fetch the boat and bring it to the beach at Oued el Ihud at the foot of the cliffs, he was eager to be off, anxious lest some unforeseen event occur which could be a snag in his plans. The arrival of Wilcox, for instance, to pay an unexpected after-dinner call—that was one idea whose infinite possibilities of calamity paralyzed him; he forced himself to think of something else.

"Have you seen our silly Jack since night before last?" asked Daisy suddenly, as if she were inside Dyar's mind. He felt such acute alarm that he made a great effort to turn his head slowly and look at her with a carefully feigned expression of preoccupation turning to casual interest. "I'm worried about him," she was saying. "And I was certainly not reassured by your little description of his behavior."

But he thought: "Night before last? Why night before last? What happened then?" In his mind the party at the Beidaoui Palace had been weeks ago; it did not occur to him that she was referring to that. "No, I haven't seen him," he said, forgetting even that he had had breakfast with him that very morning. Hugo entered, wheeling a table covered with bottles and glasses. "I've learned one thing in my life, if nothing else," Daisy said. "And that is, that it's utterly useless to give anyone advice. Otherwise I'd ask Luis to talk with him. He might be able to worm something out of him. Because I have a distinct feeling he's up to something, and whatever it is, he won't get away with it. I'll wager you ten pounds he doesn't. Ten pounds! Why have you brought just these few pieces of ice? Bring a whole bowl of it," she called after Hugo as he closed the door behind him.

"I don't know," Dyar said. "Don't know what?" he thought, suppressing a tickling desire to laugh aloud. "Jack's pretty careful. He's nobody's fool, you know. I can't see him getting into any serious trouble, somehow." He felt that he must put a stop to this conversation or it would bring him bad luck. The mere fact that he was in a position for the moment to be offhand about the subject, even though his nonchalance was being forced upon him, seemed to indicate likely disaster. "Pride before a fall," he thought. It was a moment for humility, a moment to touch wood. The expression *get away with it* bothered him. "I don't know," he said again.

"Ten pounds!" Daisy reiterated, handing him a whiskey-soda. He sipped it slowly, telling himself that above all things he must not get drunk. At the end of ten minutes or so she noticed that he was not drinking.

"Something's wrong with your drink!" she exclaimed. "What have I done? Give it to me. What does it need?" She reached out for the glass.

"No, no, no!" he objected, hanging on to it. "It's fine. I just don't feel like drinking, somehow. I don't know why."

"Aha!" she cried, as though she had made a great discovery. "I see! Your system's hyperacid, darling. It's just the moment for a little majoun. I don't feel much like whiskey myself tonight." She made a place for her glass among the bottles and tubes on the night-table, opened the drawer and took out a small silver box which she handed him.

"Have a piece," she said. "Just don't tell anyone about it. All the little people in Tangier'd be scandalized, all but the Moroccans, of course. They eat it all the time. It's the only thing allowed the poor darlings, with alcohol forbidden. But a European, a Nazarene? Shock-

ing! Unforgivable! Depths of depravity! Tangier, sink-hole of in-
iquity, as your American journalists say. 'Your correspondent has it
on reliable authority that certain members of the English colony begin
their evening meal with a dish of majoun, otherwise known as
hashish.' Good God!''

He was looking with interest at the six cubes of greenish black
candy which exactly filled the box. "What is it?" he said.

"Majoun, darling. Majoun." She reached out, took a square and
bit it in half. "Have a piece. It's not very good, but it's the best in
Tangier. My sweet old Ali gets it for me." She rang the bell.

The candy was gritty, its flavor a combination of figs, ginger,
cinnamon and licorice; there was also a pungent herbal taste which he
could not identify. "What's it supposed to do?" he asked with curiosity.

She put the box back onto its shelf. "The servants would be
horrified. Isn't it ghastly, living in fear of one's own domestics? But
I've never known a place like Tangier for wagging tongues. God! The
place is incredible." She paused and looked at him. "What does it do?"
she said. "It's miraculous. It's what we've all been waiting for all these
years. If you've never had it, you can't possibly understand. But I call
it the key to a forbidden way of thought." She leaned down and patted
his arm. "I'm not going mystical on you, darling, although I easily
could if I let myself go. J'ai de quoi, God knows. There's nothing
mystical about majoun. It's all very down to earth and real." A maid
knocked. Daisy spoke to her briefly in Spanish. "I've ordered tea," she
explained, as the girl wheeled the table of drinks away.

"Tea!"

She laughed merrily. "It's absolutely essential."

To Dyar, who had pulled his left cuff up so he could glance
surreptitiously now and then at his watch, the time was creeping by
with incredible slowness. Daisy talked about black magic, about exhibi-
tions of hatha-yoga she had seen in Travancore, about the impossibility of understanding Islamic legal procedure in Morocco unless one
took for granted the everyday use of spells and incantations. At length
the tea came, and they each had three cups. Dyar listened apathetically; it all sounded to him like decoration, like the Pekineses,
incense-burners and Spanish shawls with which certain idle women

filled their apartments, back in New York. He let her talk for a while. Then he said: "But what's the story about that candy? What is it? Some kind of dope, isn't it? I think you were cheated. I don't feel anything."

She smiled. "Yes, I know. Everyone says that. But it's very subtle. One must know which direction to look in for the effect. If you expect to feel drunk, you're looking the wrong way, it takes twice as long, and you miss half the pleasure."

"But what *is* the pleasure? Do *you* feel anything, right now?"

She closed her eyes and remained silent a moment, a slightly beatific expression coming to rest on her upturned face. "Yes," she answered at length. "Definitely."

"You do?" The incredulity in his voice made her open her eyes and look at him an instant reproachfully. "You don't believe me? I'm not just imagining things. But I've had it before and I know exactly what to expect. Darling, you're not comfortable there on the edge of the bed. Draw up that big chair and relax."

When he was sprawled in the chair facing the bed, he said to her: "Well, then, suppose you try and tell me what it feels like. I might as well get some benefit out of the stuff, even if it comes second-hand."

"Oh, at the moment it's nothing very exciting. Just a slight buzzing in my ears and an accelerated pulse."

"Sounds like fun," he scoffed. For a few minutes he had forgotten that this evening he was waiting above all for time to pass. Now he turned his arm a bit, to see the face of his watch; it was eight-twenty. He had set the meeting with Thami for no definite hour, not knowing exactly when he would be able to get away, but he had assured him it would not be after midnight. The understanding was that the Jilali would go back to town to the port, and would bring the boat to a small beach just west of Oued el Ihud, also not later than twelve o'clock. In the meantime Thami was to sit and wait, a little below the far end of the garden, so that when Dyar left the house he could lead him down across the face of the mountain, directly to the beach. Thami had insisted he would not be bored by waiting so long: he had his supper and his kif pipe with him.

"Yes," Daisy was saying. "If I let too much time go by, I shan't be able to tell you anything at all. One becomes fantastically inarticulate at a certain point. Not always, but it can happen. One thinks one's making sense, and so one is, I daresay, but in a completely different world of thought."

It seemed to him that the wind outside was rising a little, or else a window had opened a minute ago to let the sound in. He turned his head; the drawn curtains did not move. "What are you looking at?" she asked. He did not answer. At the same time he had a senseless desire to turn his head in the other direction and look at the other wall, because he thought he had seen a slight movement on that side of the room. Instead, he pulled out a pack of cigarettes and offered her one.

"No thanks, darling. I couldn't. You have a house. You see?"

"What?" He stared at her.

"I'm explaining, darling, or at least trying to. You have a house. In the middle of some modest grounds, where you're used to walking about." She waited, apparently to be certain he was following her argument. Since he said nothing, she went on. "You can always see the house. At least, from most parts of the property, but in any case, you know it's there. It's the center of your domain. Call it your objective idea about yourself."

He toyed with the pack of cigarettes, extracted one and lighted it, frowning.

"Say it's the idea of yourself by which you measure what's real. You have to keep it straight in your mind, keep it in working order. Like a compass."

He was making an effort to go along with the sense of what she was saying, but all he could follow was the words. "Like a compass," he repeated, as if he thought that might help.

"And so. You know every path, every plant, every stone on the grounds. But one day while you're out walking you suddenly catch sight of what looks like a path in a spot where you've never noticed, nor even suspected one before." Slowly her voice was taking on dramatic fervor. "The entrance is perhaps half hidden by a bush. You go over and look, and find there actually is a path there. You pull the bush aside, take a few steps down the path, and see ahead of you a grove of trees you never before knew existed. You're dumfounded! You go through the grove touching the tree trunks to be sure they're really there, because you can't believe it. . . ."

This time he jerked his head quickly to the left, to catch whatever was over there by the windows, staring at the blank expanse of unmoving white curtain with disbelief. "Just relax," he said to himself, as he turned back to see if she had noticed him; she seemed not to have. "Relax, and be careful. Be careful." Why he was adding the second admonition he did not know, save that he was conscious of an overwhelming sense of uneasiness, as if a gigantic hostile figure towered above him, leaning over his shoulder, and he believed the only way to combat the feeling was to remain quite calm so that he could control his movements.

". . . Then through the trees you see that the path leads up a hill. 'But there is no hill!' you exclaim, probably aloud by this time, you're so excited and muddled. So you hurry on, climb the hill, which is rather high, and when you get to the top you see the countryside, perfectly familiar on all sides. You can identify every detail. And there's your house below, just where it should be. Nothing is wrong. It's not a dream and you've not gone mad. If you hadn't seen the house, of course, you'd know you'd gone mad. But it's there. Everything is all right." She sighed deeply, as if in relief. "It's just upsetting to find that grove of trees and that strange hill in the middle of your land. Because it can't be there, and yet it is. You're forced to accept it. But it's how you think once you've accepted it that makes what I call the forbidden way of thought. Forbidden, of course, by your own mind, until the moment you accept the fact of the hill. That's majoun for you. You find absolutely new places inside yourself, places you feel simply couldn't be a part of you, and yet there they are. Does what I said mean anything at all to you, or have I been ranting like a maniac?"

"Oh, no. Not at all." All his effort was going to giving a sincere ring to the words. An intense silence followed, which he felt he was also making, as he had uttered the words, only it went on for an endless length of time, like telegraph wires across miles of waste land. A pole, a pole, a pole, a pole, the wires strung between, the flat horizon lying beyond the eyes' reach. Then someone said: "Not at all" again, and it was he who had said it.

"What the hell is this?" he asked himself in a sudden rage. He had promised himself not to get drunk; it was the most important thing to remember while he was at the Villa Hesperides this evening. "I'm not drunk," he thought triumphantly, and he found himself on his feet, stretching. "It's stuffy in here," he remarked, wondering if she would think he was being rude.

She laughed. "Come, now, darling. Admit you're feeling the majoun at last."

"Why? Because I say it's stuffy? Nope. I'm damned if I feel anything." He was not being obstinate; already he had forgotten the little side-trip his mind had made a moment ago. Now that he was standing up the air in the room did not seem close. He walked over to a window, pulled the heavy curtain aside, and peered out into the dark.

"You don't mind being alone here at night?" he said.

"Sometimes," she answered vaguely, wondering if his question would be followed by others. "Stop thinking like that," she told herself with annoyance.

He still stood by the window. "You're pretty high up here."

"About six hundred feet."

"Have you ever been down to the bottom?"

"Over those rocks? God, no! Do you think I'm a chamois?"

He began to walk around the room slowly, his hands behind him, stepping from one zebra skin to the next as if they were rocks in a stream. There was no doubt that he felt strange, but it was not any way he had expected to feel, and so he laid it to his own perturbation. The evening was going to be agonizingly long. "I'd like to be saying good night right now," he thought. Everything he took the trouble to look at carefully seemed to be bristling with an intense but unde-cipherable meaning: Daisy's face with its halo of white pillows, the light pouring over the array of bottles on the table, the glistening black floor and the irregular black and white stripes on the skins at his feet, the darker and more distant parts of the room by the windows where the motionless curtains almost touched the floor. Each thing was uttering a wordless but vital message which was a key, a symbol, but which there was no hope of seizing or understanding. And inside himself, now that he became conscious of it, in his chest more than anywhere else, there was a tremendous trembling pressure, as though he were about to explode. He breathed in various ways to see if he could change it, and then he realized that his heart was beating too fast. "Ah, hell," he said aloud, because he was suddenly frightened.

"Come and sit down, darling. What's the matter with you? You're as restless as a cat. Are you hungry? Or has the majoun got you?"

"No," he said shortly. "Nothing's got me." He thought that sounded absurd. "If I go and sit down," he thought, "I'll get up again, and she'll know something's the matter." He felt he must make every effort to prevent Daisy from knowing what was going on inside him. The objects in the room, its walls and furniture, the air around his head, the idea that he was in the room, that he was going to eat dinner, that the cliffs, and the sea were below, all these things were playing a huge, inaudible music that was rising each second toward a climax which he knew would be unbearable when it was reached. "It's going to get worse."

He swallowed with difficulty. "Something's got to happen in a minute. Something's got to happen." He reached the chair and stood behind it, his hands on the back. Daisy looked at him distraughtly. She was thinking: "Why have I never dared tell Luis about majoun?" She knew he would disapprove, if only because it was a native concoction. But that was not why she had kept silent. She had never told *anyone* about it; the taking of it was a supremely private ritual. The experience was such a personal one that she had never wanted to share it with another. And here she was, undergoing it with someone she scarcely knew. All at once she wanted to tell him, so that he might know he was the first to be invited into this inner chamber of her life. She took a deep breath, and instead, said petulantly: "For God's sake, sit down. You look like a Calvinist rector telling his flock about Hell."

He laughed and sat in the chair. Under the table in the shadow he saw his briefcase. The tremulous feeling inside him suddenly expressed a great elation; it was still the same sensation, but it had changed color. The relief made him laugh again.

"Really!" exclaimed Daisy. "You may as well admit you're feeling the majoun. Because I know damned well you are. At least admit it to yourself. You'll have more fun with it. You've been fighting it for the past ten minutes. That's not the way to treat it. Just sit back and let it take its course. It's in you, and you can't get rid of it, so you may as well enjoy it."

"How about you?" He would not admit it.

"I told you long ago I was feeling it. At the moment I'm about to take off on a non-stop flight to Arcturus."

"You are, are you?" His voice was unfriendly. "Personally, I think the stuff is a fake. I'm not saying it has no effect at all, but I don't call feeling jumpy and having my heart beat twice too fast, I don't call that a kick, myself."

She laughed commiseratingly. "You should have drunk your whiskey, darling. You'd have felt more at home with it. *Mais enfin.* . . ." She sat up and rang the bell. "I expect the kitchen is in a turmoil because we're taking so long with our tea."

19

ALL DURING THE DINNER Daisy talked unceasingly; often Dyar found himself replying in monosyllables, not because he was uninterested, although occasionally he had very little idea what she was saying, but because half the time he was off somewhere else in a world of his own. He did not know what he was thinking about, but his brain was swarming with beginnings of thoughts fastened on to beginnings of other thoughts. To receive so many took all his attention; even had they not been incommunicable he would have had no desire to impart them to Daisy. It was as if his mind withdrew to a remote, dark corner of his being. Then it would come out into the light again, and he would find himself actually believing that he sat having dinner at a small table in a quiet room while a woman lay in bed nearby eating the same food from a tray.

"You're awfully untalkative," Daisy said presently. "I'd never have given the majoun to you if I'd known it was going to make a statue out of you."

Her words made him uncomfortable. "Oh," he said. And what seemed to him a long time later: "I'm all right."

"Yes, I daresay you are. But you make a God-damned unsatisfactory dinner partner."

Now he became fully present, began to stammer apologies more florid than the occasion warranted. "I couldn't feel worse," he said finally, "if I'd kicked you. I don't know what was the matter with me. It must be that stuff that did something crazy to me."

"It's all my fault. Don't give it another thought, poor darling."

He would not have it that way. "No, no, no," he said. "There's no excuse." And in an excess of contrition he rose and sat down heavily on the bed beside her. The tray tipped perilously.

"Be careful, darling!" she exclaimed. "I shall have peas and wine all over me in another moment." But he had already seized her hand and was covering it with quick kisses. He was floating in the air, impelled by a hot, dry wind which enveloped him, voluptuously caressed him. For the space of two long breaths she was silent, and he heard his own breathing, and confused it with the sound of the wind that was blowing him along, above the vast, bare, sunlit valley. The skin of her arm was smooth, the flesh was soft. He pulled her further toward him, over the balancing tray.

"Be careful!" she cried again in alarm, as the tray tilted in his direction. "No, no!"

The wine glass went over first; the icy stain on his thigh made him jump convulsively. Then, very slowly it seemed to him, plates slid and tumbled toward him as the tray overturned and buried the lower part of his body in a confusion of china, glassware and warm food. "Oh!" she cried. But he held her more tightly with one arm, sweeping the tray and some of the dishes onto the floor with the other. And he scrambled up to be completely near her, so that there were only a few thicknesses of wet cloth, a fork and a spoon or two between them, and presently, after a short struggle with pieces of clinging clothing, nothing but a few creamed mushrooms.

"For God's sake, no! Not like this!" she was on the point of shouting, but as if she sensed how tenuous was the impulse that moved him, she thought: "At this very moment you're hoping desperately that nothing will happen to stop this. So you did want it to happen. Why wouldn't you admit it? Why can't you be frank? You wanted it; let it happen, even this way. Even this way." And so she said nothing, reaching out and turning off the light beside the bed. A word, she told herself, could have broken the thread by which he hung suspended from the sky; he would have fallen with a crash into the room, a furiously embarrassed young man with no excuse for his behavior, no escape from his predicament, no balm for his injured pride. "He's very sweet. And a little mad. So compact. Not at all like Luis. But could I really love any man I don't respect? I don't respect him at all. How can one respect an impersonal thing? He's scarcely human. He's not conscious of me as me. As another natural force, perhaps, yes. But that's not enough. I could never love him. But he's sweet. God knows, he's sweet."

The soft endless earth spread out beneath him, glowing with sunlight, untouched by time, uninhabited, belonging wholly to him. How far below it lay, he could not have said, gliding soundlessly through the pure luminous air that admitted no possibility of distance or dimension. Yet he could touch its smooth resilient contours, smell its odor of sun, and even taste the salt left in its pores by the sea in some unremembered age. And this flight—he had always known it was to be made, and that he would make it. This was a corner of existence he had known was there, but until now had not been able to reach; at present, having discovered it, he also knew he would be able to find his way back another time. Something was being completed; there would be less room for fear. The thought filled him with an ineffable happiness. "Ah, God," he murmured aloud, not knowing that he did so.

Beyond the windows the rising wind blew through the cypresses, bringing with it occasionally the deeper sound of the sea below. Regularly the drawn white curtains on one side of the room glowed white as the lighthouse's beam flashed across it. Daisy coughed.

"You're a slut," she said to herself. "How could you ever have allowed this to happen? But it's ghastly! The door's not locked. One of the servants may knock at any minute. Just collect yourself and do something. Do something!"

She coughed again.

"Darling, this is dreadful," she said softly, smiling in the dark, trying to keep her voice free of reproach. He did not answer; he might have been dead. "Darling," she said again hesitantly. Still he gave no sign of having heard her. For a moment she drifted back into her thoughts. If one could only let go, even for a few seconds, if only one could cease caring about everything, but really everything, what a wonderful thing it would be. But that would probably be death. Life means caring, is one long struggle to keep from going to pieces. If you let yourself have a really good time, your health goes to pieces, and if your health goes, your looks go. The awful part is that in the end, no matter what you have done, no matter how careful you may have been, everything falls apart anyway. The disintegration merely comes sooner, or later, depending on you. Going to pieces is inevitable, and you haven't even any pieces to show when you're finished. "Why should that be a depressing thought?" she wondered. "It's the most obvious and fundamental one there is. *Mann muss nur sterben.* But that means something quite different. That means we are supposed to have free will. . . ."

Far in the distance, out over the Atlantic, she heard the faint hum of a plane as the dark mountain and the Villa Hesperides were included briefly within the radius of its sound. Northward to Lisbon, southward to Casablanca. In another hour Luis might be hearing that same motor as it circled above the airport.

"Darling, *please!*" She struggled a little to free herself from his embrace. Since he still held her, she squirmed violently and managed to sit up, bathed in sweat, wine and grease. The air of the room suddenly seemed bitter cold. She ran her hand tentatively over her stomach and drew it back, disgusted. Quickly she jumped out of bed, locked the door into the corridor, drew her peignoir around her, and disappeared into the bathroom without turning on any light.

She stayed in the shower rather longer than was necessary, hoping that by the time she came out he would have got up, dressed, and perhaps cleared away some of the mess around the bed. Then she could ring, say: "I've had a little accident," and have coffee served. When she opened the bathroom door the room was still in darkness. She went over to the night table and switched on the light. He lay asleep, partially covered by the sheet.

"But this is the *end!*" she told herself. And with an edge of annoyance in her voice: "Darling, I'm sorry. You absolutely *must* get dressed immediately." He did not stir; she seized his shoulder and shook it with impatience. "Come along! Up with you! This little orgy has gone on long enough. . . ."

He heard her words with perfect clarity, and he understood what they meant, but they were like a design painted on a wall, utterly without relation to him. He lay still. The most important thing in the world was to prolong the moment of soothing emptiness in the midst of which he was living.

Taking hold of the sheet, she jerked it back over the foot of the bed. Then she bent over and shouted in his ear: "You're stark naked!" Immediately he sat upright, fumbling ineffectively around his feet for the missing cover. She turned and went back into the bathroom, calling over her shoulder: "Get dressed immediately, darling." Looking into the mirror, arranging her hair, she said to herself: "Well, are you pleased or displeased with the episode?" and she found herself unable to answer, dwelling rather on the miraculous fact that Hugo had not walked in on them; the possibility of his having done so seemed now more dreadful each minute. "I must have been quite out of my senses." She closed her eyes for an instant and shuddered.

Dyar had pulled on his clothing mechanically, without being fully conscious of what he was doing. However, by the time he came to putting on his tie, his mind was functioning. He too stood before a mirror, smiling a little triumphantly as he made the staccato gestures with the strip of silk. He combed his hair and knelt by the bed, where he began to scrape up bits of food from the floor and put them on the tray. Daisy came out of the bathroom. "You're an angel!" she cried. "I was just going to ask if you'd mind trying to make a little order out of this chaos." She lay down on a chaise longue in the center of the room and pulled a fur coverlet around her, and she was about to say: "I'm sorry there was no opportunity for you to have a shower, too," when she thought: "Above all, I must not embarrass him." She decided to make no reference to what had occurred. "Be a darling and ring the bell, will you, and we'll have coffee. I'm exhausted."

But apparently he was in no way ill at ease; he did as she suggested, and then went to sit cross-legged on the floor at her side. "I've got to get going," he said to himself, and he was not even preoccupied with the idea of how he would broach the subject of his departure; after the coffee he would simply get up, say good-bye, and leave. It had been an adventure, but Daisy had had very little to do with it, beyond being the detonating factor; almost all of it had taken place inside him. Still, since the fact remained that he had had his way with her, he was bound to behave in a manner which was a little more intimate, a shade on the side of condescension.

"You warm enough?" He touched her arm.

"No. It's glacial in this room. Glacial. God! I can't think why I didn't have a fireplace installed when they were building the house."

Hugo knocked on the door. For ten minutes or so the room was full of activity: Inez and another girl changing the sheets, Mario cleaning up the food from the floor, Paco removing grease spots from the rug beside the bed, Hugo serving coffee. Daisy sat studying Dyar's face as she sipped her coffee, noting with a certain slight resentment that, far from being embarrassed, on the contrary he showed signs of feeling more at ease with her than earlier in the evening. "But what do I expect?" she thought, whereupon she had to admit to herself that she would have liked him to be a little more impressed by what had passed between them. He had come through untouched; she had the uneasy impression that even his passion had been objectless, automatic.

"What goes on in your head?" he said when the servants had all gone out and the room had fallen back into its quiet.

Even that annoyed her. She considered the question insolent. It assumed an intimacy which ought to have existed between them, but which for some reason did not. "But *why* not?" she wondered, looking closely at his satisfied, serious expression. The answer came up ready-made and absurd from her subconscious; it sounded like doggerel. "It doesn't exist because he doesn't exist." This was ridiculous, certainly, but it struck a chord somewhere in the vicinity of the truth. "Unreal. What does it mean for a person to be unreal? And why should I feel he is unreal?" Then she laughed and said: "My God! Of course! You want to feel you're alive!"

He set his cup and saucer on the floor, saying: "Huh?"

"Isn't that what you said to me the first night you came here, when I asked what you wanted most in life?"

"Did I?"

"You most assuredly did. You said those very words. And of course, you know, you're so right. Because you're *not* really alive, in some strange way. You're dead." With the last two words, it seemed to her she heard her voice turning a shade bitter.

He glanced at her swiftly; she thought he looked hurt.

"Why am I trying to bait the poor man?" she thought. "He's done no harm." It was reasonless, idiotic, yet the desire was there, very strong.

"Why dead?" His voice was even; she imagined its inflection was hostile.

"Oh, not dead!" she said impatiently. "Just not alive. Not really. But we're all like that, these days, I suppose. Not quite so blatantly as you, perhaps, but still . . ."

"Ah." He was thinking: "I've got to get out of here. I've got to get going."

"We're all monsters," said Daisy with enthusiasm. "It's the *Age* of Monsters. Why is the story of the woman and the wolves so terrible? You know the story, where she has a sled full of children, crossing the tundra, and the wolves are following her, and she tosses out one child after another to placate the beasts. Everyone thought it ghastly a hundred years ago. But today it's much more terrible. Much. Because then it was remote and unlikely, and now it's entered into the realm of the possible. It's a terrible story not because the woman is a monster. Not at all. But because what she did to save herself is exactly what we'd all do. It's terrible because it's so desperately true. I'd do it, you'd do it, everyone we know would do it. Isn't that so?"

Across the shining stretches of floor, at the bottom of a well of yellow light, he saw his briefcase waiting. The sight of it lying there reinforced his urge to be gone. But it was imperative that the leave-taking be casual. If he mentioned it vaguely now, the suggestion would be easier to act upon in another five minutes. By then it would be eleven-thirty.

"Well," he began, breathing in deeply and stretching, as if to rise.

"Do you know anyone who wouldn't?" He suddenly realized that she was serious about whatever it was she was saying. There was something wrong with her; she ought to have been lying there contentedly, perhaps holding his hand or ruffling his hair and saying a quiet word now and then. Instead she was tense and restless, talking anxiously about wolves and monsters, seeking either to put something into his mind or to take something out of it; he did not know which.

"*Do* you?" she insisted, the words a despairing challenge. It was as if, had he been able to answer "Yes," the sound of the word might have given her a little peace. He might have said: "Yes, I do know someone," or even: "Yes, such a person exists," and she would perhaps have been comforted. The world, that faraway place, would have become inhabitable and possible once again. But he said nothing. Now she took his hand, turned her face down to him coquettishly.

"Speaking of monsters, now that I recall your first evening here, I remember. God! You're the greatest monster of all. Of course! With that great emptiness in your hand. But my God! Don't you remember? Don't you remember what I told you?"

"Not very much of it," he said, annoyed to see his chance of escape being pulled further away from him. "I don't take much stock in that sort of stuff, you know."

"Stock, indeed!" she snorted. "Everyone knows it's perfectly true and quite scientific. But in any case, whether you take stock or not—what an expression!—just remember, you can do what you want. If you know what you want!" she added, a little harshly. "You have an empty hand, and vacuums have a tendency to fill up. Be careful what goes into your life."

"I'll be careful," he said, standing up. "I'm afraid I've got to be going. It's getting late."

"It's not late, darling," she said, but she made no effort to persuade him to stay on. "Call a cab." She pointed to the telephone. "It's 24-80."

He had not thought of that complication. "I'll walk," he said. "I need the exercise."

"Nonsense! It's five miles. You can't."

"Sure I can," he said smiling.

"You'll get lost. You're mad." She was thinking: "He probably wants to save the money. Shall I tell him to have it put on our bill?" She decided against it. "Do as you like," she said, shrugging.

As he took up his briefcase, she said: "I shall see you down to the door," and despite his protestations she walked ahead of him down the stairs into the hall where a few candles still burned. The house was very still.

"The servants are all in bed, I guess," he said.

"Certainly not! I haven't dismissed Hugo yet." She opened the door. The wind blew in, rippling her peignoir.

"You'd better go up to bed. You'll catch cold."

He took the hand she held forth. "It was a wonderful evening," he declared.

"Luis will be back in a few days. You must come to dinner then. I'll call you, darling."

"Right." He backed away a few steps along the gravel walk.

"Turn to your left there by that clump of bamboo. The gate's open."

"Good night."

"Good night."

Stepping behind the bamboo thicket, he waited to hear her close the door. Instead, he heard her say: "Ah, Hugo. There you are! You may lock the gate after Mr. Dyar."

"Got to do something about *that*," he thought, walking quickly to the right, around the side of the house to the terrace where the swimming pool reflected the stars in its black water. It was a chance to take, because she would probably have been watching, to see him go out through the gate. But she might think he already had slipped out when she was not looking; otherwise it would be very bad. The idea of just how bad it could be struck him with full force as he hesitated there by the pool, and as he hurried ahead down the steps into the lower garden he understood that he had committed an important tactical error. "But I'd have been locked out of the garden, God damn it," he thought. "There was nothing else I could do."

He had now come out from behind the shadow of the house into the open moonlight. Ahead of him something which had looked like part of the vegetation along the path slowly rose and walked toward him. "Let's go," said Thami.

"Shut up," Dyar whispered furiously. At the moment they were in full view of the house.

And as she strained to identify the second person, even to the point of opening one of the doors and silently stepping out onto the terrace to peer down through the deforming moonlight, the two men hurried along the path that led to the top of the cliff, and soon were hidden from her sight.

4

Another Kind of Silence

20

DYAR LAY ON HIS BACK across the seat in the stern of the boat, his hands beneath his head, looking up at the stars, vaguely wishing that at some time or another he had learned a little about astronomy. The rowboat they had brought along to get aboard and ashore in scudded on top of the dark waves a few feet behind him, tied to a frayed towing rope that was too short. He had started out by arguing about the rope, back at Oued el Ihud when they were bobbing around out there a hundred feet or so from the cliffs, trying to attach the two craft together, but then he had decided to save his words for other, more important, things. And in any case, now that the Jilali was away from the land, he paid no attention to what was said to him, feeling, no doubt, that he was master of the immediate situation, and could afford to disregard suggestions made by two such obvious landlubbers as Thami and the crazy Christian gentleman with him. The moment of greatest danger from the police had been passed when the Jilali was rounding the breakwater, before the others had ever got into the boat. Now they were a good mile and a half from shore; there was little likelihood of their being seen.

From time to time the launch passed through choppy waters where the warmer Mediterranean current disagreed with the waves moving in from the Atlantic. Small whitecaps broke and hissed in the dark alongside, and the boat, heaving upward, would remain poised an instant, shuddering as its propeller left the water, and then plunging ahead like a happy dolphin. To the right, cut out by a razor blade, the black mountains of Africa loomed against the bright sky behind them. "This lousy motor's going to give us trouble yet," thought Dyar: the smell of gasoline was too strong. An hour ago the main

227

thing had been to get aboard; now it was to get ashore. When he felt the land of the Spanish Zone under his feet he supposed he would know what the next step was to be; there was no point in planning unless you knew what the possibilities were. He relaxed his body as much as he could without risking being pitched to the floor. "Smoke?" called Thami.

"I told you no!" Dyar yelled, sitting up in fury, gesturing. "No cigarettes, no matches in the boat. What's the matter with you?"

"He wants one," Thami explained, even as the Jilali, who was steering, struck a match and tried to shelter the flame from the wind. The attempt was unsuccessful, and Thami managed to dissuade him from lighting another. "Tell him he's a God-damned fool," called Dyar, hoping thus to enlist Thami on his side. But Thami said nothing, remaining hunched up on the floor near the motor.

There was no question of sleeping; he was much too alert for that, but as he lay there in a state of enforced inactivity, thinking of nothing at all, he found himself entering a region of his memory which, now that he saw it again, he thought had been lost forever. It began with a song, brought back to him, perhaps, by the motion of the boat, and it was the only song that had ever made him feel really happy. "Go. To sleep. My little pickaninny. Mammy's goin' to slap you if you don't. Hushabye. Rockabye. Mammy's little baby. Mammy's little Alabama coon." Those could not have been the words, but they were the words he remembered now. He was covered by a patchwork quilt which was being tucked in securely on both sides— with his fingers he could feel the cross-stitching where the pieces were joined—and his head was lying on the eiderdown pillow his grandmother had made for him, the softest pillow he had ever felt. And like the sky, his mother was spread above him; not her face, for he did not want to see her eyes at such moments because she was only a person like anyone else, and he kept his eyes shut so that she could become something much more powerful. If he opened his eyes, there were her eyes looking at him, and that terrified him. With his eyes closed there was nothing but his bed and her presence. Her voice was above, and she was all around; that way there was no possible danger in the world.

"How the hell did I think of that?" he wondered, looking behind him as he sat up, to see if the lights of Tangier had yet been hidden by Cape Malabata. They were still there, but the black ragged rocks were cutting across them slowly, covering them with the darkness of the deserted coast. Atop the cliff the lighthouse flashed again and again, automatically, becoming presently a thing he no longer noticed. He rubbed his fingers together with annoyance: somehow they had got resin on them, and it would not come off.

And as the small boat passed more certainly into a region of shadowed safety, farther from lights and the possibility of discovery, he found himself thinking of the water as a place of solitude. The boat seemed to be making less noise now. His mind turned to wondering what kind of man it was who sat near him on the floor, saying nothing. He had talked with Thami, sat and drunk with him, but during all the moments they had been in one another's company it never had occurred to him to ask himself what thoughts went on behind those inexpressive features. He looked at Thami: his arms were folded around his tightly drawn-up knees, and his head, thrown back, rested against the gunwale. He seemed to be looking upward at the sky, but Dyar felt certain that his eyes were closed. He might even be asleep. "Why not?" he thought, a little bitterly. "He's got nothing to lose. He's risking nothing." Easy money for Thami—probably the easiest he ever would make with the little boat. "He doesn't give a damn whether I get there or not. Of course he can sleep. I ought to have come alone." So he fumed silently, without understanding that the only reason why he resented this hypothetical sleep was that he would have no one to talk to, would feel more solitary out there under the winter sky.

The Jilali, standing in the bow, began to sing, a ridiculous song which to Dyar's ears sounded like a prolonged and strident moaning. The noise it made had no relation to anything—not to the night, the boat, not to Dyar's mood. Suddenly he had a sickeningly lucid glimpse of the whole unlikely situation, and he chuckled nervously. To be tossing about in a ramshackle old launch at three in the morning in the Strait of Gibraltar with a couple of idiotic barbarians, on his way God only knew where, with a briefcase crammed with money—it made no sense. That is to say, he could not find a way of believing it. And since he could not believe it, he did not really have any part in it; thus he could not be very deeply concerned in any outcome the situation might present. It was the same old sensation of not being involved, of being left out, of being beside reality rather than in it. He stood up, and almost fell forward onto the floor. "Shut up!" he roared; the Jilali stopped singing and called something in a questioning voice. Then he resumed his song. But as Dyar sat down again he realized that the dangerous moment had passed: the vision of the senselessness of his predicament had faded, and he could not recall exactly why it had seemed absurd. "I wanted to do this," he told himself. It had been his choice. He was responsible for the fact that at the moment he was where he was and could not be elsewhere. There was even a savage pleasure to be had in reflecting that he could do nothing else but go on and see what would happen, and that this impossibility of finding any other solution was a direct result of his own decision. He sniffed the wet air, and said to himself that at last he was living, that whatever the reason for his doubt a moment ago, the spasm which had shaken him had been only an instant's return of his old state of mind, when he had been anonymous, a victim. He told himself, although not in so many words, that his new and veritable condition was one which permitted him to believe easily in the reality of the things his senses perceived— to take part in their existences, that is, since belief is participation. And he expected now to lead the procession of his life, as the locomotive heads the train, no longer to be a helpless incidental object somewhere in the middle of the line of events, drawn one way and another, without the possibility or even the need of knowing the direction in which he was heading.

These certainties he pondered explain the fact that an hour or so later, when he could no longer bear the idea that Thami had not once shifted his position, Dyar lurched to his feet, stepped over, and kicked him lightly in the ribs. Thami groaned and murmured something in Arabic.

"What's the idea? You can sleep later."

Thami groaned again, said: "What you want?" but the words were covered by the steady stream of explosions made by the motor. Dyar leaned down, and yelled. "It's going to be light soon, for God's sake! Sit up and keep an eye open. Where the hell are we?"

Thami pointed lazily toward the Jilali. "He knows. Don't

worry." But he rose and went to sit in the bow, and Dyar squatted
down between the motor and the gunwale, more or less where Thami
had been sitting. It was warmer here, out of the wind, but the smell of
the gasoline was too strong. He felt a sharp emptiness in his stomach;
he could not tell whether it was hunger or nausea, because it wavered
between the two sensations. After a few minutes he rose and walked
uncertainly to join Thami. The Jilali motioned to them both to go and
sit in the stern. When Dyar objected, because the air was fresh here by
the wheel, Thami said: "Too heavy. It won't go fast this way," and
they stumbled aft to sit side by side back there on the wet canvas
cushions. Long ago the moon had fallen behind a bank of towering,
thick clouds in the west. Above were the stars, and ahead the sky
presently assumed a colorless aspect, the water beneath melting
smokelike, rising to merge momentarily with the pallid air. The Jilali's
turbaned head took on shape, became sharp and black against the
beginning eastern light.

"You sure you know where we're going?" Dyar said finally.

Thami laughed. "Yes. I'm sure."

"I may be wanting to stay up there quite a while, you know."

Thami did not speak for a moment. "You can stay all your life if
you want," he said sombrely, making it clear that he did not relish the
idea of staying at all.

"What about you? How do you feel about it?"

"Me? Feel about what?"

"Staying."

"I have to go to Tangier with him." Thami indicated the Jilali.

Dyar turned to face him furiously. "The hell you do. You're
going to stay with me. How the hell d'you think I'm going to eat up
there all by myself?"

It was not yet light enough to see the contours of Thami's face,
but Dyar had the feeling he was genuinely surprised. "Stay with
you?" he repeated slowly. "But how long? Stay up there?" Then,
with more assurance: "I can't do that. I have to work. I'll lose money.
You're paying me for the boat and to go with you and show you the
house, that's all."

"He knows I've got money here," Dyar thought savagely.
"Damn his soul."

"You don't think I'm giving you enough?" He heard his own voice tremble.

Thami was stubborn. "You said only the boat. If I don't work I lose money." Then he added brightly: "Why you think I bought this boat? Not to make money? If I stay with you at Agla I make nothing. He takes the boat to Tangier, everything is in Tangier. My boat, my house, my family. I sit in Agla and talk to you. It's very good, but I make no money."

Dyar thought: "Why doesn't he ask me why I want to stay up there? Because he knows. Plain, ordinary blackmail. A war of nerves. I'm God damned if I give in to him." But even as he formed the words in his mind, he knew that what Thami was saying had logic.

"So what d'you expect me to do?" he said slowly, proceeding with caution. "Pay you so much a day to stay up there?"

Thami shrugged his shoulders. "It's no use to stay at Agla anyway. It's no good there. What do you want to do there? It's cold and with mud all over. I have to go back."

"So I have to make you an offer," he thought grimly. "Why don't you ask me how much I've got here in the briefcase?" Aloud he said: "Well, you can stay a few days at least. I'll see you don't lose anything by it." Thami seemed satisfied. But Dyar was ill at ease. It was impossible to tell how much he knew, even how much he was interested in knowing, or to form any idea of what he thought about the whole enterprise. If he would only ask an explicit question, the way he phrased it might help determine how much he knew, and the reply could be formed accordingly. Since he said nothing, he remained a mystery. At one point, when they had been silent for some minutes, Dyar said to him suddenly: "What are you thinking about?" and in the white light of dawn his smooth face looked childishly innocent as he answered: "Me? Thinking? Why should I think? I'm happy. I don't need to think." All the same, to Dyar the reply seemed devious and false, and he said to himself: "The bastard's planning something or other."

With the arrival of daylight, the air and water had become calmer. On the Spanish side of the strait they saw a large freighter moving slowly westward, statuelike, imperturbable. The progress of the launch was so noisy and agitated in its motion that it seemed to

Dyar the freighter must be gliding forward in absolute silence. He looked in all directions uneasily, scanning the African coast with particular attention. The mountains tumbled precipitately down into the froth-edged sea, but in a few spots he thought he could see a small stretch of sand in a cove.

"What's this Spanish Zone like?" he asked presently.

Thami yawned. "Like every place. Like America."

Dyar was impatient. "What d'you mean, like America? Do the houses have electric lights? Do they have telephones?"

"Some."

"They do?" said Dyar incredulously. In Tangier he had heard vaguely that the Spanish Zone was a primitive place, and he pictured it as a wilderness whose few inhabitants lived in caves and talked in grunts or sign language. "But in the country," he pursued. "They don't have telephones out there, do they?"

Thami looked at him, as if mildly surprised at his insistence upon continuing so childish a conversation. "Sure they do. What do you think? How they going to run the government without telephones? You think it's like the Senegal?" The Senegal was Thami's idea of a really uncivilized country.

"You're full of crap," said Dyar shortly. He would not believe it. Nevertheless he examined the nearby coastline more anxiously, telling himself even as he did so that he was foolish to worry. The telephoning might begin during the day; it certainly had not already begun. Who was there to give the alarm? Wilcox could not—at least, not through the police. As for the American Legation, it would be likely to wait several days before instigating a search for him, if it did anything at all. Once it was thought he had left the International Zone, the Legation would in all probability shelve the entire Jouvenon affair, to await a possible return, even assuming that was why they had telephoned him. Then who was there to worry about? Obviously only Wilcox, but a Wilcox hampered by his inability to enlist official aid. Relieved in his mind for a moment, he stole a glance at Thami, who was looking at him fixedly like a man watching a film, as if he had been following the whole panorama of thoughts as they filed past in Dyar's mind. "I can't even think in front of him," he told himself. He was the one to look out for, not Wilcox or anybody Wilcox might hire.

Dyar looked back at him defiantly. *"You're* the one," he made his eyes say, like a challenge. "I'm onto you," he thought they were saying. "I just want you to know it." But Thami returned his gaze blandly, blinked like a cat, looked up at the gray sky, and said with satisfaction: "No rain today."

He was wrong; within less than half an hour a wind came whipping around the corner of the coast out of the Mediterranean, past the rocky flanks of Djebel Musa, bringing with it a fine cold rain.

Dyar put on his overcoat, holding the briefcase in his lap so that it was shielded from the rain. Thami huddled in the bow beside the Jilali, who covered his head with the hood of his djellaba. The launch began to make a wide curve over the waves, soon turning back almost in the direction from which it had come. They were on the windward side of a long rocky point which stretched into the sea from the base of a mountain. The sheer cliffs rose upward and were lost in the low-hanging cloudbank. There was no sign of other craft, but it was impossible to see very far through the curtain of rain. Dyar sat up straight. The motor's sound seemed louder than ever; anyone within two miles could surely hear it. He wished there were some way of turning it off and rowing in to shore. Thami and the Jilali were talking with animation at the wheel. The rain came down harder, and now and then the wind shook the air, petulantly. Dyar sat for a while looking downward at his coat, watching rivulets form in valleys of gabardine. Soon the boat rested on water that was smoother. He supposed they had entered an inlet of some sort, but when he raised his head, still only the rocks on the right were visible. Now that these were nearer and he could see the dark water washing and swirling around them, he was disagreeably conscious of their great size and sharpness. "The quicker we get past, the better," he thought, glad he had not called to the Jilali and made a scene about shutting off the motor. As he glanced backward he had the impression that at any moment another boat would emerge from the grayness there and silently overtake them. What might happen as a result did not preoccupy him; it was merely the idea of being followed and caught while in flight which was disturbing. He sat there, straining to see farther than it was possible to see, and he felt that the motor's monotonous racket was the one thin rope which might haul him to safety. But at any instant it could break, and there would be only the soft sound of the waves touching the boat. When he felt a cold drop of water moving down his neck he was not sure whether it was rain or sweat. "What's all the excitement about?" he asked himself in disgust.

The Jilali stepped swiftly to the motor and turned it off; it died with a choked sneeze, as if it could never be started again. He returned to the wheel, which Thami held. The launch still slid forward. Dyar stood up. "Are we there?" Neither one answered. Then the Jilali moved again to the center of the boat and began desperately to force downward the heavy black disk which was the flywheel. With each tug there was another sneeze, but the motor did not start. Raging inwardly, Dyar sat down again. For a full five minutes the Jilali continued his efforts, as the boat drifted indolently toward the rocks. In the end the motor responded, the Jilali cut it down to half speed, and they moved slowly ahead through the rain.

21

THERE WAS a small sloping beach in the cove, ringed by great half-destroyed rocks. The walls of the mountain started directly behind, rose and disappeared in the rain-filled sky. They leaped from the rowboat and stood a moment on the deserted strip of sand without speaking. The launch danced nearby on the deep water.

"Let's go," Dyar said. This also was a dangerous moment. "Tell him you'll write him when you want him to come and get you."

Thami and the Jilali entered into a long conversation which soon degenerated from discussion into argument. As Dyar stood waiting he saw that the two were reaching no understanding, and he became inpatient. "Get him out of here, will you?" he cried. "Have you got his address?"

"Just a minute," Thami said, and he resumed the altercation. But remembering what he considered Dyar's outstanding eccentricity—his peculiar inability to wait while things took their natural course—he turned presently and said: "He wants money," which, while it was true, was by no means the principal topic of the conversation. Thami was loath to see his boat, already paid for, go back to Tangier in the hands of its former owner, and he was feverishly trying to devise some protective measure whereby he could be reasonably sure that both the Jilali and the boat would not disappear.

"How much?" said Dyar, reaching under his overcoat into his pocket, holding his briefcase between his knees meanwhile. His collar was soaked; the rain ran down his back.

Thami had arranged a price of four hundred pesetas with the Jilali for his services; he had intended to tell Dyar it was eight hundred, and pay the Jilali out of that. Now, feeling that things were turning against him from all sides, he exclaimed: "He wants too much! In Dradeb he said seven fifty. Now he says a thousand." Then, as Dyar pulled a note from his pocket, he realized he had made a grievous error. "Don't give it to him!" he cried in entreaty, stretching out a hand as if to cover the sight of the bill. "He's a thief! Don't give it to him!'

Dyar pushed him aside roughly. "Just keep out of this," he said. He handed the thousand-peseta note to the expectant Jilali. "D'you think I want to stand around here all day?" Turning to the Jilali, who stood holding the note in his hand, looking confused, he demanded: "Are you satisfied?"

Thami, determined not to let any opportunity slip by, immediately translated this last sentence into Arabic as a request for change. The Jilali shook his head slowly, announced that he had none, and held the bill out for Dyar to take back. "He says it's not enough," said Thami. But Dyar did not react as he had hoped. "He knows God-damned well it's enough," he muttered, turning away. "Have you got his address?" Thami stood unmoving, tortured by indecision. And he did the wrong thing. He reached out and tried to snatch the note from the Jilali's hand. The latter, having decided that the Christian gentleman was being exceptionally generous, behaved in a natural fashion, spinning around to make a running dash for the boat, pushing it afloat as he jumped in. Thami hopped with rage at the water's edge as the other rowed himself out of reach laughing.

"My boat!" he screamed, turning an imploring face to Dyar. "You see what a robber he is! He's taking my boat!"

Dyar tooked at him with antipathy. "I've got to put up with this for how many days?" he thought. "The guy's not even a half-wit."

The Jilali kept rowing away, toward the launch. Now he shouted various reassurances and waved. Thami shook his fist and yelled back threats and curses in a sobbing voice, watching the departing Jilali get aboard the launch, tie the rowboat to the stern, and finally manage to start the motor. Then, inconsolable, he turned to Dyar. "He's gone. My boat's gone. Everything."

"Shut up," Dyar said, not looking at him. He felt physically disgusted, and he wanted to get away from the beach as quickly as possible, particularly now that the motor's noise had started up again.

Listlessly Thami led the way along the beach to its western end, where they walked among the tall rocks that stood upright. Skirting the base of the mountain, they followed an almost invisible path upward across a great bank of red mud dotted with occasional boulders. It was a climb that became increasingly steeper. The rain fell more intensely, in larger drops. There were no trees, no bushes, not even any small plants. Now cliffs rose on both sides, and the path turned into a gully with a stream of rust-colored water running against them. At one point Dyar slipped and fell on his back into the mud. It made a sucking sound as Thami helped him up out of it; he did not thank him. They were both panting, and in too disagreeable a humor to speak. But neither one expected the other to say anything, in any case. It was a question of watching where you put each foot as you climbed, nothing more. The walls of rock on either side were like blinders, keeping the eye from straying, and ahead there were more stones, more mud, and more pools and trickles of red-brown water. With the advance of the morning the sky grew darker. Dyar looked occasionally at his watch. "At half-past nine I'm going to sit down, no matter where we are," he thought. When the moment came, however, he waited a while until he found a comfortable boulder before seating himself and lighting a cigarette which, in spite of his precautions, the rain managed to extinguish after a few puffs. Thami pretended not to have noticed him, and continued to plod ahead. Dyar let him walk on, did not call to him to wait. He had only a half-pack of cigarettes, and he had forgotten to buy any. "No more cigarettes, for how long?" The landscape did not surprise him; it was exactly what he had expected, but for some reason he had failed to imagine that it might be raining, seeing it always in his mind's eye as windswept, desolate and baking in a brilliant sunlight.

Those of his garments which had not already been wet by the rain were soaked with sweat, for the steady climbing was arduous and he was hot. But he would not take off his overcoat, because under his arm, covered by the coat, was the briefcase, and he determined to keep it there, as much out of the rain as possible.

He kept thinking that Thami, when he had got to a distance he considered dignified, would stop and wait for him, but he had mistaken the cause of his companion's depression, imagining that it was largely pique connected with his defeat at the hands of the Jilali, whereas it was a genuine belief that all was lost, that for the time being his soul lay in darkness, without the blessing of Allah. This meant that everything having to do with the trip was doomed beforehand to turn out badly for him. He was not angry with Dyar, whom he considered a mere envoy of ill-luck; his emotion was the more general one of despondency.

Thami did not stop; he went on his way until a slight change in the direction of the gully took him out of Dyar's view. "The son of a bitch!" Dyar cried, jumping up suddenly and starting to run up the canyon, still holding his sodden cigarette in his hand. When he came to the place where the passage turned, Thami was still far ahead, trudging along mechanically, his head down. "He wants me to yell to him to wait," Dyar thought. "I'll see him in Hell first."

It was another half-hour before he arrived within speaking distance of Thami's back, but he did not speak, being content to walk at the other's pace behind him. As far as he could tell, Thami had never noticed his short disappearance. Thami climbed and that was all.

And so they continued. By midday they were inland, no longer within reach of the sea's sound or smell. Still Dyar felt that had it not been for the miles of rainy air behind them the sea would be somewhere there spread out below them, visible even now. The sky continued gray and thick, the rain went on falling, the wind still came from the east, and they kept climbing slowly, through a vast world of rocks, water and mud.

A ham sandwich, Dyar found himself thinking. He could have bought all he wanted the day before while he waited to get into Ramlal's. Instead he had gone and lain on the beach. The sunbaked hour or so seemed impossibly distant now, a fleeting vista from a dream, or the memory of a time when he had been another person. It was only when he considered that he could not conceivably have bought food then for this excursion since he had not in any way suspected he was going to make it, that he understood how truly remote yesterday was, how greatly the world had changed since he had gone into Chocron's stuffy little office and begun to watch the counting of the money.

Looming suddenly out of the rain, coming toward them down the ravine, a figure appeared. It was a small gray donkey moving along slowly, his panniers empty, drops of rain hanging to the fuzz along his legs and ears. Thami stood aside to let the animal pass, his face showing no expression of surprise. "We must be getting near," said Dyar. He had meant to keep quiet, let Thami break the silence between them, but he spoke without thinking.

"A little more," said Thami impassively. An old man dressed in a tattered woolen garment came into view around a bend, carrying a stick and making occasional guttural sounds at the donkey ahead. "A little more," Dyar thought, beginning to feel light-headed. "How much more?" he demanded. But Thami, with the imprecise notions of his kind about space and time, could not say. The question meant nothing to him. "Not much," he replied.

The way became noticeably steeper; it required all their attention and effort to continue, to keep from sliding back on loose stones. The wind had increased, and was blowing what looked like an endless thick coil of cloud from the crags above downward into their path. Presently they were in its midst. The world was darker. "This isn't funny," Dyar found himself thinking, and then he laughed because it was absurd that a mere sudden change in lighting should affect his mood so deeply. "Lack of food," he said to himself. He bumped against Thami purposely now and then as he climbed. If they should get too far apart they would not be able to see each other. "I hope you've got something to eat up in this cabin of yours," he said.

"Don't worry." Thami's voice was a little unpleasant. "You'll eat tonight. I'll get you food. I'll bring it to you. Don't worry."

"You mean there's no food in the house? Where the hell are you going to get it?"

"They got nothing to eat at the house because no one is living there since a long time. But not very far is the house of my wife's family. I'll get you whatever you want there. They won't talk about it. They're good people."

"He thinks he's going to keep me cooped up," Dyar said to himself. "He's got another think coming." Then as he climbed in silence: "But why? Why does he want to keep me hidden?" And so the question was reduced once more to its basic form: "What does he know?" He resolved to ask him tonight, point-blank, when they were sitting quietly face to face and he could observe whatever changes might come into Thami's expression: "What did you mean when you said your wife's family wouldn't talk about it?"

As the gradient increased, their climb became an exhausting scramble to keep from sliding backward. The heavy fog was like wind-driven smoke; every few seconds they were revealed briefly to each other, and even a sidewall of rock beyond might appear. Then with a swoop the substance of the air changed, became white and visible, and wrapped itself around their faces and bodies, blotting out everything. They went on and on. It was afternoon; to Dyar it seemed to have been afternoon forever. All at once, a little above him Thami grunted with satisfaction, emitted a long: "Aaah!" He had sat down. Dyar struggled ahead for a moment and saw him. He had pulled out his kif pipe and was filling it from the long leather mottoui that was unrolled across his knees. "Now it's easy," he said, moving a little along the rock to make room for Dyar. "Now we go down. The town is there." He pointed straight downward. "The house is there." He pointed slightly downward, but to the left. Dyar seated himself, accepting the pipe. Between puffs he sniffed the air, which had come alive, smelled now faintly like pine trees and farmyards. When he had finished the pipe he handed it back. The kif was strong; he felt pleasantly dizzy. Thami refilled the pipe, looking down at it lovingly. The stem was covered with tiny colored designs of fish, water-jars, birds and swords. "I bought this sebsi three years ago. In Marrakech," he said.

They sat alone in the whiteness. Dyar waited for him to smoke; the kif was burned in three long vigorous puffs. Thami blew the ball of glowing ash from the little bowl, wound the leather thongs around the mottoui, and gravely put the objects into his pocket.

They got up and went on. The way was level for only an instant, almost immediately becoming a steep descent. They had been sitting at the top of the pass. After the long hours of breathing in air that smelled only of rain, it was pleasantly disturbing to be able to distinguish signs of vegetable and animal life in the mist that came up from the invisible valley below. Now their progress was quicker; they hurried with drunken movements from one boulder to another, sometimes landing against them with more force than was comfortable. It had stopped raining; Dyar had pulled the briefcase out from under his coat and was carrying it in his left hand, using his free right arm for balance and as a bumper when it was feasible.

Soon they were below the cloud level, and in the sad fading light Dyar stood a moment looking at the gray panorama of mountains, clouds and shadowy depths. Almost simultaneously too, they were out of reach of the wind. The only sound that came up from down there was the soft unvaried one made by a stream following its course over many rocks. Nor could he distinguish any signs of human habitation. "Where's the house?" he said gruffly. That was the most important detail.

"Come on," Thami replied. They continued the downward plunge, and presently they came to a fork in the trail. "This way," said Thami, choosing the path that led along the side of the mountain, a sheer drop on its right, and on the left above, a succession of cliffs and steep ravines filled with the debris of landslides.

Then Thami stood still, one eyebrow arched, his hand to his ear. He seized Dyar's wrist, pulled him back a few paces to a huge slab of rock slightly off the path, pushed him to a squatting position behind it, and bent down himself, peering around every few seconds. "Look," he said. Half a hundred brown and gray goats came along the path, their hooves making a cluttered sound among the stones. The first ones stopped near the rock, their amber eyes questioning. Then the pressure of those following behind pushed them ahead, and they went on past in disorder, the occasional stones they dislodged bouncing from rock to rock with a curious metallic ring. A youth with a staff, wearing a single woolen cape slung over his shoulders, followed the flock. When he had passed, Thami whispered: "If he sees you, my friend, it would be very bad. Everybody in Agla would know tomorrow."

"What difference would that make?" Dyar demanded, not so much because he believed it did not matter, as because he was curious

242   PAUL BOWLES

to know exactly what his situation was up here.

"The Spaniards. They would come to the house."

"Well, let 'em come. What difference would it make?" He was determined to see the thing through, and it was a good opportunity. "I haven't done anything. Why should they take the trouble to come looking for me?" He watched Thami's face closely.

"Maybe they wouldn't hurt you when you show them you got an American passport." Thami spoke aloud now. "Me, I'd be in the jail right away. You have to have a visa to get here, my friend. And then they'd say: How did you get in? Don't you worry. They'd know you were coming in by a boat. And then they'd say: Where is the boat? And whose boat? And worst: Why did you come by boat? Why didn't you come by the *frontera* like everybody else? Then they talk on the telephone to Tangier and try to know why from the police there. . . ." He paused, looking questioningly at Dyar, who said: "So what?" still studying Thami's eyes intently.

"So what?" said Thami weakly, smiling. "How do I know so what? I know you said you will give me five thousand pesetas to take you here, and so I do it because I know Americans keep their word. And so you want to get here very much. How do I know why?" He smiled again, a smile he doubtless felt to be disarming, but which to Dyar's way of thinking was the very essence of Oriental deviousness and cunning.

Dyar grunted, got up, thinking: "From now on I'm going to watch every move you make." As Thami rose to his feet he was still explaining about the Spanish police and their insistence upon getting all possible information about foreigners who visited the Protectorate. His words included a warning never to stand outside the house in the daytime, and never—it went without saying—to set foot inside the village at any hour of the day or night. As they went along he embroidered on the probable consequences to Dyar of allowing himself to be seen by anyone at all, in the end making everything sound so absurdly dangerous that a wave of fear swept over his listener—not fear that what Thami said might be true, for he did not believe all these variations on catastrophe for an instant, but a fear born of having asked himself only once: "Why is he saying all this? Why is he so excited about nobody's seeing me?" For him the answer was to be found, of course, at the limits of Thami's infamy. It was merely a question of knowing how far the man was prepared to go, or rather, since he was a Moroccan, how far he would be able to go. And the answer at this point was, thought Dyar: he will go as far as I let him go. So I give him no chance. Vigilance was easy enough; the difficulty lay in disguising it. The other must not suspect that he suspected. Thami was already playing the idiot; he too would be guileless, he would encourage Thami to think himself the cleverer, so that his actions might be less cautious, his decisions less hidden. One excellent protective measure, it seemed to him, would be to go to the village and then tell Thami about it. That would let him know that he was not afraid of being seen, thus depriving Thami of one advantage he seemed to feel he had over him. "And then he'd think twice before pulling anything too rough if he realized people knew I had been up here with him," he reasoned.

"Well," he said reluctantly, "I'm going to have a fine time up here. I can see that. You down in the town all the time and me sitting on my ass up here on the side of a mountain."

"What you mean, all the time? How many days do you want to stay? I have to go to Tangier. My boat. That Jilali's no good. I know him. He's going to sell it to somebody else. You don't care. It's not your boat—"

"Don't start in again," said Dyar. But Thami launched into a lengthy monologue which ended where it had been meant to end, on the subject of how many pesetas a day Dyar was willing to pay him for his presence at Agla.

"Maybe I want him here and maybe I don't," he thought. It would depend on what he found and learned in the town. Plans had to be made carefully, and they might easily include the necessity of having Thami take him somewhere else. "But the quicker I can get rid of him the better." That much was certain.

Was this haggling, genuine enough in appearance, merely a part of Thami's game, intended to dull whatever suspicion he might have, replacing it with a sense of security which would make him careless? He did not know; he thought so. In any case, he must seem to take it very seriously.

"D'you think I'm made of money?" he said with simulated

ill-humor, but in such a tone that Thami might feel that the money
eventually would be forthcoming. The other did not answer.

There was an olive grove covering the steep side hill that had to
be gone through, a rushing stream to cross, and a slight rise to climb
before one reached the house. It was built out on a flat shelf of rock
whose base curved downward to rest against the mountainside as-
tonishingly far below.

"There's the house," said Thami.

It's a fort, thought Dyar, seeing the little structure crouching
there atop its crazy pillar. Its thick earthen walls once had been
partially whitewashed, and its steep roof, thatched in terraces, looked
like a flounced petticoat of straw. The path led up, around, and out
onto the promontory where the ground was bare save for a few
overgrown bushes. There were no windows, but there was a patchwork door with a homemade lock, to fit which Thami now pulled from
his pocket a heavy key as long as his hand.

"This is the jumping-off place all right," said Dyar, stepping to
the edge and peering down. Below, the valley had prepared itself for
night. He had the feeling that no light could pierce the profound
gloom in which the lower mountainside was buried, no sound change
the distant, impassive murmur of water, which, although scarcely
audible, somehow managed to fill the entire air. After struggling a
moment with the lock Thami succeeded in getting the door open. As
Dyar walked toward the house he noticed the deep troughs dug in the
earth by the rain that had run from the overhanging eaves; it still
dripped here and there, an intimate sound in the middle of the
encompassing solitude—almost with an overtone of welcome, as if the
mere existence of the house offered a possibility of relief from the vast
melancholy grayness of the dying afternoon.

At least, he thought, as he stepped inside into the dark room that
smelled like a hayloft, this will give me a chance to catch my breath. It
might be only for a day or two, but it provided a place to lie down.

Thami opened a door on the other side of the room and the
daylight came in from a tiny patio filled with broken crates and refuse.
"There's another room there," he said with an air of satisfaction.
"And a kitchen, too."

Surprisingly, the earth floor was dry. There was no furniture, but a clean straw mat covered almost half the floor space. Dyar threw himself down and lay with his head propped against the wall. "Don't say kitchen to me unless you've got something in it. When are we going to eat? That's all I want to know."

Thami laughed. "You want to sleep? I'm going now to the house of my wife's family and get candles and food. You sleep."

"The hell with the candles, chum. You get that food."

Thami looked slightly scandalized. "Oh, no," he said with great seriousness and an air of faint reproof. "You can't eat without candles. That's no good."

"Bring whatever you like." He could feel himself falling asleep even as he said it. "Just bring food too." He slipped his fingers through the handle of the briefcase and laid it over his chest. Thami stepped out, closed the door and locked it behind him. There was the sound of his footsteps, and then only the occasional falling of a drop of water from the roof outside. Then there was nothing.

22

EVEN WHEN he was fully conscious of the fact that Thami had returned and was moving about the room making a certain amount of noise, that a candle had been lighted and was shining into this face, his awakening seemed incomplete. He rose from the mat, said: "Hi!" and stretched, but the heaviness of sleep weighed him down. He did not even remember that he was hungry; although the emptiness was there in him, more marked than before he had slept, it seemed to have transformed itself into a simple inability to think or feel. He took a few steps out into the center of the room, grunting and yawning violently, and immediately wanted to lie down again. With the sensation of being half-dead, he staggered back and forth across the floor, stumbling over a large blanket which Thami had apparently brought from the other house, and from which he was extracting food and dishes. Then he went back to the mat and sat down. Triumphantly Thami held up a battered teapot. "I got everything," he announced. "Even mint to put in the tea. You want to sleep again? Go on. Go to sleep."

There was a crackle and sputter from the patio as the charcoal in the brazier took fire. Dyar still said nothing; it would have cost him too great an effort.

As he watched Thami busying himself with the preparations he was conscious of an element of absurdity in the situation. If it had been Hadija preparing his dinner, perhaps he would have found it more natural. Now he thought he should offer to help. But he said to himself: "I'm paying the bastard," did not stir, and followed Thami's comings and goings, feeling nothing but his consuming emptiness inside, which, now that at last he was slowly waking, made itself felt unequivocally as hunger.

"God, let's eat!" he exclaimed presently.

Thami laughed. "Wait. Wait." he said. "You have to wait a long time still." He pulled out his kif pipe, filled and lit it, handed it to Dyar, who drew on it deeply, filling his lungs with the burning smoke, as if he might thereby acquire at least a little of the nourishment he so intensely wanted at the moment. At the end of the second pipeful his ears rang, he felt dizzy, and an extraordinary idea had taken possession of him: the certainty that somewhere, subtly blended with the food Thami was going to hand him, poison would be hidden. He saw himself awakening in the dark of the night, an ever-increasing pain spreading through his body, he saw Thami lighting a match, and then a candle, his face and lips expressing sympathy and consternation, he saw himself crawling to the door and opening it, being confronted with the utter impossibility of reaching help, but going out anyway, to get away from the house. The detailed clarity of the visions, their momentary cogency, electrified him; he felt a great need to confide them immediately. Instead, he handed the pipe back to Thami, his gestures a little uncertain, and shutting his eyes, leaned back against the wall, from which position he was roused only when Thami kicked the sole of his shoe several times, saying: "You want to eat?"

He did eat, and in great quantity—not only of the vermicelli soup and the sliced tomatoes and onions, but also of the chopped meat and egg swimming in boiling bright green olive oil, which, in imitation of Thami, he sopped up with ends of bread. Then they each drank two glasses of sweet mint tea.

"Well, that's that," he finally said, settling back. "Thami, I take my hat off to you."

"Your hat?" Thami did not understand.

"The hat I don't own." He was feeling expansive at the moment. Thami, looking politely confused, offered him his pipe which he had just lighted, but Dyar refused. "I'm going to turn in," he said. If possible he wanted to package the present feeling of being at ease, and carry it with him to sleep, so that it might stay with him all night. A pipe of kif and he could easily be stuck with nightmares.

Surreptitiously he glanced at his briefcase lying on the mat in the corner near him. In spite of the fact that he had carried it inside his coat whenever it rained, thus drawing at least some attention to it, he thought this could be accounted for in Thami's mind by its newness; he would understand his not wanting to spot the light-colored cowhide and the shining nickel lock and buckles. Thus now he decided to pay no attention to the case, to leave it nonchalantly nearby once he had tossed his toothbrush back into it, near enough on the floor so that if he stretched his arm out he could reach it. Putting it under his head or holding it in his hand would certainly arouse Thami's curiosity, he argued. Once the light was out, he could reach over and pull it closer to his mat.

Thami took out an old djellaba from the blanket in which he had brought the food, put it on, and handed the blanket to Dyar. Then he dragged a half-unraveled mat from the room across the patio and spread it along the opposite wall, where he lay continuing to smoke his pipe. Several times Dyar drifted into sleep, but because he knew the other was there wide awake, with the candle burning, the alarm he had set inside himself brought him back, and he opened his eyes wide and suddenly, and saw the dim ceiling of reeds and the myriad gently fluttering cobwebs above. Finally he turned his head and looked over at the other side of the room. Thami had laid his pipe on the floor and ostensibly was asleep. The candle had burned down very low; in another five minutes it would be gone. He watched the flame for what seemed to him a half-hour. On the roof there were occasional spatters of rain, and when a squall of wind went past, the door rattled slightly, but in a peremptory fashion, as if someone were trying hurriedly to get in. Even so, he did not witness the candle's end; when he opened his eyes again it was profoundly dark, and he had the impression that it had been so for a long time. He lay still, displeased with the sudden realization that he was not at all sleepy. The indistinct call of water came up from below, from a place impossibly faraway. In the fitful wind the door tapped discreetly, then shook with loud impatience. Silently he cursed it, resolving to make it secure for tomorrow night. Quite awake, he nevertheless let himself dream a little, finding himself walking (or driving a car—he could not tell which) along a narrow mountain road with a sheer drop on the right. The earth was so far below that there was nothing to see but sky when he glanced over the precipice. The road grew narrower. "I've got to go on," he thought. Of course, but it was not enough simply to go on. The road could go on, time could go on, but he was neither time nor the road. He was an extra element between the two, his precarious existence mattering only to him, known only to him, but more important than everything else. The problem was to keep himself there, to seize firmly with his consciousness the entire structure of the reality around him, and engineer his progress accordingly. The structure and the consciousness were there, and so was the knowledge of what he must do. But the effort required to leap across the gap from knowing to doing, that he could not make. "Take hold. Take hold," he told himself, feeling his muscles twitch even as he lay there in his revery. Then the door roused him a little, and he smiled in the dark at his own nonsense. He had already gone over the mountain road, he said to himself, insisting on taking his fantasy literally; that was past, and now he was here in the cottage. This was the total reality of the moment, and it was all he needed to consider. He stretched out his arm in the dark toward the center of the room, and met Thami's hand lying warm and relaxed, directly on top of the briefcase.

If he had felt the hairy joints of a tarantula under his fingers he could scarcely have drawn back more precipitately, or opened his eyes wider against the darkness. "I've caught him at it," he thought with a certain desperate satisfaction, feeling his whole body become tense as if of its own accord it were preparing for a struggle of which he had not yet thought. Then he considered how the hand had felt. Thami had rolled over in his sleep, and his hand had fallen there, that was all. But Dyar was not sure. It was a long way to roll, and it seemed a little too fortuitous that the briefcase should happen to be exactly under the spot where his hand had dropped. The question now was whether to do something about it or not. He lay still a while in the dark, conscious of the strong smell of mildewed straw in the room, and decided that unless he took the initiative and changed the situation he would get no more sleep; he must move the briefcase out from under Thami's hand. He coughed, pretended to sniffle a bit, squirmed around for a moment as if he were searching for a handkerchief, reached out and pulled the briefcase by the handle. Partially sitting up, he lit a match to set the combination of the lock, and before the flame went out he glanced over toward the middle of the room. Thami was lying on his mat, but at some point he had pulled it out, away from the wall; his hand still lay facing upward, the fingers curled in the touching helplessness of sleep. Dyar snuffed the match out, took a handkerchief from the case, and blew his nose with energy. Then he felt inside the briefcase; the notes were there. One by one he removed the packets and stuffed them inside his undershirt. Without his overcoat he might look a little plumper around the waist, but he doubted Thami could be that observant. He lay back and listened to the caprices of the wind, playing on the door, hating each sound not so much because it kept him from sleeping as because in his mind the loose door was equivalent to an open door. A little piece of wood, a hammer and one nail could arrange everything: the barrier between himself and the world outside would be much more real. He slept badly.

When it first grew light, Thami got up and built a charcoal fire in the brazier. "I'm going to my wife's family's house," he said as Dyar surveyed him blinking, from his mat. There was tea and there was a little bread left, but that was all. As he drank the hot green tea which Thami had brought to his mat, he noticed that the other had pushed his own mat back to the opposite wall where it had been at the beginning of the night. "Well, that's that," he thought. "No explanation offered. Nothing."

"I'll come back later," Thami said, gathering up the blanket from Dyar's feet. "I got to take this to carry things. You stay in the house. Don't go out. Remember."

"Yes, yes," said Dyar, annoyed at being left alone, at not having slept well, at having the blanket removed in case he wanted to try to sleep now, and most of all at the situation of complete dependence upon Thami in which he found himself at the moment.

When Thami had gone out, the feeling of solitude which replaced his presence in the house, contrary to his expectations, proved to be an agreeable one. First Dyar got up and looked at the door. As he thought, a small chip of wood nailed to the jamb would do the trick. When the door was shut you would simply pull the piece of wood down tight like a bolt. Then he set out on an exploratory tour of the cottage, to search for a hammer and a nail. The terrain was quickly exhausted, because the place was empty. There was nothing, not even the traditional half candle, empty sardine tin and ancient newspapers left by tramps in abandoned houses in America. Here everything had to be bought, he reminded himself; nothing was discarded, which meant that nothing was left around. An old tin can, a broken cup, an empty pill bottle, these things were put on sale. He remembered walking through the Joteya in Tangier and seeing the thousands of things on display, hopelessly useless articles, but for which the people must have managed to find a use. His only interesting discovery was made in the corner between Thami's mat and the door leading into the patio, where behind a pile of straw matting partially consumed by dry-rot he found a small fireplace, a vestige of the days when the house had been someone's home. "We'll damned well have a fire tonight," he thought. He went back to the entrance door, opened it, and stood bathing in the fresh air and the sensation of freedom that lay in the vast space before him. Then he realized that the sky was clear and blue. The sun had not risen high enough behind the mountains to touch the valley, but the day danced with light. Immediately an extraordinary happiness took possession of him. As if some part of him already had suspected the arrival of the idea which was presently to occur to him, and which was to make the day such a long one to live through, he said to himself: "Thank God" when he saw the blueness above. And far below, on a ridge here, in a ravine there, a minute figure moved, clothed in garments the color of the pinkish earth itself. It even seemed to him that in the tremendous stillness he could hear now and then the faint frail sound of a human voice, calling from one distant point to another, but it was like the crying of tiny insects, and the confused backdrop of falling water blurred the thin lines of sound, making him wonder a second later if his ears had not played him false.

He sat down on the doorstep. It was nonsense, this being dependent on an idiot, and an idiot who had given every sign, moreover, of being untrustworthy. For instance, he had said he was going to his relatives' house. But what was to prevent him from going instead to the town and arranging with a group of cutthroats down there to come up after dark? Or even in the daytime, for that matter? What Thami did not quite dare do himself, he could get others to do for him; then he would act his part, looking terrified, indignant, letting them hit him once or twice and tie him up. . . . The scenes Dyar invented here were absurdly reminiscent of all the Western films he had seen as a child. He was conscious of distorting probability, and yet, goaded by an overwhelming desire to make something definite out of what was now equivocal (to assume complete control himself, in other words), he allowed his imagination full play in forming its exaggerated versions of what the day might bring forth. "Why did I let him out of my sight?" he thought, but he knew quite well it had been inevitable. His sojourn up here was predicated on Thami's making frequent trips, if not to the village, at least to the family's abode. "Like a rat in a trap," he told himself, looking longingly out at the furthest peaks, which the sun was now flooding with its early light. But now he knew it would not be like that, because he was going to get out of the trap. It was a morning whose very air, on being breathed, gave life, and there was the path, its stones still clean and shadowless because they lay in the greater shadow of the cliffs above. He had only to rise and begin to walk. There was no problem, unless he asked himself "Where?" and he took care not to allow this question to cross his mind; he wanted to believe he must not hesitate. Yet to make sure that he would act, and not think, he got up and went inside to where he knew Thami had left his two little leather cases—one containing the sections of the dismantled kif-pipe, and the other with the kif itself in it. He picked them both up and put them in his pocket. Since he had decided to leave the house, it now seemed a hostile place, one to get out of quickly. And so, seizing his briefcase, talking a final disapproving sniff of the moldy air in the room, he stepped outside into the open.

Once before, two days ago, he had become intoxicated upon emerging into a world of sun and air. This morning the air was even stranger. When he felt it in his lungs he had the impression that flying would be easy, merely a matter of technique. Two days ago he had been moved to feel the trunks of the palms outside the Hotel de la Playa, to raise his head doglike into the breeze that came across the harbor, to rejoice at the fact of being alive on a fine morning. But then, he remembered, he had still been in his cage of cause and effect, the cage to which others held the keys. Wilcox had been there, hurrying him on, standing between him and the sun in the sky. Now at this moment there was no one. It was possible he was still in the cage— that he could not know—but at least no one else had the keys. If there were any keys, he himself had them. It was a question of starting to walk and continuing to walk. Slowly the contours of the valleys beneath shifted as he went along. He paid no attention to the path, save to note that it was no longer the one by which he had come yesterday. He met no one, nothing. After an hour or so he sat down and had two pipes of kif. The sun still had not climbed high enough to strike this side of the mountain, but there were eminences not far below which already caught its rays. The bottoms of the valleys down there were green snakes of vegetation; they lay warming themselves in the bright morning sun, their heads pointing downward toward the outer country, their tails curling back into the deep-cut recesses of rock.

He continued with less energy, because the smoke had cut his wind somewhat, and his heartbeat had accelerated a little. In compensation, however, he felt a steadily increasing sense of well-being. Soon he no longer noticed his shortness of breath. Walking became a marvelously contrived series of harmonious movements, the execution of whose every detail was in perfect concordance with the vast, beautiful machine of which the air and the mountainside were parts. By the time the sun had reached a point in the sky where he could see it, he was not conscious of taking steps at all; the landscape merely unrolled silently before his eyes. The triumphant thought kept occurring to him that once again he had escaped becoming a victim. And presently, without his knowing how he had got there, he found himself in a new kind of countryside. At some point he had wandered over a small crest and begun going imperceptibly downward, to be now on this upland, sloping plain, so different from the region he had left. Long ago he had ceased paying attention to where he was going. The sun was high overhead; it was so warm that he took off his coat. Then he folded it and sat down on it. His watch said half-past twelve. "I'm hungry," he let himself think, but only once. Determinedly he pulled out the sections of the pipe, fitted them together, and buried the little terra cotta bowl in the mass of fragrant, moist kif that filled the mottoui. And he drew violently on the pipe, holding the smoke inside him until his head spun and his eyes found themselves unable to move from the contemplation of a small crooked bush that grew in front of him. "With this you don't need food," he said. Soon enough he had forgotten his hunger; there were only the multiple details of the bright landscape around him. He studied them attentively; it was as though each hill, stone, gully and tree held a particular secret for him to discover. Even more—the configuration of the land seemed to be the expression of a hidden dramatic situation whose enigma it was imperative that he understand. It was like a photograph of a scene from some play in which the attitudes and countenances of the players, while normal enough at first glance, struck one as equivocal a moment later. And the longer he considered the mysterious ensemble, the more undecipherable the meaning of the whole became. He continued to smoke and stare. "I've got to get this straight," he thought. If he could catch the significance of what he saw before him at the moment, he would have understood a great deal more than what was denoted by these few bushes and stones. His head was clear; all the same, he felt peculiarly uneasy. It was the old fear of not being sure he was really there. He seized a stone and from where he sat threw it as far as he was able. "All right," he told himself, "you're here or you're not here. It doesn't matter a good God damn. Forget about it. It doesn't matter. Keep going from there. Where do you get?" He rose suddenly, took up his coat and began to walk. Perhaps the answer lay in continuing to move. Certainly the natural objects around him went on acting out their silent pantomime, posing their ominous riddle; he was aware of that as he went along. But, he reflected, if he felt strange and unreal at this instant he had good reason to: he was full of kif. "High as a kite," he chuckled. That was a consolation, and if it were not enough, there was the further possibility that he was right, that it was completely unimportant whether you were here or not. But unimportant to whom? He began to whistle as he walked, became engrossed in the sounds he made, ceased his game of mental solitaire.

Little by little the uncertain trail led downward across regions of rough pastureland and stony heaths. It was with astonishment that he saw on a hillside a group of cows grazing. During the morning he had grown used to thinking of himself as the only living creature under this particular sky. If he were coming to a village, so much the worse; he would continue anyway. His hunger, which long ago had reached mammoth proportions, no longer expressed itself as such, but rather as a sensation of general nervous voraciousness which he felt could be relieved only by more kif. And so he sat down and smoked some more, feeling his throat turn a little more inevitably to the iron it was on its way to becoming. If the cows surprised him, the sight now of a dozen or more natives working in a remote field did not. Only their minuteness amazed him; the landscape was so much larger than it looked. He sat on a rock and stared upward. The sky seemed to have reached a paroxysm of brilliancy. He had never known it was possible to take such profound delight in sheer brightness. The pleasure consisted simply in letting his gaze wander over the pure depths of the heavens, which he did until the extreme light forced him to look away.

Here the terrain was a chorus of naked red-gray valleys descending gently from the high horizon. The clumps of spiny palmetto, green nearby, became black in the distance. But it was hard to tell how far away anything was in this deceptive landscape. What looked nearby was far off; the tiny dots which were the cattle in the foreground proved that—and if his eye followed the earth's contours to the farthest point, the formation of the land there was so crude and on such a grand scale that it seemed only a stone's throw away.

He let his head drop, and feeling the sun's heat on the back of his neck, watched a small black beetle moving laboriously on its way among the pebbles. An ant, hurrying in the opposite direction, came up against it; apparently the meeting was an undesirable one, for the ant changed its course and dashed distractedly off with even greater haste. "To see infinity in a grain of sand." The line came to him across the empty years, from a classroom. Outside was the winter dusk, dirty snow lay in the empty lots; beyond, the traffic moved. And in the stifling room, overheated to bursting, everyone was waiting for the bell to ring, precisely to escape from the premonition of infinity that hung so ominously there in the air. The feeling he associated with the word *infinity* was one of physical horror. If only existence could be cut down to the pinpoint of here and now, with no echoes reverberating from the past, no tinglings of expectation from time not yet arrived! He stared harder at the ground, losing his focus so that all he saw was a bright blur. But then, would not the moment, the flick of the eyelid, like the grain of sand, still be imponderably weighted down with the same paralyzing element? Everything was part of the same thing. There was no part of him which had not come out of the earth, nothing which would not go back into it. He was an animated extension of the sunbaked earth itself. But this was not quite true. He raised his head, fumbled, lit another pipe. There was one difference, he told himself as he blew the smoke out in a long white column that straightway broke and dissolved. It was a small difference, self-evident and absurd, and yet because it was the only difference that came to him then, it was also the only suggestion of meaning he could find in being alive. The earth did not know it was there; it merely was. Therefore living meant first of all knowing one was alive, and life without that certainty was equal to no life at all. Which was surely why he kept asking himself: am I really here? It was only natural to want such reassurance, to need it desperately. The touchstone of any life was to be able at all times to answer unhesitatingly: "Yes." There must never be an iota of doubt. A life must have all the qualities of the earth from which it springs, plus the consiousness of having them. This he saw with perfect clarity in a wordless exposition—a series of ideas which unrolled inside his mind with the effortlessness of music, the precision of geometry. In some remote inner chamber of himself he was staring through the wrong end of a telescope at his life, seeing it there in intimate detail, far away but with awful clarity, and as he looked, it seemed to him that now each circumstance was being seen in its final perspective. Always before, he had believed that, although childhood had been left far behind, there would still somehow, some day, come the opportunity to finish it in the midst of its own anguished delights. He had awakened one day to find childhood gone—it had come to an end when he was not looking, and its elements

remained undefinable, its design nebulous, its harmonies all unre-
solved. Yet he had felt still connected to every part of it by ten
thousand invisible threads; he thought he had the power to recall it
and change it merely by touching these hidden filaments of memory.

The sun's light filtered through his closed eyelids, making a blind
world of burning orange warmth; with it came a corresponding ray of
understanding which, like a spotlight thrown suddenly from an unexpected direction, bathed the familiar panorama in a transforming glow
of finality. The years he had spent in the bank, standing in the teller's
cage, had been real, after all; he could not call them an accident or a
stop-gap. They had gone by and they were finished, and now he saw
them as an unalterable part of the pattern. Now all the distant
indecisions, the postponements and unsolved questions were beyond
his reach. It was too late, only until now he had not known it. His life
had not been the trial life he had vaguely felt it to be—it had been the
only one possible, the only conceivable one.

And so everything turned out to have been already complete, its
form decided and irrevocable. A feeling of profound contentment
spread through him. The succession of ideas evaporated, leaving him
with only the glow of well-being attendant upon their passage. He
looked among the pebbles for the beetle; it had disappeared along the
path. But now he heard voices, nearby. A group of turbaned Berbers
came past, and looking at him without surprise went on, still convers-
ing. Their appearance served to bring him back from the interior place
where he had been. He took the pipe to pieces, put it away. Feeling
drunk and light-headed, he rose and followed behind them at a
discreet distance. The path they presently chose led over a hill and
down—down across a wilderness of cactus, through shady olive
groves (the decayed trunks were often no more than wide gnarled
shells), over cascades of smooth rocks, through meadows dotted with
oleander bushes, becoming finally a narrow lane bordered on either
side by high holly. Here it twisted so frequently that he lost sight of
the men several times, and eventually they disappeared completely.
Almost at the moment he realized they were gone, he came unexpectedly out onto a belvedere strewn with boulders, directly above the
rooftops, terraces and minarets of the town.

23

SOMETIMES ON FRIDAY mornings, Hadj Mohammed Beidaoui would send one of his older sons to fetch the last-born, Thami, where he was playing in the garden, and the little boy would be carried in, squirming to prevent his brother from covering his cheeks with noisy kisses all the way. Then he would be placed on his father's knee, his face would momentarily be buried in the hard white beard, and he would hold his breath until his father's face was raised again, and the old man began to pinch his infant cheeks and smooth his hair. He remembered clearly his father's ivory-colored skin, and how beautiful and majestic the smooth ancient face had seemed to him framed in its white silk djellaba. When he thought of it now, perhaps he was referring in memory to one particular morning, a day radiant as only a day in spring in childhood can be, when his father, after sprinkling him with orange flower water until he was quite wet and almost sick from the sweet smell, had taken him by the hand and led him through the streets and parks of sunlight and flowers to the mosque of the Marshan, through the streets openly, where everyone they met, the men who kissed the hem of Hadj Mohammed's sleeve, and those who did not, could see that Thami was his son. And Abdelftah and Abdelmalek and Hassan and Abdallah had all been left home! That was the most important part. The conscious campaign to seek to gain more than his share of his father's favor dated from that morning; he had waged it unceasingly from then until the old man's death. Then, of course, it was all over. The others were older than he, and by that time disliked him, and he returned their antipathy. He began to bribe the servants to let him out of the house, and this got several of them into trouble with Abdelftah, master of the household then, who was short-tempered and flew into a rage each time he learned that Thami had escaped into the street. But it was the street with its forbidden delights that tempted the boy more than anything else, once the world had ceased being a place where the greatest good was to climb into his father's lap and listen to the flow of legends and proverbs and songs and poems that he wished would never come to an end. There was one song he still recalled in its entirety. It went: *Ya ouled al harrata, Al mallem Bouzekri. . . .* His father had told him all the boys of Fez ran through the streets singing it when rain was needed. And there was one proverb which he associated intimately with the memory of his father's face and with the sensation of being held by him, surrounded by the mountains of brocade-covered cushions, with the great lanterns and high looped draperies above, and no matter how often his father acceded to his pleas to repeat it, always it was fresh with a mysterious, magical truth when he heard it.

"Tell about the day."

"The day?" Old Hadj Mohammed would repeat, looking deliberately, cunningly vague, and pulling at his lower lip while he rolled his eyes upward with a vacant expression. "The day? What day?"

"The day," Thami would insist.

"Aaah!" And the old man would begin, and begin at the same time the dovening motion which accompanied the utterance of any words that were not extemporaneous. "The morning is a little boy." He made his eyes large and round. "Noon is a man." He sat up very straight and looked fierce. "Twilight is an old man." He relaxed and looked into Thami's face with tenderness. "What do I do?" Thami knew, but he remained silent, waiting breathless, spellbound for the moment when he would take part in the ritual, his eyes unwaveringly fixed on the ivory face.

"I smile at the first. I admire the second. I venerate the last." And as he finished saying the words, Thami would seize the frail white hand, bend his head forward, and with passion press his lips against the back of the fingers. Then, renewed love in his eyes, the old man would sit back and look at his son. Abdallah once had spied on this game (of the brothers he was the nearest Thami's age, being only a year older), and later when he got him alone, he had subjected Thami to a series of tortures which the boy had borne silently, scarcely offering resistance. It seemed to him a small enough price to pay for his father's favor. "And if you tell Father I'll tell Abdelftah," Abdallah had warned him. Abdelftah would devise something infinitely worse—of that they were both certain—but Thami had laughed scornfully through his tears. He had no intention of telling; to bring to his father's attention the fact that the others could be jealous of his participation in this sacred game would have meant to risk losing his privilege of playing it.

Later it was the streets, the hidden cafés at Sidi Bouknadel that closed their doors leaving the boys inside sitting on mats playing ronda and smoking kif and drinking cognac until morning; it was the beach where they played football and, pooling their money, would rent a caseta for the season, which they used for drinking competitions and the holding of small private orgies whose etiquette demanded that the younger boys be at the entire disposal of the older ones. And above all it was the bordels. By the time Thami was eighteen he had had all the girls in all the establishments, and a good many more off the street. He took to staying away from home for several days at a time, and when he returned it would be in a state of dishevelment which infuriated his brothers. After his sixth arrest for drunkenness Abdelmalek, who was now the head of the family, Abdelftah having moved to Casablanca, gave orders to the guards of the house to refuse him entrance unless he was in a state of complete sobriety and properly dressed. This meant, more than anything else, that he would no longer receive his daily spending money. "This will change him," he said confidently to Hassan. "You'll see the difference very soon." But Thami was more headstrong and resourceful than they had suspected. He found ways of living—what ways they never knew—without needing to return home, without having to forego the independence so necessary to him. And since then he never had gone back, save now and then for a moment of conversation with his brothers at the entrance door, usually to ask a favor which they seldom granted. There was nothing basically anti-social about Thami; hostility was alien to him. He merely had expended almost all his capacities for respect and devotion upon his father, so that he could not give the traditional amount of either to his brothers. Also he would not agree to pretend. He did not respect them and he had had too much contact with European culture to believe he was committing a sin in refusing to feign a respect which custom demanded but which he did not feel.

It was at the annual moussem of Moulay Abdeslam, where serious men go for the good of their souls, that Thami had met Kinza, among the tents and donkeys and fanatical pilgrims. The situation was one with which Moslem tradition is totally unprepared to deal. Young men and women cannot know each other, and if by some disgraceful chance they happen to have managed to see each other alone for a minute, the idea is so shameful that everyone forgets it immediately. But to follow it up, to see the girl again, to suggest marrying her—it would be hard to conceive of more outrageous conduct. Thami did all these things. He went back to Agla at the same time as she did, got to know the family, who were naturally much impressed with his city ways and his erudition, and wrote to Abdelmalek saying that he was about to be married and thought it time he received his inheritance. His brother's reply was a telegram bidding him return to Tangier at once to discuss the matter. It was then that the two had their serious falling-out, since Abdelmalek refused outright to let him touch his money or his property. "I'll go to the Qadi," threatened Thami. Abdelmalek merely laughed. "Go," he said, "if you think there is anything about you he doesn't already know." In the end, after lengthy discussions with Hassan, who thought marriage, even with a shamefully low peasant girl, might possibly be a means of changing Thami's ways, Abdelmalek gave him a few thousand pesetas. He fetched the whole family from Agla and they had a wedding in Emsallah, the humblest quarter of Tangier, all of which nevertheless seemed magnificent to Kinza and her tribe. In due time all but the bride returned to the farmhouse on the mountain above Agla, where they lived working their fields, gathering the fruit from their trees and sending the children to tend the goats on the heights above.

To them Thami was a glamorous, important figure, and they had been overjoyed to see him come knocking at the door the previous evening. They were not so pleased, however, to learn that he had a Nazarene with him, up in the other house, and although he had managed last night to slide over it by talking of other things and then leaving suddenly, he could see that his father-in-law had not finished expressing his views on the subject.

At the house they told him that the men were down in the orchard. He followed the high cactus fence until he came to a gate made of sheet tin. Where he knocked, the sound was very loud, and it was with a certain amount of mild apprehension that he waited for someone to come. One of the sons let him in. An artificial stream ran through the orchard, part of the system which irrigated the entire valley with the spring water that came out of the rocks above the town. Kinza's father was watering the rose-bushes. He hurried back and forth, his baggy trousers hitched above his knees, stooping by the edge of the channel to fill an ancient oil can that spouted water from all corners, running with it each time, to arrive before it was empty. When he saw Thami he ceased his labors, and together they sat down in the shade of a huge fig tree. Almost immediately he brought up the subject of the Nazarene. Having him in the house would make trouble, he predicted. No one had ever heard of a Spaniard living in the same house with a Moslem, and besides, what was the purpose, what was the reason for such a thing? "Why doesn't he stay at the fonda at Agla like all the others?" he demanded. Thami tried to explain. "He's not a Spaniard," he began, but already he foresaw the difficulties he was going to meet, trying to make the other understand. "He's an American." "Melikan?" cried Kinza's father. "And where is Melika? Where? In Spain! Ah! You see?" The oldest son timidly suggested that perhaps the Nazarene was a Frenchman. Frenchmen were not Spaniards, he said. "Not Spaniards?" cried his father. "And where do you think France is, if it's not in Spain? Call him Melikan, call him French, call him English, call him whatever you like. He's still a Spaniard, he's still a Nazarene, and it's bad to have him in the house." "You're right," said Thami, deciding that acquiescence was the easiest way out of the conversation, because his only argument at that point would have been to tell them that Dyar was paying him for the privilege of staying in the house, and that was a detail he did not want them to know. The old man was mollified; then, "Why doesn't he stay at the fonda, anyway? Tell me that," he said suspiciously. Thami shrugged his shoulders, said he did not know. "Ah! You see?" the old man cried in triumph. "He has a reason, and it's a bad reason. And only bad things can happen when Nazarenes and Moslems come together."

There was a halfwit son who sat with them; he nodded his head endlessly, overcome by the wisdom of his father's utterances. The other sons looked at Thami, slightly embarrassed at hearing these ideas, which they supposed he must consider ridiculously old-fashioned. Then they talked of other things, and presently the old man returned to watering his flowers. Thami and the sons retired to a secluded part of the orchard where they could not be seen by him, and smoked, Thami feeling that under the circumstances he could not very well insult the family by returning to the house on the mountain solely to take food to the Christian. They passed the day eating, sleeping and playing cards, and it was twilight when he took his leave, not having dared to suggest that they give him food again, nor even finding the courage to ask for the use of the blanket. But he could not go back up to the house without food, for Dyar would be ravenous by now, and this meant that he must go into Agla and buy supplies for dinner. *"Yah latif, yah latif,"* he said under his breath as he followed the path that led downward to the village.

*

There was little doubt in Dyar's mind, as he stumbled along the cobbled road that led through the town gate, that the place was Agla. He had merely come down by a very wide detour, by going around to the back of the mountain, and then returning to the steep side once again. Thus there was a real possibility of his running into Thami, who, it now occurred to him, would be convinced he had run away in order to avoid having to pay him what he owed him. Or no, he thought, not at all. If Thami were after everything, such a detail would naturally be of no importance. In that case the meeting would bring matters to a head very quickly. The men he had chosen to help him would be nearby; by some casual gesture as they walked along the street together, he and Thami, in full view of the populace, the signal would be given. Or they might even be with him. The only hope would be to defend the briefcase as though his whole life were locked inside. Then, when they got it open and found it empty, he might possibly be far enough away to escape.

The tiny streets and houses were smothered with whitewash, which glowed as if all during the day it had been absorbing the sunlight and now, at dusk, were slowly giving it off into the fading air. It all looked, he thought, as though it had been made by a pastry-cook, but probably that was only because at the moment he did not need much imagination for things to look edible. With infallible intuition he chose the streets that led to the center of town, and there he saw a small native restaurant where the cooking was being done in the entrance. The cook lifted the covers of the various copper cauldrons for him; he looked down into them and ordered soup, chickpeas stewed with pieces of lamb, and skewered liver. There was a small dim room behind the kitchen with two tables in it, and beyond that a raised niche covered with matting where several rustics squatted with enormous loaves of bread which they tore into pieces and put into the soup. For Dyar the assuaging of his appetite was a voluptuous act; it went on and on. What he had ordered at first proved to be completely inadequate. Thami had told him that the desire for food after smoking kif was like no other appetite. He sighed apprehensively. Thami and his kif. How would he feel when he realized his prisoner had escaped, taking with him even Thami's own pipe and mottoui? He wondered if perhaps that might not be considered a supreme injury, an unforgivable act. He had no idea; he knew nothing about this country, save that all its inhabitants behaved like maniacs. Maybe it was not Thami himself of whose reactions he was afraid, he reflected—it might be only that Thami was part of the place and therefore had everything in the place behind him so to speak. Thami in New York—he almost laughed at the image the idea evoked—he was the sort no one would even take the trouble to look at in the street when he asked for a dime. Here it was another matter. He was a spokesman for the place; like Antaeus, whatever strength he had came out of the earth, and his feet were planted squarely upon it. "So you're afraid of him," he remarked to himself in disgust. He looked through the bright kitchen out into the black street beyond. "Afraid he might walk in that door." He sat perfectly still, somehow expecting the idea to conjure up the reality. Instead, an oversized Berber appeared in the doorway, his djellaba slung loosely over one shoulder, and ordered a glass of tea. While he waited the five minutes it always took to prepare the tea, (because the water, while hot, was never boiling, and the mint leaves had to be stripped one by one from the stalk) he stood staring at Dyar in a manner which the other at first found disconcerting, then disturbing, and finally, because he had begun to ask himself the possible reason for this insolent scrutiny, downright frightening. "Why does he block the door like that?" he thought, his heart beginning to beat too fast in a sudden wave of desperate conjecture. For the moment there was only one answer: one of Thami's henchmen had arrived to keep watch, to prevent his escape. They were probably posted in every café and eating-place in the town. For the first time it occurred to him that they might do their work on him in Thami's absence, with Thami conveniently seated in some respectable home, laughing, drinking tea, strumming on an oud. And this possibility seemed in a way worse, perhaps because he had never been able to see Thami in the role of a brutal torturer, the tacit understanding with his own imagination having been that things would somehow be done with comparative gentleness, painlessly. He looked up once again at the Neanderthal head, the deep furrows in the slanting forehead and the brows that formed a single ragged line across the face, and knew that for such a man there were no halfway measures. Yet he could not see any baseness in the face, nor even any particular cunning—merely a primal, ancient blindness, the ineffable, unfocused melancholy of the great apes as they stare between the cage bars.

"I don't want any of this," he told himself. You didn't try to outwit such beings; you simply got out if you could. He rose and walked over to the stove. "How much?" he said in English. The man understood, held up his two hands, the fingers outspread, then raised one lone forefinger. Turning his back on the giant in the doorway, so as to hide as well as possible the fistful of bills he pulled out of his pocket, he handed the cook a hundred-peseta note. The man looked startled, indicated he had no change. Dyar searched further, found twenty-five pesetas. Dubiously the cook accepted it, and pushing aside the Berber in the entrance, went out into the street to get change. "But good God," Dyar thought, seeing the prospect of a whole new horizon of difficulties spreading itself before him. No change for a hundred pesetas. Then a thousand pesetas would be just ten times as hard to get rid of. He moved his shoulder a little, to feel the twelve hundred and sixty thousand-peseta notes against his skin, around his middle. He stood there, conscious of the huge Berber's gaze, but not for an instant returning it, until the cook came back and handed him fourteen pesetas.

When he went out into the street he turned to the right, where there seemed to be the greater number of passers-by, and walked quickly away, looking back only once just before he forced himself through the middle of an ambling group, and being not at all surprised to see the Berber step out of the restaurant and start slowly in the same direction. But Dyar was going rapidly; the next time he turned around to look, he was satisfied that he had lost him.

The whitewashed cobbled street was full of strollers in djellabas moving in both directions; the groups saluted each other constantly as they passed. Dyar threaded his way among them as unostentatiously as he could for a man in a hurry. Sometimes the street would turn into a long, wide flight of stairs with a shop no bigger than a stall on each step, and he would run lightly all the way down, gauging his distances with care to be sure of not plunging into a group of walkers, not daring to look up to see what effect his passage was having on the populace. When he came out into an open space lined on one side with new one-story European buildings he stopped short, not certain whether to continue or go back. There was a café over there with tables and chairs set out along a narrow strip of sidewalk, and at the tables sat Spaniards, some of whom wore the white uniforms of officers in the Moroccan army. His instinct told him to stay in the shade, to go back into the Moroccan town. The question was: where would he be safer? There was no doubt that the greater danger was the possibility of being stopped and questioned by the Spanish. Yet the fear he felt was not of them, but of what could happen back in the streets he had just come from. And now as he stood there clutching his briefcase, the people pushing past him on both sides, his mind still muzzy from the kif, he saw with terror that he was hopelessly confused. He had imagined the town would be something else, that somewhere there would be a place he could go into and ask for information; he had counted on the town to help him as a troubled man counts on a friend to give him advice, knowing beforehand that he will follow whatever advice he gets, because the important thing is to do *something*, to move in any direction, out of his impasse. Once he had been to Agla, he had thought, he would know more about his situation. But he had not understood until now how heavily he was counting on it, partly perhaps because all day he had been thinking only of escaping from Thami. However, at this moment he was conscious that the props that held up his future were in the act of crumbling: he never had had any plan of action, he could not imagine now what he had ever intended to "find out" here in the town, what sort of people he had thought he would be able to see in order to get his information, or even what kind of information he had meant to get. For an instant he looked upward into the sky. The stars were there; they did not tell him what to do. He had turned, he had started to walk, back through the town's entrance gate into the crooked street, but his legs were trembling, and he was only indistinctly aware of what went on around him. This time, since a part of the mechanism that held his being together seemed to have given way, he somehow got turned off the principal street which led steeply upward, and let his legs lead him along a smaller flat one that had fewer lights and people in it, and no shops at all.

24

SOMETIMES THERE WAS the dribbling of fountains into their basins, sometimes only the sound of the fast-running spring water under the stones, behind the walls. Occasionally a single large night-bird dipped toward the ground near a lamp, its crazy shadow running swiftly over the white walls; each time, Dyar started with nervousness, cursing himself silently for not being able to dislodge the fear in him. He walked slowly now, overtaking no one. Ahead, when the way was straight enough, he sometimes caught sight of two men in dark robes, walking hand in hand. They were singing a song with a short vigorous refrain which kept recurring at brief intervals; in between was a lazy variation on the refrain which followed like a weak, uncertain answer to the other. This in itself Dyar surely would not have noticed, had it not been for the fact that each time the meandering section began, just for the first few notes, he had the distinct impression that the sound came from somewhere behind him. By the time he had stopped to listen (his interest aroused not by the music, but by his own fear) the two ahead had always started in again. Finally, in order to be sure, he stood quite still for the space of several choruses, while little by little the voices of the two ahead grew fainter. There was no longer any doubt in his mind; a querulous falsetto voice was singing the same song, coming along behind him. He could hear it more plainly now, like a mocking shadow of the music that went on ahead. But from the strategic spaces that were left in the design of the melody and rhythm by the two men for the single voice in the rear to fill in, he knew immediately that they were conscious of the other's participation in the song. He stepped back into a recess between the houses, where there was a small square tank with water pouring into it, and waited for the owner of the single voice to go by. From in here he could near nothing but the hollow falling of the water into the cistern beside him, and he strained, listening, to see if the other, on noticing his disappearance, would stop singing, change the sound of his voice, or in some other manner send a signal to those who went ahead. If only he had a good-sized flashlight, he thought, or a monkey-wrench, he could hit him on the back of the head as he went past, drag him into the dark here, and go back quickly in the other direction. But when the lone vocalist appeared, he turned out to be accompanied by a friend. Both were youths in their teens, and they stumbled along with the air of not having a thought in their heads, beyond that of not losing the thread of the song that floated back through the street to them. He waited until they had gone past, counted to twenty, and peered around the corner of the house: they were still going along with the same careless, unsteady gait. When they had disappeared he turned and went back, still by no means convinced that when they noticed his absence ahead of them, they would not hurry to confer with the other couple and set out with them to look for him.

Because fear is without any true relationship to reality each time he left a lighted patch of street and entered the dark, he now expected the singers and their friends to be somewhere there waiting, having taken a short cut and got there before him. An iron arm would reach out of an invisible doorway and yank him inside before he knew what was happening, a terrific blow from behind would fell him, and he would come to in some deserted alley, lying in a pile of garbage, his money gone, his passport gone, his watch and clothes gone, with no one to help him either here or in Tangier or anywhere else. No one to cover his nakedness or to provide him with even tomorrow morning's meal. From the jail where they would lodge him they would telephone the American Legation, and he would soon see Tangier again, a thousand times more a victim than ever.

Going by each side street and passageway he opened his eyes wider and stared, as if that might help him to see through the darkness. Back on the main street, climbing the long stairs, where the light from the stalls spilled across the steps, he felt a little better, even though his legs were hollow and seemed not to want to go where he tried to direct them. There was some comfort in being back among people; all he had to do here was walk along his head down and not look up into their faces. When he had got almost back up to the place where he had eaten, he heard drums beating out a peculiar, breathless rhythm. Here the street made several abrupt turns, becoming a series of passageways that led through the buildings. He glanced up at the second-story window overlooking the entrance to one of these tunnels, and saw, through the iron grillework, the back of a row of turbaned heads. At the same instant a peremptory voice in the street behind him called out, *"Hola, señor! Oiga!"* He turned his head quickly and saw, fifty feet back, a native in what looked like a policeman's uniform and helmet, and there was no doubt that the man was trying to attract his attention. He plunged ahead into the darkness, made the first turn with the street, and seeing a partially open door on his right, pushed against it.

The light came from above. A steep stairway led up. The drums were there, and also a faint, wheezing music. He stood behind the door at the foot of the stairs, not having pushed it any further shut than it had been. He waited; nothing happened. Then a man appeared at the top of the stairs, was about to come down, saw him, motioned to another, who presently also came into view. Together they beckoned to him. *"Tlah. Tlah. Agi,"* they said. Because their faces were unmistakably friendly, he slowly started to mount the steps.

It was a small, very crowded café with benches along the walls. The dim light came from a bulb hung above a high copper samovar which stood on a shelf in a corner. All the men wore white turbans, and they looked up with interest as Dyar entered, making room for him at the end of a bench by the drummers, who sat in a circle on the floor at the far end of the room. Over here it was very dark indeed, and he had the impression that something inexplicable was taking place on the floor almost at his feet. The men were looking downward through the smoke at a formless mass that quaked, jerked, shuddered and heaved, and although the room shook with the pounding of the drums, it was as if another kind of silence were there in the air, an imperious silence that stretched from the eyes of the men watching to the object moving at their feet. As his own eyes grew accustomed to the confused light, Dyar saw that it was a man, his hands locked firmly together behind him as if they were chained there. Until this moment he had been writhing and twisting on the floor, but now slowly he was rising to his knees, turning his head desperately from side to side, an expression of agony on his tortured face. Even when, five minutes later, he had finally got to his feet, he did not alter the position of his hands, and always the spasms that forced his body this way and that, in perfect rhythm with the increasing hysteria of the drums and the low cracked voice of the flute, seemed to come from some secret center far inside him. Dyar watched impassively. He was completely hidden by the ranks of the men who stood near him looking at the spectacle, and more of whom kept crowding up; from the door he was invisible, and the consciousness of that gave him momentary relief. Someone passed him a glass of tea from the other end of the long table. As he held it under his nose, the sharp fumes of hot spearmint cleared his head, and he became aware of another odor in the air, a spicy resinous smell which he traced to a brazier behind one of the drummers; a heavy smudge of sweet smoke rose constantly. The man had begun to cry out, softly at first, and then savagely; his cries were answered by rhythmical calls of *"Al-lah!"* from the drummers. Dyar stole a glance around at the faces of the spectators. The expression he saw was the same on all sides: utter absorption in the dance, almost adoration of the man performing it. A lighted kif pipe was thrust in front of him. He took it and smoked it without looking to see who had offered it to him. His heart, which had been beating violently when he came in, had ceased its pounding; he felt calmer now.

After a day passed largely in the contemplation of that far-off and unlikely place which was the interior of himself, he did not find it difficult now to reject flatly the reality of what he was seeing. He merely sat and watched, content in the conviction that the thing he was looking at was not taking place in the world that really existed. It was too far beyond the pale of the possible. The kif pipe was refilled several times for him, and the smoke, rising to his head, helped him to sit there and watch a thing he did not believe.

According to Dyar's eyes, the man now at last moved his hands, reached inside his garments and pulled out a large knife, which he flourished with wide gestures. It gleamed feebly in the faint light. Without glancing behind him, one of the drummers threw a handful of something over his shoulder and resumed beating, coming in on the complex rhythm perfectly: the smoke rose in thicker clouds from the censer. The chanted strophes were now antiphonal, with "*Al-lah!*" being thrown back and forth like a red-hot stone from one side of the circle to the other. At the same time it was as if the sound had become two high walls between which the dancer whirled and leapt, striking against their invisible surfaces with his head in a vain effort to escape beyond them.

The man held up his bare arm. The blade glinted, struck at it on a down beat of the drum pattern. And again. And again and again, until the arm and hand were shining and black. Then the other arm was slashed, the tempo increasing as the drummers' bodies bent further forward toward the center of the circle. In the sudden flare of a match nearby, Dyar saw the glistening black of the arms and hands change briefly to red, as if the man had dipped his arms in bright red paint; he saw, too, the ecstatic face as an arm was raised to the mouth and the swift tongue began to lick the blood in rhythm. With the shortening of the phrases, the music had become an enormous panting. It had kept every detail of syncopation intact, even at its present great rate of speed, thus succeeding in destroying the listeners' sense of time, forcing their minds to accept the arbitrary one it imposed in its place. With this hypnotic device it had gained complete domination. But as to the dancer, it was hard to say whether they were commanding him or he them. He bent over, and with a great sweep of his arm began a thorough hacking of his legs; the music's volume swelled in accompaniment.

Dyar was there, scarcely breathing. It could not be said that he watched now, because in his mind he had moved forward from looking on to a kind of participation. With each gesture the man made at this point, he felt a sympathetic desire to cry out in triumph. The mutilation was being done for him, to him; it was his own blood that spattered onto the drums and made the floor slippery. In a world which had not yet been muddied by the discovery of thought, there was this certainty, as solid as a boulder, as real as the beating of his heart, that the man was dancing to purify all who watched. When the dancer threw himself to the floor with a despairing cry, Dyar knew that in reality it was a cry of victory, that spirit had triumphed; the expressions of satisfaction on the faces around him confirmed this. The musicians hesitated momentarily, but at a signal from the men who bent solicitously over the dancer's twitching body they resumed playing the same piece, slowly as at the beginning. Dyar sat perfectly still, thinking of nothing, savoring the unaccustomed sensations which had been freed within him. Conversation had started up; since no one passed him a pipe, he took out Thami's and smoked it. Soon the dancer rose from where he lay on the floor, stood up a little unsteadily, and going to each musician in turn, took each head between his hands from which the blood still dripped, and planted a solemn kiss on the forehead. Then he pushed his way through the crowd, paid for his tea, and went out.

Dyar stayed on a few minutes, and after drinking what remained of his tea, which had long ago grown cold, gave the qaouaji the peseta it cost, and slowly went down the steps. Inside the door he hesitated; it seemed to him he was making a grave decision in venturing out into the street again. But whatever awaited him out there had to be faced, he told himself, and it might as well be now as a few minutes or hours later. He opened the door. The covered street was deserted and black, but beyond the farthest arch, where it led into the open, the walls and paving stones glowed as the moonlight poured over them. He walked out into a wide plaza dominated by a high minaret, feeling only acute surprise to find that none of his fear was left. It had all been liberated by the past hour in the café; how, he would never understand, nor did he care. But now, whatever circumstance presented itself, he would find a way to deal with it. The confidence of his mood was augmented by the several pipes of kif he presently smoked sitting on the ledge of the fountain in the center of the plaza.

A hundred feet away, in a café overlooking the same plaza, Thami was lamenting having left his pipe and mottoui behind in the house. He had to accept the qaouaji's generosity, and it was embarrassing to him. With the number of parcels he had, he was understandably loath to set off up the mountain, and besides, he had just eaten heavily. He had wanted very much to buy a bottle of good Terry cognac to drink that night, but his money had proved insufficient for such a luxury. Instead, he had got a large mass of majoun, at the same time making a firm resolution to demand his five thousand pesetas as soon as he got back up to the house. The extra money he had been promised could wait, but not that initial sum. Dyar would be in no mood to give it to him, he knew, but after all, he had the upper hand: he would simply threaten to leave tomorrow. That would bring him around.

Dyar sat, watching the strong moonlight flood the white surface of the plaza, letting his mind grow lucid and hard like the objects and their shadows around him. (At noon the kif had had a diffusing effect, softening and melting his thought, spreading it within him, but now it had tightened him; he felt alert and fully in touch with the world.) Since the situation was worse than he had imagined, because of the patent impossibility of his getting change for the notes anywhere in Agla, the only thing to do was to spend a little money improving that situation. It would mean taking Thami into his confidence, but it was simple, and if he could instil into him the idea that once a man has agreed to be an accomplice he is as guilty as his companion, he thought the risk would not be too great. The fact that he had already dismissed as childish and neurotic the fear which had driven him out of the house and along the mountainside all day, did not strike him as suspect or worthy of any particular scrutiny. The important thing, he thought, was to get over the border into French Morocco, which was many times larger than the Spanish Zone, where he would be less conspicuous (because, while he might be taken for French, he could never pass for a Spaniard), and where the police were less on the lookout for strangers. But before that they would have to have change for the banknotes. Feeling the need to walk as he made his plans, he rose and went across to the dark side of the plaza, where small trees lined the walk. Without paying attention to where he was going, he turned off into a side street.

Every day for the next week he would send Thami down here to Agla for provisions, and each time he would give him a thousand peseta note with which to purchase them. He was confident Thami could get change. That way at the end of the week they would at least have enough to start south. He would also give Thami five hundred pesetas a day until they were across the border, with a promised bonus of an extra five thousand when they were in French territory, and a hundred on each thousand-peseta note Thami could change into francs for him once there were there. Assuming he were able to get it all changed, this project would cost him over two thousand dollars, but that was a small price to pay for being in the clear.

From ahead came the noise of voices raised in angry dispute. Although the plaza out there was empty, the town was by no means entirely asleep. Turning a bend in the street he came out upon a small square darkened by a trellis of vines overhead. A group of excited men had gathered around two small boys who apparently had been fighting; they had started by being onlookers, and then, inevitably, had entered into the altercation with all the passion of the original participants. The rectangles of yellow light that lay on the pavement came from the shops that were open; in contrast the mottles of moonlight in dark corners were blue. He did not stop to watch the argument: walking along the white street in the moon's precise light was conducive to the unfolding of plans. The commotion was such that no one noticed him as he passed through the shady square. The shops, which seemed to belong primarily to tailors and carpenters, were empty at the moment, having been deserted at the first indication of a diversion in the street. The way twisted a little; there was one more stall open here, and beyond, only the moonlight. It was a carpenter's shop, and the man had been working in the doorway, building a high wooden chest shaped like a steamer trunk. The hammer lay where he had left it. Dyar saw it without seeing it; then he looked at it hard, looked involuntarily for the nails. They too were there, a bit long, but straight and new, lying on a little square stool nearby. Only when he had passed the shouting group again and had got so far beyond that he could no longer hear the hoarse cries, the hammer and one big nail in his coat pocket, did he realize that for all his great clarity of mind sitting by the fountain smoking his kif, he had been unbelievably stupid. What were the hammer and nail for? To fix the door. What door? The door to the cottage, the rattling door that kept him from sleeping. And where was the cottage, how was he going to get there?

He stood still, more appalled by the revelation of this incredible lapse in his mental processes than by the fact itself that he could not get to the house, that he had nowhere to sleep. This kif is treacherous stuff, he thought, starting ahead slowly.

Back in the deserted plaza he seated himself once again on the edge of the fountain and pulled out the pipe. Treacherous or not, like alcohol it at least made the present moment bearable. As he smoked he saw a figure emerge from the shadows on the dark side of the plaza and come sauntering over in his direction. When it was still fairly far away, but near enough for him to see it was a man carrying a large basket, it said: *"Salam."* Dyar grunted.

"Andek es sebsi?"

He looked up unbelieving. It was impossible. The stuff was treacherous, so he did not move, but waited.

The man came nearer, exclaimed. Then Dyar jumped up. "You son of a bitch!" he cried, laughing with pleasure, clapping Thami's shoulder several times.

Thami was delighted, too. Dyar had eaten, was in a good humor. The return to the house with its attendant furious reproaches no longer had to be dreaded. He could broach the subject of the money. And there was his own kif-pipe, whose absence he had been so lately regretting, right in Dyar's hand. But he was nervous about being here in the plaza.

"You're going to have trouble here," he said. "It's very bad. I told you not to come. If one moqqaddem sees you, 'Oiga, señor, come on to the comisaría, we look at your papers, my friend.' Let's go."

The moonlight was very bright when they had left the town behind and were among the olive trees. Halfway up the mountain, among the ragged rocks, they sat down, and Thami took out the majoun.

"You know what this is?" he asked.

"Sure I know. I've had it before."

"This won't make you drunk for an hour yet. Or more. When we get to the house I'll make tea. Then you'll see how drunk."

"I know. I've had it before, I said."

Thami looked at him with disbelief, and divided the cake into two unequal pieces, handing the larger to Dyar.

"It's soft," Dyar remarked in some surprise. "The kind I had was hard."

"Same thing," Thami said with indifference. "This is better." Dyar was inclined to agree with him, as regarded the flavor. They sat, quietly eating, each one conscious in his own fashion that as he swallowed the magical substance he was irrevocably delivering himself over to unseen forces which would take charge of his life for the hours to come.

They did not speak, but sat hearing the water moving downward in the gulf of moonlight and shadows that lay open at their feet.

25

"HOME AGAIN!" Dyar said jovially as he went inside the house, greeted by the close mildewed smell he had said good-bye to so long ago. "Let's make that fire before we blow our respective tops." He tossed the briefcase into a corner, glad to be rid of it.

Thami shut the door, locked it, and stared at him, not understanding. "You're already m'hashish," he said. "I know when I look at you. What are you talking about?"

"The fire. The fire. Get some wood. Quick!"

"Plenty of wood," said Thami imperturbably, pointing to the patio with its crates. Dyar stepped out and began to throw them wildly into the center of the room. "Break 'em up!" he shouted. "Smash 'em! It's going to be God-damned cold in here without any blanket. We've got to keep the fire going as long as we can."

Thami obeyed, wondering at the surprising transformation a little majoun could work in a Christian. He had never before seen Dyar in good spirits. When he had an enormous pile of slats, he pushed it to one side and spread the two mats, one on top of the other, in front of the fireplace. Then he went out into the kitchen and busied himself building a charcoal fire in the earthen brazier, in order to prepare the tea.

"Ah!" he heard Dyar cry in triumph from the patio. "Just what we wanted!" He had unearthed several small logs in one corner, which he carried in and dumped beside the fireplace. He joined Thami in the kitchen. "Give me a match," he said. "My candle's gone out." Thami was squatting over the brazier, and he looked up smiling. "How do you feel now?" he asked.

"I feel great. Why? How do you feel?"

Thami handed him his box of matches. "I feel good," he answered. He was not sure how to begin. Perhaps it would be better to wait until they were lying in front of the fire. But by then Dyar's mood might have changed. "I wanted to buy a big bottle of cognac tonight, you know." He paused.

"Well, why didn't you? I could do with a drink right now."

Thami rubbed his forefinger against his thumb, back and forth, expressively.

"Oh," said Dyar soberly. "I see." He went back into the other room, stuffed some paper into the fireplace, put some crate wood on top, and lighted it. Then he walked over to the darkest corner of the room and keeping his eye on the door into the patio, pulled out five notes from the inside of his shirt. "This'll show him I'm playing straight with him," he said to himself. He returned to the kitchen and handed the money to Thami, saying: "Here."

"Thank you," Thami said. He stood up and patted him on the back lightly, three pats.

"When you come in I'll talk to you about the rest of it." He went out into the patio and stood looking up at the huge globe of the full moon; never had he seen it so near or so strong. A night bird screamed briefly in the air overhead—a peculiar, chilly sound, not quite like anything he had heard before. He stood, hearing the sound again and again in his head, a long string of interior echoes that traced an invisible ladder across the black sky. The crackling of the fire inside roused him. He went in and threw on a log. He crouched down, looking into the fire, following the forms of the flames with his eyes. The fireplace drew well; no smoke came out into the room.

They were putting their feet carefully on the square gray flagstones that led through the grass across the garden, having to step off them at one point onto the soaked turf to avoid the hose with the sprinkler attachment. It went around and around, unevenly. Mrs.

Shields had pulled down all the shades in the big room, because the sun shone in and faded the "drapes," she said. Once the windows were shut, the thunderstorm could come whenever it liked; it had been threatening all afternoon. Across the river it looked very dark. It was probably raining there already, but the rolling of the thunder was more distant. Far up the valley toward the gap it groaned. There was wild country up there, and the people did not have the same friendliness they had here where the land was good. Mrs. Shields had let the hose spot her dress. It was a shame, he thought, looking closely at the paisley design.

He did not want to be in the house when they left. Turning to the empty rooms where the air still moved with the currents set up by their last-minute hurryings, feeling the seat of a chair in which one of them had sat, because of that a little warmer than the others, but the warmth still palpable after they had gone, seeing the cord of a window-shade still swinging almost imperceptibly—he could not bear any of those things. It was better to stay in the garden, say goodbye to them there, and wait to go in until the house was completely dead. And the storm would either break or it would growl around the countryside until evening. The grapes are getting ripe, she said as they passed under the arbor. And the sailboats will be making for the harbor. He stood against a cherry tree and watched the ants running up and down across the rough brown bark of the trunk, very near his face. That summer was in a lost region, and all roads to it had been cut.

Thami came in, carrying the burning brazier. He set it down in the middle of the room, went and got the teapot and the glasses. While he waited for the water to boil, blowing from time to time on the glowing coals, Dyar told him of his plans. But when he came to the point of mentioning the sum he had, he found he could not do it. Thami listened, shook his head skeptically when Dyar had finished. "Pesetas are no good in the French Zone," he said. "You can't change them. You'd have to take them to the Jews if you did that."

"Well, we'll take 'em to the Jews, then. Why not?"

Thami looked at him pityingly. "The Jews?" he cried. "They won't give you *anything* for them. They'll give you five francs for one peseta. Maybe six." Dyar knew the current rate was a little over eight. He sighed. "I don't know. We'll have to wait and see." But secretly he was determined to do it that way, even if he got only five.

Thami poured the boiling tea into the glasses. "No mint this time," he said.

"It doesn't matter. It's the heat that does it."

"Yes." He blew out the candle and they sat by the light of the flames. Dyar settled back, leaning against the wall, but immediately Thami objected. "You'll get sick," he explained. "That wall is very wet. Last night I moved my bed, it was so wet there."

"Ah." Dyar sat up, drew his legs under him, and continued to drink his tea. Was the hand on the briefcase explained away for all time? Why not, he asked himself. Believing or doubting is a matter of wanting to believe or doubt; at the moment he felt like believing because it suited his mood.

"So, are you with me?" he said.

"What?"

"We stay a week, and you go every day and change a thousand pesetas?"

"Whatever you say," said Thami, reaching for his glass to pour him more tea."

The room was getting taut and watchful around him; Dyar remembered the sensation from the night at the Villa Hesperides. But it was not the same this time because he himself felt very different. The bird outside cried again. Thami looked surprised. "I don't know how you call that bird in English. We call it *youca*."

Dyar shut his eyes. A terrible motor had started to throb at the back of his head. It was not painful; it frightened him. With his eyes shut he had the impression that he was lying on his back, that if he opened them he would see the ceiling. It was not necessary to open them—he could see it anyway, because his lids had become transparent. It was a gigantic screen against which images were beginning to be projected—tiny swarms of colored glass beads arranged themselves obligingly into patterns, swimming together and apart, forming mosaics that dissolved as soon as they were made. Feathers, snow-crystals, lace and church windows crowded consecutively onto the screen, and the projecting light grew increasingly powerful. Soon the edges of the screen would begin to burn, and the fire would be on each side of his head. "God, this is going to blind me," he said suddenly; he opened his eyes and realized he had said nothing.

"Do you know what they look like?" Thami asked.

"What what look like?"

"*Youcas.*"

"I don't know what anything looks like. I don't know what you're talking about!"

Thami looked slightly aggrieved. "You're m'hashish, my friend. M'hashish *bezef!*"

Each time Thami spoke to him, he raised his head and shook it slightly, opened his eyes, and made a senseless reply. Thami began to sing in a small, faraway voice. It was a sound you could walk on, a soft carpet that stretched before him across the flat blinding desert. *Ijbed selkha men rasou. . . .* But he came up against the stone walls of an empty house beside a mountain. The fire was raging behind it, burning wildly and silently, the door was open and it was dark inside. Cobwebs hung to the walls, soldiers had been there, and there were women's silk underclothes strewn about the empty rooms. He knew that a certain day, at a certain moment, the house would crumble and nothing would be left but dust and rubble, indistinguishable from the talus of gravel that lay below the cliffs. It would be absolutely silent, the falling of the house, like a film that goes on running after the sound apparatus has broken. *Bache idaoui sebbatou. . . .* The carpet had caught on fire, too. Someone would blame him.

"I'm God damned if I'll pay for it," he said. Regular hours, always superiors to give you orders, no security, no freedom, no freedom, no freedom.

Thami said: "*Hak.* Take your tea."

Dyar reached forward and swam against the current toward the outstretched glass shining with reflected firelight. "I've got it. *Muchas gracias, amigo.*" He paused, seemed to be listening, then with exaggerated care he set the glass down on the mat beside him. "I put it there because it's hot, see?" (But Thami was not paying attention; already he was back in his own pleasure pavilion overlooking his miles of verdant gardens, and the water ran clear in blue enamel channels. *Chta! Chta! Sebbatou aând al qadi!*)

"Thami, I'm in another world. Do you understand? Can you hear me?"

Thami, his eyes shut, his body weaving slowly back and forth as
he sang, did not answer. The perspective from his tower grew vaster,
the water bubbled up out of the earth on all sides. He had ordered it all
to be, many years ago. (The night is a woman clothed in a robe of
burning stars. . . .) *Ya, Leïla, Lia. . . .*

"I can see you sitting there," Dyar insisted, "but I'm in another
world." He began to laugh softly with delight.

"I don't know," he said reflectively. "Sometimes I think the
other way around. I think. . . ." He spoke more slowly. "We . . . .
would be better . . . . . . I think . . . . . if you can get through
. . . . if you can get through . . . . Why can't anyone get through?"
His voice became so loud and sharp here that Thami opened his eyes
and stopped singing.

"*Chkoun entina?*" he said. "My friend, I'm m'hashish as much
as you."

"You get here, you float away again, you come to that *crazy*
place! Oh, my *God!*" He was talking very fast, and he went into a
little spasm of laughter, then checked himself. "*I've* got nothing to
laugh about. It's not funny." With a whoop he rolled over onto the
floor and abandoned himself to a long fit of merriment. Thami listened
without moving.

After a long time the laughter stopped as suddenly as it had
begun; he lay quite still. The other's little voice crept out again: "*Ijbed
selkha men rasou . . .*" and went on and on. From time to time the
fire stirred, as an ember shifted its position. Every small sound was
razor-sharp, but inside there was a solid silence. He was trying not to
breathe, he wanted to be absolutely motionless, because he felt that
the air which fitted so perfectly around him was a gelatinous substance
which had been moulded to match with infinite exactitude every
contour of his person. If he moved ever so slightly he would feel it
pushing against him, and that would be unbearable. The monstrous
swelling and deflating of himself which each breath occasioned was a
real peril. But that wave broke, receded, and he was left stranded for a
moment in a landscape of liquid glassy light, greengold and shimmer-
ing. Burnished, rich and oily, then swift like flaming water. Look at it!
Look at it! Drink it with your eyes. It's the only water you'll ever see.
Another wave would roll up soon; they were coming more often.

Ya Leïla, Lia. . . . For a moment he was quite in his senses. He lay there comfortably and listened to the long, melancholy melodic line of the song, thinking: "How long ago was it that I was laughing?" Perhaps the whole night had gone by, and the effect had already worn off.

"Thami?" he said. Then he realized it had been almost impossible to get the word out, because his mouth was of cardboard. He gasped a little, and thought of moving. (I must remember to tell myself to move my left hand so I can raise myself onto my elbow. It must move back further before I can begin to pull my knees up. But I don't want to move my knees. Only my hand. So I can raise myself onto my elbow. If I move my knees I can sit up. . . .)

He was sitting up.

(I'm sitting up.) *Is this what I wanted? Why did I want to sit up?*

He waited.

(I didn't. I only wanted to raise myself onto my elbow.) *Why?* (I wanted to lie facing the other way. It's going to be more comfortable that way.)

He was lying down.

(. . . from the gulf of the infinite, Allah looks across with an eye of gold. . . .) *Alef leïlat ou leïla, ya leïla, lia!*

Before the wind had arrived, he heard it coming, stirring stealthily around the sharp pinnacles of rock up there, rolling down through the ravines, whispering as it moved along the surface of the cliffs, coming to wrap itself around the house. He lay a year, dead, listening to it coming.

There was an explosion in the room. Thami had thrown another log onto the fire. "That gave me designs. Red, purple," said Dyar without speaking, sitting up again. The room was a red grotto, a theatre, a vast stable with a balcony that hung in the shadows. Up there was a city of little rooms, a city inside a pocket of darkness, but there were windows in the walls you could not see, and beyond these the sun shone down on an outer city built of ice.

"My God, Thami, water!" he cried thickly. Thami was standing above him.

"Good-bye," said Thami. Heavily he sat down and rolled over onto his side, sang no more.

"Water," he tried to say again in a very soft voice, and trem-
blingly he made a supreme effort to get to his feet. "My God, I've got
to have water," he whispered to himself; it was easier to whisper.
Because he was looking down at his feet from ten thousand feet up, he
had to take exquisite care in walking, but he stepped over Thami and
got out into the patio to the pail. Sighing with the effort of kneeling
down, he put his face into the fire of the cold water and drew it into his
throat.

When it was finished he rose, threw his head up, and looked at
the moon. The wind had come, but it had been here before. Now it
was necessary to get back into the room, to get all the way across the
room to the door. But he must not breathe so heavily. To open the
door and go out. Out there the wind would be cold, but he must go
anyway.

The expedition through the magic room was hazardous. There
was a fragile silence there which must not be shattered. The fire,
shedding its redness on Thami's masklike face, must not know he was
stealing past. At each step he lifted his feet far off the floor into the air,
like someone walking through a field of high wet grass. He saw the
door ahead of him, but suddenly between him and it a tortuous
corridor made of pure time interposed itself. It was going to take
endless hours to get down to the end. And a host of invisible people
was lined up along its walls, but on the other side of the walls, mutely
waiting for him to go by—an impassive chorus, silent and without
pity. "Waiting for me," he thought. The sides of his mind, indistinguishable from the walls of the corridor, were lined with messages in
Arabic script. All the time, directly before his eyes was the knobless
door sending out its ominous message. It was not sure, it could not be
trusted. If it opened when he did not want it to open, by itself, all the
horror of existence could crowd in upon him. He stretched his hand
out and touched the large cold key. The key explained the heaviness in
his overcoat pocket. He put his left hand into the pocket and felt the
hammer, and the head and point of the nail. That was work to be done,
but later, when he came in. He turned the key, pulled open the door,
felt the bewildered wind touch his face. "Keep away from the cliff," he
whispered as he stepped outside. Around him stretched the night's
formless smile. The moon was far out over the empty regions now.

Relieving himself against the wall of the house, he heard the wind up here trying to cover the long single note of the water down in the valley. Inside, by the fire, time was slowly dissolving, falling to pieces. But even at the end of the night there would still be an ember of time left, of a subtle, bitter flavor, soft to the touch, glowing from its recess of ashes, before it paled and died, and the heart of the ancient night stopped beating.

He turned toward the door, his steps short and halting like those of an old man. It was going to require a tremendous effort to get back to the mat, but because the only thing he could conceive of at this instant was to sink down on it and lie out flat by the fire, he felt certain he could make the effort. As he shut the door behind him he murmured to it: "You know I'm here, don't you?" The idea was hateful to him, but there was something he could do about it. What that thing was he could not recall, yet he knew the situation was not hopeless; he could remedy it later.

Thami had not stirred. As he looked down from his remote height at the relaxed body, a familiar uneasiness stole over him, only he could connect it with no cause. Partly he knew that what he saw before him was Thami, Thami's head, trunk, arms and legs. Partly he knew it was an unidentifiable object lying there, immeasurably heavy with its own meaninglessness, a vast imponderable weight that nothing could lighten. As he stood lost in static contemplation of the thing, the wind pushed the door feebly, making a faint rattling. But *could* nothing lighten it? If the air were let in, the weight might escape of its own accord, into the shadows of the room and the darkness of the night. He looked slowly behind him. The door was silent, staring, baleful. "You know I'm here, all right," he thought, "but you won't know long." He had willed the hammer and nail into existence, and they were there in his pocket. Thinking of their heaviness, he felt his body lean to one side. He had to shift the position of his foot to retain his balance, to keep from being pulled down by their weight. The rattle came again, a series of slight knockings, knowing and insinuating. But now, did they come from the mat below him? "If it opens," he thought, looking at the solid, inert mass in front of him in the fire's dying light, his eyes staring, gathering fear from within him. "If it opens." There was that thing he had to do, he must do it, and he knew what it was but he could not think what it was.

A mass of words had begun to ferment inside him, and now they bubbled forth. "Many Mabel damn. Molly Daddy lamb. Lolly dibble up-man. Dolly little Dan," he whispered, and then he giggled. The hammer was in his right hand, the nail in his left. He bent over, swayed, and fell heavily to his knees on the mat, beside the outstretched door. It did not move. The mountain wind rushed through his head, his head that was a single seashell full of grottoes; its infinitely smooth pink walls, delicate, paper-thin, caught the light of the embers as he moved along the galleries. "Melly diddle din," he said, quite loud, putting the point of the nail as far into Thami's ear as he could. He raised his right arm and hit the head of the nail with all his might. The object relaxed imperceptibly, as if someone had said to it: "It's all right." He laid the hammer down, and felt of the nail-head, level with the soft lobe of the ear. It had two little ridges on it; he rubbed his thumbnail across the imperfections in the steel. The nail was as firmly embedded as if it had been driven into a coconut. "Merry Mabel dune." The children were going to make a noise when they came out at recess-time. The fire rattled, the same insistent music that could not be stilled, the same skyrockets that would not hurry to explode. And the floor had fallen over onto him. His hand was bent under him, he could feel it, he wanted to move. "I must remember that I exist," he told himself; that was clear, like a great rock rising out of the sea around it. "I must remember that I am alive."

He did not know whether he was lying still or whether his hands and feet were shaking painfully with the effort of making himself believe he was there and wanted to move his hand. He knew his skin was more tender than the skin of an overripe plum; no matter how softly he touched it, it would break and smear him with the stickiness beneath. Someone had shut the bureau drawer he was lying in and gone away, forgotten him. The great languor. The great slowness. The night had sections filled with repose, and there were places in time to be visited, faces to forget, words to understand, silences to be studied.

The fire was out; the inhuman night had come into the room. Once again he wanted water. "I've come back," he thought; his mouth, gullet, stomach ached with dryness. "Thami has stayed behind. I'm the only survivor. That's the way I wanted it." That warm, humid, dangerous breeding-place for ideas had been destroyed. "Thank God he hasn't come back with me," he told himself. "I never wanted him to know I was alive." He slipped away again; the water was too distant.

A maniacal light had fallen into the room and was hopping about. He sat up and frowned. The ear in the head beside him. The little steel disc with the irregular grooves in it. He had known it would be there. He sighed, crept on his hands and knees around the ends of the drawn-up legs, arrived in the cold, blinding patio, and immersed his face in the pail. He was not real, but he knew he was alive. When he lifted his head, he let it fall all the way back against the wall, and he stayed there a long time, the mountains' morning light pressing brutally into his eyelids.

Later he rose, went into the room, dragged Thami by his legs through the patio into the kitchen and shut the door. Overpowered by weakness, he lay down on the mat, and still trembling fell into a bottomless sleep. As the day advanced the wind increased, the blue sky grew white, then gray. The door rattled unceasingly, but he heard nothing.

26

THE POUNDING on the door had been going on for a long time before, becoming aware of it, he began to scramble up the slippery sides of the basin of sleep where he found himself, in a frantic attempt to escape into consciousness. When finally he opened his eyes and was back in the room, a strange languor remained, like a great, soft cushion beneath him; he did not want to move. Still the fist went on hitting the door insistently, stopping now and then so that when it began again it was louder after the silence that had come in between.

There were cushions under him and cushions on top of him; he would not move. But he called out: "Who is it?" several times, each time managing to put a little more force into his unruly voice. The knocking ceased. Soon he felt a faint curiosity to know who it was out there. He sat up, then got up and went to the door, saying again, his mouth close to the wood: "Who is it?" Outside there was only the sound of the casual dripping of water from the eaves onto the bare earth. "So it's been raining again," he thought with unreasoning anger. "Who is it?" he said, louder, at the same time being startled as he put his hand to his face and felt the three-day beard there.

He unlocked the door, opened it and looked out. It was a dark day, and as he had expected, there was no one in sight. Nor was he still any more than vaguely interested in knowing who had been knocking. It was not indifference; he knew it concerned him vitally—he knew that he should care very much who had stood outside the door a moment ago. But now there was not enough of him left to feel strongly about anything; everything had been spent last night. Today was like an old, worn-out film being run off—dim, jerky, flickering, full of cuts, and with a plot he could not seize. It was hard to pay attention to it.

As he turned to go back in, for he felt like sleeping again, a voice called: "Hola!" from the direction of the stream. And although he was having difficulty focusing (the valley was a murky gray jumble), he saw a man who a second before had been standing still looking back at the house turn and start walking up toward it. Dyar did not move; he watched; on the top of his head now and then he felt the cold drops that fell singly, unhurriedly, from the sky.

The man was a Berber in country clothes. As he drew near the house he began to walk more slowly and to look back down the path. Soon he stopped altogether, and stood, obviously waiting for someone behind him. From between the rocks two figures presently emerged and climbed up across the stream, around the curve in the path. Dyar, remaining in the doorway, observing this unannounced arrival, feeling sure that it meant something of great importance to him, was unable to summon the energy necessary for conjecture; he watched. When the two figures had reached the spot where the lone one stood, they stopped and conferred with him; he waved his arm toward the house, and then sat down, while they continued along the path. But now Dyar had begun to stare, for one man was wearing a uniform with jodhpurs and boots, while the other, who seemed to need assistance in climbing, was in a raincoat and a brilliant purple turban. When the two had got about halfway between the seated Berber and the house, he realized with a shock that the second person was a woman in slacks. And an instant later his mouth opened slightly because he had recognized Daisy. Under his breath he said: "Good God!"

As she came nearer and saw him staring at her she waved, but said nothing. Dyar, behaving like a small child, stood watching her approach, did not even acknowledge her greeting.

"Oh!" she exclaimed, gasping a little as she came on to the level piece of ground where the house stood. She walked toward the door and put her hand out. He took it, still looking at her, unbelieving. "Hello," he said.

"Look. Will you please not think I'm a busybody. How are you?" She let go of his hand and directed a piercing glance at his face; unthinkingly he put his hand to his chin. "All right?" Without waiting for an answer she turned to the man in the chauffeur's uniform. *"Me puedes esparar ahí abajo."* She pointed to the native waiting below. The man made a listless salute and walked away.

"Oh!" said Daisy again, looking about for a place to sit, and seeing nothing but the wet earth. "I must sit down. Do you think we could go in where it's dry?"

"Oh, sure." Dyar came to life. "I'm just surprised to see you. Go on in." She crossed the room and sat down on the mat in front of the dead fireplace. "What are you doing here?" he said, his voice expressionless.

She had her knees together out to one side, and she had folded her hands over them. "Obviously, I've come to see you." She looked up at him. "But you want to know *why*, of course. If you'll be patient while I catch my breath, I'll tell you." She paused, and sighed. "I'll lay my case before you and you can do as you like." Now she reached up and seized his arm. "Darling" (the sound of her voice had changed, grown more intense), "you must go back. Sit down. No, here, beside me. You've got to go back to Tangier. That's why I'm here. To help you get back in."

She felt his body stiffen as he turned his head quickly to look at her. "Don't talk," she said. "Let me say my little piece. It's late, and it's going to rain, and we must leave Agla while there's still daylight. There are twenty-seven kilometers of trail before one gets to the *carretera*. You don't know anything about the roads because you didn't come that way."

"How do you know how I came?"

"You *do* think I'm an utter fool, don't you?" She offered him a cigarette from her case and they smoked a moment in silence. "I saw the little business in the garden the other night, and I thought I recognized that drunken brother of the Beidaoui's. And I had no reason to doubt his wife's word. According to her he brought you here. So that's that. But all that's of no importance."

He was thinking: "How can I find out how much she knows?" The best idea seemed to be simply to ask her; thus he cut her short, saying: "What have they told you?"

"Who?" she said drily. "Jack Wilcox and Ronny Ashcombe-Danvers?"

He did not reply.

"If you mean them," she pursued, "they told me everything, naturally. You're all bloody fools, all three of you, but you're the biggest bloody fool. What in *God's* name did you think you were doing? Of course, I don't know what Jack was thinking of in the first place to let you fetch Ronny's money, and he's so secretive I couldn't make anything out of his silly tale. It wasn't until I met Ronny yesterday at the airport that I got any sort of story that hung together at all. Ronny's an old friend of mine, you know, and I can tell you he's more than displeased about the whole thing, as well he may be."

"Yes," he said, completely at a loss for anything else to say.

"I've argued with him until I'm hoarse, trying to persuade him to let me come up here. Of course he was all for coming himself with a band of ruffians from the port and taking his chances on getting the money back by force. Because obviously he can't do it by legal means. But I think now he understands how childish that idea is. I made him see how much better it would be if I could get you to come back of your own accord."

Dyar thought: So Ashcombe-Danvers is an old friend of hers. He's promised her a percentage of everything she can get back for him. And he remembered Mme. Werth's reservation at the hotel in

Marrakech; Daisy might as well have been saying to him: "Do come back and be a victim again for my sake."

"It's out of the question," he said shortly.

"Oh, is it?" she cried, her eyes blazing. "Because little Mr. Dyar says it is, I suppose?"

He flushed. "You're God-damned right."

She leaned toward him. "Why do you think I came up here, you bloody, bloody fool, you conceited idiot? God!"

"I don't know. I'm wondering, myself," he said, tossing his cigarette into the fireplace.

"I came," she paused. "Because I'm the biggest fool of all, because through some ghastly defect in my character, I—because I've somehow—let myself become fond of you. God knows why! *God* knows why! Do you think I'd come all the way here *only* to help Ronny get his money back?" ("Yes, you would," he thought.) "He's better equipped for a manhunt than I am, with his gang of cutthroats from the Marsa." ("She doesn't believe any of that. She thinks she can do the job better," he told himself.) "I'm here because Ronny's a friend of mine, yes, and because I should like to help him get back what belongs to him, what you've stolen from him." (Her voice trembled a little on the word *stolen*.) "Yes, of course. All of that. And I'm here also because what will help him happens to be the only thing that'll help you."

"Do my soul good. I know. Walk in and make a clean breast of it."

"Your soul!" she snapped. "Bugger your soul! I said help you. You're in a mess. You know damned well what a mess you're in. And you're not going to get out of it without some help. I want very much to see you through this. And if I must be quite frank, I don't think anyone else can or will."

"Oh, I know," he said. "I don't expect anybody to take up a collection for me. Nobody can help me. Fine. So how can you?"

"Don't you think Luis knows a few people in Tangier? It's a question of getting you and the money across the frontier. In any case, I've borrowed a diplomatic car. With the CD plates one goes right through, usually. Even if we don't it's all seen to. You run no risk."

"No risk!" he repeated, with a brief laugh. "And in Tangier?"

"Ronny? What can he do? I assure you he'll be so delighted to see his money, he'll—"

He cut her short. "Not that," he said. "I'm not worried about that. I'm just thinking."

She looked puzzled an instant. "You don't mean the check you accepted from that hideous little Russian woman?"

"Oh, Jesus," he groaned. "Is there anything you don't know?"

"In the way of Tangier gossip, no, darling. But everyone knows about that. She's been ordered to leave the International Zone. Day before yesterday. She's probably already gone. The only useful thing Uncle Goode's done since she arrived in Tangier. I don't know what the official American attitude would be toward your sort of stupid behavior. But that's a chance you'll have to take. I think we've talked about enough, don't you?"

"I guess we have," he said. It was a solution, he thought, but it was not the right one, because it would undo everything he had done. It had to be his way, he said to himself. He knew what the other way was like.

"Do you think we could have some tea before we leave?" Daisy inquired suddenly. "It would help." ("She doesn't understand," he thought.)

"I'm not going," he said.

"Oh, darling, don't be difficult." He had never seen her eyes so large and serious. "It's late. You know God-damned well you're going. There's nothing else you can do. The trouble is you just can't make up your mind to face Jack and Ronny. But you've *got* to face them, that's all."

"I tell you I'm not going."

"Rot! Rubbish! Now come! Don't disgust me with your fear. There's nothing more revolting than a man who's afraid."

He laughed unpleasantly.

"Come along, now," she said in a comfortable voice, as though each sentence she had uttered until then had succeeded in persuading him a little. "Make some good hot tea and we'll each have a cup. Then we'll go back. It's that simple." As a new idea occurred to her, she looked around the room for the first time. "Where's the Beidaoui boy? Not that I can take him; he'll have to get back by himself, but I daresay that offers no particular problem."

Because what had been going on for the past half-hour had been in a world so absolutely alien to the one he had been living in (where the mountain wind blew and rattled the door), that world of up here, like something of his own invention, had receded, become unlikely, momentarily effaced itself. He caught his breath, said nothing. At the same time he glanced swiftly over her shoulder toward the kitchen door, and felt his heart make a painful movement in his chest. For an instant his eyes opened very wide. Then he looked into her face, frowning and not letting his eyelids resume their natural position too quickly. "I don't know," he said, hoping that his expression could be interpreted as one of no more than normal concern. With the wind, the door had swung outward a little, and a helpless hand showed through the opening. "I haven't seen him all day. He was gone when I woke up."

Now his heart was pounding violently, and the inside of his head pushed against his skull as if it would break through the fragile wall. He tried to play the old game with himself. "It's not true. He's not lying there." It would not work. He knew positively, even without looking again; games were finsihed. He sat in the room, he was the center of a situation of whose every detail he was aware; the very presence of the hand gave him his unshakable certainty, his conviction that his existence, along with everything in it, was real, solid, undeniable. Later he would be able to look straight at this knowledge without the unbearable, bursting anguish, but now, at the beginning, sitting beside Daisy in the room where the knowledge had been born, it was too much. He jumped to his feet.

"Tea?" he cried crazily. "Yeah, sure. Of course." He stepped to the front door and looked out: the chauffeur and the guide were still sitting down there in the gathering gloom, on opposite sides of the path. "I don't know where he is," he said. "He's been gone all day." It was still raining a little, but in a moment it would fall harder. A dense cloud was drifting down from the invisible peaks above. In the wet gray twilight everything was colorless. He heard a sound behind him, turned and stood frozen as he watched Daisy rise slowly, deliberately, walk into the patio, her eyes fixed on the bottom of the kitchen door. She pulled it all the way open, and bent down, her back to him. He was not sure, but he thought he heard, a second later, a slight, almost inaudible cry. And she stayed crouching there a long time. Little by little the dead, flat sound of the falling rain spread, increased. He started to walk across the room toward the patio, thinking: "This is the moment to show her I'm not afraid. Not afraid of what she thinks." Because of the rain splattering from the eaves into the patio, she did not hear him coming until he was almost in the doorway. She looked up swiftly; there were tears in her eyes, and the sight of them was a sharp pain inside him.

He stood still.

"Did—?" She did not try to say anything more. He knew the reason: she had looked at his face and did not need to finish her question. She stood only a second now in front of him, yet even in that flash many things must have crossed her mind, because as he stared into her eyes he was conscious of the instantaneous raising of a great barrier that had not been there a moment before, and now suddenly was there, impenetrable and merciless. Quickly she walked in front of him into the room and across to the door. Only when she had stepped outside into the rain did she turn and say in a smothered voice: "I shall tell Ronny I couldn't find you." Then she moved out of his vision; where she had paused there was only the rectangle of grayness.

He stood there in the patio a moment, the cold rain wetting him. (A place in the world, a definite status, a precise relationship with the rest of men. Even if it had to be one of open hostility, it was his, created by him.) Suddenly he pushed the kitchen door shut and went into the room. He was tired, he wanted to sit down, but there was only one mat, and so he remained standing in the middle of the room. Soon it would be dark; stuck onto the floor was the little piece of candle the other had blown out last night when the fire was going. He did not know whether there was another candle in the kitchen, nor would he look to see. More to have something to do than because he wanted light, he knelt down to set the stub burning, felt in his pocket, in all his pockets, for a match. Finding none, he stood up again and walked to the door. Out in the murk there was no valley, there were no mountains. The rain fell heavily and the wind had begun to blow again. He sat down in the doorway and began to wait. It was not yet completely dark.

—Amrah, Tangier

Paul Bowles: 1948

PAUL BOWLES has lived for many years as an expatriate
American in Tangier, Morocco. He is the author of four
highly acclaimed novels: *The Sheltering Sky, Let It Come
Down, The Spider's House,* and *Up Above the World.* In
1979 Black Sparrow Press published Bowles' *Collected
Stories 1939–1976,* about which Gore Vidal wrote, "His
short stories are among the best ever written by an
American." This latter volume collected all of Paul
Bowles' short fiction, much of it long out of print and
unavailable, written over a period of more than thirty
years, and presented these stories for the first time as an
entity.